ROBYN CARR

WILD MAN CREEK

MIRA®

ISBN-13: 978-0-7783-1757-9

Wild Man Creek

Printed in U.S.A.

For Martha Gould,
high on my list of most admired women, with
thanks for her loyal support and tireless affection.

WILD MAN
CREEK

Prologue

Jillian Matlock was a natural in the business world and her ability to anticipate surprises and challenges was legendary. After many successful years in communications it never once occurred to her that she'd be tricked. Set up. Taken for a fall.

One busy Monday morning Jillian wondered only briefly why Kurt Conroy hadn't shown up for work. Kurt worked for her in Corporate Communications at the San Jose software manufacturer, Benedict Software Systems. He was the director of PR. He was also her boyfriend, though no one in the company knew that. She'd spoken to him last night but he never mentioned a thing about not feeling well or taking some personal time.

Right now she had bigger fish to fry as she had just had a call from her boss, Harry Benedict, President and CEO. As Vice President of Corporate Communications, such a summons was fairly routine for Jillian. She had several face-to-face meetings with Harry each week. He was her boss, mentor and friend.

She gave his office door a couple of short courtesy raps before entering. The question about Kurt's absence was immediately answered—he was seated in front of the president's desk.

"Well, good morning," she said to Kurt. "I wondered where you were. You didn't mention taking the morning off."

It took several beats before she noticed that Kurt could not meet her gaze and Harry was frowning darkly. She sat in the other guest chair and it still didn't quite register that something was wrong. Very wrong.

"We have a situation," Harry said, looking first at Kurt, then at Jillian. "Mr. Conroy has notified me that he intends to file a sexual harassment complaint, he has hired an attorney to represent him and he is here to suggest a settlement of terms that will help us all avoid a lawsuit." Harry swallowed and his frown darkened.

For another long moment Jillian was on another planet. Someone had been sexually harassing her *boyfriend?* "My God," she said, stunned. "Why didn't you say something, Kurt? Who would do this to you?"

Kurt finally looked her in the eye and then he smirked. "Funny, Jillian," he said. "Very funny."

She unconsciously drew her eyebrows together. "What's going on here?" she asked, looking between Kurt and Harry.

Harry cleared his throat, clearly uncomfortable. "Mr. Conroy alleges that you are the guilty party, Jillian."

"What?" she said, automatically shooting to her feet. "What the hell…?" She stared at Kurt. "Have you lost your *mind?*"

"Please, sit down, Jillian," Harry said. Then he looked at Kurt and said, "Take the rest of the day off, Kurt. I'll be in touch later."

Without a word, without a backward glance, Kurt rose

and left the office of the president, quietly closing the door behind him.

Jill looked at Harry. "Is this some kind of sick joke?"

"I wish," Harry said. "I can't wait to hear your take on this, Jill."

She gave a short laugh of disbelief. "My take? I thought I had a *boyfriend!* Harry, Kurt and I have been seeing each other for months! It was completely consensual and only became—" she struggled for the right word "—serious…very recently! He pursued me! And trust me, our private relationship had nothing to do with work! He had been promoted long before I ever went out with him."

"You were seeing him secretly?" he asked.

"I'd prefer to describe it as 'discreetly.' I helped Human Resources put together the corporate policy years ago, when the company was so young. No problem with dating or marrying inside the company, but not within the same department. According to that policy, one of us would have had to change departments. Obviously Kurt would have to make the change, since he's the subordinate. But his only experience is in PR and my department was the only place he had a good fit. We worked *well* together! Or so I thought…"

Harry shook his head. "You were instrumental in putting that policy in place, Jillian. In fact, if I remember, it was your idea in the first place."

She scooted to the edge of her seat. "Yes, but it wasn't developed because of the threat of sexual harassment! Sexual harassment is *never* consensual, and it's never confused with dating—it's always extortion of some kind. We—I mean the Human Resources team—were concerned about complaints inside departments from employees alleging promotion based on favoritism. *That's* why dating within a department was a bad idea.

We also created a policy saying employees shouldn't be late, shouldn't dress inappropriately and shouldn't park in the president's spot!"

She got a smile out of Harry for that. It was a small smile.

"I thought, given time and training, Kurt might be a good successor to me. And before you ask, my opinion is not because I liked him but because there was no one else more qualified. I know how you hate to go outside the company to fill positions if there's opportunity internally for our employees." The seriousness of this situation was becoming brutally apparent and Jill took a moment to pass her hand across her brow and then gaze across the room.

"Well, that's a coincidence," Harry said, passing her a folder. "Kurt sees himself as your successor, as well. Have a look at this."

Jill's hands actually trembled a bit as she lifted the cover of the folder and looked at a collection of memos, emails, printouts of text messages and miscellaneous notes. The first email she looked at came from her and it said, How am I doing? I could use shoulder rub! "Harry, this had nothing to do with a relationship! After a grueling meeting, he emailed me and asked me how I was holding up! In fact…" She looked closely at the date. She shook her head. "I wasn't even dating him then!" She would have to plow through months of old emails. Months of *deleted* emails. Months of inane, trivial messages.

Then there was a page of text exchanges and, highlighted in yellow, from her cell phone, was the message *I miss you!* "But this is completely innocent," she said, turning it toward Harry. "I'd have to check my calendar, but I think I was out of town. And I did. I did miss him!"

And in that instant she knew what he'd done—he'd set her up.

"God," she muttered. "Playful messages between two people who worked for the same company. How did I never smell this coming? How could I have been so wrong?"

A glance through some of the pages revealed similar brief, affectionate comments that any woman might have made to the man in her life, and there was no way of knowing if they were sent during work hours or at other times. In her mind these were innocent romantic gestures that were nonthreatening. But among them all she couldn't find a single thing that came from Kurt.

He had been the seducer; most likely all his responses had been verbal...and untraceable.

"Harry, he said flirtatious and seductive things to me, but the difference is, he has no paper trail! I was never afraid to send an email or text like this—I trusted him." She shook her head. "Do you see how slim this file is, Harry? You'd think in months of dating there would be a lot more, wouldn't you? But we were very professional around the office. I'll have to go through my records of emails and texts, but surely I'll find what I need to reveal that he was his sexy, flirtatious self and I responded because I believed we were a couple!"

"I don't suppose you can remember anything significant off the top of your head?" Harry asked with a lift of his bushy, graying eyebrow.

"Well, there's a jewelry store manager who'd probably be happy to testify that Kurt was just as attentive and romantic as could be when he talked me into looking at rings after dinner one evening, but that wouldn't be in print, would it," she said with an unhappy laugh. "We had agreed to keep our relationship private until one of us had identified a part of the company to which we could move. I was the more likely candidate to make a move even though Kurt was subordinate to me. You've been tempting me with VP of Marketing for a year now and I warned Kurt that if that came through for me, he might not be ready to take on Corporate Communications, or that you might not be ready to give it to him. He told me our relationship was far more important than his next promotion." She dropped her chin and fought back the tears. "I can't believe this is happening." She looked up. "I believed him, Harry!"

"He also has office mates who have witnessed inappropriate touching and…and he's kept a log. A very *detailed* log of events."

Thinking back over the past several months Jillian had to admit that he had charmed a lot of people—all the women in the office loved him; he was funny and cute and oh so helpful. Jillian thought she had behaved perfectly in the office; she had been very conscious of the need for that level of professionalism. But had she given his shoulder a loving pat? Touched his back in a quick caress? Smiled into his eyes? Kurt was a couple of years younger than she, handsome, sexy and bright—she'd had no idea just *how* bright! To orchestrate something as complex as this took planning and brainpower. He should have used those skills on his job!

Oh how she wished her denial could hang on a bit tighter, a bit longer. As the tears welled she bit down on her lower lip to keep her chin from quivering. "Does it say in his log that he had to ask me a dozen times to even meet him for a drink after work, something which is completely appropriate between coworkers? Or how about a few nights ago, when he drew a bath for me and—"

Harry held up a hand. "Stop. I'm not an idiot and I'm

not angry with you. I know what's happening here. You've been with me from the beginning, Jill. You helped build this company. I know you wouldn't do something like this. But unless you have some compelling evidence to the contrary, we have ourselves a problem. And keep this in mind, please—if an accusation like this was his objective, dating his boss probably wasn't necessary in the first place. He could have singled you out as his victim *without* your cooperation."

"But why?" she asked desperately.

"I don't know," Harry said earnestly. "Maybe an investigation will reveal that."

Jill had to grit her teeth to keep from crying. She'd never cried in front of Harry. She was his right arm, his sidekick, his protégé. One of the things she was most proud of was that, young as she'd been when she'd started with Harry and a brand-new company, she'd never wimped out. Their products were in the category of wealth management software—everything from customized accounting systems for businesses, to budget and bill-pay software for the average home computer. Some of their clients were huge, bringing a lot of money and challenges to the company; but she was tough and she faced everything with courage and ingenuity. Awful things could happen on the job—like failed software or the threat of losing a big client to a competitor. In PR, Jill's job was to keep a positive face on the product and on customer service. They'd been in tight spots from time to time when the future of the company hung in the balance, but Jill didn't cry. She *fought!*

Her boss saying he still believed in her almost put her over the edge. It almost made her cry. She stiffened her spine. "What does he want?" she asked weakly.

"A settlement of some kind. And your resignation."

She lifted the folder of incriminating evidence. "Is stuff like this even admissible?"

"In civil court, very probably. In the newspapers, absolutely."

"Harry, I thought he cared about me. He flirted first, for a long, long time! Are we going to let him win?"

Harry leaned forward, clasping his hands on the top of his desk. "I'd like nothing better than to stand and fight, Jill. Never once in ten years have I seen any indication that you were less than professional, loyal or honest. I never had an employee put in longer hours, work harder or give me more of her personal life. You've become a member of my family! If there's some part of you that would take advantage of a junior employee, I never saw it. Either I'm no judge of character, or the little bastard conned us all. And if I'm no judge of character, I managed to build a real successful software manufacturing company in spite of it.

"So, this is our reality—it looks like he's stacked the deck pretty good. We've faced issues like this before and we've always managed them in-house wherever possible. HR and our attorneys will look at the complaint and evidence and meet with him. If they find it's potentially damaging, I will do everything in my power to keep you and the company out of court. Bear in mind we have twenty-five hundred employees who shouldn't have to take this risk with us. Much as it galls me, we might have to cut our losses."

"And that means?" Jill asked.

"At the moment, I want you to take the rest of the week off. I want you to go home knowing that I'll do everything I can to protect the company and you in the clinches. If I have to make a sacrifice, Jill, I won't let you down. I'm not going to throw you to the sharks. At the very least, I'll make sure a confidentiality agreement is a priority in any settlement so your future prospects won't hear about this mess. Half my competitors have been after you for the past five years anyway."

"But I made my choice a long time ago. I chose BSS."

"I know this," he said. "Get yourself a lawyer, Jill. Just in case you need one. Don't go through this alone, and don't rely on me when I have a whole company to protect."

"Will you give him a ton of money?"

"Not if I can help it."

She laughed ruefully and wiped a hand under her nose. "You've made me rich," she said. "He'd have been better off marrying me. He's not that good in PR. He was coming along, but he had a lot to learn. You're getting the worst end of the deal."

"Even if he wins, no way he'll stay here," Harry said confidently. "We're a stepping stone. My bet is he would flaunt his title, take credit for some work he didn't do and land himself a bigger job with Microsoft or Intel. Where he would promptly fall on his face."

"Unless he finds a woman to seduce," she said quietly.

"I know you don't see this now, but you're going to survive this. You're smart, you're good and you're going to land on your feet. Try to be patient while we work this out. Just keep your head."

And your heart, she thought.

"Take the week for now," Harry said. "If there's any way out of this, believe me, we'll take it. I just want you to be prepared for the worst. In case. And, obviously, you can't discuss this with anyone—litigation pending." Harry stood. The meeting was over. He stuck out his hand. "I'm sorry this happened. I wish you'd have come to me about the relationship a long time ago. Dating someone isn't that big a deal. We could've worked with that. You're not the first office romance. You'll hardly be the last. But by keeping him secret for professional reasons, you gave him opportunity."

"I thought I was covering for you," she said. "I just didn't want to put you in a difficult position because of a choice I made."

When she clasped her mentor's hand, he held on. "This is so unlike you. My biggest worry about you was that you had no life—this job took everything you had and more! What was it about him, Jill?" Harry asked softly. "How did he get you to take chances like this?"

She laughed without humor. Kurt had had obvious flaws, but she overlooked them because no one's perfect. He was cute and seemed thoughtful, but he wasn't the sharpest knife in the drawer. If he hadn't pursued her, she might not have noticed him! She just shook her head pathetically. Was it because he was the only man she'd had time for? No wonder office romances flourished. They were convenient! "You might not believe this, Harry, but he had to invest a *lot* of time to get me to take a chance on him. And maybe it all boiled down to that—he was relentless and I was lonely. If he wins this battle, you'll be getting one lousy Corporate Communications exec. He can barely tie his shoes or make a phone call without leadership. You're going to have to fire him."

"I'm sure he's figured all that out," Harry said.

"God, I'm sorry," she said. "Harry, I'm sorry. I feel like such a fool!"

Despite her better judgment, Jill tried to contact Kurt. He did not answer his cell or his door, and after she'd left about fourteen voice mails in a barely controlled voice she realized she was only making her situation worse.

Wasn't the plot clear? He'd benefit from her hysteria! She'd look guiltier! She made herself stop.

Jill met with a lawyer who contacted Harry, the head of HR and the BSS General Counsel. She had turned over a backup of her personal hard drive and her company computer, along with her cell phone and the contents of her desk. Since she had not been trying to set up a sting, her evidence against Kurt was just not there. But, if nothing else, Jill's legal counsel should be able to keep the investigation in the company at the HR level and not let it get as far as the Equal Employment Opportunity Commission or a civil court.

A week turned into two and Jillian was nearly jumping out of her skin. She was getting cabin fever, holed up in her San Jose town house with nothing to do but surf the internet on her new laptop.

And then Harry called.

"It's looking good for our side," he said. "By far the most damaging case against you is going to be the testimony of two employees who believe they witnessed harassment—two employees who shall remain nameless. And, to be fair, if he was manipulative enough, they might just think that's what they saw."

"Right," she replied with sarcasm. There were only fifteen employees in Corporate Communications; she could guess *exactly* who the women were. Both older than Jillian by a good fifteen years, they tended to sparkle stupidly whenever Kurt was around.

"What I'd like you to do is step out of the fight, Jillian. Rather than a resignation, I'd like you to take a leave of absence. At least three months. I'm going to put someone else in the position you'd be vacating—I'm going to bring in a consultant. Kurt will get his vested options and, unsurprisingly, he's agreed to a confidentiality agreement."

"Unsurprisingly?"

Harry laughed. "He doesn't want his complaint against his supervisor to follow him any more than you'd like it to follow you. I'm telling you—he's going to be moving along. And I'm not done looking into his past." Harry lowered his voice and said, "You never told him what you're worth, did you?"

"I don't know," she said honestly. "I don't think so. It's not something I talk about. Why?"

"Because if you had, he'd never settle this easily. He's getting a nice option package, but it's nothing by comparison to what you've made in ten years. He should have taken the time to read old prospectuses, or stolen a look at your portfolio."

Jillian had a clever financial planner; she'd engaged her services after her first modest bonus. Together they decided that twenty-four hours a day and seven days a week was enough time to give one company. It made no sense to sit on the stock and options, so Jillian exercised or sold them and invested her money elsewhere. While she made more and more money from BSS, her planner made more and more in other investments.

The money hadn't mattered to her as much as the job—or as much as Harry's vision and faith in her.

"What am I supposed to do for three months?" Jill exclaimed.

"I don't know. Take a breather. You have plenty of money. Take a trip or a few classes or something. Unwind and let this fade—take some time to think about where you want to go. Don't leap into anything—I know you love to be spontaneous! Try to learn to relax and enjoy life—get your strength back. I'd venture to say that in a few months he'll be out of here and there's nothing in our settlement preventing you from coming back if you feel like it. There's also nothing preventing you from making a change. You have your life back, Jillian. Think about that."

She *had* thought about that. It *terrified* her. She longed for the days they worked till 4:00 a.m., snarfing down cold pizza and Red Bull to keep going, putting together a public offering, or preparing for a board meeting with a critical vote the following morning. She loved the deadlines, the crush to bring up the company profits before the quarterly report, the chilling fear and excitement of the audits, the gatherings of the suits to put together the prospectus. It was Jillian who was the PR guru, who put the spin on the company's viability to the Board, the Securities and Exchange Commission, the brokers, the public. It was Jill who scrambled and took all Harry's hard work and vision to the finish line with him.

She wasn't sure *how* to slow down and she was pretty sure she didn't want to.

Despite Harry's instructions about confidentiality, Jill shared her current predicament with her one trusted intimate, her sister and best friend, Kelly. Kelly was a busy sous-chef in a five-star San Francisco restaurant, and their time together was limited, but they talked and texted daily. The greatest comfort in her secret dialogue with her sister was that Kelly wanted to kill Kurt—metaphorically anyway.

"Kurt better never try to have a meal in my restaurant," Kelly said hatefully.

"I'm sure he knows better," Jill replied. "He's figured everything else out."

"I'm just saying… I know how to make it look like an accident…."

"Shush, for all I know he's recording my phone!" Jill

took a breath. "And now, having realized that's actually a possibility, you have to let him live."

"Bummer," Kelly said. "He's a pig. I never liked him. Did I tell you that?"

"No, you *did* like him! He charmed you, too, which makes us equally stupid. Ah, God, what happened to me? I mean, I'm no Einstein but I've never been so naive! Truthfully? I didn't think he was smart enough to do something like this!"

"You're impulsive," Kelly said. "You always have been. You see something you want and you just go for it."

"I wasn't that impulsive," Jill argued. "He courted me for a long time before… Oh never mind. Harry was right—even if I fought and won, it would become public, and his accusation would taint me for a long, long time!"

"Here's my biggest question." Kelly asked, "How could he get one over on everyone and yet be such a dud in PR? Isn't that good PR? Knowing how to put a good spin on things, sell things, convince people they want what they don't even know they want?"

"In a nutshell," Jill said wearily. "He should have applied as much energy to his job."

"Well—you helped build the little empire that is BSS," Kelly said. "And it didn't turn out the way you wanted, but you made a ton of money and your money made a ton of money. A whole bunch of software and dot-com corporations sputtered out, but yours did great. You should be able to get anything you want! Let's think ahead for a sec. What's your first, best idea?"

"I'm taking Harry's advice. A little time off," she said. "Then I'll rethink the next job.…"

"That surprises me. My little sister would usually hit the ground running! In spite of Kurt's efforts to wipe you out, your reputation is sterling. If anyone calls Harry for a recommendation, it'll glow! You can go just about anywhere you—"

Jillian's voice was so soft Kelly barely heard it. "But I'm still too wounded."

Kelly was silent for a moment. "Oh, baby…"

"You know what I felt so guilty about while I was seeing Kurt? I worried that he cared far more for me than I did for him! But all the while he was loving me, he was plotting how he could really screw me."

"He's a bastard…."

"I've never had trust issues before," Jillian said very quietly. "I always had good instincts about who couldn't be trusted. I could always tell the minute I met someone if I could trust them, and I was seldom wrong. But now…"

"You just need a little time," Kelly said.

"Now," she repeated, "I'll never trust another man. If I do, it'll be a miracle."

There was silence between them.

"I'm taking off for a while, Kell," Jillian said. "A vacation, some peace and quiet, a break in the action. Harry's right—I owe it to myself to think."

"Where will you go?" Kelly asked. "Do you need me with you?"

Jillian chuckled at the offer. "I know you can't leave work. No, I'm going to make this trip solo. I don't know where I'm going yet but don't worry, I'll be fine. I just need a little time to absorb this whole situation. A little time to heal."

Kelly sighed into the phone. Then she said, "Seriously, he better never look for a meal in my restaurant because I do want him dead. And I hope he got that on tape!"

One

It gave Jillian a sense of relief to pack a few bags, lock up her small town house in San Jose and just drive away. Nothing could make a woman want to run for her life like being used and betrayed by a man.

To appease Kelly, she drove only as far as San Francisco for her first leg of an unknown trip. That night she had dinner in her sister's restaurant. It was so hard to get a table in the five-star restaurant where Kelly was the head sous-chef that those people willing to wait usually stood around the bar for two hours after checking in with the maître d', and that was if they had a reservation. The chef de cuisine was a man named Durant, known only by one name, and he was regionally famous. But Jillian was seated immediately, and at an excellent, semiprivate table. Then she was served every specialty the restaurant had by the best of the waitstaff. Kelly must have called in a lot of favors to make it happen.

After dinner, Jill drove over to Kelly's small San Francisco flat where she planned to stay the night. Kelly didn't get home from the restaurant until well after one in the morning, so the girls had their chance to visit over a late breakfast together. Kelly asked, "What now?"

"Many possibilities," Jill said. "Maybe Tahoe. I've never been to Sun Valley, Idaho. The point is not where I'm going so much as just driving. Watching the miles stack up in the rearview mirror—figuratively and literally putting things behind me. I'll stay in big, comfortable, anonymous hotels or resorts, relax, eat good food, watch all the movies I've missed over the past ten years and do many, many bookstore prowls. Before I go back to the grind I'm going to see if I can remember what having a life was like."

"You have your phone, of course?"

Jillian laughed. "Yes. I'll keep it charged in the car, but I'm not taking calls from anyone except you and Harry."

"Will you do something for me?" Kelly asked. "Will you please just text me in the morning every day and let me know where you are? And can we talk before I start work in the kitchen? Just so I know you're all right?"

Jillian was so far from all right it was almost laughable. She felt like an utter nutcase. Her attention span and focus were so disturbed that driving was probably not a great idea. But traveling by air to a vacation spot like Hawaii or Cancun, or being held prisoner on a cruise ship were so unappealing that she rejected those ideas immediately. She wanted her feet on the ground; she wanted to get her mental awareness back. She felt almost as if she didn't know herself anymore. The inside of her car, alone, made total sense to her. There she could think, undisturbed, and try to get things in perspective.

But she put on a brave face. "You bet," she said to her sister. Then she smiled. "If you call, I'll answer if I have a signal."

Right after they said their goodbyes Kelly left for work and Jillian got in her car and immediately drove east. She was halfway to Lake Tahoe when she remembered the vacation she'd taken with Kelly and two girlfriends the previous autumn. They'd driven to Vancouver—which was an excellent option for right now—but on the way home they'd stopped off at some dinky little town in the mountains—she couldn't even remember the name. While they were there they'd wandered into an estate sale and the old house where it was held reminded her of the house she and Kelly had grown up in with their great-grandmother. Nostalgia had flooded her and she'd become almost teary with remembering, even though the two houses had very little in common. The other image that came to mind were the little cabins along a river where they'd stayed for a couple of days—nice little cabins, remote yet comfortable. They had left the windows open at night and slept to the sounds of nature, the river rushing by, the wind whistling and humming through the huge pines, the quacks, caws, honks and calls of wildlife. They'd put their feet in the icy river last fall, watching trout jump and turning leaves flutter into the water. It had been lovely. Soothing.

With those thoughts in mind, Jill made a turn and headed north. She'd go up through Napa—that would point her in the right direction. Those little cabins weren't like a motor lodge or Holiday Inn, not the kind of place you could show up at midnight asking for a room. It was owned and run by a guy named Luke and his young wife; they lived on the property.

Jill spent the second night on the road at a little roadside inn in Windsor, probably halfway to her destination. First thing in the morning, she headed north again. Even a phone call to Kelly hadn't produced the exact name of the town, but Jillian knew roughly where it was.

A couple hundred miles and a few wrong turns led Jill

to a remote intersection in Northern California where she saw a couple of guys had parked their pickups at odd angles. They were clearly just passing the time. She pulled up alongside. "Hi, guys," she said. "There's a little town back in here somewhere. I had dinner at a place called Jack's—I think—and there are some cabins along a river run by a guy named—"

One of the men pulled his hat off his head and smoothed his thinning hair over his freckled scalp. "Luke Riordan owns those cabins in Virgin River. Luke and Shelby."

"Yeah!" she said. "That's it! Virgin River! I must've missed the turn, never saw the sign."

The other guy laughed. "Ain't no sign. You didn't miss it by much," he said. "Up 36 a quarter mile. It's a left. But to get to Luke's you're gonna wanna go another left after 'bout another mile and a half up that hill. Then you'll go down again, then around a curve at the bottom of the mountain. Your second left ain't marked, but there's a dead sequoia stretched out by the side of the road right where you turn. Big mother. Then you'll prolly see the river. Take that road along the river to the cabins. Ain't far."

She laughed. It might've been one of her first belly laughs in a couple of weeks! Yeah, she remembered the dead tree, the up, down and around of the road. "I remember now—I remember the dead tree. Thanks. Thanks so much!"

Off she drove in the direction of the first left and then the dead tree, laughing as she went. She was laughing at how different it was! She might as well have traveled to a different country—these people were as removed from iPhones and iPads and daily stock reports and board of director meetings as she was from fly-fishing and camping. And now that she'd seized on this idea and spontaneously found herself in Virgin River, of all places, she realized hardly anything in her baggage was going to be right for this kind of break. Thinking she might end up at some hotel resort in a place like Sun Valley she'd packed her country club casual—clothes she had on hand for corporate events or company picnics. She had linen slacks, a couple of stylish but casual dresses, wraparound skirts, sweater sets, that sort of thing. Low heels; lots of low heels. She had exactly one pair of Nike walking shoes and two sweat suits, and they both had designer labels.

As she recalled, Virgin River was very rugged, not to mention cooler. And boy, was it wet! It was early March; it had been drizzling on and off all day. It was a little bleak—except for the new green growth on the trees and the eruptions of plant life all along the side of the road.

Also muddy! Her pretty little Lexus Hybrid was splattered and filthy.

Jill followed the road along the river and when she came into the cabin compound she saw that Luke was on top of one of the cabins doing a little roof repair. He turned toward her as she pulled in. She stopped the car, got out and waved at him.

He smiled before climbing down his ladder. "Hi," he said when he got to the bottom. He grabbed a rag out of his back pocket to wipe off his hands.

"Any chance you remember me, Luke?" she asked him. "I came up here last fall with my sister and girlfriends. We spent a couple of days in one of your cabins. You invited us to the estate sale—that old woman's house."

He laughed. "Sure I remember you, but I don't remember your name."

"Oh—sorry. I'm Jill. Jillian Matlock. I apologize. I didn't even call ahead. I just thought if you had a vacancy…"

"This is a lucky time of year for vacancies," he said, grinning. "Lucky for you, anyway. Good time of year for me to make repairs anytime the rain lets up. You have your choice of cabins. The key's hanging on a hook inside the door."

"Thanks, I remember. Hey, if I stayed a few days, would that be okay?"

"No hunters, very few fishermen and the summer folks don't show up until June. June through January are busy for me, but early spring is a light load. What are you going to do around here for a few days?"

"I don't know." She shrugged. "Rest, sleep in, explore... It is safe to explore, right?"

"If you stay away from marijuana grows, but they're usually hidden. Bear aren't all the way awake yet. Fish? You fish?"

"Not since I was about seven or eight," she said.

"Art will teach you," Luke said. "There's an extra rod and reel in the shed. Art knows where. In fact, anything you might need, we probably have an extra one. Just remember—the river is up—snow from the mountains is melting. And the weather is wet two out of three days. Just let us know what you need." He looked her up and down. She was wearing jeans, heels, a silk blouse and suede blazer. "Um, Shelby's got some waders she'd let you borrow. Those shoes will be wrecked in no time."

"That's so nice of you, Luke."

"Just want you to enjoy yourself and be comfortable, Jillian."

Jillian knew she would have to buy some knocking around clothes; stuff that could hold up for long walks, fishing or sitting under a tree with a book. The next day she drove to a bigger town and texted her sister from the parking lot of the Target in Eureka.

You'll never guess where I ended up! Virgin River! Remember Virgin River?

Jillian was trying on jeans before a response came back. Kelly's text said, Why?

To relax and unwind and think, was Jillian's reply.

Jill bought some lace-up boots for possible hiking, jeans, cargo pants, sweatshirts and sweatpants without designer labels, a rain slicker and a hoodie, some warm pajamas and a bunch of socks. She was going to just decompress in the natural, cold, wet beauty. She wasn't giving up civilization altogether—she had her laptop, portable DVD player, iPad, iPhone and several DVDs she'd been meaning to watch.

But relaxation was easier said than done. Jill had fantasized for years about taking time off, having a break, but after a few years of such fantasies she had to admit that wasn't what she wanted at all. She wanted to work! Perform! Compete! Knock herself out! Win! She thrived on success, on the praise of her staff, her boss.

Jillian had been fresh out of college with a brand-new marketing degree and a bunch of credits toward her MBA when Harry Benedict offered her a low-paying job in a start-up firm. His start-up capital was limited, but he needed a few key people—a CPA, a software engineer and someone to pull together marketing demographics for his software products. Jillian could be that marketing person if she was willing and able to take a gamble. Harry had a good track record; he'd successfully started several companies, all of which he subsequently sold. What he offered her was an opportunity—to learn from him, get in on the ground floor of a new, high-tech manufacturing business and grow professionally.

Kelly was right about her—she was impulsive. She'd jumped at the chance. She had not been in a hurry to land the biggest job on the planet but the one with the most challenge and excitement. Plus, she liked Harry; liked his gruff, no-nonsense ways; liked his confidence and experience. His drive was addictive. She remembered one late night when they were still working at four in the morning, he'd said, "When we stop having fun, we're outta here, right?" She bet on him just as he bet on her. And she missed him so much.

There was nothing more fun than helping to build a company. She became close to the Benedict family, rose in Harry's software development and manufacturing business and, in fact, helped to formulate the company from its start-up to the day it went public. At the age of twenty-nine she had been made the vice president of Corporate Communications with a full staff and had become one of Harry's inner circle execs. Along the way she'd collected bonuses, stock options and her salary grew along with her responsibilities. Careful investments meant that she had a significant portfolio that was well diversified.

Over the past ten years the only vacations she was successfully able to indulge in were those with her sister and their two best friends from high school. They were four women of diverse occupational interests who were all hardworking, ambitious, competitive and single. They managed to get away once a year for a week to ten days. Other than those vacations, Jillian didn't know what to do with time off.

The thing that had always worked for both Jill and Kelly was hard work to turn their big dreams into successful realities. Kelly's plans had been more focused right from the beginning—culinary school to line cook, to line cook in better and better restaurants, to sous-chef, to head chef to her own restaurant one day. Jillian's path had never really wavered. After college, she jumped into the first opportunity that felt right. But both their paths proved to work. Kelly was definitely going in the direction she'd always planned and Jill had a nice nest egg from her ten successful years at BSS.

But, for now, Jill's days were pretty simple. She enjoyed fishing with Luke's helper, Art, a man in his early thirties who had Down Syndrome. They didn't even talk much but she could tell Art enjoyed it immensely. She napped every afternoon, read, or watched movies late into the night, walked along the river in the early morning or dusk and drove around Humboldt County, taking in the landscape, the towns and the people—the people so unlike those she'd been used to in Silicon Valley. Though she appreciated invitations for dinner from the owners, she declined Luke and Shelby's offers and remained on her own.

It was hard to change patterns and habits that had been ten years in the making—she bought prepared dinners that were easy to warm and eat, as if she were still putting in those long days. She was so happy to have time to read again, to indulge a few real girlie novels, but the love scenes only made her cry.

By driving to an open area, Jill was able to talk to Kelly at least once a day.

"Are you doing all right?" Kelly asked. "Any idea what's next?"

"I'm kicking around a few ideas," Jillian said. Truth

was she had absolutely *no* ideas. "I don't want to say anything out loud until I've done some more thinking...."

"How about your poor battered heart?"

"Hah! My heart is *fine*. I hate him and I want to *kill* him."

"Good for you!" Kelly said approvingly.

In fact, Jill's heart was in shreds. She still couldn't believe the same man had supported her, comforted her, praised her—then betrayed her. It had been so long since her heart had hurt like this—maybe since high school? College? She hadn't been a total workaholic since joining BSS—she had dated a bit. But Kurt had the distinction of having really reeled her in.

And there was something else she was having real trouble dealing with—she wasn't sure if she mourned more for the lost relationship or the lost job.

Ironically, it was that weird old house and the memories it invoked that had originally made her think of Virgin River as her escape. Yet it took her three days of fishing, walking, reading and just thinking before she recalled how it made her feel. She wanted to go back to see that house.

And, oh! The house had changed in the six months since she'd seen it last! It was now simply beautiful! So different from when she had last seen it. It was painted white with tan and brown trim; the shutters were dark, the trim lighter. The gables were decorated and the turrets at the front end of the structure stood as proud as those at any castle. The porch had been reinforced and painted tan and white; new doors and windows had been installed. It was a stunning, refurbished house that might be a hundred years old but that looked as fresh and new as the day it had been built.

And if the house wasn't amazing in itself, the grounds were as fabulous as she remembered—manicured shrubs, flowers just coming up and lining the base of the house and walk, trees sprouting buds. She identified hydrangea and rhododendron along with some other bushes that would burst into flower in another month. She walked slowly around the house and lawn, taking it in, sighing and oohing and aahing. She went up onto the porch and peeked into the window, seeing that, as she suspected, the place was empty. No one lived here.

This was not really like the house she and Kelly had grown up in—her nana's house was so much smaller, a little three-bedroom with the downstairs bedroom off the kitchen no bigger than a large closet. But it, too, had been an old Victorian clapboard with gables and a big yard, and front and back porches.

Jillian and Kelly had been on their own for several years now. When they were only five and six years old there had been a car accident; their father was killed and their mother was left an invalid. Their already-elderly great-grandmother took them on, along with their mother, who needed daily care. The girls grew up in that little house in an older neighborhood in Modesto, California. Because their mother was in a wheelchair and had very limited mobility even in that, she slept downstairs in an old-fashioned hospital bed while the girls shared one upstairs bedroom and Nana had the other one. Their mother was the first to go when the girls were in high school; their great-grandmother passed when they were in their twenties. She'd been in her early nineties.

Walking around the back porch, Jill realized that the last time she'd been here she'd sat in a rusty porch chair that the old woman who'd lived here had died in. Now she sat on the porch steps, leaned against the post and looked out at the huge yard—big as a football field up to the tree line. Most of the property was taken up by an enormous garden that needed weeding for spring planting.

It was so quiet here Jill could hear herself think. And what she thought was, *How could he touch me the way he did when he knew he was going to steal my job, destroy my reputation and break my heart? How does one human being do that to another?* And she began to cry again, something she only allowed herself to do when she was completely alone. How could he say the things he said? she wondered. *Jillian, marry me. Jillian, you're the best thing that ever happened to me. Jillian, I can't live without you, and I mean that. You're so much more important to me than any job.*

It was the deliberateness of the premeditated lies that was incomprehensible to her. Oh, Jill knew how to tell small lies, how to tell a fat girl in a bright red dress that the color was good on her, that she was late because of traffic, that she'd only just gotten the message, that sort of thing. But how do you hold a naked person, whisper those loving things when all along your plan is to throw them under the bus? This was something she could *never* do to another human being.

Tears ran down her cheeks as she walked around the backyard, eventually gravitating to a large aluminum storage shed. Still sniffing, she pulled open the unlocked double doors and found a riding lawnmower along with all of the old woman's gardening tools. She didn't want to disturb things, but thought it was harmless enough to pull out a spade. She went to work on the huge backyard garden, turning soil in the muddy patch. The woman who had lived here was eighty-six when she died, Jill had been told. Yet she had gardened a small farm. That was just like her nana.

When they were little girls, Nana had Jill and Kelly

working in the garden, the kitchen, and though Nana had never had much formal education, she taught them to read so they could take turns reading to their handicapped mother. They had garden, kitchen and house chores until they officially moved away. They worked hard through childhood, but it was good work. It probably set them up to never fear hard work. Nana used to say, "God blesses me with work." And oh, was Nana blessed! She took in laundry, ironing, sold her canned vegetables, chutneys, sauces and relishes and helped her neighbors. There was some Social Security for herself and the girls who had lost their father. They worked to the bone and barely got by.

It was the absence of work *and* love that hurt Jill's heart. She dug at the garden and cried, ignoring her tears and getting herself all muddy. When the spade didn't pull out a weed, she was on her knees giving it a tug.

There were seeds and bulbs in the shed and judging by the new green growth all around, it was planting time. About three hours after she had arrived she had a large portion of the huge garden tilled, weeded, turned and had even pushed some old, stored bulbs of unknown type that she'd found in the shed into the ground. Instinctively she knelt and scooped up some soil, giving it a sniff— her nose was a little stuffy and rusty, but she couldn't detect any chemicals. She hadn't seen any pesticides in the shed; she suspected the old woman had been an organic gardener. She kept digging and weeding. And all the while she cried soft, silent, painful, cleansing tears.

"Um, excuse me," a man said.

She was on her knees, mud up to her elbows. She gasped, sat back on her heels and wiped impatiently at the tears on her cheeks. She looked up at a very tall man; he looked somewhat familiar, but she couldn't place him.

"Everything all right?" he asked her.

"Um, sure. I was just, um, remembering my great-grandmother's garden and I—well I guess I got a little carried away here." She stood up and brushed at her knees, but it did no good.

He smiled down at her. "Must have been quite the garden. Hope gardened like a wild woman every summer. She gave away almost all of her produce and complained about the wildlife giving her hell. But she must'a loved it, the way she went after it." He tilted his head. "You miss your grandma or something?"

"Huh?"

"Well, if you'll pardon me, seems like maybe you're crying. Or something."

"Oh!" she said, wiping at her eyes again. "Yes, I was missing her!"

"That isn't going to help much, with your hands all dirty," he said. He pulled a handkerchief out of his pocket. "Here. Come on out of the mud. Wipe off your face before you get that dirt in your eyes."

She sniffed and took the clean, white handkerchief. "This your house now?" she asked, wiping off her face, amazed by the amount of dirt that came off on the cloth.

He laughed. "Nah. I worked on it, that's all." He stuck out his hand, then lifted his eyebrows—her hand was caked in mud. He reconsidered and withdrew his hand. "Paul Haggerty. General Contractor. I build and rebuild and restore around here."

"Jillian Matlock," she said, looking down at what had happened to her perfectly manicured, executive business-woman's hands. Destroyed. She pulled her hand back and wiped it on her jeans. "Whose house is it then?" she asked.

"The town's. Hope left the house, land and her trust to the town."

"Ah, that's right! I was here last fall. I came to the estate sale and someone told me about that. So what's going to happen to it?"

He stuck his hands in his pockets, rolled back on his heels and looked skyward. "Been a lot of talk about that. They could make it a museum, an inn, a town hall. Or just sit on it awhile. Or sell it—but with the economy down, it probably won't pull a good sale price just now."

"So no one really owns it?" Jillian asked.

"The town does. The guy in charge is Jack Sheridan. He has a bar in town."

"No new owner?" she asked.

"Nope."

"Gee, I'd love to see what you did inside."

He grinned. "And gee, I'd love for you to, but you're a mess!"

She looked down at herself. "Yeah. I lost my head. Got a little caught up in clearing her garden and getting it ready. For what, God knows."

"It's not locked," Paul said. "But I'd consider it a personal favor if you'd wipe your feet before going in."

She was shocked; her eyes were round and amazed. "Not locked?"

"Nope," he said with a shrug.

"So…no Realtor has the listing yet?" Jill asked.

"Not as far as I know, but then I barely finished with the redo. Jack would be the one to talk to."

"Tell you what, this will make you happy. I'm going to go home.… Um, I'm staying in a cabin out by the river.…"

"Riordans'," he said with a smile.

Boy, this was a tight group, she thought. "Right. If it's all right with you, I'll come back out here tomorrow morning and give myself a little tour. I'll be all clean and won't track dirt in your house."

His grin was huge. "And I thank you from the bottom of my heart. I painted and waxed those floors." Then he blushed a little. "Well, I got it done."

She smiled right back at him. "I know what a general contractor does. So, what does a place like this usually go for?"

"Who knows?" he said. "Put it in Fortuna, maybe seven hundred and fifty thousand. Restored, maybe a million. Lot of rooms in that house but only a couple of baths—I added one small one with a shower to make it three. Put it in a place like Menlo Park or San Jose—three million. Problem with real estate right now—it's worth whatever you can get."

"I hear that," she said. "Listen, I'm going to take off." She looked at the handkerchief. "I'll, um, launder this for you."

"Not to worry. I have a few."

"I'm going to clean up and come back tomorrow, look through the house, if you're sure it's okay."

"It's okay. Half the town's been through the house. They're real nice about not leaving marks or tracks and that's appreciated."

"Gotcha," she said with a laugh.

"Maybe I'll swing by, in case you have questions," he said. "About what time you want to do that?"

She lifted her eyebrows in question. "Nine?"

"Works for me," he said. "I thought I'd stop by Jack's Bar and get some eggs out of Preacher first."

"Oh yeah, I remember him. He's the cook! Maybe I'll join you for breakfast."

"You'd be more than welcome."

The next morning Jillian got up and put on some of her city clothes, as opposed to the new jeans and sweats she'd been wearing for her days on the river. Even she had to admit the difference, sans mud and tears, was pretty remarkable. She chose pleated slacks, silk tee and linen jacket along with some low heels. From what she knew of this little town, it wasn't necessary to dress up, but she primped anyway.

And a part of her, a large part, couldn't wait to get back to work where looking good was as much a part of the job as performing well. She smiled at her reflection and thought, *Not bad. Not bad at all.*

Over breakfast Paul explained to her that there were still a few things to finish in Hope's old house, but it had come a long way in the past six months. "We found it stacked to the ceiling with junk and collectibles, but it was in amazingly sound condition for its age. It didn't take too much restoration—mostly cosmetic work. That's one big house. Wish I'd had stock in the paint company."

"What's your interest in that old house?" Jack asked as he refilled their coffee cups. "Wanna open a bed-and-breakfast?"

"God, no!" she said with a laugh. "Clean up after people? Cook for them? Nah, never! I'm just kind of curious. I grew up in an old house with a big garden out back—though the house was much smaller. But it had porches, a big yard, big kitchen.... When my great-grandmother died my sister and I sold it. It wasn't near where either of us lived and worked. It made absolutely no sense to keep it, but I always regretted that it was gone. My great-grandmother had lived in that house since she was a teenager who was brought from France to marry a man she'd never met! She was half-French, half-Russian, and that was the way things were done then. Then she and her husband—who died long before I was born—lived there. It was her one-and-only home in this country and she nurtured it."

They chatted for a few more minutes and then when it was time to leave, Jack decided he wanted to tag along; he hadn't checked on the house in a good week.

Even though the house was immense from the outside, it didn't quite prepare Jillian for the inside, which was huge and beautiful. This was the second time she'd actually been in the house; for the first time it was void of furniture and people.

Right inside the front door was what they used to refer to as a front room. Past it was the dining room; to the left a staircase and farther left on the other side of the staircase, a sitting room. The walls were textured and painted pale yellow, trimmed in white. Upstairs were three bedrooms, a large bathroom with claw-foot tub and pedestal sink, and a sunroom that stretched the length of the house over the back porch. On the third floor, two bedrooms, one medium-sized bath and what would now be referred to as a loft—a big open space between the bedrooms at the top of the stairs.

"This area was the attic and the two bedrooms were partially finished—walls up, but that's it. It didn't take much to finish them," Paul said. The bedrooms on the third floor had window seats in the turrets and there was a metal spiral staircase that led to the roof and a widow's walk. The widow's walk was accessed through a door that pushed open easily and stood ajar. The walk was large, probably twelve feet long, but only six feet wide.

"A widow's walk in a forest?" Jillian asked.

"I don't know where old Percival came from—he was Hope's husband—but I bet there was an ocean nearby. This is a sea captain's house, complete with widow's walk. And the view is amazing."

Indeed, Jillian could see over the tops of the trees, down into the valley where there were vineyards. Way out west she could see what had to be sea fog; on the other side of the house she could see a couple of farms, some roads and a piece of the Virgin River. "How much of this land was hers?" Jillian asked.

"Most of the town property belonged to Percival but after he died Hope sold it off. She only kept ten acres," Jack said. "She said when she was younger she had a couple of vegetable patches that were so big she was a legitimate farmer. When I moved to town and Hope was already in her eighties, she was still gardening in that big plot behind the house."

Jillian looked down, and sure enough, saw a great big backyard almost completely taken up with the garden, along with a thick copse of trees that included a few tall pines, but also spruce, hemlock, maple and cedar. There were also lots of thick bushes and ferns. This long, thick copse of forest separated the backyard from another large meadow that could be easily transformed into a second huge garden, but there was no visible way to get to it except through the trees. There didn't seem to be a path or road.

"How do you get back there?" Jill asked Jack, pointing. "To that big meadow behind the trees?"

"Drive all the way around," he said. "Through town, past farms and vineyards. Hope gave up that second garden and let trees and brush grow over the access drive. Those trees are likely thirty years old and fully grown. I imagine she planned to sell that back meadow off, but either didn't get around to it or had no takers."

"This is amazing. This house should be an inn. Or maybe a commune. Or a house for a very large family. And one little old lady lived here all alone."

"For fifty years," Jack said. "Percival married himself a sixteen-year-old girl when he was near fifty. I bet he was hoping for a big family."

"I wonder if they were in love," Jillian idly commented as they headed downstairs.

"As far as I can tell they were together till he died, but no one knows much about them—at least about their personal lives. No one around here remembers Percival McCrea and there's no question, he pretty well founded the town. He was the original landowner here and if he hadn't left everything to his widow, and she hadn't doled it out to friends and neighbors, there wouldn't be a Virgin River."

Something seemed odd about the house and Jillian wasn't sure what it was until they arrived in the spacious kitchen. She noticed that not only were there no appliances, there weren't any plumbing fixtures! She gasped suddenly and said, "You don't leave the place unlocked because it's so safe around here, but because there's nothing in here to steal!"

Paul shrugged. "I didn't want a door kicked in or window broken so someone could look around for something to steal. Unless they can figure out a way to get that claw-foot tub down the stairs, there isn't anything to take. I guess they could steal the doorknobs, but that's a real enterprising thief. I have a better front door with a leaded glass window stored in my garage for once the place is inhabited. Leaded glass is expensive. I have all the plumbing fixtures to install later. It is pretty safe around here, though. I mean, I never lock my door but Valenzuela, our town cop, says there's the odd crime here and there and a person with a brain would just lock the damn door."

Jillian just turned around and around in the great big kitchen while the guys talked. In addition to a lot of cupboard space and countertop, there was room for a double subzero fridge and an industrial-size stove top, two double ovens, a couple of dishwashers....

"And I love this," Paul said, pulling open a couple of bottom drawers in the work island. "My idea. Extra refrigeration, probably useful for fresh produce or marinating meat. On the other side—warming trays."

At the nonworking end of the kitchen was a very large dining area, large enough for a long table that would seat twelve. Over by the back door was a large brick hearth. The entire back wall was all windows that looked out onto the porch and the yard beyond. Below the windows were built-in drawers and cupboards. On one side of the dining area was a beautiful built-in desktop.

Continuing the tour, Paul said, "We've got one small bedroom here and we added a small bath, which was easy to do since we had access to the kitchen plumbing. I think this was set up to be the maid's quarters. But near as we could tell, Hope lived in this small area of the kitchen for at least the last several years. It's where she kept a big recliner, her filing cabinets, her TV and computer. Furnace works just fine, but I think she kept warm in front of the fire and, as we know, she chopped her own wood. If I owned the house, I'd trade that wood fireplace in for a gas—"

"Not me," Jack said. "I like the smell of the wood. I like to chop wood."

"Wood fires are hard on the chimney and interior walls, and sparks aren't healthy in dry forests," Paul argued.

Jillian barely heard them. She was looking out the window into the backyard. For about three hours yesterday she had been transported. She might've cried as she dug in the garden, but it had been the first time since leaving San Jose that she'd truly felt like herself. She was at home in that dirt! She could imagine living in the kitchen!

It seemed like a great place to live with all those windows looking out onto the garden. She'd be happy sleeping in a recliner.

Her nana had spent many a night sleeping upright. She'd fall asleep with a book in her lap and sometimes she wouldn't even bother going up to bed. Then of course there was Jillian's mom—there were times Nana stayed downstairs all night because she needed tending.

I should remember my early years as traumatic, difficult, Jill thought. *Why don't I? Why doesn't Kelly?*

"Jillian, look," Paul said. He put a hand on her shoulder and pointed out the window. Right at the tree line, a doe and fawn picked their way cautiously into the yard. "Whoa, that guy's brand-new—he can hardly stand up!"

Then a second fawn appeared, a twin, and the doe nudged him in the rear with her nose, moving him along. They stayed close to the trees.

Jillian's chin could have hit the floor. "God," she said in a breath. "God."

"Probably looking for Hope's lettuce crop," Jack said with a laugh. "The deer used to drive her nuts."

"She used to come in to Jack's for her drink every night, covered in garden mud, and say she was going to start shooting 'em," Paul added. "Jack? You think there are deer skeletons all over that back patch?"

"You know what? Now that you mention it, we never found a gun when we cleaned out Hope's house! That old biddy was all talk!" Jack exclaimed.

Jillian whirled around and faced Jack. "Rent it to me!" she said.

"Huh?" both men replied.

"Rent it to me! The house. And yard of course."

"Wait a minute," Jack said. "I hadn't even considered that…"

"Well, consider it. I mean, even if the house is paid for, there's taxes, right? And bills—water, electric, etc. You probably don't want to try to sell it in this bad real estate market, being all the way out here in the country and all. Until you can figure out what you want to do, rent it to me."

"For how long?" he asked.

"I don't know," she said, shaking her head. "How about a little while, like for the summer." She shrugged. "Six months?"

"Don't you have a job or something?" Jack asked, hands on his hips.

"Nah," she said with a smile and shake of her head. "I've taken a leave of absence. I need a little downtime before I go back or change directions. And yesterday I started on the garden. It reminded me of growing up, of my great-grandmother's garden. And it felt better than just working so hard at learning to relax a little or being confused about what I want to do next. So?"

Jack took a deep breath. "Jillian, you can have full access to the garden as much as you want. Go for it. Rent something your size and come over every day, putter to your heart's content.…"

"But if I rent this house I can put a table or recliner here and see it in the morning. Come on. At least until you have a better idea."

"You sure you want to make a commitment like that? Because this is a big place and it might be out of your price range."

"Well, how much?"

Jack rolled his eyes, then met hers. "I have no idea. I haven't even had the property appraised yet," he said.

She laughed at him. "Why don't you do a little research and figuring and let's at least talk about it. We could put a plan in place—one that doesn't leave me suddenly homeless or you unable to take a good offer on the house. Really, we can work this out easy." She looked back out the window at the deer. "Yeah, I think this might work for me for a while."

Jillian thought about what Harry had said to her. His suggestion that she try to learn to relax seemed enormous and vague to her, but suddenly the idea of getting closer to nature not only made sense, it held a lot of appeal. After ten years in skirts and heels, racing around the pristine offices of BSS, Jill wanted to dig in the ground, enjoy the sunshine and wildlife and beauty of this remote place. *While I dig and plant and weed, I'll think about my options. I need a lot of think time, and I have to put time between my downfall at BSS and my return. Or my new start. And for sure I need to try to understand how I could be taken by a dimwit like Kurt!*

Jill wasn't naive about everything—she knew that, despite the confidentiality agreement, word would have leaked and she would be exposed as the bad guy she wasn't.

"I don't know..." Jack fumbled.

"Think about it," she urged. "Talk to some folks for advice, if you have advisors. I have very good references. I have a little money socked away. I'll come to the bar tomorrow to see if you have more questions, more ideas. What's a good time?"

"Afternoon. Two to three-thirty."

She stuck out her hand, which was clean, right down to the trimmed and scrubbed nails. "I'll be there." She shook Paul's hand, as well, thanked them both and nearly skipped out of the house.

Two

Colin Riordan pulled up   s brother's house and cabins still asking himself if this was a good decision. The
past several months had been grueling and since he had
to be somewhere, this place would serve his purposes for
now. He'd been in treatment of one variety or another for
so long he could hardly remember back when he had considered himself pretty tough and well-balanced. In fact,
if his left arm and leg didn't ache with such relentless
regularity, he'd barely remember the accident.

And, yeah, the occasional nightmare would remind
him. Lying in a tangled, burning heap that had once been
an airborne Black Hawk, being pulled free by his boys
before he burned to death. Yeah, that was the beginning
of the end. He rubbed his short, trimmed beard; he could
feel the scars on his right cheek. He was scarred on his
cheekbone, down his neck and on his shoulder, back,
upper arm and left side.

He'd traded in his sports car for a Jeep Rubicon; he got
out of it, happy to stretch his legs. He wasn't planning to
stay here with Luke and Shelby. He'd come up to Virgin
River with his brother Aiden about a month ago and had
managed to find a two-room cabin buried deep in the

forest beside a mountain creek. He made arrangements to rent the place until hunting season opened in the fall.

Luke stepped out onto his front porch, eight-month-old Brett balanced on his hip. "Hey," he said. "How was the drive?"

Horrible, Colin thought, fighting the urge to rub his leg, his back, his arm. "Terrific. Quicker than I thought." He couldn't quite disguise the slight limp as he walked toward the porch and saw Luke's eyes dart to his leg. "Just stiff, Luke," Colin said. He went up the steps and reached for the baby. "C'mere, Bud. Did you remember that trick I taught you?"

Brett reached out for him with a wet, droolly smile. Of all the shocks Colin had shouldered in the past six months, this was one of the biggest—that he'd bond with a baby! He'd never been crazy about kids, didn't want any, tended to give them a wide berth, but this one just got under his skin. In his eight months of life Colin had only seen little Brett maybe five times—right after he was born, once when Luke came to visit while he was in treatment in Tucson and brought the kid along and last month—that accounted for three. And yet...

The baby grabbed Colin's nose; Colin made a noise and a face. Brett giggled wildly and did it again. And again. And again. Finally Colin said, "Just like your father—easily entertained."

"Come on in," Luke said.

"I'm not staying. I just wanted to swing by, say hello, let you know I'm in the area. I'm going out to the cabin."

Luke looked annoyed. "Can't you stay here just one night?"

"Can you give me a break? I've been living with people for six frickin' months and I am sick of living with people!" Shelby stepped outside, wiping her hands on a dish towel. "Hi, sweetheart," Colin said, his mood instantly lightened. "Tell your husband I want my own place and I want to be alone for a while and I have earned it."

"Yes, you have. Come in for a soda or cup of coffee. Fifteen minutes, then Luke will leave you alone."

"You went to see Mom," Luke accused. "You stayed with Mom for a few days. Why not one night here, till you get your bearings?"

"I have my bearings! And I only went to see Mom to placate her so she wouldn't come to see me!"

"Oh, Colin, she's just being a good mother," Shelby said. "I hope I'm as good a mother as Maureen is."

Colin looked at Brett. "You hear that, bud? You'd better look out."

Shelby made a face at him. "That's going to cost you five more minutes. Now come in here, let me give you something to drink at least. And we should pack you up a little care package—sandwiches or milk and eggs—something to tide you over till you can get to the grocery store."

Colin tilted his head. "Not a bad idea," he said. That was something he'd always liked about women—the way they seemed to want to feed you. The other things he liked, he probably wasn't going to experience. Certainly not out here in the boonies.

Luke held the door open and Colin walked in. "Weren't you alone for three days of driving?" he asked to his back.

"I want to be alone while I'm not driving."

"What will you do?"

"I will unload a few things, settle in and listen to the inside of my own head for a while."

"Well that oughta scare the shit outta you," Luke said.

"Should we be saying *shit* around the kid here?"

"Aw, I forget sometimes," Luke said.

Colin sat at their kitchen table, still holding Brett on his lap. He accepted a cup of coffee from Shelby and made sure it was pushed out of the baby's reach.

Colin had an attack of conscience because he was being difficult, as usual. Bad stuff had happened to him, his brothers had all come running, stuck by him for six months while he tried to get his head and body back and here he was, just being an asshole. He threw Luke a bone. "Hey, any chance you have a little time this week? I got permission to install a satellite dish at that cabin. I can pick it up, but the installation is going to require some climbing."

"You don't want to be climbing," Luke agreed.

"No," Colin said, shaking his head. "I hear the only thing worse than getting a titanium rod shoved into one femur is when they do it to the other one." He grinned. "But, I think I'm going to need internet. Stuck out in the woods, it's my easiest way to stay in touch and buy things I need."

"Sure. Just say when," Luke said, clearly pleased to be allowed to do something to help.

"And with all my stuff in storage, any chance you have an extra gun? Mine are with my household goods."

"Worried about bear?" Luke asked.

"Not necessarily. Might be a little worried about growers. I heard there are pot growers around."

"Been a long time since we've had any trouble with pot growers—they tend to stay away from Virgin River and hang closer to Clear River. But, you should have a gun—bear are coming out with the cubs. Man, you get between a bear and her cub and it isn't pretty. I have a rifle I never use."

"Um, any chance you have a high-caliber handgun?"

Colin asked, trying to stretch out his left arm and wincing at the pain.

"Still can't get the best out of that arm, huh?" Luke asked, nodding toward the affected limb.

"It's coming along. It's the elbow, man. It might never be right. The breaks in the humerus seem okay now, but I went through a shoulder problem from—never mind all that. I'll take the rifle if that's all you have."

"I have a Magnum locked up, but the thing is, if you shoot a bear with it, you might only piss him off."

"The noise could scare him away, though," Colin said.

"Hmm, yeah," Luke said with a tilt of his head. "I haven't fired it in a while. You'll have to clean it, fire it, make sure—"

"Great, thanks, uhh..." Colin said. Then he smiled a bit lamely and said, "My buddy Brett seems to be very relaxed, sitting here on my lap. I think he's going to need a little change. You might want to brace yourself."

Colin had rented himself a pretty good little cabin. Furnished, but not fancy; electricity and indoor plumbing. It was lacking a few things—good, natural light, for one. When Colin had looked at it with Aiden the previous month, he lamented the dark shadows in the cabin, but he could live with that. He brought bright lights with him to illuminate the place for those days when it was too wet to paint outside. He looked forward to taking his painting, his easel, canvas and paints to a higher spot outdoors, to a clearing, and taking advantage of the good, natural light when the weather permitted. What the cabin did have was a quiet, secluded space in the forest with a creek. Or brook. Or whatever you called a baby river. That meant wildlife. And wildlife was what Colin wanted.

Colin had always been a gifted artist, but it had never

interested him as much as flying and sports. He'd always doodled; in high school he was the one stuck with all the posters, signs, lettering, even chalk renderings of team players. High school counselors and art teachers wanted him to go to college to study art, but he'd been after something a lot more exciting.

It was ironic that Colin had wanted to fly since the first time he looked into the sky and saw aircraft above him, and yet Luke was the first in their family to do it. Luke always remarked that Colin followed him into Black Hawk helicopters, but that was not so. Luke had gone into the Army ready for any assignment from artillery to KP when he was offered a Warrant Officer School slot and from there flight school. Luke had stumbled into a flying career. Colin had dreamed of flying jets or helicopters since he'd been about six years old; he had enlisted with that as his single objective. He couldn't wait to get off the ground!

Art was his sideline, just as it had been in high school. He was good at caricature and entertained his Army buddies with his drawings. He'd done an oil portrait of the five Riordan boys, ages ten to eighteen; he'd copied it from a photo and given it to his mother. He'd painted a huge, wallsize mural of a Black Hawk in a house he'd owned about ten years ago and when the new owner bought it he swore he'd keep it on that wall forever. But all that had been for fun. While in treatment—all kinds of treatment—he'd been drawing and painting. Ballroom dancing or squash certainly weren't options for rehab.

The injuries Colin sustained from the crash led to addiction to Oxycontin, which led to being arrested for buying from a dealing doctor, which led to addiction treatment, which led to depression, which led to… Put all the pieces together and he'd been in one form of therapy or another for six months. Colin had been painting with oils, watercolors and acrylics for a few months now, one of the only parts of his past he'd been able to hang on to and something that was now part of his therapy. It slowed him down enough to let his mind move easily rather than crazily. He'd painted all the bowls of fruit and landscapes he could stand, but the thing that got his juices flowing was painting wildlife.

He was frighteningly good at it for a man who hadn't been professionally trained. He could replicate some of the best wildlife portraits he found; then he discovered his own images through the lens of a camera.

He had taken one, and only one, professional art instruction in his life after high school and that was in the nuthouse. He went from the hospital to physical therapy to drug rehab to depression rehab—and it was in the third rehab that some wise guy counselor suggested a bona fide art instructor, since painting had become so crucial to Colin's recovery

The art instructor had said, "The hardest part of training a painter is showing him how to introduce emotion into his work, and you do it naturally."

And Colin had said, "Don't be ridiculous—I don't have emotions anymore."

After repeating this to his assigned counselor, they had decided to slowly reduce and eliminate the antidepressants and *increase* the group therapy sessions. To that idea Colin had said, "Can't you just shoot me instead?"

It had worked in spite of Colin's dislike of those touchy-feely group-hug sessions. He must have been ready to come off the antidepressants. Now he was glad; his senses were no longer dulled by drugs of any kind.

He'd never even considered art as a career. But why would he? He was into fast, edgy living; he was a combat-trained Black Hawk pilot who lived hard. He drove a sports car too fast, occasionally partied too much, played amateur rugby, had too many women, went to war too often. And then it all came crashing down on him, literally. In slowly learning to pick up the pieces of his lost life, he reclaimed his art. Art moved slow and exercised feelings he had been able to ignore for a long time.

Now, after many long months, he was released to pursue his continued healing and his art. He had a good digital camera with an exceptional zoom lens. Obviously wildlife couldn't pose for him—but he could catch them in the wild, get several photos and work from them.

Though he wouldn't admit it to anyone, Colin was looking forward to really getting into his art and to reclaiming the life he had nearly lost.

As promised, Luke helped Colin get the internet up and running, talking a little more than he used to. It was probably the influence of living with a woman. Colin recalled that most women had that talking gene hardwired.

Colin spent the next couple of days cautiously prowling around the forest, confirming to himself that he'd made a good choice. He liked the quiet; he enjoyed the sounds in the woods. He liked to sit on his rough-hewn porch at dawn and dusk, still and quiet, camera at the ready, and watch the wildlife that would gather at the creek—everything from a black bear fishing for trout to a puma looking for a drink. He caught a good shot of a fox; a distant photo of a buck; the head of a doe peeking out of the brush; an amazing American eagle in flight.

He went out exploring, rain or shine, but was careful with his hiking, and since spotting the bear fishing in his creek, never went out without the gun. He watched his step and moved slowly; he wasn't kidding about the second titanium rod. He had no interest in breaking any more bones.

Being outdoors in the crisp March spring was energizing for him. It seemed to drizzle two out of three days, but although he couldn't paint outdoors in wet weather, Colin certainly didn't mind being exposed to the elements. And watching the new spring growth begin to emerge was a new experience for him. He'd never noticed things like new vegetation, the quality of the air and the perfect stillness of the forest before now. He'd never moved slow enough to take notice.

On a rare sunny day he took his easel and paints and drove up an old dirt road past a vineyard and a couple of farms. He set up in a meadow and went back to work on the eagle he had started a few days ago. He clipped his photo to the top of the canvas and found himself wondering, *What does it feel like up there? Tell me what it's like to know you can just step off a limb and soar...*

Just then he heard a wild rustling in the trees not far away. He put down the palette and brush and pulled the .357 Magnum out of his belt at the small of his back. He took a stance in the direction of the noise, his pulse picking up speed, and aimed in the direction of the sound. But the creature who broke through the trees was not a black bear. It was a girl in sweatpants, red rubber boots, a dirty T-shirt and ball cap with her ponytail strung through the back. He knew it was a girl by her vaguely female shape and her deafening scream as she dived to the ground, facedown, with her hands over the back of her head.

Colin calmly engaged the safety and tucked the gun back in his belt. "It's all right," he said. "I'm not going to shoot you. You can get up."

She lifted her head and looked up at him. "Are you crazy?"

Now there were some pretty big brown eyes, he thought. Very pretty. "Nope. Not crazy. I was expecting a bear."

She lifted herself up slowly, sitting back on her heels. "Why in the world were you expecting a *bear?*" she demanded.

"They're starting to come out of hibernation now, with cubs. I've seen a couple. Thankfully at a safe distance."

She huffed. "Don't you know they're more afraid of you than you are of them?"

He smiled lazily. "Better to be safe. On the off chance I'm not that scary," he offered with a shrug. He bent to pick up his palette and brush.

"Amazing," she said with an irritated tone. "I have yet to hear *anything* that sounds like an apology!"

She was really pissed, and for some reason, it made him smile. He tried to keep it a small smile, asking himself why he found her so amusing. He gave a half bow, partly to conceal his grin. "Sorry if I startled you," he said. "And sorry you startled me. You weren't in any danger—I wouldn't shoot something I couldn't positively identify."

"Very lame attempt," she said. "What are you doing here?"

All right, he was standing in front of an easel, holding a paint palette and brush. "Taxidermy?" he responded with just a touch of his own sarcasm.

She stood and brushed at her dirty sweatpants. "Cute," she said. "Very cute. I mean, *on my property?*"

"Oh, this is yours? The roads were open and there were no signs. The light's good here. My place is buried in the forest where it's pretty dark—all I have is artificial light. If this is a problem, I'll move on...."

"But how did you get here? Where is the road? Because this is my—I mean, I don't own it, but I rent that house back there," she said, pointing over her shoulder where the top of a large Victorian could be seen above the trees. "And aside from cutting down some trees, I couldn't figure out how to get to this clearing back here. I could see it from the widow's walk, but there didn't appear to be any access."

"And yet, here you are," he pointed out with a smile. "Posing as a bear."

She brushed at her cheeks, which only moved the dirt from her hands onto them. But Colin was taking closer stock of her and starting to see things he'd missed when she first burst through the trees and threw herself to the ground. Like a very delicious female shape—lean and sexy but with curves in all the right places, and a lot of chestnut-colored hair that was escaping that ball cap to fan her face. Her lips were full and peachy; her skin like ivory with a few light freckles across her nose; those eyes were amazingly large and deep and shadowed by thick lashes. He had a sudden urge to taste that mouth, that smart, sassy mouth.

"It wasn't easy," she said. "I plowed through those trees and bushes to ask you how you got here with all your stuff." She turned up a palm; it was bleeding. "See, the last owner let the trees and shrubs between her backyard and this clearing grow in, and I wanted to get back here with gardening equipment, but I couldn't see how…"

He looked at her palm, looked her up and down and asked, "Was it really dirty coming through there?"

"Huh? Oh!" she laughed. "I've been gardening. I mean, farming—you can't call what I've been doing gardening. I've gone a little nuts. See, stuff is already coming up. I've looked up the planting cycle online and if I hurry I can catch up. I have to get all my seeds and starters in the ground before April, and that actually puts me a little behind. Vegetable seeds should be in the ground early March; tomatoes should be started. Except the squashes and melons—there's time for them yet. And I've already had birds, deer, rabbits—"

He took a step toward her. "What are you doing about them?" he asked.

She shrugged. "I have a horn. A cow horn. It's loud. The birds fly, the deer run. But I hate it. I don't hate scaring off birds so much, but the doe come with their fawns and I don't really want them to go, but if I don't scare them off and they dig up the garden, all my work is for nothing. And the only reason to garden is to watch it grow. Deer trampling my new plants isn't going to get me—"

"Don't you garden to eat it or sell it?" he asked.

"Honestly, I haven't thought that far ahead. Right now I garden to garden."

He took a step toward her. He stuck out a hand. "Colin Riordan," he said.

She looked down at her bleeding palm.

"Oh, damn, let me take care of that," he said. He went to the opened hatchback of the Jeep and found a clean rag. When he got back to her, he wrapped it around her cut. Then he stuck out his hand again.

"Jillian," she said, shaking his hand cautiously. "Are you related to Luke and Shelby?"

"You know them?"

"I stayed in one of their cabins until this place turned up and I rented it."

"I'm Luke's brother, also known as Uncle Colin."

"Pleasure," she said. "Now how did you get here?" He turned around and she did a quick study of his back; she had another look at the big, scary gun in his waistband.

She also couldn't help but admire his broad, muscled shoulders, narrow waist and long legs.

"See that road?" he asked, pointing. "It's a crappy road, bumpy and overgrown from lack of use, but the Rubicon can take it, no problem. And the road kept going up, past a vineyard, past a couple of farms, and I stayed on it. Up was my objective. Up was where the sun was."

"How far did you have to stay on that road?" she asked.

"I'm not sure. Maybe as long as a half hour?"

She sighed. "Well, Uncle Colin, you can get sun a lot easier. My place on the other side of the trees is a couple of turns off 36. You can paint in my front yard or backyard. I don't mind and you'd be a lot less trouble that way. You won't need a gun and I won't need to duck all the time. But I've been planting bulbs around the house and drive and walk, too, so try not to step on the new plants."

"Jillian, when does all the wildlife pester the garden?" he asked.

"Dawn. In fact, right up till eight o'clock. They're back again at dusk. They probably hang out back here. I'm sure they stay around the trees. They're so cautious when they come out."

"Show me your garden," he said.

"It isn't easy," she said. "You might want to go down that road and around to 36 and come up the front way."

"If you can do it, I can do it," he said. "So? Let's do it."

She sighed, shrugged and turned to walk back into the trees. With the rag wrapped around her hand she carefully parted the growth. It wasn't exactly a narrow copse, and there was no path, and because she was not totally familiar with the property she wasn't entirely sure of the most direct route back to the house. She hadn't been in the house long and the only part of the property she knew was what surrounded the house.

Finally they came through and arrived at the garden area. A large, rectangle portion of it was tilled, turned and planted. The place was *huge.* There were stakes along some rows, marking the plants. Then there was the house. Astonishing.

Colin took off his straw cowboy hat and rubbed a hand over his head. "Whoa," he said. "Look at that house! You rent that?"

"Mainly for the kitchen window, back porch and yard. That part of the house reminds me of where I grew up."

He took in the garden. "That's quite a farm you got there. You been at this a long time?"

"Like I said, I was trying to catch up…"

He looked down at her. He lifted the brim of her ball cap. "How long?"

She shrugged. "Maybe ten days. Maybe a little less. A week?"

"Did you start from scratch?"

"Oh, no. I think that garden has been there for fifty years or so, but I can't tell how much of it was used by the woman who used to live here. If she was an experienced organic gardener, she probably planted stuff in alternating sections just to regenerate the soil. I could see the established rows. I weeded, tilled, started planting seeds. I've planted less than a quarter, but I'm ready to plant more."

He whistled. "No wonder you're covered in dirt."

She laughed at him. "There's a tiller in the shed, but I like the hoe and shovel and trowel and cultivator. I like to get close to the garden. My nana used to say the secret to excellent gardening was to be close to the dirt and the plants. Besides, dirt washes off."

"You've been doing this for a week?" he asked. "Jesus, girl, got a little OCD going on there?"

"Maybe a little," she said with a grin. "When I get into something, I just really get into it. I bet it's that way with your painting."

Colin shook his head. "It's not like that. I'm not obsessed."

"Well, I'm not *obsessed*," she returned, insulted. "It's just when I take on a job, I like to do a good job!"

"Yeah," he said absently, moving closer to the garden— the long, perfect rows, the stakes, the starter plants here and there. "Mostly seeds?"

"And some seedlings," she said. "Some bulbs around the ends—she had some in her shed. I have no idea what they are, but we'll find out. I suspect tulips, irises, daffodils and lilies. I put some along the front of the house, too. I have some new starters up on the porch, so I'm getting the bed ready. And I have some baskets to hang around the porch—it's a new thing, cherry tomatoes that grow out of the bottom of the hanging basket." She grinned at him. "Very handy for dinner go pluck your tomatoes on the porch. I wanted to try it. And all the bushes surrounding the side of the house back to these trees? Rhododendron and hydrangea. And lots of lilacs. I love lilacs."

He took in the house—enormous, wide porch, three stories. He nodded toward it. "That's a lot of house. You live there alone?"

She leaned on one leg, hand on her hip and threw him a look. "Where I come from, gentlemen don't ask questions like that. I have protection and very large locks."

He grinned at her. "I'm rarely accused of being a gentleman, but I'm not dangerous. Besides, I didn't ask because I intend to break in and steal your gardening tools, I asked because it's a very big house. Where do you come from?"

"San Jose."

"Then what are you doing up here, in this big house?"

She showed him her palms, one wrapped in a rag. "Taxidermy," she said.

He chuckled at her. Smart-ass kid, he thought. "I can see that. Before gardening, how did you pass the time?"

"I was a corporate person. Software industry. It was too stressful, so I'm taking some time off. I…ah…oh never mind…"

"What?" he asked.

"I haven't had a proper vacation in a long time so I'm relaxing and thinking about what I want to do next. I think while I garden."

"A multitasker," he said with grin. "What do you do when it rains?"

"Same thing, only a lot wetter," she said.

"Well, if you see someone prowling around out here at dawn on a clear day, don't get scared. And no horn, okay? If there are deer, I'd like to get some shots."

"Pictures?" she asked.

"Exactly."

"Why?" she wanted to know.

He turned and started to walk away from her. "Because animals won't pose for me. Later, Jillian."

She watched as he disappeared into the thick copse of trees behind her garden. And while he'd seemed a nuisance at best, she was suddenly sorry to see him go.

Jillian went inside, cleaned up her cut hand, bandaged it and covered it with a latex glove. She went back to her garden and worked through the afternoon, but it wasn't quite the same. The painter showing up—it was like a little tease and she realized how much better it felt to have a little break in the day and some conversation. Then she remembered she had heard that Hope McCrea had gone to Jack's every day for that end-of-day whiskey. Jillian didn't crave a whiskey, but it might be nice to have a glass of wine and some dinner. And some company.

Risking the garden to the wildlife at dusk, she went inside to shower. Clean, hair dripping, dressed in her robe, she padded up to the third floor and looked out one of the bedroom windows. She could barely see over the trees, but she was able to make out Colin just now packing up the back of his Jeep. The sun was beginning to lower; his painting light was obviously dwindling.

She blew her hair dry, put on some of her nicer slacks, gave her short nails a whisk of clear polish and left the house.

Colin was sitting at the bar passing the time with a draft and a new acquaintance, Dan Brady. Colin learned that Brady worked construction for Paul Haggerty and could be found at Jack's once or twice a week for a beer. As for Colin, this was exactly the third beer he'd indulged in since getting out of treatment. In fact, while he wasn't particularly tempted to overindulge in beer, he never kept any at his cabin. He was on a completely different path these days.

He was just giving himself a silent pat on the back for how well he was keeping his messed-up life together when she walked in. Dan Brady was still talking but Colin didn't hear a word he said. He didn't even recognize her at first; he just glanced at her and thought she was one fine-looking woman when he realized it was Jillian, the gardener. She smiled right at him. In fact, she smiled like she was happy to see him. He almost glanced over his shoulder to be sure she was smiling at him. Except for the pink nose and cheeks and smattering of freckles, she looked almost entirely different.

First of all, she not only had a shape, it was an awesome shape. Oh man, that was a nice chest—not too big, not too small. She was kind of tall for a girl, but would still be small up against his six-three frame. Her chestnut hair fell to her shoulders in a smooth, silky curtain that called out for big, male hands. Narrow waist, firm butt, trim thighs. Her pink lips were heart-shaped and that smile cut right through him. Her smile almost brought him to his knees. She had a clean and classy girl-next-door look about her; not his usual type but he felt the kind of physical response that suggested he might like to make her his type.

She jumped up on the stool beside Colin. "I didn't expect to see you again so soon," she said and nodded hello to Dan.

"Whew," he said. "You clean up *good*. You don't look like the same girl."

She frowned right before she laughed. "Do women usually thank you for saying things like that?"

Jack was instantly in front of her, slapping down a napkin. "How's it going, Jillian?" he asked.

"Great, Jack. What can you give me in a nice, woody Chardonnay?"

"Screw top or cork?"

"Oh, let's go crazy and go with the cork." He reached in his cooler and pulled out an opened bottle of Mondavi, showing it to her. "Perfect," she said.

"You two already know each other?" Jack asked as he poured.

"I caught him painting out on the property, back behind that stand of trees."

"Meet Dan Brady," Jack said. "Dan, Jillian Matlock rents Hope's old house. You did some work on that house, didn't you?"

Dan gave her a nod. "I never painted so much in my life. How many people live with you out there?" he asked.

"Just me," she said, taking a sip of her wine.

Dan leaned an elbow on the bar. "What in the world are you doing out there?"

"She's gardening and thinking," Colin answered for her.

"Gardening?" Dan asked. "Why?"

She shrugged. "Because I can. I learned as a little girl. I'm very good at it. We have some farmer's chromosome in the family, I think."

"What are you growing?" Dan asked.

"Salad," she said with a smile. "I got the root vegetable seeds in first, then the lettuce—three kinds. Swiss chard. Scallions, leeks, cucumbers, beans. Next I'll sow the squashes, but I'm nursing along some tomato starters up on the porch. My great-grandmother started everything from seed, but she'd always start certain ones like tomatoes in little trays on the back porch until they were strong before they went in the ground."

"Sounds nice," Dan said. "And what are you thinking about that brings you out our way?"

"Well, I'm taking a leave from a corporate PR job and I intended to think about what I'd like to do next, where I'd like to work next, but all I can think about is gardening." She got a wistful look on her face. "I'm growing the standard stuff, but you can't imagine the stuff my nana grew! White asparagus, cherry peppers, red brussels sprouts, tomatillo, red romaine… Oh, there was Purple Cape and baby eggplant. She grew a tomato called Russian Rose that was so delicious we ate them like apples—they could get up to two pounds. The ones we didn't eat she stewed and canned. She was French and Russian but could make the most amazing Italian sauce—the neighbors bought it from her sometimes."

Colin made a face and shivered. "The only thing worse than green brussels sprouts would have to be red ones...."

"What the hell is Purple Cape?" Dan asked.

"Purple cauliflower."

"My mother gardened like mad, made all of us weed, but as far as I know no one got the bug," Colin said. "I've never even seen the stuff you mentioned."

She shook her head. "You don't see it every day, that's for sure. You'd see some of that stuff in five-star restaurants. They garnish their meals with them. They're grown in small, special, commercial gardens and come at a high price. They're always organic like my great-grandmother's garden was and dining patrons know that if the chef is using them he or she has knowledge, skill, creativity and style. I'd give anything to grow some of that stuff."

"Why don't you?" Dan asked.

She laughed at him. "They don't have seeds for that stuff at the Eureka garden shop. They're pretty much limited to the stuff you see every day. My nana brought her first seeds from her own garden in France and reproduced them from her fruit and vegetables every year."

"You just haven't looked far enough," Dan informed her. "Do you use a computer?"

"*Use* one?" she asked with a laugh. "The job I just left was as a corporate officer for a software manufacturer!"

"Research those seeds," he said. "Trust me, someone has them. And if they can grow pot year-round up here, they can find a way to grow special tomatoes. A sheriff's deputy once told me that if the same energy was put into hybrid vegetables as was put into pot, we'd have fifty-pound watermelons."

"Pot?" she asked. "They grow pot year-round up here?"

"Sheltered," Dan said with a nod. "Irrigated, grow lights run on generator, fertilized with chicken shit." He grinned. "Organic!"

"Boy, you know a lot about growing pot."

"That's a fact. Did time, too," he said. "I wasn't a full-time gardener, however. I was strictly a businessman." He drained his beer. "Wish I'd heard about these high-dollar veggies. That might've been a smarter move. They even sell greenhouses on the internet, but you don't want to be growing your pot in a glass house." Then he smiled, obviously not embarrassed at all by his experience growing illegal drugs.

For a moment Jillian was lost in thought and she wasn't paying attention to the rest of the conversation. She knew her eyes got a little round and thought her mouth might be standing open. She absently shook Dan's hand and said it was a pleasure to meet him, but Colin said something to her that she didn't even hear. An onslaught of information and ideas ran through her brain so fast her eyes almost rolled back in her head. Could she actually find her great-grandmother's seeds and grow those things very few people managed to grow?

"Hey," Colin said, giving her arm a jiggle. "You all right?"

She shook herself and refocused. "Yeah. Fine. Jack?" she called. He came right over. "That guy? Dan?" she asked in a near whisper. "He did time for growing pot?"

Jack gave the bar a wipe. "Yup. Had some serious family crisis and needed emergency money, so he dove in. It must've been a bad situation to make him do something like that because he's a real stand-up guy. But you gotta admire the guy—he did his time and got himself a legit life. He's well liked around here."

"Wow. How about that."

"Lots of stories in this naked city…"

"He doesn't seem real shy or embarrassed about it…"

"Well, first off, everyone knows, so no point in pretending. Second, I think there's a part of him that kind of enjoys being infamous." Jack smiled. "Notorious. When you get down to it, though, he's just a real good guy. Lot of us have those rough patches, catch us doing things we wouldn't ordinarily do."

"Tell me about it," she said thoughtfully. "Hmm. Listen, I'm going to need a hand. Like handyman help, out at the house…"

"Aw. Jillian, I'd love to help, but—"

"No," she said with a laugh. "I want to *hire* someone! I'm not looking for a favor!"

"Oh. Well in that case…" Jack walked down to the end of the bar, spoke briefly with a handsome young man in his early twenties who was sitting there, then brought him back behind the bar to face Jillian. He introduced him as Denny Cutler. "Denny's been looking for something permanent around here. He's a friend of mine and I can vouch for him."

"Nice to meet you, Denny," Jill said, putting out her hand.

"Ma'am," he said.

"I need some help with a few things. I have to buy a truck first of all, preferably an old truck that runs well. I'm going to need to haul things for the yard and garden. Know anything about trucks?" she asked.

"Some," he said, flashing her an engaging grin.

"When you say that, I hope it means you know enough. I'm also thinking about cutting down some trees and making a path to a back meadow. Oh, and I have to erect a fence to keep the deer and rabbits out of the lettuce. It'll be a long fence."

"Wow," he said. "Sounds like stuff I can get done, but I don't have the equipment."

"Can the equipment be rented?" she asked.

"I can certainly find out. I worked for a landscaper one summer in high school. Worked me to death, but I learned a couple of things. Thing is, it's been a long time, so I might not be as fast as you want."

"Do you work hard?"

"That I do," he said with a nod. "There's another thing—it would have to be temporary. Like Jack said, I'm looking for a good full-time position. I have résumés and applications out there, but it's a tough job market. I could use a project, but if I get a call…"

"Understood," she said. "What's your fee?"

He looked a little thunderstruck. "I have no idea, ma'am."

"Okay, that's going to have to stop. I'm Jillian or Jill or Miss Matlock if you're feeling very formal, but I'm thirty-two years old and ma'am kind of rubs me the wrong way. How's sixteen an hour? That's double minimum wage."

"Whoa!" Colin and Denny said at once.

"What?" she asked.

Denny grinned largely. "Yeah. I mean, yes, ma'am, that'll work."

"Jillian. It's Jillian. I'll see you tomorrow morning by eight. Jack can give you directions. And would you mind telling him I'll need a dinner to go?"

"You bet, ma'—Jillian. Thanks. I'll do my best." And he walked away to speak to Jack.

She turned to find Colin leaning his head into his hand, elbow resting on the bar. "That was almost un-believable."

"I'm good at delegating," she said, lifting her wineglass. Then she shook her head. "What the heck was I thinking? Or not thinking? Seeds on the internet? Why not?"

"Maybe you were too busy digging in the dirt?" he suggested.

"No, that's not it. My mind was in the past, not the future. I was thinking about the old garden, not the new garden."

"Time for a fence?" he asked.

"If the wildlife gets into my radishes and lettuce, no big deal. But I won't sacrifice Purple Calabash, tomatillo or Russian Rose! Besides, there's a couple of apple trees on the property—the deer will be fine. Well fed, in fact."

"And the rabbits?"

"I'm afraid they're on their own."

"Thirty-two, huh?" he asked. "I woulda put you at about twenty-five."

She laughed at him. "I guess that's better than having you 'put me' at forty-five!"

Jack wandered over and she asked, "Can I get something to go, Jack? Anything? I have to get home."

"House on fire, Jillian?" he asked.

"I hope not. I just got a tip about seeds from your local expert, Dan, and I want to get on the computer."

"Let me go dish you up a little something," he said, heading for the kitchen.

She took another sip of her wine, smiling.

"Just how long *is* your rental lease?" Colin asked.

She turned toward him excitedly. "Don't you get it? If I can find the seeds and make it work, that's all I need to know. I can do that in a few months, but I have that house and land through the summer. And you can't imagine how happy it would make me to grow some of that rare stuff my nana used to grow."

Colin left the second half of his beer on the bar and stood to leave. "Good luck with that," he said, smiling at her. "Ma'am."

Three

Jillian talked Jack out of what remained of that opened Chardonnay and took it home along with some of Preacher's wonderful meat loaf, garlic mashed, green beans, bread, a small container of tomato gravy and a slice of chocolate cake. She ate the cake first with another glass of Chardonnay while browsing online, researching seeds and plants. Damn if Dan Brady wasn't right! Specialty seed catalogues by the dozens! Of course she had no idea how authentic the seeds were or how the finished fruit or vegetables would taste, but this was the first step—seeds were available. And while they were slightly more expensive than ordinary garden shop seeds, they were still priced low.

That night, after talking with Dan, was the first of many such nights. Jillian, like Hope McCrea before her, lived in the kitchen with the fireplace, her computer and desk. From her recliner she could eat on a tray, surf the Net and see that vast garden through the kitchen windows.

That first night, though, she was up almost all night, researching, shopping, ordering, reading gardening blogs. She finally nodded off in the recliner at about 4:00 a.m. only to wake at around six, before the sun. Taking a closer

look Jill realized there would be no sun this morning—
it was drizzling. *Perfect!* she thought. She had important errands.

The best part about this climate was that the drizzle
didn't stop her from working in the garden, and there was
seldom a heavy, driving rain. But it was so deliciously
wet, it would quench the thirst of a garden so well!

Denny arrived at seven-forty-five, and she loved that
he was early and ready to work. Jillian was also ready
to roll. He came to the front door and she invited him
in; she took him through the empty living room, dining
room and into the kitchen. "Want a cup of coffee for the
road?" she asked.

"Sure. Thanks. Where are we going?"

"First, to get a truck. I need a truck to carry supplies
too large for my Hybrid. How do you take your coffee?"

When he didn't answer immediately, she looked up
to see him staring at her living quarters. Her quilt was
draped in the recliner, there was a tray for eating there,
a pillow for sleeping, a newly purchased small TV, computer, necessities. "Denny?" she said.

He looked back at her. Although he frowned in some
confusion she couldn't help but notice he was a tall, handsome youth. He had short-cropped hair, expressive brown
brows over deep chocolate eyes. Eyes that were showing
concern at the moment. "I hope you have a bed somewhere, Miss Matlock. That doesn't look real comfortable."

"Are you kidding? It's fantastic! I don't think I've ever
been more comfortable. And it's probably better for my
back, neck and whatever.... Coffee?"

"Black," he said. Then he just shook his head and she
laughed.

By noon they had a truck—an '02 Ford with a nice big
bed. They had gone to the fencing company together to

order chain-link fencing for her big garden. They loaded up the posts in the truck bed, but the rest of the chain link would be delivered in a couple of days. She sent Denny off in the truck to take care of renting equipment, a crew or both to take down some trees and grade a level passage to the back meadow. While they were off doing chores in separate vehicles, she went about the business of buying some garden supplies. She had found a company online that would test her soil for chemicals and bought the appropriate containers for shipping. Hopefully, there had been no pesticides in that dirt for many, many years. She needed to know the pH, which nutrients were present or missing, all the sort of thing the company promised to provide.

She visited more than one lawn and garden store and asked about pure poultry manure fertilizer for organic gardening and was rather surprised by the smiles and lifted eyebrows. "I'm growing tomatoes, not marijuana," she informed the clerks who helped her.

"Some do," was the response.

When she found a good price, she bought several large bags and had them held to be picked up by Denny in the truck. She bought a gas-powered tiller and put it in the back of her Lexus along with a gas can she could fill up on the way home.

Before heading back to the Victorian, she stopped off at Jack's Bar. As she entered, he came out of the back. "Well, there's my landlord," she greeted, smiling at him. "I have a couple of things to run by you."

"Something to drink while you run?" he asked. "Cola?"

"Coming up."

"I think you should come out to the house when you have time. I'd like you to come up to the widow's walk with me so we can see a lot of the acreage. You know how the drive to the house runs up the road and forks at the southeastern corner in front? Part of the drive curves to the left in front of the house and the other part goes straight along the eastern side of the house to the back."

"It always seemed like that was the obvious place for a freestanding garage, behind the house," Jack said.

"It's just a gravel drive, so I was wondering something. If I extended it through the trees for access to the back meadow, would you go along with that idea?"

"Good idea," he said. "But I'm sorry to say, I don't think it would be responsible for me to invest any more in that house. That's something an owner should do. Someday."

"Well, here's what I'm offering," Jill said. "I want to put a couple of portable greenhouses back in that meadow, a sheltered place to start some plants. I'm going to fence the plot behind the house to keep the wildlife out, but I'm going to use that back meadow for the greenhouses. I found them online for a few hundred dollars each and they're easily movable."

He leaned both hands on the bar and looked at her closely, quizzically. "Jillian, aren't you taking this gardening thing a bit far?"

"Oh, definitely. To the next level. I want to try some special fruits and vegetables back there. Denny's out getting estimates on excavation crews and the cost of leasing equipment. I'm not talking an asphalt drive, but more of a wide path, wide enough to accommodate one vehicle and, of course, I'll cover the cost. It's really not going to be that expensive—we won't have to take out more than ten trees. In fact, getting some gravel to match what's already down on the drive will probably be the most expensive part."

"Um, Jillian, have you considered going a little slower? A little smaller? I mean, what you're really doing is experimenting, and it seems like an awful big, expensive experiment."

She smiled. "I've been told I can be impulsive, but it usually works for me to go with my gut instinct. Of course, I'll be leaving the extended road when my lease is up, so it should improve the property. For right now, that's what I need to be able to access that meadow. Oh, and thank you for Denny—bright kid. I like him. He thinks I'm a little nuts, but he's awful cute, totally polite and he does exactly what I ask him to do. So—will you come out to the house, look over my plans and give me your approval?"

"I'll come out after breakfast is done," he said. "See you tomorrow."

"Great!" she said, slapping the bar.

He couldn't help but laugh. "Jillian, where did all this come from?"

"From my great-grandmother," she said, taking a sip of her cola. "When she was teaching us to garden, cook, read, clean, sew, she said she was preparing us for life. Well, life has changed a lot in the years since she was my age, but somehow the lessons haven't really changed. They've *evolved.* And I want to be part of that."

Jillian went home and was scooping dirt from several different sections of the garden into small plastic cups with lids and labeling them when Denny returned and came over to report on his activities and progress.

"There is not a lot of work around these days so I was able to have a tree crew come out first thing tomorrow to give you a final estimate," he said. "I hope that works for you. It'll take them two days to cut through those trees. I found a guy who can grade the area and level it out. You can worry about the gravel after that. And I rented a posthole auger so I can get started on the fencing in the meantime."

She smiled very happily at his business sense. "Perfect," she said, sitting back on her heels in the dirt. "Will they come even if it's kind of wet?"

He gave a nod. "Like I said, not so much work around these days. I think I got you a good price because of that. And you get a discount if you let them have the trees. They'll process it into usable lumber."

"Seriously?" she asked, standing up.

"Not huge, but still..."

"Did you shop around a little bit?"

"Three businesses," he said with a nod. "They were pretty much in line. I went with the one who was available right away." Then he got a worried look. "Was that all right? That I made a decision? And rented the post digger?"

"That's what I expected you to do, get it done," she said, balancing all her little containers to take them into the house. "Want to quit for the day or do you want to make a run to FedEx for me? I need to send in the soil samples."

"I'll work till you can't take any more of me," he said with a grin.

She stopped in her tracks, smiled at him and said, "You're my kind of guy, Denny."

"And you're my kind of boss, Miss Matlock."

Jillian thought often about the fact that her best friend was her sister and had been since they were toddlers, yet they were complete opposites in almost every way. They didn't even look alike, Jillian being a tall, slender brunette and Kelly, a shorter, rounder, blonde. Jill's skin tanned nicely while Kelly's tended to burn; Jill had always leaned toward academics while Kelly, the chef, was more artistic. And while even Jill could admit she had a tendency to be impetuous, Kelly always cautiously planned every detail of her life.

Jill had always relied heavily on Kelly, who had a very nurturing personality. When Jill was twelve and started her period, it was Kelly who showed her the ropes. And whenever Jill's heart was broken, whether it be by a boy or just a disappointment, it was Kelly, the more steady of the two of them, who propped her up and encouraged her.

Even while she was in Virgin River, busy with her new garden, Jillian talked to Kelly every day, usually right before Kelly went to work in the afternoon. She liked to climb up to the roof and sit on the widow's walk where her cell reception was best and talk to Kelly, filling her in on her growing plans by the day. By the end of her third week she told Kelly, "There's a bunch of construction equipment parked by the side of the house, a big stack of tree trunks waiting for a flatbed and the road to the back meadow is almost finished. The fencing finally arrived and Denny is working on the posts. Two ten-by-twelve-foot greenhouses are on the way and I've started to till the soil where they're going to be positioned. I can plant both in the ground and in starter trays under the protective domes. It's going to be a two-tiered operation.

"And," Jillian went on, "I put my town house in San Jose on the market."

"You did *what?*" Kelly nearly shrieked.

"I sent the key to my agent by FedEx along with a personal check for a cleaning crew to get it all cleaned up and spiffy. I realized I'm done with that place, Kell," she said. "I'm not attached to it."

"But are you staying there—in Virgin River? Is that the new plan?"

"Honestly? I don't know."

"But what if Harry calls you and asks you to come back to BSS?" Kelly asked.

"I'll cross that bridge when I get to it. For right now, I'm enjoying myself here. I don't know when I've had more fun."

"But Jill, don't you have a plan?"

"Sort of. I want to garden through the summer. I have to see what I can grow. If I had to give up and leave now, it would break my heart! Besides, even if I ended up back in San Jose in the fall, I'd want to rent something for a while. When I think about that town house, I realize it just doesn't feel like home. This feels more like home at the moment, and it's not really even the house, but more the property."

"But are you relaxing?" Kelly asked. "Taking stock of your life? Thinking about what's next?"

Jillian laughed. "In much the same way people relax by running marathons," she said. "I'm busy all day, researching gardens on the computer till late at night."

"And just how do you propose to make a living?" Kelly, the practical one, asked.

"Thanks to ten good years at BSS, a nice exit package and a clever financial planner, I don't have to worry about that right now. But I've been thinking about selling vegetables."

"That sounds profitable," Kelly said facetiously. "I was thinking something a little more long-term."

Jillian just laughed at her. "Jealous?"

"Green!" Kelly said. They both knew that in spite of the fact that Jill was known to jump into the deep end of the pool and Kelly thought everything through with relentless planning, Jill had made a ton of money from BSS and Kelly a relatively poor sous-chef.

"I'm thinking of selling fancy high-end fruits and veggies, the kind your restaurant and other five-star restaurants would buy. But let's not get ahead of ourselves. Right now all I want to know is if I can grow them—then I'll think about the next step."

"I'd better come up there," Kelly said. "I think you've lost your mind...."

Jill laughed. "It's just the opposite, Kell. I feel like I suddenly found it! You know, when was the last time I was this excited? Probably when Harry offered me a chance to work with him to start BSS! I didn't know anything about the software industry, but I knew I could do it! And this? Kelly, I *know* about this! Nana taught us in her own garden how to grow some of this stuff. The Russian Rose! White asparagus! Purple Calabash! And I found the seeds. I already have the seedling cups ready. I bought a truckbed full of chicken shit!"

"An asparagus bed takes up to three years..."

"Then I'd better get it started," Jillian said.

"Aren't you spending an awful lot of money?"

"Nah. My biggest expense right now is Denny, my new assistant. But he's such a great guy and good worker he's helping me speed up this whole process, so he's worth every cent."

"You could run into areas you don't understand, like permits, licensing, agricultural restrictions, that sort of thing. I'd never buy exotic, organic fruits or vegetables from a grower who hadn't passed all the agricultural inspections."

"Kelly, lighten up. No one knows how to hire a consultant like I do—I've done it a hundred times in an industry I didn't understand nearly as well as I do this one. Can't you be a little more positive?"

"Maybe when I stop shaking..."

"Oh, brother. I'd better get this up and running before

you buy your own restaurant. You'll go through so many lists and checkpoints, the place will never open. You'll never get it open without me."

"Seriously, I might have to come up there, make sure you're not totally crazy."

"You're certainly welcome, but you'll have to bring your own recliner."

Colin parked his Jeep near the turnoff into Jill's driveway so the motor wouldn't frighten off early morning wildlife. He walked up the drive and before getting far he noticed a few things. The drive was a muddy mess for one thing, marked with the tire tracks of large equipment. As he neared the house he saw there was a forklift, wood chipper and a little Bobcat backhoe all parked in a row along the tree line east of the house. As he walked around the house he saw a wide path had been cut through the copse of trees to the back meadow, all the huge, felled trees stacked and ready to be taken away.

"Morning," she said.

He whirled around in surprise to see Jillian sitting on the back porch steps wearing purple furry slippers, draped in a quilt and holding a steaming cup of coffee in both hands. It wasn't even 6:00 a.m.

"Morning. What's going on here?"

"A little excavation. I needed access to that back meadow. And we've just about got the garden fenced. I'm afraid we scared off the wildlife for the time being, but I'm sure they'll be back when things quiet down."

"Are things going to quiet down?"

"Sure. Gardening is a serene occupation. But for now there's been some noise. I'm putting up a couple of greenhouses back there behind the trees. Everything should be finished in a week, unless Denny can't figure out how to erect the greenhouses. If we have to get more help, it could take longer. Want a cup of coffee, since you've come all this way?"

He held his camera out to the side, glancing at it. Useless now, he thought. "Sure."

"I'll get it for you and bring it out. There's no place to sit in the house. How do you take it?"

"A little cream."

"Will two percent milk do?" she asked.

He gave her a slight smile. "Yeah. That'll work fine." She pulled the quilt around her and shuffled into the house, into the kitchen. She poured and dressed his coffee.

"There's no furniture in here," he said from behind her. He had followed her inside.

She turned around while stirring. "Sure there is. I have a recliner and all my important stuff—computer, printer, TV. I had to ask Jack to throw a stovetop and refrigerator in here, even though I'm sure the eventual owner will want custom stuff that actually fits the space the builder provided. There's room for lots of large, high-end kitchen appliances—stuff with all the bells and whistles. I just needed the occasional flame and a small refrigerator. I mostly use the microwave."

"Do you have a bed somewhere?"

"Is that important? I'm very comfortable in the recliner and, since I'm not expecting any company it'll do just fine for now…unless my sister comes to be sure I haven't completely lost my mind." She smiled and said, "I told her she'd have to bring her own recliner."

He reached for the coffee. "Why is she worried about that? Because you're living in the kitchen and are planting the back forty?"

Jill chuckled. "You have no idea how perfect this is. When I turn out the lights and the TV I can see the stars from that chair. If it's clear, that is. And it's going to be clear a lot more often in summer. I stand guard, trying to train the deer and bunnies to move along to the next farm. In the early morning, just as the mist and fog are lifting, I can watch the land come to life. I don't usually go outside before seven, but it was such a nice morning today. Actually, I half expected you to show up."

He sipped his coffee. "Where are your clothes?"

She pulled the quilt around her. Her hair was still mussed from sleep and her cheeks kind of rosy and he wanted to pull her into his arms for just a little touch. A little taste. "I'll get dressed in a while," she said.

"No," he said with a laugh. "Your wardrobe. Your luggage. You obviously don't keep them in the kitchen."

"Oh, that—there's a closet in that bedroom—one of two closets in the whole house. Maid's quarters, we think."

"Ah," he said. "So, I guess this means you're going full speed ahead?"

"With the growing? Oh, yes. I'm so charged up I can hardly sleep at night. Want to go outside? Sit on the porch? I mean, there could be a totally crazy deer out there that hasn't been completely intimidated by the excavation noise."

"Sure," he said. "And you can tell me about your greatest expectation for this exercise."

"I think," she said as they went back out the door, "that I'm trying my hand at becoming a commercial farmer. I don't know if it'll work until I know if I can grow the stuff, but I could farm exotic, rare, heirloom fruits and vegetables. The kind that are hard to produce. I would sell them to high-end restaurants that are looking for new and unique, fabulous foods."

He sipped again. "Going to buy a fleet of trucks to deliver them to big cities?"

She laughed. "Nope. Going to call UPS or FedEx and send them overnight. They're delicate—none of them have a long shelf life. And they're not used in mass quantities, usually as side dishes or garnishes."

"How do you make money doing that?"

She shrugged. "You become the best, with the best marketing campaign. And, of course, you start small and regionally. I've already identified target cities with five-star restaurants. I wouldn't ship to New York—it's too far. But shipping to Portland, Sun Valley, Seattle, Vancouver, San Francisco and the surrounding areas would not be a problem."

He chuckled. "I have to admit, it's gutsy and it actually sounds reasonable."

"It's completely reasonable! There is one 'x' factor… and that's whether I can grow these rare, old seeds. I bought product from several different seed companies and I'll check them out. My great-grandmother canned some, sold some fresh off the porch—we had a hard time getting by back then and she had lots of ways to supplement her income. This is a whole different story. If it works, buyers will order ahead of season, so I have to know I can deliver. It'll take me six to eighteen months to figure that out."

"But how long are you renting…?"

"Through summer. But things like moves and leases can be worked out. The one thing I can't control is whether or not I can grow the stuff."

"So, you'll have fruit trees, too?" he asked.

"No trees," she said, shaking her head. "There are a few apple trees on the property, but I'm not planting trees…"

"But you said fruits…"

"Tomatoes, tomatillo, melons, et cetera—are all considered fruits." She smiled.

He felt a little pang of something. A jolt of some kind. She was awful cute. Incredibly smart and very cute.

Colin was a little startled. *Cute* was not in his vernacular. He felt those sizzling jolts when he was with women he would describe as *hot* or *sexy* or *edible*, but he had never before felt a single nerve-tingle for *cute*. He was too jaded for that. He reasoned this was probably only because he hadn't been with a woman for so long and, further, because he assumed he probably wouldn't be again, at least not for a very long time. And certainly not this one—although she was smart as a whip, she was too "girl next door." He was attracted to women in low-cut tops with generous cleavages, microscopic skirts and four-inch heels. The kind of women you wouldn't want your mother to meet.

"Is the eagle painting done?" she asked him.

"Done? Oh, no," he said. "That won't be done for a while. Maybe another few weeks."

"Wow. Don't you get bored, spending so much time on one painting?"

"I have several going at one time. I keep going back, improving, changing, fixing, getting them right. It's hard to know when it's really done. And sometimes when you think they're finished, they're not. More often, when you think they're *not* finished, they really are. Sometimes knowing when to stop is more important than knowing when to keep working on it."

"And then you sell them?"

He shook his head. "Haven't ever sold one."

She sat up straighter and her quilt slipped off one shoulder exposing her striped pajamas. They were almost little-girl pajamas. "Never sold one? How do you make a living?"

Again he chuckled. "I'm independently wealthy."

"How nice for you. Do you plan to ever sell any or are you doing this for fun?"

"Right now painting them is more important than selling them," he said.

"What kind of market is there for a…an *eagle?*"

He smiled at her. Straight to the point, wasn't she? "Huge," he said. "I didn't realize that when I got hooked on animals. Wild animals, not kittens or puppies. I liked them better than bowls of fruit…."

She got a teasing grin on her face. "Better than nudes?"

He matched her grin. "I've never painted any nudes." He lifted an eyebrow. "Was that an offer?"

She burst out laughing and he found the sound was perfectly charming. *Charming?* Yet another word Colin had never used before, but it suited her. And son of a bitch if it didn't *charm* him!

"Oh, believe me, you can do way better than me! Maybe I could strip, wear my garden gloves, straw hat and rubber boots—that should get you a big *Playboy* commission!" And she laughed some more while he got an irresistible image in his head that he wanted to paint. "But seriously, who buys paintings of animals?"

"Wildlife art," he said. "Look it up on Google sometime. It surprised the hell out of me."

"So," she said, sipping the coffee, "you've been at this for a while?"

What the hell, he thought. Everyone else probably knew, given his brother lived here. "I was in the Army. I was a pilot and crashed in a helicopter. I broke a bunch of bones, got some burns, was in therapy for six months trying to get back on my feet, and I painted." He shrugged.

"I've always done some drawing and painting, but it kinda looks like this is how I'm going to spend my time, at least for now. The Army retired me. So," he said with a nod of his chin, "I'm trying to get good."

"Oh," she said, serious. "Sorry about the crash. You all right now?"

"Getting there. I get a little stiff and sore, but otherwise, pretty good."

"And you're here because…?"

"Because my brother is here and there's also an abundance of wildlife. I have another brother in Chico, but no deer or fox or eagles around his house. I rented a cabin till hunting season opens in September. I should be ready to hit the road by then. Meantime, I can paint. My cabin is in a valley by a stream, very isolated. I'm already getting some good pictures of animals there."

She sat up a little straighter. "What happens when hunting season starts?"

"I'll be moving on. Oh, I'm sure I'll visit sometimes. But before I decide where I'll live next I'm planning to spend six months in Africa. The Serengeti. Maybe even head over to the Amazon."

"Big game," she said. Her eyes gently closed and he wondered if she could be visualizing it in her head the way he was—large canvases of elephants, lions, tigers, wildebeests.…

"Big game for me—tiny, weird little vegetables for you. How do you think we're going to do?"

"I don't know how you're going to do, Colin, but I'm going to kick some ass. I'm a marketing and public relations expert and I was taught to grow by the best—my nana. She could throw a diamond in the ground and grow a diamond vine." She grinned. "You don't know me but, trust me, I haven't been this excited in a long, long time."

Four

Colin tried to limit dinner at Luke's to once a week. He was accustomed to being on his own. It bothered him that he actually enjoyed it and it made him wonder if he was losing some of his independent edge. He was fond of Shelby; that sweet young thing was a treasure whom Luke surely couldn't deserve. He got the biggest kick out of Brett. The baby was crawling now and trying to pull himself up on the furniture. Colin still had a problem with Luke and probably always would. Maybe because he was the oldest of the Riordian boys, Luke always took a patriarchal attitude—at least with Colin—acting as if he was the parent and this got on Colin's last nerve.

There should be a statute of limitations on big-brothering. They were only two years apart in age and Luke was not smarter or more experienced. Colin felt that after the age of thirty, brothers of all ages should become equals.

When he got to Luke's, his brother met him on the porch. "Good, you're here a little early. I need to talk to you. Let me get you a cola."

"Skip it," Colin said. "What's on your mind?"

Luke took a deep breath. "Jack mentioned you stopped

by for a beer. I asked him if he was sure that was a beer and he said he was sure."

Colin put his hands on his hips. "So, let me guess. You informed him he shouldn't sell me a beer?"

Luke shook his head. "No, but I'm counting on you making a decision not to order one."

"Why don't you just stay out of it, Luke? I'm capable of managing my own life."

Luke shook his head. "Colin, you can't be doing that—you know that. Alcohol is a drug!"

Colin ground his teeth. "I didn't come here so you could micromanage me. Believe me, I learned more in treatment than you'll ever know. I want you to let me make my own decisions. I'll be fine."

"Listen," Luke said, clearly trying to be patient. "I know you're still coping with a lot of stuff. I'm just trying to keep an eye on things so I can help and—"

"That's what I don't want, don't you get that? I don't want you keeping an eye on a lot of things!"

"Beer is not the answer!" Luke nearly shouted. "Believe me, three beers in six months is not me looking for answers! You gotta back off before you really piss me off!" Colin shouted back.

"I know you've had some challenges, but—"

"Some *challenges?*" Colin asked hotly. "I lost my *life!* I lost my career, the one thing I really lived for—flying! I lost my body and, for a while, my brain! You gotta stay off what's left of my fucking back!"

"Yeah, I just don't want you to lose it all again! Christ, man, you got your painting! You're getting along!"

"You call this getting along? You think this is what I *want?*"

"Colin, it'll get better, you just have to—"

"I have to try to stay steady!" Colin yelled. "*You* have to back off!"

And with that he turned, nearly jumped down the porch stairs, got into his Jeep and got the hell out of there before he got any hotter. Any more stupid. Luke had always gotten to him, or he'd always gotten to Luke; he wasn't sure which. But he'd wanted to throw a punch. Nothing could be more ridiculous than that—Luke would've swung back, and while his body was so much better, it was not ready for a fight. Five years ago he'd have whipped Luke's ass, but now? He was still healing; brittle and off balance. He'd probably just end up rebreaking some things.

He went home. Where he *wished* he did have a beer! He was no longer hungry. He turned on his bright lighting, brought out the four-by-four canvas of the buck. He attached two photos to the top of the canvas—one of the animal he'd caught on camera at the river and a second of a nicer-looking background. He was usually able to get a little lost in the painting, but not this time. And when he heard a car or truck engine about a half hour later, he steamed up all over again. How like Luke to follow him with the fight!

But it wasn't Luke.

"We'd better have a talk," Shelby said from behind him. She'd let herself in.

He turned, palette and brush in hand. "I thought you were Luke."

Shelby closed the door and walked into his brightly lit cabin. "Some advice," she said. "If you want to keep Luke out, it would be best to try the door locks."

He put down the palette and brush. She was such a beautiful, tiny thing in her boots and jeans, suede jacket, hair down to her butt. She was twenty-seven, but she looked even younger. "Aren't you afraid of a typical Riordan screaming match?" he asked her.

"You wouldn't dare," she said. "Riordan men have a lot of flaws, but they're always civil to women. Let's talk. This has to stop."

"Shelby, Luke had no reason to jump on me. I wasn't using drugs of any kind. I just had a couple of beers, a few weeks apart...."

"Not that, I don't care about that. This is about the conflict you have with Luke and he with you. He claims not to know how it all started, but that doesn't matter. He's your brother. He cares about you. Somehow you and Luke have to come to terms. There's no reason to tear up the rest of the family over whatever it is."

"The rest of the family learned to live with it by the time we were eight and ten," he said.

"I didn't," she replied. "Brett didn't."

He was stunned silent for a moment. Briefly ashamed. "Aw, Shelby..."

"I can understand how it gets on your nerves to feel like someone's always watching you. If we hadn't nearly lost you, maybe Luke would go a little lighter..."

"Doubtful," Colin said. "He has a tendency to take charge. Taking charge is fun for him. Not so much for me."

"He loves you. He cares."

"He's a control freak," Colin said.

"Also true," she said. "And so are you or you'd just answer his concerns without a fight every time."

Colin was suddenly deflated and he sat down in the nearest chair, hanging his head. When he lifted it, his eyes were sad. "Please," he said to Shelby. "Sit down for a second."

She sat in the chair nearest him, leaning toward him, her hands on her knees.

Colin took a deep breath. "I have been alerted about problems with cross-addiction. For several months I didn't even gargle with mouthwash that contained microscopic amounts of alcohol. I've never been a big drinker. Oh, there were times I could overdo it with my boys, but I wasn't irresponsible—no DUIs in my history, no bar fights, no issues. I don't think a beer once a week or month is going to be a problem for me. But still—there isn't any liquor of any kind in this cabin. Go ahead," he said. "Check."

"I'm not going to check."

"I never had a drug or drinking problem, but over a month of lots of Oxycontin right after the crash is a whole different animal. It's powerful stuff and I was having a lot of pain. I think it's possible if I'd had my medicine flipped to a nonnarcotic after a week or two I wouldn't have faced this problem, but that's hindsight. I have to go forward with the knowledge that I tried to buy it on the street, I was that panicked at the thought of running out. That's addict thinking. Trust me, I'm aware."

"Why couldn't you just talk to Luke about it?" she asked.

"It's complicated," he said. "First of all, Luke never listens. He never minds his own goddamn business. He's real judgmental, which happens when you know everything. And I have bigger problems—I'm trying like hell to get some kind of life! This isn't what I had in mind."

"The paintings, Colin," she said, letting her hand wave at the room, gesturing at all the paintings nearly done, leaning against the walls or up on easels. "They're so good. Just amazing."

"But this is not what I planned. I like to draw, paint, build... But I *love* to fly! I wasn't going to stop—I was going to fly until the FAA stopped me. I knew the Army would force me out eventually, but I planned on doing civilian rescue chopper flying or news chopper or corporate flying. But now, with a history of drug treatment and hospitalization for depression, that's out of the picture. Even I wouldn't hire me."

"I'm sorry, Colin. But I think it was the right decision. Treatment."

"No argument there. I was only on the oxy merry-go-round for a month—I was in the pen with people who'd been addicted for years. To that and to even worse stuff. Multiple stuff. Now I might be just kidding myself, and we'll see, but those folks coming out of long-term addiction to multiple drugs probably shouldn't risk the occasional beer. I used oxy for thirty days and don't really know how long my addiction was and, by the grace of God, I got caught the *first time* I tried to buy it on the street. My chances of getting beyond that? I'd say they're good! To tell you the truth, that's the least of my problems—I don't even want a painkiller. I have aches and pains, but a life I didn't choose was left to me. And I have a big brother who can't back off and let me figure things out."

"The lifestyle change must be so hard for you."

"You have no idea," he said. "If it's not bad enough that I'm starting over, I'm forty with a sketchy record of rehab and other stuff, and a whole crop of twenty-five-year-old hotshots ready to fill my slot. Now look, I'm not going to go off the deep end. I'm not going to complain or take drugs or drink myself into a blind stupor, but if Luke doesn't stop riding me and taking my temperature all the time, I might just go completely crazy. Or deck him. Or move. After all—most of this is his fault."

Shelby sat up a bit straighter. "Luke's fault?"

"I struggled to keep up with him my whole life. I admired him so much, I watched every move he made. But I wanted to be a helicopter pilot from the first time I saw one banking across the sky. Then Luke stumbled into a chopper pilot slot in the Army and made it look fun and easy. He made it look like it was his idea. For me, it was way more than that." He leaned toward her. "Shelby, it was the best thing I ever did in my life. It became my passion, my lover, my best friend. I know Luke hates this, but I was good. I was a natural. If Luke was good, and he was, then I was *incredible.* That machine was made for me. I love flying."

"Luke said your first words when you became conscious after the wreck were that you were going to fly again."

"I wasn't able to pull that off," he said.

"I'm not sure you have to give it up," Shelby said. "Maybe for a while, while you heal body and soul, but not forever. Let's not fall off that bridge yet."

"Aw, skip it. There are plenty of ex-Army chopper pilots out there looking for work, Shelby. Shake a tree and ten of 'em fall out."

"So? Then?"

"Down the road I might find a flying job of some kind that's a little out there—something the average family man wouldn't take. To and from oil rigs, wilderness stuff, I don't know. That's in the future. Right now I'm going to see how it works to paint for a while. I don't hate it. I never hated it. My mom and all my high school teachers wanted me to go to college and study art, but art was just too tame for me. But now I'm a little slower, so… I just don't know if it's going to be enough. The reason I came up here instead of going to Montgomery where Sean lives or Chico where Aiden is—there's some wildlife here. I need a little more time to get stronger. I'm working with some weights. I'm making an effort. But this isn't permanent, me being here. This is temporary."

"We know that."

"I'll visit more often than I have in the past," he said. "That little guy, I think he needs me to offset his father...."

"Be nice now," Shelby said with a smile. "That's the man I love."

"Imagine," he said with a laugh. "I don't know how he caught you."

Shelby stood. "I caught him. He fought me all the way."

Colin stood. "See? He's an inferior being."

"Now that I know you're fine, even if you are missing a good dinner, I'm taking off."

"Tell him what we talked about. Tell him I'm sorry I lost it. I don't hate him. I just need him to give me space."

She looked over her shoulder at Colin. "I'll tell him what we talked about. *You* tell him you're sorry and what you need. You're grown-up men. By now you should be able to do this."

"We can't ever seem to get there," Colin said.

"Try harder," she suggested.

"Did you give Luke this lecture?" Colin asked.

"Not this one," she said. "He didn't get the gentle one." And then she was out the door.

An hour later there was a knock at the cabin door and Colin swore. He yanked open the door and Luke was standing there, a brown paper bag in his hand. "I hope we're about done with the Luke and Shelby show now," Colin said.

Luke didn't respond to that. He said, "Shelby's not that much of a cook.... Don't tell her I said that, either. But she's got a few things she never screws up, like this meat loaf. It's Preacher's recipe, I think. You wouldn't want to miss it."

"I already had something to eat," Colin lied.

"Put it in the refrigerator for tomorrow night. And I'm going to stay out of your business."

Colin lifted a brow. "Was that an apology?"

"Nope. I don't think I'm up to that yet because, although I take some responsibility, you are a huge pain in the ass. Here," he said, pushing the bag toward him.

Colin took the bag. "She chewed your ass, didn't she?"

Luke shook his head. "Worse. She cried."

"Shelby cried?" Colin asked. "Aw, Jesus. Come in here."

"I don't feel like it. You didn't make her cry. I did. And I'm not going to ever do that again. I really can't take it when she's unhappy. I know that makes me just a real wimp in your very manly eyes, but that woman..." He shrugged lamely. "My life was pretty much an empty barrel till she came along and slapped me into shape. So there—now you know I'm not tough...."

"What the hell did you say to make her cry?" Colin asked a bit meanly.

"It wasn't what I said to her, you idiot. It's what I said to *you!*"

Colin shook his head. "I'm a little lost here, pal."

"Yeah, because you're not that bright. We had yet another argument, me and you, and right after Shelby told me I was a stupid asshole, she said if I do one more thing to alienate you or cause you to move away before you plan to, I was going to be pretty hard to forgive."

"Then she cried?" Colin asked.

Luke shook his head. "She said she didn't give a flying fuck how I felt about you or how you felt about me, but *she* loves you. And yes, sweet little Shelby did so say *flying fuck.* And she loves you and Brett loves you and she wants you in our lives and I'd better make it right with you or she was never going to forgive me."

Colin was completely stunned for a second. It wasn't hard for him to imagine Shelby yelling at Luke, giving him the business. It wasn't hard to imagine her getting downright pissed because the boys were fighting again; women got sick of that fast, witness their mother. But loving him? Bringing into focus that Brett loved him? They all loved him? When he was singularly unlovable? How was that possible?

"I'm assuming she means she loves you like a brother," Luke said. "That better be it, too, or the fighting's just begun."

Colin broke into a grin in spite of himself. "And then so has the crying, I guess."

"Go ahead and joke, but she's a good woman. Too good for me, that's for sure. I have to really scramble to stay good enough for her, but it's a job I'm up to. So eat the goddamn meat loaf, come to dinner next week or sooner and I'll stay out of your business."

"Done," Colin said.

"Done," Luke said, putting out a hand.

Colin shook the hand. "Thanks for the meat loaf. It'll be great tomorrow night."

"You're welcome," Luke said. He turned to go.

"Luke," Colin called. Luke turned around. "Tell her we kissed and made up and that we won't make her cry anymore."

"I plan to." And with that, he left.

Colin closed the door, but this time he locked it. He was done with this complicated family bullshit for the night. Just being part of the Riordan clan was a contact sport.

He put the bag on the table and removed the little plastic containers that were inside—meat loaf, mashed potatoes, peas, gravy. He got a plate out and dished himself a healthy portion of each item. There was more than enough for two nights. He dug in appreciatively; Luke was right about this—it was excellent. He was also right about Shelby not being a great cook, but she was good enough. And she had qualities that were way more important than being good in the kitchen.

He shoveled the food into his mouth. They loved him? He knew they accepted him; he knew Brett had kind of taken to him. He just never thought there was a possibility Shelby cared deeply enough to threaten her marriage with tears and ultimatums and fights over wanting him to be around. She must be pretty sure of Luke's commitment to do that. Oh—it was only family love, not romantic. He'd never had a single romantic thought about her; it just didn't compute, not with her being so wildly in love with Luke and all. And vice versa.

He'd had a girl or two wildly in love with him, as a matter of fact. But he'd never met a girl he felt the same way about. Never met a woman he felt so strongly about he'd do anything to make her happy.

Suddenly and without much warning, he felt satisfied, and not because of the meat loaf. He got all emotional inside and thought, it's the damn wreck, the pills and flirtation with depression—he'd never been like that before. He wasn't that easy to touch.

But he was completely and deeply touched. Maybe in all those years that the helicopter was his lover there had been a hole inside that needed to be filled by actual human beings. People who would take a risk, a chance, a bet that he would come through, that he was worth it.

Yup, he definitely felt a gap he couldn't fill with adventure or challenge or pure recklessness. He could feel it; there was a yearning.

A tear ran down his cheek, and he didn't brush it away. And he wasn't sure why not.

* * *

It wasn't spoken of again. Colin had dinner with Luke and his family a few days later. He rolled around on the floor with Brett, though he still couldn't lift the hefty baby boy over his head with his left arm. He looked at Luke's plans for a small, four-port RV hookup station behind the house and cabins. He'd hired an electrician and plumber; there would be some digging for waste disposal, a separate waterline for potable water hookup, a new electrical unit installed, some concrete poured and a little landscaping to finish it off. Each hookup port would have a small patio surrounded by shrubs and flowers and a community path to the river. Ultimately, in addition to his cabins, Luke would have hookup facilities for those who vacationed in motor coaches, including his mother and George.

Colin considered it a successful evening—no arguing with Luke—and he was ready to say good-night. He thanked Shelby for a fantastic dinner with a sweet kiss on her cheek.

A few days later Colin went into Jack's Bar and discovered Luke taking a beer break at the same time. It was fated. They didn't sit together but were at right angles to one another up at the bar. Colin thought about ordering a cola, but he was ready for his weekly beer and he was damn well having it.

Luke raised his own brew in a toast and burning there in Luke's eyes were the questions—how many? How long?

Should we talk about this? Are we in a crisis? But to his credit, Luke said nothing. Colin knew that took a lot of willpower. When Luke stood to leave Colin waved him over, threw him a bone for the sake of peace. "I'm only having one beer and I'm staying for dinner, but tell Shelby we talked and we're good."

"I'll do that."

* * *

The day after dawned bright; the sun was coming up earlier as spring marched across the land. Colin went out looking for wildlife and late in the morning he drove to the Victorian house the old way, past the farms and vineyards, up the side of the mountain, until he got to that back pasture he'd discovered a couple of weeks ago. But it had changed—the road, nothing more than graded dirt was now covered in fine gravel. Passing through the trees Colin saw there was a small greenhouse erected, with the frame up for a second. The Plexiglas panels were lying on the ground beside it.

Jillian was amazing, all that she dared to do on a whim. He didn't see her anywhere, but he was curious about what she might have inside that greenhouse. The door was standing open and he looked inside. She was laying there, on the ground, flat on her back, looking up. Her hands were crossed over her stomach and her eyes were open.

He went in and stood over her. "Do you feel as ridiculous as you look?" he asked her.

She didn't even glance at him. "I want to see and feel what the seedlings will see and feel. My nana used to *taste* the soil."

"But you wouldn't go that far," he said.

She sat up and smiled at him, teasing him. "It tastes just fine," she said.

He crouched to get eye level with her. "You didn't really put dirt in your mouth. You're just leading me on."

"Think what you like," she said. "Why are you here? Looking for deer?"

"I wanted to see what you'd accomplished. You've been a busy little girl." He stood up and looked down at her. "Why is the other greenhouse only framed?"

She put out a hand for a lift up off the ground. "Denny, my associate, had a job interview and we couldn't get it finished yet. Those were our terms, remember—he's hunting for more permanent work and I knew that going in." She brushed off the butt of her jeans with her hands. "I hope he doesn't take it—he's working out real well for me. On the other hand, if he stays on much longer I'm going to have to make adjustments, pay social security, provide some benefits, maybe bribe him with better pay and then find things for him to do."

"I'm pretty impressed by the way you're just going for it. You got this idea, and that's all it was. I saw it happen—I was there. When Dan told you how to find your special seeds and how they grow pot around here, I saw your eyes light up and next thing I know, the property is full of equipment and you are just taking *off!* That's incredible. Brave and impressive. You're a gutsy little broad. I admire that in a woman."

She felt her whole body get warm; she looked at him in a whole new way. Jillian was a sucker for a man who admired her. She already found him attractive, but that was easy since he truly was. Suddenly he was also desirable. After having so many people, including the sister she admired so much, think she was out of her mind to go this far, Colin said he was impressed. She saw him through new eyes. She wanted to run her fingers through his neatly trimmed beard and the curly hair pulled into a short ponytail. She noted some subtle scarring on the right side of his neck that disappeared into his shirt collar, but it didn't strike her as unsightly. His brown eyes were kind of sultry and sexy; his arms looked so strong and capable, his hands so big. And, he either had a sock in his drawers or possessed an admirable package. She jerked her eyes back to his face only to find him grinning.

"Why, thank you," he said, acknowledging that he'd caught her. "But why don't you let me take you out to lunch first."

She ran a hand through her hair. "First?" Best to just play dumb.

"Before a lot of dirty, mindless sex."

"All right, I'm just going to have to ask you to leave now."

"Aw, get over it. How about I take you somewhere for food, no obligation. I'm hungry and it's lunchtime."

She sighed. "I'm a mess. I'm not going anywhere."

"Jill, even when you're a mess, you're just pretty as hell."

"Hmm. Pretty as hell," she mimicked. "I bet the women just faint when you say that."

He laughed at her and she noticed the most beautiful white, straight teeth.

"I thawed some stuff for lunch," she said. "If you can behave yourself, you can have Denny's half since he's a no-show."

"And then—"

"Don't push it." She started walking, headed for the new road that would lead her to the house.

"Let's ride," he said. He couldn't help laughing at her. "Then I can park the Jeep by the back porch."

She stopped walking and shot him a damning look.

"I'm crazy to even let you near my back porch," she told him.

He went around to the driver's side. "I figured you for a better sense of humor. Come on, lighten up. Get in."

There was probably good reason she was a little squeamish when teased like that, given her sexual harassment experience. But she reminded herself that Colin couldn't sue her and she couldn't sue him, so why was she getting all excited....

And excited was what she was getting, though she tried hard to pretend otherwise, and to keep her eyes off his body. He was a big, beautiful man and when he grinned and played and teased, she felt a little weak in the knees. She felt like a girl, and it wasn't a bad feeling.

She got in the Jeep and said, "I could teach you gardening...."

"And I could teach you painting, but at the end of the day I wouldn't be a gardener and you wouldn't be a painter."

"I think you're right about that." She relented. "I really wish I could do what you do, however. That eagle was brilliant."

He cast her a glance as he drove through the trees. "Really? Then maybe if you're very good I'll show you the bear, fox, mountain lion and deer. And also the ones I made up without photo models." He pulled right up alongside the house and threw the Jeep into Park.

She got out and on her way up the porch steps she said, "Why do I have to earn it by being good? Don't you feel like bragging?"

"It's better when you beg," he said, his voice low. "It's always better when you beg."

She knew there was some kind of sexual innuendo in that, but she didn't let him see that she noticed it. She went across the porch and into the kitchen, washed her hands and headed to the refrigerator. She started pulling things out—a plate of Italian sausages, a plastic bowl of onions and peppers, a bag of sandwich rolls. "Sausage and peppers?" she asked.

"No kidding? That sounds great. And lookie here," he said, sitting on a stool at her work island. "Furniture!"

She popped the peppers and sausages into the microwave. "I didn't want to go overboard," she said, smiling in spite of herself.

"You're safe," he laughed. "No one will accuse you of overdecorating." He watched her get out plates, slice the rolls the long way, get the warmed sausage and peppers out of the microwave, nuke the sliced rolls and build them sandwiches. His was much larger and meatier than hers. She put a couple of canned colas on the work island and claimed a stool across from him. "What will we do if Denny shows up for lunch?" he asked.

"Not to worry," she said. "There's baloney and cheese." Then she bit into her sandwich.

"So, what gives a young girl like you the ambition to go after something like this?" he asked. "On such a large scale?"

She chewed and swallowed. "First of all, I'm not a young girl anymore. Thirty-two is a very respectable age and not so much younger than you."

"Ah, I get it. You're offended by being called a girl?" he asked.

"Not really, as long as you stipulate my being an adult."

"You're definitely an adult," he admitted with a laugh. "Your ambition? The confidence that goes with it?"

"Originally? Probably from my great-grandmother. Nana." She put down her sandwich. "Nana had ONE daughter, an only child. My great-grandfather was an older man when they married and died before that daughter was grown. That daughter, my grandmother, had a son out of wedlock, which in the fifties was still a big scandal, a huge embarrassment." She took another bite, put down her sandwich and chewed. "So," she said, wiping her mouth. "My grandmother was very young and she left the little baby boy with Nana so she could chase after the man, the baby's father. Nana said she chased him and never returned. Maybe something happened to her, or maybe she just ran off for good. So my nana raised her grandson alone, and then, like the poor woman was born under an unlucky star, there was an accident that left our father dead and our mother an invalid and Nana took us all in—my crippled mother and me and Kelly, aged five and six. She was already an old woman then," Jillian said, shaking her head. "I don't know how she managed. But she was amazing. No matter how tough things got, she was totally positive. And brave? Oh my God, she was so fearless! She might've been the smartest woman I've ever known but she didn't consider herself smart. She didn't have much formal education but she spoke five languages! And she sure as hell had no money, so she pushed us real hard to study and get scholarships and make something of ourselves." She took another bite, chewed slowly, swallowed and said, "Which we did."

Colin hadn't bitten into his sandwich for a while; he was listening raptly. His own upbringing had had its challenges—there wasn't a lot of money, his mother's garden was important to the subsistence of the family, they'd gone to Catholic school on partial scholarship and it had been impossible to afford to send five sons to college. But his growing up wasn't anything like hers!

He tried not to react. He ate some of his sandwich. "Got yourself a scholarship, did you?"

"I did. Kelly was tougher—she wanted to be a chef, to study cooking. Getting financial aid for culinary institutes, especially abroad, was almost hopeless. But, we managed. So, I did pretty well and was barely out of college with a marketing degree and looking for work when I was approached by this guy who was starting a company—a software manufacturing company. He found me in the college Who's Who—I had a good GPA. But, you could have fit what I knew about software manufacturing between the slices of this bun," she said, holding up what was left of her sandwich. "He offered me a job. Low pay to start, insane hours, reasonable benefits, but if we could pull it off, stock and bonuses. I told him I didn't know anything about his business and he said, 'Research. Learn.' And I did. He'd successfully started a few companies and before I even accepted the job, I knew everything about him I could ever know. I knew his birth weight! Harry Benedict—I love that guy. He not only gave me a chance, he taught me, let me perform, put me on the ground floor and I helped take that company to one of the most successful public offerings on record. I was with them for ten years when it was time for a change, time to move on." She smiled at him. "I was taking a leave of absence to relax, to get a little thinking space, but I sank my hands in this dirt, remembered my nana and whoops...." She shrugged. "I'm back in the garden. And relaxation is about the last thing I want."

"And you're happy?" he asked.

She laughed. "I didn't think I was *unhappy* at BSS with Harry and a growing company, but this is better, surprisingly."

"Your great-grandmother taught you to garden?"

"Yes," Jillian said. "The old way. Small garden. Now the internet is teaching me," she said, swinging an arm wide to indicate her "office" of chair, computer, et cetera. "Things have obviously changed. Who taught you to paint?"

"I don't know," he said with a shrug. "My pictures weren't smeary like the other kids and the teachers moved me along. They took advantage of me, too—made me do all their art and posters and lettering. By the time I got to high school I was doing murals. They wanted me to study art in college, but I wanted the Army."

"Really? What was it about the Army?" she asked him.

"Low, fast, scary, dangerous combat choppers. I wanted to fly. I thought I wanted Cobras first, but I started out in the Huey and moved into Black Hawks and found out I loved them. I did twenty in the Army. So, why aren't you married?" he asked.

She burst out laughing. "I couldn't get a weekend off. Harry worked me to death."

"Seriously," he pushed.

"Seriously! I dated sometimes." He had an earnest look on his face. "Okay, I dated a little. I had a guy for a few months, but we broke up."

"Why?"

"Not important. And very over."

"But why? Was he abusive?"

"He never spoke meanly or hit me. Give it up. I'm not telling you and you'll never figure it out."

"He cheated?" Colin asked.

"Probably, but that isn't what broke us up. Really, rest your brain. This one hasn't reached the Dear Abby column."

He studied her for a moment. "Hmm," he said. "At first glance you're a muddy little girl. On closer inspection you're a complicated woman."

"I'm sure there was a compliment in there somewhere...."

"And beautiful," he added with a smile, pleased to note that by her expression he had surprised her.

"Oh, you must be very lonely and hard up. My sister,

Kelly, whom you've never met, is really the beautiful one. I get by. But she's a knockout."

"*She's* a knockout?" he asked, straightening suddenly, eyes wide. "Jillian, you are hot! I mean, I've only seen you dressed up once, but anyone who can pull off hot without fussing around is completely hot. Besides you look like that actress, what's her name…"

"Yeah," she said, leaning her chin in her hand as if bored. "I remember seeing her."

"Seriously. She got an Academy Award. Sandra Somebody. And I like that you don't fuss much. I never liked fuss," he lied. He'd always been overly attracted to fuss and couldn't remember why. "Besides, you're trying to grow stuff." And looking so earthy, so healthy, so naturally beautiful. And *hot*. The way her firm little butt filled out those cargo pants, he wanted to drool. He thought she was wearing a tank top under a T-shirt, no bra, and her breasts were just exactly the right size. And she was delicious looking.

"It isn't working," she said. "I realize it's a small town and there aren't too many single females here, but I'm not looking for a fling. I'm very busy."

"I'm not bullshitting you," he insisted.

Again she burst out laughing. "Oh, Colin, you're going to have to practice up on that lying. You're awful at it."

"I'm not lying," he said, straight-faced. "You're a beautiful woman."

"Right," she said, waving a hand. "Whatever. And you're a lovely man. But I have seeds waiting." She lifted a brow. "You about done there?"

He took the last bite of his sandwich, chewed and swallowed. "For now," he got out in spite of his full mouth. *For now*, he thought.

Five

Denny peeled the cap off his head as he walked into Jack's Bar.

"Well now," Jack said brightly. "How goes the chasing of fame and fortune?"

"Fame?" Denny asked with a laugh. "I hope not!"

"The job search? Didn't you have interviews today?" Without being asked, Jack served him up a beer.

"Two. Stocking and loading dock for a big grocer and some ranch work clear on the other side of the valley—Ferndale—where they have six hundred people and sixty thousand cows."

Jack laughed. "See any potential in either one?"

"Oh, the grocer is going to make me president of the company pretty quick if I just jump on board and work my tail off for minimum." He sipped his beer. "When have I heard that before? I'm just as glad."

"Glad?"

Denny shrugged. "I know it's only temporary, but I like what I'm doing for Jillian. I'm busy every minute, the pay is good and did you know she talks all the time?"

Jack laughed. "Why does that not surprise me?"

"It's not chatter, exactly—she talks about growing,

about the interesting varieties of fruits and vegetables you hardly ever see that her great-grandmother used to grow, that she brought from the old country. Plus I do so many different things—sometimes I chop trees or build greenhouses and sometimes I poke little tiny seeds into little cups of dirt. And then Jillian describes what will happen to those seeds, step by step, talking about the acidity of the soil, the ground temperature, the altitude, how everything plays together…and I'd kinda hate to miss it."

"How long do you think she'll keep you on?" Jack asked him.

"No telling," he said with a shrug. "We're almost caught up with work for now. But she's got a lot of growing going on and, if I know her, she's going to put up a couple more greenhouses. She's talking about it. There's room in that meadow. She'll have to heat 'em, irrigate 'em, and once the fall and winter come…who knows what will be involved. She's been talking about seeing some grow lights in her future." He took another swallow of his beer. "Sounds like she might be renting awhile. You okay with that?"

Jack shrugged. "I'm not going to find a buyer next winter unless things change in this economy by a lot. And she's keeping the place nice and paying the bills."

"Good," Denny said. "I'm kind of getting into this…."

"Have you told her that, son?" Jack asked.

Denny got a startled look on his face. Then he answered, simply, "No."

"You should let her in on the secret. Tell her you're enjoying the work. Can't hurt. Might help."

"Yeah… Might…" He cleared his throat. "I did get some good news today. The Sheriff's Department will be hiring in three to six months. I have my app in at all the law enforcement and fire departments."

"Good for you!"

"Oh, by the way, I didn't have to go to Jillian's at all today so I drove out to your place and did a few things around the yard—picked up the dog doo and ran the lawn mower around the grassy area. I cut under the play set, edged around the slide and legs and under the jungle gym."

Jack whistled. "That must've taken forever."

"Slow and steady," Denny said.

Jack gave the bar a wipe. "You know you don't have to do that, Denny. I really appreciate it, but I don't expect it."

"You let me stay there rent-free for two months, right up to Christmas! I'll be a long time paying that back."

"There's no debt," Jack said. "Apparently it's the smartest thing I've ever done—there's been a lot of free labor. How are things going down at the Fitch house?"

"Great. That room over the garage is perfect, all the privacy I want, no one to clock in with, nice folks. Mrs. Fitch is trying to replace all the girlie, flowery stuff in the room with manly stuff," he said with a grin. "I told her that doesn't matter. She must be worried about my sexual preference."

"I think I'm worried about it," Jack joked. "You getting out much at all?"

"I took out a girl named Mindy a few times. She's a waitress at a restaurant up in Arcata—nice girl. We had fun, then her ex-boyfriend turned up. I should'a just killed him. I'm on the hunt again."

"Be careful, buddy," Jack said. Jack looked around to be sure they weren't overheard. "And what about that other matter? The one that brought you up here? The search for your biological father?"

"Hmm," Denny said. "I'm pretty sure I found him. I'm just moving real slow. It shouldn't come as any surprise—he's married with a family. I don't want to mess up his situation."

"Is he a good guy? I know that was high on your list of concerns."

"Very good guy as far as I can tell. I've gotten to know him some. He has no idea who I might be, so there's no pressure there. There is one thing I hadn't counted on— I'm kind of committed to this place now. No matter how the guy reacts to me, I feel like staying here."

"That shouldn't be a problem, son. There's plenty of room here for everyone. So maybe you and the old man won't ever be best buddies, but isn't it enough if you at least know about each other, accept each other, get along? Hell, what if you need a kidney someday?"

Denny laughed. "You sure do have a practical side, Jack. I hope he doesn't ask me for an organ right after I break it to him."

Jack grinned. "You never know. Maybe he's been patiently waiting for the day! You want dinner?"

"Not tonight. I'm headed over to Fortuna to meet Mindy's possible replacement for a fish dinner." He lifted a brow. "My first question will be whether there's a boyfriend in her recent past."

"Good luck with that."

Denny drained his beer, headed out the door and left Jack thinking, *What a good kid.* And, not for the first time, he thought how glad he was Denny happened into his bar. They'd become pretty good friends. Since his young protégé, Rick, was now married to his teenage sweetheart, Liz, and in college full-time in Oregon Jack didn't see him too often, just when he had enough time to come back to town to check on his elderly grandmother. They emailed and talked on the phone regularly, but Jack had been missing the presence of a good-natured young man. After having taken on so many young Marines in his career, it was natural for Jack. In fact, Denny was only a couple of years older than Rick and he reminded Jack of him in many ways.

The bar was very busy for a late-March evening; it seemed like a lot of his friends had chosen this night to have dinner together and most of the neighborhood stopped by. Jack was able to have dinner with Mel and the kids as long as he ate in short shifts between serving tables and bussing them. His brother-in-law, Mike, spent a little time behind the bar, pouring drafts and drinks; Mike was a more than adequate stand-in bartender and the cost of his labor was right—totally free. Being a small farming and ranching town that kept early hours, by eight-thirty there were only a few stragglers left and Jack helped out in the kitchen a little bit. By nine he was starting to envision his house, quiet with the kids in bed, his wife relaxed and sitting up with her laptop, writing emails or surfing the Net, researching, reading medical blogs. He loved going home to his family at night.

The door opened and Denny walked in, scrubbing that ball cap off his head. "Oh-oh," Jack said. "Does this mean Mindy's potential replacement didn't answer the question right? The recent-boyfriend question?"

"Nah, that went fine. Her name is Crystal, by the way." He shrugged. "Nice enough girl. No bells went off, though."

"I was just about to pour that end-of-day shot," Jack said. "Can I get you something?"

"Maybe I'll join you," Denny said. "I know you're a Scotch man. Make mine Canadian, will you?"

Jack got the glasses ready. "You act like maybe the date didn't go so well." He reached for a bottle and because it was Denny, made it a good Canadian.

"Date was fine. I just had something on my mind so if it wasn't perfect, I have no one to blame but myself."

"What's up?" Jack asked.

Denny took a breath. "I've been meaning to talk to you about this. Some of it I told you when I came up here last fall—about looking for my father. And—that my mom's boyfriend's name is on my birth certificate, but he took off when I was about seven or ten or something. He came and went a few times before he went for good and after that last time, I only talked to him if I made the contact. Me and my mom…we weren't sorry to see him go. You know all that…."

"What's wrong, son?"

Another deep breath. "My mom's name was Susan Cutler. Ring any bells with you, Jack?"

"Did I know her?" he asked.

"For just a little while. You dated her for a couple of months back when you were at Fort Pendleton. I guess you were about twenty."

"If I was twenty and at Fort Pendleton and dated your mother, I didn't see much of her," Jack said. "I imagine I'd have been in training there."

"Sounds about right. You were just a couple of kids, younger than me." He pulled an old and worn envelope out of the inside of his jacket pocket. "She had a hard time talking about when she was young. She always felt like she let me down. She never married, exposed me to a father figure who was a pure jackass, ended up raising me alone. She didn't let me down—my mom was awesome. But, since she had trouble looking me in the eye and talking about it, she wrote me this letter. *Then* we talked about it. Would you read it?"

Jack lifted a brow. "You really want me to?"

"It's not very long. Yeah, I'd like you to read it." He put it on the bar and pushed it toward him.

Jack locked eyes with him as he pulled the envelope over. He wasn't sure he liked where this was going. He opened it and read, Denny, my dearest, We both know this cancer is not going away, that it's only a matter of time, and there's something I have to tell you, but it's so hard for me I'm putting the facts in a letter and then, if you want to, we can talk about it.

When I was twenty, I fell in love. Oh, I truly did, but I made the mistake of falling in love with a twenty-year-old Marine who was shipping out in a couple of months and didn't want any commitments. He was good to me, a wonderful young man with a nice family, and we had a real good time together. We laughed so much! He was so kind and tender, but also strong and fearless. And as I was warned, he left. He told me from the first time he held my hand—there was an expiration date on our romance.

I was pretty brokenhearted, but I started dating Bob, also a Marine at the time, but not the best man in the world. I realized after a few weeks that I was pregnant and I knew Bob wasn't the father. I'm sorry, Denny—I lied to you all these years because I was ashamed and sorry; also because I was afraid of what Bob would do to us if he knew I lied to him. The finest man I ever knew left, I never tried to find him because we had an agreement—no commitments. I let Bob and you think that Bob was your father. So… We know how Bob turned out—not only a bad example, but a poor excuse for a man—abusive, mean, unfaithful. The day he left for good was probably our best day. And now I feel like I'm failing you with this awful cancer. Denny, I'm not afraid to die, I'm just afraid to leave you with questions, and thinking you have a father with scary DNA you can't be proud of! The truth is, Bob was not your father. Your father's name is Jack Sheridan. I don't know where he ended up or what became of him, but you can believe you did have a father you could be proud of.

There was more to the letter, but Jack let his hand drop to the bar while he stared, wide-eyed and openmouthed at Denny. He looked him straight on and said, in his Jack way, "Are you *shitting* me?"

Denny paled. "No, sir. You're the guy I came to find."

"Are we *sure?*" he asked.

"After the letter," Denny said, "we talked about it. She was a young girl, but girls that age think they know everything—her words, not mine. She worked at Camp Pendleton. She got that job to meet guys, she said, but ended up working there for about ten years, a civilian employee. But she said she didn't screw around. She liked to go out, go dancing, go to movies, parties, that kind of thing. I have some pictures," he said, going back into that pocket. "She was so pretty." He passed the pictures across the bar.

Jack frowned. She didn't look twenty in the pictures, but older than that. He said nothing, just waited for Denny.

"She said when she met you, she just lost it. Totally fell for you, but you had some orders pending and said you could only date if it was understood…"

Jack shook his head sadly. "That sure sounds like Jack Sheridan…." He looked at the photos. Both of them were studio portraits taken with a much younger Denny. She was an attractive brunette with a sweet smile and a handsome little son. He wanted to bang his head on the bar. She looked vaguely familiar but he couldn't remember her. He wanted to remember her so much he ached inside.

"She told me about your parents—your dad was some kind of stock broker or something. And your four sisters—two older, two younger and the little one still in grade school. But the part that embarrassed her and kept her from being honest with me—she started dating Bob right away after you left because she was so lonely and so heartbroken with you gone. And she realized she was pregnant and Bob couldn't be the father by a month." He shook his head. "She said there was no one else, Jack. And I know she was my mom, but I believe her anyway."

"Denny, when I was twenty, I was at Pendleton for a few months. I remember dating a girl named Ginger for a while, but I was all caught up in the Corps. Ginger broke it off with me because I wouldn't think serious." He shrugged. "There might've been a couple of girls here and there, but I don't remember any who could've been in love...."

"I know what being twenty in the Marines is like, Jack."

Jack didn't read the rest of the letter. He slid it across the bar toward Denny. "You've been up here for months," Jack said.

"Yeah. It took me a while to get to know you, then I had to be sure the truth wouldn't make your life harder, then... Then there was the time it took to get up the courage. Because once I let it out, I couldn't take it back. You know?"

Jack lifted his shot and threw it back. With shot glass in hand, he pointed at Denny's drink. "You'd better drink that, son."

Denny lifted the drink, but paused. "Look, I get it if you say this isn't the happiest day of your life."

Jack scowled. "Drink," he said. When Denny put down the glass Jack said, "Any man would be proud to

Robyn Carr

have you for a son. Any man, me included. I'm just having a real hard time with the facts, with knowing what kind of man I was, that I'd scare a woman off telling me she's pregnant because I can't be bothered with the responsibility. And I'm having a real goddamn hard time thinking I had the kind of relationship that would bring me a son and… And I can't remember her."

Jack leaned on the bar. "Accidents happen all the time, Denny, but I gotta be honest with you—I was careful. Not stupid careful—I was always armed with protection. When you talked to your mother, did she say anything like that we *knew* there was a problem? Like a blowout or something?"

"I couldn't get into that with her, Jack. She was my mother. And she was sick."

Jack felt his chest go tight. Here he was thinking about himself when this kid had discovered one man was not his father and another was—all when his mother was dying! And he was thinking about whether his condom had a hole in it? "What kind of cancer, Denny?"

"Breast, then it spread. She was so young, she didn't get checked, didn't get good medical care. It was an aggressive cancer. We spent five years beating it back then it would pop up somewhere else, then more chemo, then a few good months that looked promising, then— Thing is, she couldn't beat it. And she wanted me to have the truth before she died." Denny swallowed. "We don't have to tell anyone, Jack."

Jack just shook his head. "That's not the important thing, Denny. It's not about keeping it a secret…." He shook his head. "There are some truths about me, son— one of 'em is that until I met Mel, I hadn't met a woman I was tempted to settle down with, to start a family with, but I never thought of myself as cruel. Maybe I've just been lying to myself about that. There must have been a reason your mom wasn't brave enough to look for me, to tell me about you...."

"Lots of reasons," Denny said. "She never blamed you. She was with a guy who thought I was his and he wasn't a nice guy. He never even married her. I can't think of a thing my mom ever did that was bad or wrong, but he slapped her around anyway. She was too scared of him to tell the truth, to break free and try to find you. By the time he was out of the picture, too many years had passed."

"It never once occurred to me to tell a woman that even if I didn't feel like being married, I could be responsible..." Jack's voice faded out.

"Soldiers, Marines, they do things like that," Denny said. "I did that. I was with a girl right before Afghanistan and I told her I didn't want to be worrying about attachments while I was—"

Jack put a hand over his forearm. "Denny, even if I couldn't have been a husband, I could have been a father. I should have been supporting you, knowing you, teaching you. Not easy for a Marine, a single Marine at that, but I would have liked to have tried. At the least, I could have been there for you when you were losing your mother. I could have been waiting for you to come home from war." He shook his head. "I'm sorry, son. I'm sorry I didn't know. But I know now."

Denny smiled. "Hey. I don't expect anything. I just wanted to know you, that's all. Really, I didn't think I'd be this lucky, to find out you're a guy I actually like, a guy I'd want for a friend even if there wasn't any other connection. But Jack, you don't have to do anything. I like things the way they are." He grinned boyishly. "I don't need a kidney or anything. I can support myself just fine."

Jack poured another couple of shots. "I usually limit myself to one, but it's a big night. You should move back out to the guesthouse if you want. Rent free, of course."

"What I want is to take care of myself. It's what I'd want to do even if you'd been around the past twenty-four years. In fact, from what I know of you so far, I bet it's what you would have raised me to do."

Jack lifted his glass. "You're probably right about that."

Right at that moment Preacher came into the bar from the kitchen. "I'm gonna have to learn to wash up faster if I want company for that shot," he said. "You're getting ahead of me."

"Let me pour you one," Jack said. "Wait till you hear the news. Uncle Preacher."

Mel sat cross-legged on the king-size bed, her laptop pushed to the side, while Jack paced and talked, telling her the story Denny had told him. He would periodically stop pacing, bend at the waist and lean both hands on the bed and add something emphatic. Dramatic. Then he'd pace again.

"Unbelievable," she finally said. "Then again, not. There's even a slight resemblance. But then, I took Rick for your son when I first met him. How many more of them do you think are out there?" she asked.

"Do you think you're being *funny?*"

"Um, not really," she said. "I thought I was being a little concerned."

"Listen, I'm telling you the absolute truth when I say that this is the last thing I expected to hear. I was seriously very, very cautious. I got an A in biology. I didn't take chances."

"Till you got to me?" she asked.

"Frankly, yes! You were entirely different! I was completely in love with you! I wanted to be with you forever! I totally lost my mind!"

"Could you please not raise your voice? First of all, I didn't do this to you and second, the kids are sleeping."

He scrubbed a hand over his face. "Sorry. Sorry."

"Jack, condoms aren't a hundred percent. Sometimes there's a malfunction—a little hole, a leak, a tear. And, as we've proven, you're pretty potent. Are *you* worried you're going to be getting more news like this?"

"Not so much that." He sat down on the bed. "Mel, I can admit to playing it kind of loose when I was young and there was the occasional real short-term relationship.... Not as many as you might think. But either I'm getting old and losing my memory or I was only with Denny's mom once or maybe twice. Mel, my girlfriends, such as they were, might not have always been memorable, but I don't remember Denny's mom at *all*. She looks kind of familiar, but I can't tie her to a single date, event, conversation, anything. And yet, she told Denny all about my family! Not the kind of stuff I share with a girl I've been out with once or twice."

"Denny was around over the holidays, Jack. I'm sure you talked about your family all the time."

He shook his head. "She told him I had a little sister still in grade school. We must have been close—when I was twenty, Brie was only ten. And she took me being in the Marines real hard."

"Maybe you were drunk," Mel said with a shrug.

He straightened. "As a well-known fact, personally and across the board, I didn't have much sexual success when drunk. I did, however, have blissful memory loss."

"Maybe it'll all come back to you. But Jack, are you sure this information is accurate? I mean, maybe the person who's not remembering real well was Denny's mom. Although…"

"Although…?" he prompted.

"I have to say, my experience is that women generally know who got them pregnant, unless there were multiple partners in a very tight period of time. Men seem to be more prone to blow off the average encounter while most women take these things very seriously."

"I know this," he said. "I know men and women look at things like sex differently and, I admit, I can't remember the phone number of every woman I slept with, but that letter said she was *in love* with me. That she fell *hard.* It happened a time or two—that a woman's feelings for me were stronger than mine for her, and when that happened, I had to move along before someone got hurt real bad. I have four sisters. I listened to them wail and cry over some dipshit boy who led them on then disappeared, just took what he could get and didn't call again. I wasn't going to do that to a girl, so I bit the bullet and broke it off. And when I had to do that it wasn't easy and I remember *every one.*"

Mel pulled a face. "I have to give you credit for that, Jack. It's rare. Most guys would rather leave the country than have an honest conversation about their feelings."

"Don't overpraise me. I'm not sure I did a good job of it, but I did fess up that I wouldn't turn out to be a good boyfriend, that there was no future in me. Hell, I loved the Marines—there really wasn't room for one other woman in my life."

"Except your sisters," she pointed out.

"Yeah, well I was stuck with them," he said. "Do you have any idea how much I don't want to tell my dad about this?" He covered his face with his hands, leaning elbows on his knees.

"Well, Jack, given the fact you don't remember Denny's mom or the period of time he was conceived, before you tell the whole family and the whole town, I recommend you get a little evidence more concrete than a posthumous letter. You two need to do a little blood test. Make sure you're related."

Jack looked devastated. "Aw, Mel, I can't do that to the kid. Think of all he's been through. And I've known him coming up on six months now and he's a good young man. Can I really question his dying mother's confession without hurting him?"

"If you'd gotten this letter a year after he was conceived asking for your involvement and support and didn't remember being with the mother, wouldn't you, in the kindest possible way, say you were completely willing, but a blood test would be in the best interest of everyone involved?"

"That would be obvious after only a year," he said. "The man is twenty-four. He's lived for this moment. I've already disappointed him for a couple of decades. I don't want to question him even more."

"I appreciate that and I like him very much. But, Jack, it's not all about Denny. There's you, too. And then there's David and Emma...."

"David and Emma don't care whether there's a blood test...."

"They might if they ever need a bone marrow transplant."

"If there's ever a medical situation, believe me we'll jump right on that blood work."

"Well, this is your situation," Mel said. "I'm just along for the ride and I have no trouble accepting Denny as your son. Honestly, I have no trouble accepting Rick as your son, though you don't share a single chromosome—

I think of him as a son, too. I was ready to adopt a baby that wouldn't be ours biologically and I never doubted for a second that we'd love him as much as our own biological children. Jack—keep an open mind. Your relationship with Denny doesn't have to change. Even though you didn't bring him up it's obvious you care about him—no blood test would change that. But it would lend evidence to the claim." She shrugged. "Could give you both enormous peace of mind."

Jack was quiet for a long time. Finally he said, "I'll keep it in mind. But I know now is not the time."

Six

Jillian knew she'd see Colin again before too long. She had been thinking about him, knew he was more than a little curious about her, just as she was intrigued by him, but she didn't expect him to walk right in her back door at six-thirty in the morning. She was standing at the kitchen sink in her pajamas, filling egg cartons with dirt from a big bag of potting soil. She wasn't wearing sexy pajamas but they were a bit revealing. She was braless and the curve of her breasts was clearly visible. And she was a tiny bit glad.

"Good morning," she said. "Don't you knock?"

He lifted his arms—one brown paper grocery sack in each. "No free hands."

"You could have knocked. You could have used the toe of your boot."

"I'll try like hell to remember that. Have you had breakfast?"

"I was just about to eat some Froot Loops."

"Ugh," he groaned. "Poison. I'll make breakfast. What are you doing?"

"Making seed cups. Preacher's been saving me his egg cartons—they're perfect." She brushed the dirt off her hands into the bag. "I'll move this bag of dirt and get dressed."

"Not on my account—you look good." He put his grocery bags on the work island. "I'll move the dirt to the back porch for you. How do you like your eggs?"

"Benedict?"

"Second choice?"

"Steamed. Medium. Firm whites, plenty of yellow yolk."

He smiled at her. "You're trying to trick me. You think I can't deliver. I'm a pretty good cook. Breakfast is my specialty." His eyes dropped to her breasts and he seemed to sway slightly; he almost moaned. "Go ahead, get dressed. I'll get busy in the kitchen."

She was smiling as she went into the little bedroom off the kitchen and closed the door. Well, they were even now. She'd been caught glancing at his crotch and he'd taken a survey of her chest. She couldn't miss the reaction—he had paled, and if she was not mistaken, he had subdued a shiver. Since her breasts were completely adequate and still quite perky she assumed he liked them just fine. She never thought of them as anything special but, in the grand scheme of things, they were nicely shaped and large enough for a man's hands.

Jillian had been thinking about Colin a lot lately because she was undeniably attracted to him. This wouldn't have happened in her old life. She'd been too busy while employed at BSS, putting in her sixty-to-eighty-hour weeks. It had been hard to get her attention at all under all the excitement and anxiety of her high-pressure job. Probably one of the only reasons Kurt had burrowed into her romantic life was because they spent so much time working together.

But here, mostly alone, in this completely alien environment, not only did Colin appeal to her in a very basic and earthy way, the idea that they were both transients and wouldn't be in the same town longer than a few more months was a definite upside as far as she was concerned. She was a long, long way from trusting a man again, but she had discovered, since meeting Colin, that she wasn't all that far from wanting one.

By the time she pulled on some jeans, a bra and a T-shirt, and had combed her hair and applied a little lip gloss, she could already make out the good smells coming from the kitchen. She followed her nose and sat on one of the two stools at the kitchen island. He was busy at the stove and when he glanced over his shoulder at her, she smiled and said, "Do you suppose we could try something very old-fashioned? Like planning ahead?"

"We could try," he said. "But if that was a rule, I wouldn't be here now. And you'd hate that. Plates?" he asked.

She pointed to the cupboard above the stove. And then she just watched in fascination while he moved around her kitchen. She liked the way his butt filled out his jeans—his legs were awful long. So were his arms, she noticed. His hands were big, but he was surprisingly graceful. He fried bacon and sausage together, steamed the eggs, warmed the croissants, pulled a package of smoked salmon from his grocery bag along with a jar of capers and a container of cream cheese and put those in the center of the work island. He opened drawers until he found utensils; he folded paper towels for napkins. And right before sliding the eggs and meat onto plates he quickly, and thinly, sliced a red onion onto a small plate. And voilà! He was sitting down across from her.

"Not bad," she said.

"Not bad? You are cruel! Considering what I had to work with, this is a feast! Picnic-style, but a feast!"

She laughed. "You're right. Plus it beats the hell out of Froot Loops."

"Do you really eat those things?"

"I love them," she said with childlike passion, her mouth full of smoked salmon rolled around some cream cheese and capers. "You forgot the tomatoes."

"I'm waiting for the Russian Rose," he replied, and then he winked. "Seriously, a moment of truth, this is all I can cook well—breakfast. I make a mean omelet, too. I can turn a steak or hamburgers on the grill, but the rest? It's a complete mystery to me."

"If you're going to cook one thing then why breakfast?" she asked.

"I love breakfast."

She put down her fork. "Have you been married?"

"No. Why?"

She picked up her fork and dug into her eggs. "I just had this picture in my head of some sweet wife getting up at 4:00 a.m. to make perfect eggs before sending you off to your helicopter. And I kind of hated that vision."

"I've never found a single woman in all my years of looking who would do that for me, so I did it for myself. And why would you hate that?"

She shrugged. "I always put in long hours. I really wanted a wife."

He leaned toward her. "Jillian, honey, the whole world wants a wife. But we're gonna have to make do. Now, what's on your agenda today?"

"Moving all the seed cups from the porch into the greenhouses! Dan Brady—our friend from the bar—is going to come out later and show us how to install some lights. I won't use chemical fertilizer on the seedlings, but I'm not above artificial lighting if it helps. I have a little golf cart kind of thing on order with a flatbed in the back—the kind landscapers and gardeners use—and it should be here today or tomorrow. That'll get me between the gardens and greenhouses and this house. And, if you look closely at the front garden, you'll see the veggies are coming up! Shoots from the carrots, leeks and scallions—little blossoms from the lettuce. There's a lot to do." She scooped up some sausage, egg and croissant and said, "You know, this may be your only talent, but you're very good at it."

A corner of his mouth lifted. Then the other corner. Then he showed her his beautiful, straight, sexy teeth and said, "It's not my only talent, Jilly."

Oh, yes, she *wanted* him. She didn't necessarily want to keep him, but she wanted him. Her cheeks grew so pink, she could feel them burn.

"Oh, right," she said. "There's also flying and painting."

He grew instantly somber. And quiet.

"Uh-oh," she said. "I think I hit a raw nerve there."

He chewed and swallowed before he said, "I wasn't ready to be done flying yet. The accident pretty much forced me out of the Army."

"What about civilian flying?"

"I wouldn't pass a physical now," he said. "But while I'm in Africa, I plan to look around at some of the flying over there. Might be a place to give it a go." He shrugged. "Maybe they don't look so closely at things like titanium rods and elbow screws." He didn't mention that it might be a bit more than the rods and screws that could keep him from passing a physical in the U.S. There could be a little issue about drugs and depression...

"It's not just big game that has you running off to Africa," she thoughtfully observed. "You crave adventure."

He shrugged and ate. "I don't know about that," he

said. "A little action, maybe. Something that demands a little more of me than cleaning the paint off the brushes."

"Are you bored?"

"Sometimes, yeah."

"Is that why you're hanging around my back porch?"

That brought a grin out of him. "I get a kick out of you, that's all."

"You sure it's not because I'm the only single woman within pitching distance?" she asked, lifting a shapely brow.

"That's not it," he said. "In fact, you're not the only single woman around here. There are tons of single women in this area. Maybe not right on this mountain, but I have a car. And I like to eat out."

"Bet you don't realize how much we have in common."

"Enlighten me," Colin said.

"Well," Jill began, putting down her fork and blotting her lips with her napkin, "I was also forced out of my job, more or less. It was a major coup for one of my subordinates. I'm sure you've seen similar things in the military. Getting rank must be competitive."

He was speechless for a moment. "You were fired?"

"No, I was replaced. I took a leave. It was down to him or me and I wanted to stand and fight, but my boss, mentor and very good friend recommended I take a little time off rather than resign or face the threat of termination. I hired a lawyer to negotiate my exit." She tilted her head. "Such is the executive experience."

"Sounds mystifying to me."

"Yeah, it probably does. Harry, my mentor and boss, had many philosophies he shared with me over the years. Always have your eye on where you're going next, train your replacement, know when you've reached the peak of your performance level and, probably the one he used when he counseled me, sometimes the needs of the company supersede the needs of the individual employee even if the employee is getting screwed."

"You call that good advice? Go away quietly when you're getting screwed?"

"No, Colin—go away *successfully*. And if I'd been better prepared and taken Harry's advice, I would have known exactly where I was going next. I didn't take that advice seriously—I had always toyed with the idea of my own marketing consulting business, but hadn't devoted any real brainpower to it. I thought I'd take a few weeks to consider my options, but then I got sidetracked." She smiled.

"How'd you get forced out by a subordinate?" he asked.

She shook her head. "Part of my settlement included a confidentiality agreement."

"I won't tell."

"And neither will I. My old boss, Harry, started several successful companies, taking them all public. He was once forced out as a president and CEO—he never took those things personally. He said you know you're important when an entire board of directors gives you the boot. His response to that was to get a good exit package and start a new company that was stronger and bigger. If you're going to swim with the sharks and get the big bucks, your position is always touch-and-go."

"Well, there's something we don't have in common—big bucks."

"You said you were independently wealthy."

"Not as independently as you apparently are—I'm a retired Army Warrant Officer. My income was never large and doesn't seem to have the potential to be, but there's a check each month and it gets me by."

"You should rethink that potential thing. I looked up

wildlife art... I researched it on the web. Some paintings and prints draw impressive sale prices. So—you can get mad at the crash, come out swinging a paintbrush and do better than you could with the military."

"The best revenge is to live well?"

"Yeah. And I am—thing is, I didn't plan this. Even if I can't make it go, I'm having a lot of fun." She looked briefly upward. "I didn't start all this with the idea of fun in mind. I just wanted to garden. And, right now, this feels really good."

Colin removed the plates from the table and took them to the sink. "That's what I'm not having as much of out of the cockpit. That felt really good and just painting full-time is a poor substitute," he tossed off. "You need furniture, Jillian," he said, while thinking about how nice it would be to sit with her on a sofa for a couple of hours.

She joined him at the kitchen sink. Sometimes their hands briefly touched as they passed plates to each other. "I need a golf cart, some lights and, before too long, I'm going to need a good indoor irrigation system for the greenhouses."

"Where will you go when you leave here?" he asked.

"Totally up in the air," she said. "But if I can grow stuff I'll be in the market for some rural property priced right with the best climate and soil conditions. Anything can be moved, Colin. Plants can even be relocated. Jack promised me six months, but he might be inclined to give me a little more time if things are going well. We'll see what happens over the summer."

He turned to her while drying his hands on the dish towel. "I have my plane ticket to Africa already," he said. "I booked early to get a good price on first class—I'm too damn tall to make that long flight in coach. September 1."

She smiled at him. "Then we also have that in common—

we'll be making the most of the summer. And, um, Colin? I haven't told anyone else that I was forced out of my last job. Not that it matters, but a lot of people wouldn't understand. They'd think I'm just a loser."

"We're even again—Luke doesn't know I have a plane ticket."

Colin really didn't get it. Jillian wasn't his type at all. He had always been drawn to women who looked like they wanted sex, and soon. Women who dressed to draw attention to their breasts, legs, hips or butts. Not slutty-looking women, though he didn't discriminate—he liked them, too. More like the soccer mom who was wearing her "out to be seen" dress-up clothes that fit nice and snug. Not to mention plenty of accessories and makeup. Colin developed his style with women early in his flying days; he was smooth—flirty and sexy and ultimately successful. He had never had a shortage of female company, that's for sure. One of his favorite things was to wash lipstick off his favorite organ in the morning-after shower, something that hadn't happened often enough in the recent past.

But this woman was different. Jillian was a whole new being. Right above some very delicious-looking breasts was a fresh, wholesome, beautiful face with large dark eyes that burned in his memory for hours and a smile that knocked him out. And in that head? Some very sexy, unbelievable intelligence. Man, she was *way* too smart for him. When she talked about corporate strategy, she turned him on. When she talked about growing her fancy seeds, she turned him on. When she ate her eggs and croissant, she made him want to tackle her and lower her to the ground and start peeling off her clothes.

He thought about her all morning. After breakfast he

took his painting of the buck to a meadow that got a lot of sun and set up the easel. All the while he asked himself if he'd been off the antidepressants just long enough to get good and horny, or if this woman was just about the finest, rarest woman he'd come across in a very long time.

A small herd of deer—doe and fawns and one buck—wandered along the bottom of the foothills and he snapped a few shots with his zoom. Beautiful extended family out there, does nudging the fawns along, buck tall and standing guard. He wondered if he could paint something as detailed and expansive as a herd.

But then his thoughts returned again to Jillian—so pretty, so fresh, so sexy, so smart. He tried to think about other women—he'd run into a couple when visiting art galleries over in the coastal towns, good-looking women who had been happy to give him business cards. There were a couple of women back in Georgia who had kept in touch after his accident. There were even a couple of old girlfriends he could resurrect without much effort. He was far from rich but could easily afford a plane ticket so he could do some visiting if it was a simple matter of getting with a woman. Anything to somehow scratch this itch and put the confusion to rest.

But his brain and his body were completely tuned in to Jillian. She was a kooky little dish, that one, with her recliner and no furniture, her seed cups, getting excited over her golf cart. Then there was something about the way she could read him. *I was forced out of my job, too.*

And now they shared confidences—his plane ticket and her job loss. He couldn't remember ever doing that before. It was strangely alluring.

Colin wasn't a religious man at all, but he had a powerful core faith that had strengthened since being pulled out of a Black Hawk wreck he shouldn't have survived by fellow pilots who risked their own lives by landing and coming to his rescue. So he lectured God that it was a bad idea to put this quality female in his path because he was a little vulnerable and she seemed like a first-class woman who shouldn't be hurt by an irresponsible wild man like him.

Wild man? That persona was now mostly in the past. He might still have the soul of a wild man, but at the moment he was just a man in need of a woman.

He was pulled out of his thoughts when he heard the sound of horse hooves and turned to see a man riding toward him. His Jeep was still on the road outside the fence, the hatch up in back, so he rested the palette and brush on the ground and waited.

As he got closer, Colin could see the man was Native American with a feather in his cowboy hat and a long braid down his back. Colin didn't know much about horses but he knew a pretty one when he saw it. This one was incredible; chestnut in color, young and muscular. The man rode right up to him and stopped, not dismounting but stretching out his hand from his position in the saddle. "How you doing?" he said. "I'm Clay Tahoma."

"Colin Riordan," he said, shaking the hand. "Am I trespassing? I didn't see any signs."

"There should be signs posted on the fence, but it's no problem for you to paint here—it's things like target practice, off-season hunting and poaching we dislike. This is a back pasture—it belongs to Dr. Nate Jensen, the vet who owns Jensen Large Animal Clinic. It's private property, but you're welcome here as long as it's unoccupied. It isn't likely we'd ever leave a difficult horse this far away from the clinic. Just be careful, that's all. Look around first. Mind the fence. A broken-down fence can be catastrophic for us." Clay leaned down from his horse to peer at the painting—it was the four-point buck. "Awesome," he said. "That's probably not paint by number."

Colin laughed. "I got a great shot of them with the zoom," he said, pointing at the small herd of deer in the distance.

"They're headed for the river," Clay said, "taking the youngsters out for a stroll. I'm a friend of Luke's and Shelby's—they mentioned you'd be here for a while."

"Seems like everyone's a friend of Luke's and Shelby's...."

"I think everyone is a friend of everyone else around here. I've only been here since last August myself." He nodded toward the painting. "That's beautiful work. I have a cousin who paints—Native American art. He's now some high mucky-muck artist in Sedona, but he grew up next door to me on the reservation, Navajo Nation. Where are you showing your work?"

"I haven't had a showing or a sale. Right now I'm just painting."

"Lots of Native and wildlife work around Albuquerque, Sedona, Phoenix... Might be time for a road trip."

Colin laughed. "Maybe. When I'm ready."

"Looks like you're ready, but what do I know." Clay tipped his hat. "I want to check the back pastures and roads. I'm sure I'll be seeing you around again. Nice meeting you."

"And you," Colin said.

Colin watched as Clay rode away from him. Lots of people seemed interested in the idea that he start selling his work. They didn't know that putting a price tag on his art wouldn't change anything. He still wanted to get up in the air.

And he still wanted to get with Jillian Matlock.

* * *

Colin worked away for the rest of the day and managed to last until 8:00 p.m. before he headed back over to her place. He drove up alongside the house and parked. Before he even got out of the Jeep he saw her sitting on the back porch step in the dark, leaning against the post, a throw wrapped around her. She had lit a large candle and had a glass of wine in a real wineglass; Jillian was living so sparsely he was surprised she wasn't drinking her wine out of a coffee cup. He got out and just leaned against the Jeep, looking at her.

The second their eyes connected, before either of them said anything, he sensed it. There was mutual attraction.

"I knew you'd be back, but I didn't know it would be this soon," she said.

"What made you think so?"

"I saw it in your eyes," she said with a shrug. "Lust."

"Listen, there are a couple of things on my mind," he said, walking over to her. He sat on the same step but leaned against the opposite post, facing her. "That last boyfriend of yours—what did he do to you?"

"Not telling," she said, shaking her head. "Maybe someday, but not now. Besides, it shouldn't concern you."

"It does. Is there any chance that if I'm just an idiot, I could do the same thing to you? Really mess you up bad?"

She laughed at him. "Colin, I'm surprised! You didn't strike me as the kind of guy who really worried about that kind of thing!"

"You're probably right about that. In my world… In the world I come from, I'd see a pretty girl and talk to her for a few minutes, get her phone number, take her someplace, get a read on her expectations and usually end up in bed. It sometimes lasted a few times or maybe a few weeks or maybe a few months. That Army post was like a small town and a guy had to be careful not to get things all stirred up. But I had no idea what a small town was until I came here."

"Ah," she acknowledged. "You're worried about your reputation?"

"No," he said, shaking his head. "I could give a shit about what people think of me. But if you've got some baggage from that last boyfriend—"

"No baggage," she said, shaking her head. "Well, that's not entirely honest—I must have some because if he walked up the drive right now, and if I had a gun, it would be so hard not to shoot at him."

"Now, see, getting shot is not on my list of things I'd like to do. That's why I'm asking what he's wanted for."

She couldn't help but laugh. "You're completely safe. His behavior and insult cannot be duplicated and besides, I don't want another boyfriend. Period."

He leaned toward her. "But do you ever want to settle down or something? Get serious, get married, all that? Someday? Because I have other plans and I don't want everyone in this town pissed at me, and feeling sorry for you and upset with Luke and Shelby for letting me come here."

"I know, Colin," she said. Jill took a sip of her wine. "The Serengeti. For the big game, for a possible extension of your flying career, for a life that's not so tame."

"Is it possible you really do understand?" he asked her.

"I believe I do. Besides, I'm not looking for a relationship. Don't want one," she said, shaking her head. "And I don't think you do, either." He just shook his head.

"It would be a shame if you gave up painting, however. I don't know much about art, but I suspect you're exceptional."

He scooted a little closer to her; he could feel his eyes growing hot as he looked at her. Hot and bright. "Well, that's just it, Jilly—you know how your mentor told you to always know what you were going to do next? Painting is what I want to do *next*. I can't fly forever—but I can paint for as long as I can stand up and hold a brush. But 'next' isn't here yet. I can fly another twenty years. And while I fly, I should also paint and get better so that when I'm done flying, there's more painting to do. See what I mean?"

She gave her head a nod. "Sounds perfectly reasonable, Colin. Why are you being so high-strung about it?"

"I don't want a girlfriend," he said flatly.

"Understandable," she said. "I can see how that would really complicate your plans. But I get the distinct impression you want *something*."

He reached out one of those long arms and toyed with her hair. "I've thought about you all day long. I started thinking about you before today. You and your strange little vegetables, your corporate strategy and your freckles. And other things."

"Yes, I caught you treating yourself to a stare. Tit for tat, if you'll pardon the pun."

He laughed. He hadn't realized until this very moment how sexy humor was. "Thing is, Jilly, not only am I attracted to you, I actually *like* you."

"Be very careful, Colin. I wouldn't want *you* to get hurt." Then she smiled at him.

He grabbed both sides of her throw and pulled. "Come closer," he said, edging her toward him. He slipped a hand around to the back of her neck under her hair and leaned toward her, and gave her the briefest of kisses. A test.

"I've never kissed a man with a beard," she said.

"You'll have to let me know how you like it." And he went after her mouth more seriously, moving over her lips until they opened and then sweeping the soft inside of her mouth with his tongue. She moaned and her arms came around his neck. He moved from her lips to her neck and whispered, "God, Jilly, you smell good."

"Soap," she whispered. "And you showered, too."

"Were we planning this?" he asked her.

"I was planning to keep you from doing anything like this," she said. But she'd been thinking about him all day, too. "The problem is, I thought about you, too. And if I'm honest, I wasn't opposed to the idea," she said, wiggling still closer. *Because this isn't a relationship*, she thought. *This is a kind of fling. This is different from anything I've ever experienced.* And it was strangely unscary.

He pulled her even closer, onto his lap, kissing her hungrily, pulling her chest against his, eating her mouth, feeding her kisses that were deep, hot and consuming. Groaning. Sighing. When he slipped his hand beneath her T-shirt and fondled a naked breast, she let her head fall back in a lovely moan. He repositioned her legs so that she straddled his lap. Her instincts took over; she pressed against him. She might think having a man in her life was impractical, especially this man, but he felt good way down where feeling good really mattered.

He lunged against her suddenly, his big hands on her waist, pulling her down against his erection. "Aw, God," he said, pushing against her. "Damn, that's good…" Jillian loved the taste of his mouth; she plunged her fingers into his long hair, freeing it from the ponytail. God, all that thick, curly hair—what she'd give to have hair like that. What she'd give to feel it brushing against her belly. She couldn't remember ever wanting like this, so hard, so fast. She had absolutely no intention of thinking it over. She was spiraling, falling, diving into him. And all she really wanted at the moment was him diving into her.

He lifted her shirt to look at her breasts and she directed his mouth to her nipple. With a groan, he went there, licking, pulling it into his mouth where it immediately turned to a hard pebble, exactly the right size, and he sucked on her greedily, making little noises.

Colin felt the heat racing through him, and then she was grinding against him, moving her pelvis against him. He was really close to going completely out of his mind. He held both her breasts in his hands and whispered against her open mouth, "Oh man, do I want you *bad*..."

"Hmm..."

"We can't."

"Can't what?" she whispered back, gyrating deliciously.

"I don't have anything. Protection."

"Why *not!*" she pleaded in a desperate whisper.

"Because the last time I had sex was shortly before I was pulled out of a burning helicopter.... I'll take care of it, though.... I wanted this to happen, but I didn't know it would."

She put her hands against his cheeks, looked into his eyes and said, "Take care of it now!"

"Easy, Jilly. Another day won't kill us."

"It *might!*"

He chuckled. "I didn't know I'd make this kind of progress with you or I would have been better prepared. I'm sorry."

"Let's just... You know..." She sighed deeply. "Let's just do something that doesn't require protection."

"Can't," he said. He pressed his lips against her throat. "If I get any closer to your skin, if I taste you, I'm going to lose my mind and get up inside you and blow my brains out. Whether I want to or not. I'm too hot. No control on this end."

"Colin, you can't really be doing this to me! You started this!"

"I know. I know. I wasn't thinking, which happens a lot when I'm close to you. But I'll be back, Jilly, and it'll be worth the wait."

"But I should be pushing you away!" she said.

He chuckled against her lips. "I love you this way. You're just like you should be. But we have to stop.... In just a second..."

"Don't you dare leave me like this." Then she stroked his bearded face. "We'll be all right. It's a good time of the month to take a chance and there's morning-after help...."

"Too scary," he said, shaking his head. Too many issues, too much risk. "We should get it right the first time." He gently moved her off his lap. "I have to go while I can still walk."

She was almost panting, her breath was coming so hard.

He leaned down and touched her lips. "I'll see you soon. And next time I won't leave you. Go take a nice, warm, bubbly bath and... Well, you'll be fine." Then he smiled.

"If you leave me like this, don't bother to come back!" she said meanly.

He lifted her chin, stared deeply into her eyes and said, "Oh, I'll be back. And you're going to be glad, I promise. This will never happen to us again." He stood to his full height. "I didn't mean for it to go like this, Jilly. I'll make it up to you."

"You'd better," she said, but she said it more softly.

Seven

When Denny asked Jack what he wanted people to know about their situation Jack said, "It's best to start off with the truth. That way there are fewer details to remember. Unless you'd like to keep it under wraps—so far only Mel and Preacher know."

Under wraps? Denny shook his head. "I'm not embarrassed. The opposite, in fact. But now *you...*"

Jack put a strong hand on Denny's shoulder and said, "As surprises go, this is one of the better ones I've had. If I have any regrets it's that I never knew, that I wasn't a father to you. I'm going to feel bad about that for a long time."

"If we're going to have a good relationship now, you're going to have to let go of that one. I'm not upset about it. My mom did the best she could for me. She protected me whenever she could. She warned me—twenty years after the fact, even five years after the fact, that the Marine who is my father could be a very different man from the one she knew when she was twenty. We know all about that, Jack. There were wars and stuff—some guys can deal, some can't. She said she thought it would be best if I'd just enjoy the knowledge that the guy she was with when I was conceived, the one whose DNA I have, was a standup guy when she knew him. Someone I could be proud of." He smiled a little. "That was nice, knowing that. But I know it wasn't part of her game plan that I go looking for you."

"I'm going to have to call my dad," Jack said. "He's seventy-four now...."

"I think you told me that before.... Before you went to Sacramento over the holidays..."

"In perfect health," Jack said. "But even with that, he has less time to get to know you as family than I have."

Denny gave a laugh. "I never had much family, much less the number I'm related to now! I mean, I had grandparents when I was real little, but I barely remember them. What's your family going to think of this? Of me? I mean, you totally get that I don't want anything, right?"

"Of course, son," Jack said. "Mel thinks we should verify all this with a blood test."

"Sure. I can do that. When?"

"We'll get to that. Right now I think we have more pressing issues. Even though we're already friends, now we have to know each other on a completely different level."

"How do we do that?" Denny asked.

"Do you fish?" Jack wanted to know.

Denny shrugged. "I dropped a line a couple of times...."

"That's not fishing. When's your next day off from the Jillian farm?"

"Any day I ask for," he said.

"Ask for a day. That's when I teach you real fishing. Fly-fishing. That's the best place I can think of for a couple of men to get to know each other better."

"Sounds good," Denny said with a laugh.

"But I am gonna call my dad," Jack said. "You think I'm finally old enough that he can't ground me?"

Jillian had a date to have sex, but she didn't know when or where.

After seeing Colin she spent the next day puttering around the property and every now and then she would feel the heat rise to her cheeks as she remembered that not only had she been close to doing the deed on her back porch, she had yelled at Colin for not finishing the job. Should a woman apologize for that? And what exactly would the wording be? *"Sorry I was such a wild, demanding, easy woman?"*

She'd never before in her life offered herself up like a main course. *Never.* And all that after stipulating she had no interest in a boyfriend or a relationship! Didn't sex constitute a relationship? For the love of God!

She hadn't had many partners, but she'd made each one work for her. She'd always had absolute expectations of it lasting, or she wouldn't have gone that far. When Kurt was pursuing her she held out for a couple of months before she finally gave in and, really, she could have held out longer.

And yet with Colin? Arguably the hottest man she'd ever kissed and here she was with a different set of expectations—that they would have *no* expectations!

But then she'd never met a man like Colin before. Something about him made her want him wildly.

"You feeling okay, Miss Matlock? Jillian?" Denny asked.

"Huh?" she said, turning to look at him. He was hauling another flat of seed cups into the greenhouse. "What?"

"I asked if you were feeling okay. You look a little, I don't know, flushed. And you're awful quiet."

"Sorry, I'm concentrating," she said, marking more of her seed cups. "I feel fine, though." In fact, she felt turned on. Every time she thought about Colin pulling her onto his lap, thought about straddling him and pushing against his erection, a new quivering jolt of electricity would flash through her panties. This was as confusing as it was exciting—Jillian had been around plenty of attractive men in her day and it was hardly the first time she'd felt the rising heat of desire, but never so much, so fast, so powerful. There was some crazy chemistry going on with Colin.

What if he decided it wasn't in his best interest to come back? After the way she'd behaved?

This whole situation with Colin was not a world she was familiar with. In her world people exchanged phone numbers and if a man interested you, you gave him your business card, email address and office number. You didn't go after him like a hungry cat on the back porch and then yell at him for not going all the way! She didn't even know how to reach him or where he lived and the only way he could reach her was by driving to her house—without an appointment.

"I'm completely out of my mind," she muttered.

"What's that, Miss Matlock?" Denny asked.

"I'm completely out of my mind…. To think I can grow Purple Calabash. And, for the love of Christ, will you please call me Jillian! Or Jill!"

He laughed at her. "Sure thing, Jillian. And if anyone can grow it, I bet you can. You know, there's something I've been meaning to say."

She turned toward him. "What's that, Denny?"

"I don't know how to say it. I like the work here—

I guess that's how you say it. I'm kind of into it. I hope you still need me when the seedlings sprout, when the fruit comes in."

She smiled happily at that. "I like that. I'll keep you busy as long as I can. It all depends on the plants."

"I get that—if they don't come in strong, it's not working."

"That's about it."

"So there's this other thing," he said. "I know I'm younger than you by about eight years, but—"

She stiffened. She got serious. "You aren't going to ask me to adopt you, are you, Denny?"

"No," he said with a laugh. "I was wondering if I could take you out to dinner. Just to Jack's, but it's about the best dinner around."

All of a sudden she had a cold feeling rush through her. "We can't ever," she said, maybe a little more harshly than she meant to. She took a deep breath; this young man was the furthest thing from a schemer she knew. "If we have dinner together at Jack's, which I'd like to do, we have to go Dutch. You work for me. I would be exploiting you by dating you."

"Seriously?" he asked with a laugh.

"As a heart attack," she said.

"Whoa," he said. "I wouldn't see it as exploiting. I'd kind of see it as a miracle. But I wasn't really thinking of it as a date, Jillian. I was more thinking of it as a thank-you. For the work, the job."

She caved; she smiled back. "You are the best guy," she said. "Okay, here's a secret. Are you good for it? A secret?"

"They'll have to rip my tongue out," he said.

"I'm kind of seeing someone."

"Oh, let me guess. The painter?"

"Now why would you say that?" she asked, hands on her hips.

"I don't know. Because no one else came to mind? But I won't tell anyone if you don't want me to."

"It's casual...." Jill said self-consciously. "Unofficial. That's why I said 'kind of' and never expected you to guess...."

"I won't tell. But I notice you do get a little happy when he comes around."

Oh, *happy* didn't touch it, she thought. She got crazy, liquid, wild and demanding—a complete out-of-body experience. That's what *happy* did to her.

"Well, if it doesn't work out with the painter, let me know," Denny said, grinning at his own joke. "Seriously, Miss... Jillian, I was just being social. I wasn't planning to propose or anything. I just thought it might be good if you got out more." Then he smiled. "You know, do the town."

"That's cool. I guess I misinterpreted your intention. Because rule number one—you can't get away with dating your boss."

"Aw, I never thought of it that way. I admit, I didn't expect the boss thing—I expected the age thing."

"Well, there's that, too," she said. And then, because he was such a darling young man and such a hard worker, she added, "but you are mature for your age."

His chest puffed up and his eyes twinkled. "Thank you, Miss Matlock. So are you."

At that, she threw a fistful of manure at him.

When you're basically a farmer and not sure when your brand-new potential lover could be coming to call, it's hard to know when is a good time to shower off the dirt and grime. Now that the sun was setting later, Jillian liked to put in a longer day in the garden, but given the possibility that Colin could show up unannounced, she sent Denny off at five and then jumped in the shower.

She shaved above the knees, a desperate and obvious move. She put lotion on her entire body, blew her hair so it would be thick and soft, even put on a little makeup. But when she dressed it was in a comfy sweat suit—a soft, clean, powder-blue set. She slipped into the fluffy slippers. When she walked out of the maid's quarters, there he was, sitting in her recliner, feet raised up, paging through a seed catalog. She put her hands on her hips and let out a sigh.

"I heard the shower and didn't want to scare you," he said. "But if you're really determined to keep people like me out, there are always locks."

She *wasn't* determined to keep him out! She had never been so glad to see anyone and tried not to let that show on her face. "I'm kind of surprised you came back," she said. "I don't know what came over me last night. I don't think I was very nice to you."

He tossed the catalog aside. "When a woman gives me hell for leaving her unsatisfied, I take that very seriously." He hoisted himself out of the chair. She blushed and he chuckled. Then he said, "I can see why you like this recliner—it's a good chair. Have you eaten?"

She shook her head.

"Would you like me to take you out for a meal?" he asked.

She ground her teeth and pinched her eyes closed. When she opened them she found him grinning at her, making fun of her. *Should I feed you before I scratch your itch?* His teeth, so white against that brown beard just about did her in.

"You don't invest a lot in your women, do you, Colin?" she asked.

"Oh, Jilly, I give them everything I've got. Know what I'd like to do?" he asked her. "I'd like to go up on the roof and have a look at the sunset from there. You game?"

She showed him a little smile. "I love it up there. You can see forever—almost all the way to the ocean."

"Take me up to the roof, Jilly," he said, his voice hoarse and his eyes glowing.

The climb was three flights and she heard him moan a little behind her as they tackled the last staircase. She looked over her shoulder. "Okay?"

"I should do more of this," he said. "My leg still gets stiff and sometimes it's not real strong. But I'm keeping up with you."

"Just watch your step—there's not much I can do if you fall off the roof." But it wasn't a dangerous roof—it was flat, about six by twelve, surrounded by an eighteen-inch tall, decorative, wrought-iron border. If this house had been built on the coast in the 1800s, the wife of a sea captain would have climbed up to the roof to scan the horizon, watching for the sight of sails, waiting for her man to return to her.

And when Colin reached the top he snatched off his hat, ran a hand over his head and said, "God." He turned full circle and took in the view. "This is better than I imagined."

"You like to be up high," she said.

"Ironically, not so much. I'm kind of afraid of heights. A lot of pilots are. We like flying—we don't like hanging close to edges of cliffs and stuff. This is good, though. Feels secure in a way." He dropped down, sitting on the roof. "Come here," he said. And when she sat, he pulled her between his long legs, his knees raised, her back against his chest, his arms around her waist, and they faced in the direction of the coast, the sunset. "Now see, that's beautiful. I'm full of good ideas."

"I sit up here and talk to my sister on the cell phone," she told him. "The connection is weak on the first floor of the house and outside with all the trees. But up here it's good. And I love it up here, especially at sunrise and sunset." She glanced at him over her shoulder. "I spotted you the first time from up here."

"That's why this spot is all cleaned off—you come up here a lot...."

"I swept it so I could sit up here. I just haven't gotten around to bringing up any chairs."

He pulled the hair away from her neck and put his lips there. "Hmm. Nice," he said. One hand slipped under her shirt. He sucked on her neck and grabbed a bare breast at the same time. "Hmm," he said. "Even nicer. So glad you didn't get overdressed."

She laughed lightly, then he gave her nipple a tender pinch and she gasped with pleasure. She scooted farther back against him.

"Do me a favor, Jilly," he whispered. "Unlace those boots for me."

"You better tell me what's going to happen here first," she said.

"Anything you want," he answered hoarsely. "Everything you want."

"On top of the house?"

His other hand went under her shirt and he held a breast in each hand. "With the setting sun?" he asked. "Nice and easy, nice and slow, nice and out of your mind?"

"That's a little crazy!"

"We're not going to fall off—there's a little fence. And

I get the impression you are a little crazy." He kissed her neck again. "You're not any more tame than I am."

"But I never knew it," she said. "I thought I was on the very conservative side." Then she groaned and reached for his boot laces, untying and loosening them. He used the toe of one to push off the heel of the other and within just a second, both boots were sitting behind him, out of the way. He reached a hand behind his neck, gathered up his T-shirt and pulled it over his head. "I'm scarred, Jilly. You should see it before it takes you by surprise and scares you. It might turn you off."

She hated to have his hands off her breasts, but she pushed them aside and turned toward him. Kneeling in front of him between his legs, sitting back on her heels, she saw the scarring. It wasn't terrible but it was obvious. The texture of his skin was rough and discolored, kind of wavy. It ran down his neck, over his shoulder, down his upper arm, upper back, upper chest. There were also a couple of tattoos—a decorative armband on his left arm, some Asian lettering on the right side of his chest. The scarring stopped right at the lettering. She ran her small hand over the skin, very lightly, very carefully.

"This isn't scary, Colin. Does it still hurt?"

He shook his head. "My leg sometimes gets stiff and my elbow drives me nuts, but I get better every day. I'm healed enough to make love." And then he slipped his hand around her neck and pulled her mouth onto his, moving over her lips slowly, deeply, with heat and passion. While he had her in that lip-lock, he slipped a hand down the back of her sweatpants, rubbing her butt softly, sweetly. Next he pulled on her shirt, lifting it over her head and leaving her bare to his gaze. He sucked in his breath. "You are gorgeous."

She laughed at him. "I think I'm probably average."

He leaned toward her and tongued a nipple. "Hmm, not in my book. You stop my breath, you're that beautiful." He still had that shirt in his grip and shook it out. He reached around her and spread it on the roof behind her, easing her back onto it. Then he leaned over her and gave her breasts a lot more serious attention. "Nothing, nothing average here. You taste better than I remembered. God, I want you so bad."

"And this time, we're ready?" she asked a little breathlessly.

"And able," he said, reaching into his back pocket and pulling out a small, square, foil packet. He put it in her hand. "And you're in charge of safety."

"Safety first," she said, accepting the condom.

He spread her legs and lowered himself onto her, his mouth on her mouth, rubbing his erection against her parted legs. He moaned. "Good God… I hope you're in a hurry."

She reached a hand down between their bodies, just running it over the bulge in his pants, bringing another low moan from him.

"Sweetheart," he said in a strained whisper. "I really need you out of these pants." He was pulling on her sweats as he spoke. "Really. And really quick."

"It's only going to make it harder. Faster."

"Baby, it can't get much harder. And we're going to have to go a little faster. I'm on a hair trigger here. You seriously turn me on."

She didn't resist him; she let him pull down the sweats, pull them over her knees and away. He flung them behind him and looked at her in the dusk, the sight of her naked making his breathing quicken. "Man," he said, one big hand covering her crotch in a soft caress, one of his fingers sliding into the soft, moist folds. "Good. Oh, so good…"

She reached for the snap on his pants, found the zipper and drew it down, slipped her hand in for the briefest touch, but then his fingers on her clitoris caused her to almost lose her mind and she lay back down, arching up to him.

He covered her with his body and devoured her mouth in a consuming kiss, roving the inside of her mouth with his tongue, playing with her tongue, and then he licked a path down her body, laving her breasts with his mouth, kissing his way down over her belly, spreading her legs and diving into her core with his tongue, moaning his pleasure all the time. She held on to his head, lifted her hips against his face, making her own desperate sounds while he tortured her with exquisite kisses.

And then he stopped, lifting his mouth up to hers. "You taste wonderful. I could get drunk on you. I want to stay down there for hours."

"Umm," she moaned. "Okay," she said weakly.

He chuckled and pulled that foil packet from her hand. "You're not going to be in charge of safety anymore— you're not paying attention."

"I am sooo paying attention," she whispered, but her eyes never opened and she was reaching for him. "Oh God." She sighed. "Hurry."

"Hurry is what we're all about right now," he said. "Jilly, I have to be inside you. Tell me you're ready...."

And then she felt him, holding himself above her with the strength of only one arm, gently probing in her very center.

"You okay, sweetheart?" he asked in a whisper.

"Okay..." She reached her hand down to touch him, to wrap around him, to lead him. And when she realized his length and girth, she sighed hungrily. She might've gasped. This was more man than she'd ever had in her hand, in her body.

"You worried about it?" he asked her.

"Worried," she whispered. "And dying for it."

"We'll try to go slow and easy," he said. "I won't hurt you."

He gave her clitoris a few more strokes while he covered her mouth with his and he entered her in a long, slow, easy movement, burying himself deep within her, holding there while she got used to him. Then he started to move, slowly at first, but as she bent her knees and pushed against him he moved faster, harder, deeper. He left her mouth to suck on a nipple and that was the magic—she threw her head back, dug her heels in to lunge her pelvis against him, cried out and he felt it, felt her entire pelvis begin to tighten, shudder, vibrate, drenching him in a hot liquid.

"Oh, honey," he whispered against her lips. "That's it, that's it...."

He held her tight against him with one big hand on her little rump, hanging on there as long as he could and when he sensed she was complete, he pounded into her in several hard, long strokes, letting himself go. To his shock and awe, she started to come again and the pleasure that gave him blew him to the next universe. He wanted to say the perfect thing about that, about how free and beautiful she was, but instead all he got out was a series of moans, grunts and grateful, unintelligible sounds. At the end of it all, breathless, he said, "My God. Sweet. Sweet!"

She went completely limp in his arms, head lolling, eyes closed, the faintest smile on her lips. He slipped his arms under her shoulders and tried to lift her but her head just dropped back. He chuckled softly, touched his lips to her exposed neck and asked, "Are you completely unconscious?"

"Maybe," she whispered. "Ohhhh…"

"Let's get you dressed," he murmured between kisses.

"Not yet. In a minute." And then she tilted her pelvis to keep him where he was, right inside.

"The sun's going down. I don't want you to get cold."

"Then stay where you are and I won't."

"Jilly, Jilly, you're a little greedy."

"You would be too if you were me…." He pulled out, sitting back on his heels between her bent knees and she said, "Awww…"

"I'll put you to sleep again later," he said. "I'll take you home with me tonight."

"Why?" she said, struggling to sit up.

"Because I have a *bed*."

"Do you have food?"

He nodded. "Nothing fancy, but food."

"You could make me breakfast for dinner." She reached behind her and grabbed her T-shirt. He held it for her to shrug into. Then she felt around. "Where are those sweats…"

It was dusk and both of them were running their hands around the roof looking for clothes. Finally Colin leaned over that little eighteen-inch wrought-iron fence and said, "Uh-oh."

Jillian leaned over the rail and saw, on the roof of the second-story sunroom, one man's boot, one man's T-shirt, one cowboy hat, one woman's fluffy slipper, one pair of powder-blue sweatpants and one small, gold, foil package, opened and empty. She looked at Colin. "Well, that pretty much tells the whole story."

Jillian would have thought that her experience on the roof, having been so completely satisfying, would have held her for a while. Long enough to eat dinner, at least.

But, no. By the time Colin had driven her deep into the woods to his cabin, she was crazy with wanting him all over again. And by the way he grabbed her around the waist and wrestled her gently to his bed, he was in the same agonizing condition.

Jillian had never in her life experienced lovemaking like this. It was as if he'd known her body and her needs forever. He drove her wild, made her beg as he said he would and delivered an astonishing series of climaxes that shook her to the marrow of her bones. Again she collapsed in his arms, panting; again he chuckled proudly.

Then came a shower, then some food. Then she said, "You should probably take me home."

"Why? You have a better deal at home? Seed catalogs in a recliner or me, naked and ready and right next to you in case you need me?"

"You do make a compelling argument...."

He pulled her close and said, "Sleep with me tonight, Jilly. I promise two things—I won't try to make you give all your nights to me."

"That was one promise. What's the second?"

"I'm going to have to buy you a bed. I don't think I can do it in that recliner and I'm not going up on the roof again...."

So she stayed with him. With the warmth of his body curled around her she slept deeply, soundly, and in the night she woke to the sensation of his hands gently stroking her, caressing her, and she rolled over and opened up to him. She was like a rosebud that came into full, fast, multilayered bloom, rich with the color of pleasure, and deep with the fullness of satisfaction. He rocked her world to the core. Better still, by the way he shuddered and groaned his pleasure, it was obvious she rocked his.

Jillian was aware of a profound difference with Colin

from any other intimate experience she'd known. Normally she would feel vulnerable and unsure until she'd known a man intimately for some time. With Colin, whom she'd known hardly at all, she felt completely safe and protected. And while it usually took her a while to trust and let go of her inhibitions, she held nothing back from him. She was surprised by the force of her own voice, crying out with abandon, and the sound of his hushed, raspy voice encouraging her, urging her to let herself go.... To let it *all* go...

It was her first night with him and rather than holding back until she knew him better, she found herself slipping down his body and pulling him into her mouth. His hands in her hair, the growl of pleasure rumbling through him fed a deep need in her and she loved it. And when pushed as far as he could be pushed, he pulled her up, flipped her over in one deft movement, applied his protection and took her; he took her to heights she couldn't remember ever exploring before.

She was completely limp and full, nourished to her very soul. And she slept in her lover's arms as she had never slept before. In the early dawn she opened her eyes to find him watching her, gently smoothing her hair away from her brow. He gave her a brief kiss. "Jilly, I think that was the best night of my life."

She put her hands on his cheeks. "Thank you, Colin. Thank you for saying that."

"We have something, you and me."

She laughed brightly. "We had something several times. Don't you ever wear out?"

"Not with you. Just when I think I've had my fill, I touch you and feel the hunger again. It's morning—we should get up."

"We should..."

"Can you take me one more time?" he asked, running a finger over her lips, lips that were plump and pink from so much kissing. "Just one more time if I promise to be gentle?"

"Maybe just once more," she whispered, pulling that finger into her mouth and sucking it. She let go of it and said, "You don't have to be too gentle...."

His breath caught and he moaned. "Baby, you blow my mind."

"And other things," she said with a laugh.

But he wasn't laughing; he was inside her before she even saw him coming, rocking her, devouring her, pushing her to her absolute limit, falling with her into the sweet aftermath of sheer, blinding pleasure. All she could say, when she caught her breath, was, "Oh... *Colin!*"

Eight

Jillian hadn't even thought about how she was going to handle the clothes and shoes and other paraphernalia that landed on the sunporch roof, but apparently Colin had. When he took her home after their first night together, he examined the sunporch from the inside and found a couple of skylights. He came back later with an A-frame ladder, screwdriver and can-do attitude; he removed a skylight, got up on the ladder and poked his head through the hole, reached onto the roof with a long-handled broom and retrieved their stranded items.

"Thank you for doing that," she said. "I might not have thought of it."

"No problem. I really like those boots and I know you're attached to the furry slippers." He lifted her chin for a kiss goodbye. "Will you come to my cabin tonight?"

"You can't keep me away."

Jillian began driving herself to Colin's cabin in the woods when the sun set and the day was done. She was so grateful that he asked her every morning if she'd come back again that night because she wasn't sure how she'd admit to him that sleeping with him was so perfect that she wanted to be in his arms every night. He never put her through that; he always told her how much he wanted her beside him.

"You talk in your sleep," he informed her.

"No way!"

"You murmur about peat moss, mulch, smudge pots, shears…. It's not about me or sex or what you want me to do to you next, but about your garden."

"Are you feeling offended? Slighted?"

"No," he said with a smile. "Because when you're conscious, you yell to me what you want, what you need, how you feel, what you're going to do to me. Sweetheart, I am anything but slighted. Over and over and over again."

Four days after their first night a bed was delivered to Jillian's house and set up in her downstairs bedroom. Since first telling her he was going to make sure she had a bed, Colin hadn't mentioned it again. She left Denny in charge that afternoon and headed for Fortuna to buy linens and groceries. Would he come to help christen the bed, knowing it had been delivered?

He did.

Every morning they decided where they would spend the night. Sometimes the big old Victorian; sometimes the little cabin in the woods by the creek. She loved that creek at night, with a bit of moonlight filtering through the tall trees, and at dawn, with wildlife creeping close to the cabin for a drink.

"I've never had so much sex in my life," she confessed to him. "I'm surprised I can walk."

"Funny, I'm walking better than ever," he said.

What was very interesting to her was that she'd never felt so secure in a relationship in her life and yet she should probably feel the most vulnerable. They had entered into this liaison because they were driven physically, knowing that this was a brief space of time during which they were both planning their next lives—lives that did not include each other. He was going off to find wild animals and perhaps an edgy flying job in another country; she wasn't likely to spend much more time in a six-bedroom Victorian when all she really needed was a little living space and a lot of gardening space. It was temporary, yet it felt so safe, so permanent.

She played her cards pretty close to her chest for a couple of weeks and concentrated on developing her gardening operation. She had irrigation installed in her portable greenhouses, bought the kind of grow lights Dan Brady recommended and then paid him to help Denny set them up. Denny picked up the generators Dan suggested as the alternative to running wiring all the way from the Victorian, and together they got them operational.

By day she gardened and Colin painted. By night they had dinner together and then lay in each other's arms, sometimes making wild love, sometimes enjoying the comfort of togetherness.

In April sprouts popped out of the ground and appeared in her seed cups—*strong* sprouts. She smiled on them; she kissed them. She believed the fullness in her heart brought them out in a rush of glory and she knew, *knew* they would be hearty plants. When her fingers touched the soil, they were fingers that held in their memory the most powerful and beautiful physical love imaginable and she believed the seeds could tell and responded.

And then, *finally*, on a call to her sister she said, "I'm having a love affair."

"Are you now?" Kelly asked with a laugh. "I thought you'd sworn off men. You sure didn't last long. Who's the lucky guy?"

Jillian explained about Colin, about how she met him,

how she responded to him as though he was made for her. She told Kelly that he planned to leave at the end of summer and that she wasn't sure where she'd settle down—it would all depend on the harvest. It was probable she'd dismantle her greenhouses after the fall harvest and begin looking for a plot of land just right for her gardens. "If I can make my organic crops work, this might be my next job."

"Wait, wait, wait," Kelly said. "Are you in love?"

"I don't know. Do I have to be? I've never experienced anything like this before. We're so right together it's almost scary."

"But it's all over in September?" Kelly asked.

"We came into this knowing our lives were going in opposite directions, that this was a holding pattern. I've never felt better about things. Isn't it funny that in every relationship I've ever been in, all my worry was focused on the future, on where it would go. This time I'm focused on where it *is.* And it's all good."

"But Jillian, will you change your plans? Ask him to change his? Will you tell him you love him?"

She just laughed. "All I plan right now is that I wake up each morning knowing that for the whole day I have the most wonderful man in my life and a whole bunch of seedlings who seem to be responding to my happiness. I might be crazy or just hopeful, but I swear his paintings, which were awesome to begin with, are getting even better. They're growing, too. Seriously."

"My God, I think you've been hypnotized. You aren't growing anything you can smoke, are you?"

"No, but I got a lot of my advice on local crops from a pot grower. He's the one who tipped me on how to find the right seeds, how to irrigate and power the greenhouses. He's a very smart man."

"He's the one you're sleeping with?" Kelly gasped.

"No," she laughed. "I mean yes, Colin is very smart, but this was a man I met in the bar, not the same one I'm sleeping with."

"Jesus and Mary—do I have to kidnap you and get you deprogrammed?" Kelly asked sharply. "I feel like I don't even *know* you!"

"Isn't it wonderful? I loved my job at BSS, but until I got up here and stuck my fingers in the ground, I didn't know life could be so satisfying. I haven't thought about that rat race for weeks."

"But Colin's *leaving* you!"

Jillian became serious. "Listen, Kell—I suffered for weeks over a scoundrel, a conniving jerk who cost me so much, who trapped me and tricked me and took from me what was mine, what I'd built! I'll take a few months with this good, solid, awesome man to six years with a loser like Kurt. Colin's plans for Africa were made before he even met me, and my plans for the garden were already coming into focus. This is the arrangement, Kelly, this is how it will be—it was the first thing we knew about each other and is completely nonnegotiable. I'm not going to spoil something as perfect as this by trying to change him to suit me. I'm not that crazy."

"That's big talk, for now," Kelly said.

"But I am big," Jill said confidently. "I had no idea how big till I came up here and tested myself. I'm up to this— this is better than anything I've experienced and I'm not going to put barriers in the way. I'm going to live it and love every second of it. And right now there's no mistaking he's just as content as I am. And you know what else? I think it really does make your complexion better!"

Colin drove by Luke's cabins around noon, just to check in on the family. He'd made it a point to stop by from time to time because he had declined every invitation for dinner for about three weeks. He and Jillian had other things to do every night. He found Luke, Shelby and Luke's helper, Art, in the kitchen, having some lunch. "Sometimes I love my timing," he said, grinning.

Shelby smiled and said, "Sit down and let me make you a sandwich. I love your timing, too."

"What have you been doing with yourself?" Luke asked. "You've been pretty scarce."

"Not much," he said with a shrug. "Painting. Hunting things to paint—hunting with the camera."

Just as Shelby put a sandwich in front of Colin, there was a little fussing from the upstairs bedroom and she went to look after Brett. Art finished his sandwich and headed out the door for a little fishing. That's when Luke asked Colin if he could babysit for a few hours on Saturday night.

"Sure," Colin said. "What do you need?"

"It's what Shelby needs—she's on spring break, but goes back to school Monday. She needs a date night. Pretty soon she's going to hunker down to study for her finals and, if I know my wife, she won't come up for air until after the tests. Before all that kicks in, I need to take her away from the river. Give her a break from the baby. Think you can handle that?"

"We have an understanding, me and Brett," Colin said. "I can handle it. There's not going to be a problem."

"We've never left you alone with the baby," Luke said. "Do you know what to do?"

Colin shrugged. "Write it down for me. We'll be fine."

"Want to come back for dinner tonight?" Luke asked.

"Thanks, but I'll just settle for lunch today. I'm busy."

"You're not kidding. We've barely seen you for weeks!"

Colin just smiled. "That's a good thing. It means I'm busy. Being productive."

"Don't forget we've got Aiden's wedding in Chico next month. Want to ride down with us?"

"Thanks for the reminder," Colin said. "I might drive myself and take the opportunity to look around some, maybe spend a couple of days in the Bay Area. But really, it's nice of you to offer."

A half hour later, as Colin was getting ready to leave he stopped on the porch and looked at Luke's Harley. "Hey, would you loan me the bike for a few hours?"

"You up to that?" Luke asked.

"Yeah, Ma—I can handle it," he said with a laugh. "I'd like to take it up some of those mountain trails. I'll bring it back in a couple of hours."

"It's a heavy bike, Colin, and if you're still kind of—"

"I'm good," he said. He put a hand on Luke's shoulder. "I won't hurt the bike or myself. I promise."

"I'm not that worried about the bike, man."

"Aw," Colin said with mischievous grin. "That's sweet." Then he laughed. "It'll be okay, Luke. I'll bring it back before dinner."

"I guess so," Luke said with a shrug, digging into his pocket for the key.

"Here are the keys to the Jeep, in case you have to move it or use it or something. I'll see you later." And Colin was on the Harley and driving away before Luke could change his mind.

Shelby came onto the porch carrying Brett just in time to see Colin headed down the drive. "Where's he going?"

Luke turned and looked at her, a frown wrinkling his brow. "You notice anything different about Colin?"

"Like?" she asked.

"Like he's all mellow and actually *nice?*"

"I've always thought Colin was *nice*."

"But to me?" Luke asked. "He's really smoothed over. You don't suppose he's taking drugs again, do you?"

"Luke, you have no reason to ask that, just because the two of you can finally get along for a half hour. Besides, if Colin wanted drugs I doubt he'd hang around you. He'd go someplace none of his brothers could find him."

"I guess," Luke relented. "It's just... I'm not used to... Ah hell, maybe he's just starting to feel a lot better. I'm not used to him being calm, nice and agreeable. He said he'd babysit Saturday night."

"Good. See if you can just focus on *me* for a while," she said, patting his cheek and giving him a smile.

He smiled back. "I can do that, yeah. In fact, I don't have to wait for date night to do that. Does Brett have any more naps scheduled today?"

Colin drove to the Victorian and went around to the back where he found both Jillian and Denny working in the garden. She got to her feet when she heard the motorcycle coming toward them. When Colin pulled off his helmet and revealed himself, she laughed and walked toward him, wiping her hands on her jeans.

"What in the world is this?" she asked.

"My brother's Harley. Come for a ride with me."

"I'm working. I'm planting."

"You work seven days a week. Tell Denny he's on his own for a while. Come for a ride with your boyfriend."

"Have you upgraded yourself to boyfriend?"

Colin winked at her. "I'll tell him you're going for a ride with your sex slave..."

"Okay, *you* aren't allowed to talk to anyone about us," she said. "I think you like to make trouble. I can't, Colin. I'm all dirty."

"I like you dirty." He grinned evilly. Seductively. "Come on. Really, come on."

She sighed. "I have to wash my hands, my face, brush my teeth...."

He shook his head. "You don't have to get all prissy— you're going to get bugs in your teeth anyway. Hurry up—I have to return it before Mother Luke starts to worry and sends out a search party."

"Let me talk to Denny."

Jill went back to see Denny and, to his credit, he had gone right back to work and didn't stand to stare. "I'm going for a ride with Colin, Denny. I might be back before you're done for the day... I might not. But you know what to do here, right?"

He looked up at her over his shoulder. "Transplant the starters according to your chart and mark them."

"Exactly. Thanks."

Then he smiled and asked, "So *now* is it official?"

She smiled right before she said, "Shh. Still casual." Such a lie! There was *nothing* casual about it, but that was her business. She ran into the house, washed up quickly, tossed off her muddy jeans and shirt, grabbed some clean clothes and was out the door so fast it would be obvious to anyone she was dying to get on that bike with him. It must certainly have been obvious to him— he was smiling. He handed her a helmet; she pulled it on and mounted the bike.

Ah God, she thought as they roared down the driveway and up highway 36. This is almost as good as sex, hanging on to him, laying her head on his back and smelling him, having this monstrous machine vibrating underneath her.

Not a lot of talking goes on while riding a motorcycle and Colin hadn't explained if he had a destination in mind. He just drove, then got off the Highway onto a narrow side road that wound up into the hills. They passed by the occasional isolated cabin, but they were getting too high for crops, too remote for livestock. The road wound around and around the mountain, the views were awesome, the drop-offs harrowing, the dirt road beneath the tires was kicking up a lot of dust. And she *loved* it.

She was oblivious to the time, but when she looked at her watch she realized they hadn't been gone that long—about thirty minutes. Colin stopped the Harley on a grassy plateau with a beautiful view, propped it up on its stand and got off. He pulled off his helmet and reached for her hand to help her off.

She pulled her helmet off. "This is beautiful! How often have you been up here?"

"Never," he said. "I thought we'd end up in the woods, but this road looked interesting. I haven't been on a bike in years."

"You managed it like you ride every day."

"I was at Luke's today. I saw that bike and thought—perfect. I've been wanting to get you alone…."

"You have me alone every night, Colin," she said with a laugh.

"To talk," he explained.

Her mouth dropped open. She looked a little stricken. "Are you dumping me?" she asked. "I'm not even quite used to you!"

"No, baby." He grabbed her around the waist and pulled her against him. "I'm going to give you a chance to dump me."

"But why would I—"

"That's what we're going to talk about."

He couldn't resist; he gave her a deep, penetrating kiss, holding her body up against his for a long, sensual moment.

When he released her mouth and her body, all he could say was, "Ahhhh… God, I think I'm addicted to you!"

A little weak in the knees, which was usual for her when he did things like that, she said, "Shew, are you a wanted felon or something?"

He sat on the soft grass and pulled her down with him. They sat cross-legged, facing each other. "Close," he said as he moved to take both her hands in his. "You know I had a bad accident, a crash." She nodded and waited, wide-eyed. "I probably should've died in it but, thanks to my boys, I made it through. They pulled me out. I was pretty roughed up."

"You were critical," she inserted. "Someone told you?" he asked, surprised. "Lucky guess," she said with a shrug.

"Yeah," he affirmed. "Lots of broken bones, burns, et cetera. I don't mean to make excuses, but I was in a lot of pain. I got addicted to OxyContin. When the doc cut me off, I tried to buy it illegally and ended up getting arrested. I got lucky and went to treatment—probably thanks to my brother, Aiden, who came to help. All my brothers came to help me at one time or another—I was a real load. I think I've been a load for about forty years—a lot of cocky attitude and defensive behavior. Anyway, I spent months in treatment, first for the injuries, then for the addiction, then for depression. That's really why the Army is done with me, but at least they retired me. No civilian operation would hire me with all that on my résumé—at least that's my assumption. Baby, when I came to these mountains I was half-alive. There are a lot of tire tracks across my body."

"Do you think I'd hold all that against you?" she asked him.

"Nah, I know you wouldn't. There's something about you, something so unique and beautiful, something I've never had in my life before. But you need to know some truths—that half of what happened to make me who I am right now was just an accident, but half was me angry that I wasn't going to get that life back. Some of that Oxy ride and depression, that was me mourning my life, the life I lost. Jilly, I loved who I was before the accident. I *loved* flying that chopper—it takes some talent to keep the greasy side down, to maneuver it into tight spots, to keep it out of the line of fire. The scarier it was, the better I liked it. I was good at it. It gave me such a *rush*, I can't even explain...."

She just smiled at him and gently raked her nails through his beard. He pressed her hand against his cheek.

"When I wasn't in the helicopter, I did other things for that rush, that charge. I played amateur rugby—just amateur, but no less rough. I liked a little hockey when we could get a few guys together. I drove too fast, I dived off cliffs, para sailed, skied, scuba dived. Anything that would duplicate that excitement. My brothers all think I'm reckless. They always called me the wild man or crazy man. I didn't feel reckless or crazy—I think I just like putting it all on the line. I liked the challenge."

"It's funny," she said. "When you make love to me, you don't seem crazy. You're a little wild," she added with a grin. "But you take very good care of me."

"That's how I felt in my old life," he said. "A little wild, but in complete control."

"You dived off cliffs? You said you didn't like heights," she reminded him.

He smiled almost sheepishly. "That would somehow make it better. The thing is, Jilly—this guy who paints and limps up the stairs? This is not who I am. This is only me getting back to who I *really* am. You might be the best woman who ever came into my life...but I'm *still* going to Africa and I might even stay there, fly in the bush."

"What exactly does that mean? Fly in the bush?"

"Simply, operating aircraft in dangerous, inhospitable regions of the world. It's the next-best thing to flying in combat. If I don't like what Africa has to offer, I'll check out New Zealand, Alaska, South America. I don't even dislike the idea of flying in a mercenary operation—a civilian in a war zone. All that matters to me is that I get my life back—I just can't get over feeling I was robbed. I'll be ready to slow down someday, but honey, that's not going to be for a long while. I'm sure not ready for a steady diet of slow and easy now."

She smiled gently. "Are you afraid I'm going to ask you not to go?"

"Maybe a little bit," he said, shaking his head. "Mostly, I'm afraid I'm going to hurt you."

"Because you give me everything you've got night after night and pretty soon that's going to end?"

"Something like that," he said.

"But, Colin, I understand about the rush!"

He sat back a bit. He almost stuttered. "No offense, Jilly, but I have to think what I'm talking about is a little more dramatic than sticking a seed in the ground or picking a tomato."

She laughed. "You know I'm not just a little gardener, Colin. I helped build a major software corporation. I worked eighty-hour weeks bringing that company to one of the biggest public offerings in that industry. I wasn't diving off literal cliffs, but figurative cliffs, betting everything on the outcome of an IPO. The pressure was intense, the fiduciary risk was high, the potential for failure extreme and the potential for success over the moon. And I *loved* it! Loved it! It felt like Olympic Gold every time we succeeded." She laughed. "Or every time we failed to fail. I gave every day, every weekend, every holiday to keeping that company strong and successful. You call Harry Benedict today and ask him which three executives he would credit with helping him make BSS a household name and a multi-multimillion dollar company and one of them would be me. I guarantee that. When that was taken away from me, I nearly crumbled. It was hard to live without the risk, the daily pressure."

He looked completely perplexed for a moment. "But you were able to walk away and stick little seeds into the dirt and—"

She was shaking her head. "I was driven out, which is what happens to big kids who swim with sharks. And it nearly killed me. I was terminated even though my old boss, Harry, considers it a leave of absence. He told me to take a break, to think, to learn to relax. There might be an opportunity for me to go back to BSS—that's kind of up in the air. But for now I'm gardening and thinking and feeling more like a real person every day. But, Colin, I don't think I've lost my edge. I still feel that edge inside me every day—that rush.

"I'm not going to try to change you, Colin. I understand.... And I know what it feels like to be robbed of the life that felt perfect." She shrugged. "You do it your way—going after the big adventure. I'll do it my way. I don't want you to feel like you're missing something in your life. I'm not that kind of person."

He looked a bit stunned. "Okay, that makes you the first woman in the history of the world who isn't pissed because her man is off chasing some excitement."

"You're arrogant," she said with a laugh. "You assume you're the only person with needs, with dreams. I like what I'm doing and even though I haven't been invited,

I don't want to go to Africa or Alaska or New Zealand. One compromise we should make, though."

"What?" he asked.

"Before you leave, you should try to sell a painting or two, just to see what happens. Not to keep you from going, but to show you what you've got to look forward to. I don't think you know. I don't think any of us really knows what we've got or who we are until we risk it, put it to the test. You're perfectly willing to risk your life, but shy away from risking your ego or your art. You're a wimp, Colin." And then she smiled.

He was speechless; he'd never known a woman like this in his life. He'd never encountered this kind of self-less support.

"So," he finally said. "You think you'll go back to BSS?"

"I honestly don't know. Some days I think so. And some days I feel that part of my life is moving farther and farther away. My life is mostly calm and quiet right now, but I'm happy."

He looked a little confused. "But what are you doing for that edge?"

She grinned at him. She ran her fingernails down through his beard. "You," she said softly, leaning toward him. "I'm doing *you*."

That took him a moment. Then he suddenly wrestled her to the ground and went after her mouth like a dying man. When he broke from kissing her, he was out of breath, hard as a baseball bat and his eyes were glowing like embers. And he said, "I think I have to have you, right here, right now."

She ran her fingers through his longish, curly hair. "Now *this* is going to be difficult to give up...."

Nine

Come date night, Luke had a difficult time focusing on his wife because his thoughts were consumed with his brother Colin. When Colin appeared for his babysitting duties earlier that evening, he was not alone. He brought a woman, and not just any woman, but Jillian Matlock! Luke couldn't stop speculating on that odd match all through what was supposed to be a special dinner in Arcata with Shelby.

"I don't know why you should be so shocked," Shelby said. "They make a handsome couple. And Jillian's very nice."

"He's a wreck. He's all screwed up. Plus he looks a mess," Luke argued. "I guess he used to be okay-looking, if you like the big, dumb type, but look at him now!"

Shelby shook her head. "I don't know what's the matter with you—Colin is a very handsome man! That scarring he got in the accident doesn't detract from his good looks at all. And he is far from dumb! Luke," she said gravely, "sometimes you just wear me out!"

"It's not just the burn scars, which I admit aren't that noticeable, but what about that long hair and beard? You just don't understand, Shelby—he's just a grunt like me, and Jillian is like some big corporate vice president! I figured she came up here and started poking around in the dirt because she doesn't have to work. She's rich, made all her money in the software industry. Even if I didn't know that about her, I'd know she was smart. Not just a little smart, but very smart! Smarter than any Riordan I've ever met."

"How ridiculous—all the Riordans are smart and handsome. Aiden's a doctor for heaven's sake."

"Well, that's Aiden," Luke said, cutting off a piece of his steak. "He's always been a nerd."

Shelby just shook her head. The Riordan men were all drop-dead gorgeous and pretty damn smart, Luke's current idiocy notwithstanding.

"But that's not the half of it, Shelby—I'm telling you, Colin doesn't lean toward smart, beautiful, classy chicks like Jillian. He goes more for the pole-dancer type." He chewed thoughtfully on his steak. He swallowed. "Course, so did I. I should never have been lucky enough to find you. You're way outta my league."

She lifted an eyebrow. "Are you trying to make up?"

"Oh, baby, I'm not saying that to flatter you—it's just the God's truth!" He shook his head. "To think Colin got all his rough edges filed down nice and smooth by *Jillian*. I thought it had to be illegal drugs." He chewed another bite of meat. "I can't wait to call Aiden!"

"Why don't you just, for once, mind your own business?" she asked.

He shrugged. "I'm a Riordan," he said simply.

Much later that night, after pie and coffee with Colin and Jillian, far too late to be placing phone calls, Luke dialed up Aiden.

"What?" Aiden answered gruffly.

"I didn't wake Erin, did I?" Luke asked. "I'm sorry if I did, but this just couldn't wait."

"Are you drunk dialing, man?"

"Colin's got himself a woman. He was so relaxed and pleasant, I was sure it was drugs, but it's a woman."

"Big surprise," Aiden said. "Colin always seems to have a woman somewhere. What else is new? And what does this have to do with me at…" He paused as if to look at the clock. "Jesus, it's eleven-thirty! The only people allowed to call me at eleven-thirty are in labor!"

"This one would just knock you out," Luke said. "She's not only really smart, I think she's probably rich and she's beautiful! I only see her in her dirty gardening clothes most of the time and she even makes those look like high fashion, she's so pretty. And she's real, real clean-cut. She has freckles!"

"Good for him," Aiden said tiredly.

"But you know Colin," Luke insisted. "He tends to go for girls who are—Shelby, honey? Put your hands over your ears for just a sec." Back into the phone he said, "He likes the real slutty ones. Ow!" he yelled when he received a wop on the back of the head. He dropped the phone and when he got back on the line all he heard was a dial tone.

Aiden had hung up on him.

As the cloudy April skies led to a bright sunny spring, Jack was conscious of tongues wagging all over Virgin River. New relationships were always springing up, so the emergence of a couple of newcomers who had hooked up—Jillian and Colin—didn't throw the River crowd too much. They were used to watching unexpected love bloom all the time.

But when the new relationship between Jack and

Denny Cutler came out of the closet, the talk really launched into high-speed chatter.

"It's probably too late for a baby shower," Connie observed. Connie and her husband owned The Corner Store across the street from the bar.

"Oh, I don't know," Jack replied with a wink. "Denny's looking for some better fishing equipment."

Denny was proving to be a pretty good angler in a very short period of time, but casting and catching trout was secondary in importance to getting acquainted on a new level. Before this revelation they'd talked about everyday things from the Marines to car engines, but now Jack felt the need to fill Denny in on the Sheridan family tree. And being the only son in his family, he had always been very close to his father, so he tried to tell Denny everything about Sam Sheridan, his new grandfather. And he told him all the things he could remember of his growingup years, things he wouldn't ordinarily talk to a friend about—subjects ranging from Boy Scouts to high school football to having sisters.

To Jack's great relief, he learned that Denny's life hadn't been all stormy seas. When Denny was a real little guy his mother might've had a hard time with her difficult and sometimes abusive partner, but Denny was cushioned from much of it by loving grandparents. His "father" left the scene not long prior to his grandparents' passing, leaving just him and his mom and a small inheritance that helped them get by. "Me and my mom had a good life. She even dated a real nice guy, a man by the name of Dan Duke—we stay in touch even though they never got engaged or anything. I played football and he never missed a game. We were like a family. She found that cancer the first time when I was barely seventeen. When I went into the Marines at eighteen, we both thought she had it licked—she was doing so well. But no. She died when I was twenty-one—almost five years from start to end. I'm gonna be honest with you, Jack. That's the hardest thing I ever went through."

"I know, son. I lost my mom when I was in my thirties and it was terrible, and I still had a big family around. Preacher, he lost his mom when he was a senior in high school and he had no other family. He moved in with his football coach."

Denny chuckled. "I moved back in with the Marines," he said.

"I'm surprised you didn't come and find me right away," Jack said.

"I had to think about it for a long time," he answered. "What if I found you and you turned out to be like Bob?" He shook his head. "I had to put a plan together in my head. My mom got involved with him too fast. I wasn't going to make that mistake."

"You had a pretty solid plan, I'll give you that," Jack said. "Even if it took years."

"I tripped and fell along the way an awful lot. All that business of losing my mom, going to Afghanistan and no father that I knew of—I did some lame-ass things. I had a girl, Becca. I didn't want her to suffer if anything happened to me, so I just broke up with her." He turned and looked at Jack. "Lame. I really cared about that girl."

"You check back in with her lately?"

"When I got back, but she was still mad. She said she was with someone else. Who can blame her, huh?"

"Sometimes we just do the best we can," Jack said. "Sometimes our best isn't worth all that much."

Jack had spent a lot of time thinking about things lately—like for example the fact that he couldn't remember Susan Cutler. He couldn't remember if she was

"Susan," "Sue" or "Susie." That led to thoughts of how he had put together *his* master plan when he was all of eighteen or twenty—the only kind of plan that a sexually driven young man has. If we have an understanding, me and the woman, and if we're careful, have protection, we're consenting adults, he had told himself. We aren't obligated to each other; we're not going to be sad or hurt when we pull apart because from the start we knew it was just for now, not forever.

What a lot of happy horseshit that was.

Clearly he must have had such an arrangement with Susan Cutler and twenty-four years later the sheer idiocy of such a plan was all too apparent—he'd had a son for more than two decades and had done exactly nothing for him.

He just couldn't figure out in his head how he could've worked that out differently. He'd never felt in love enough to marry and the idea of living without any sex? Sex had always worked real well for him—he found doing without hard to imagine. But at the moment, standing beside Denny, fishing with him, listening to him tell about his mom dying, breaking up with his girl, going to war, all without the support of a father...? It made Jack kind of wish he'd just taken the matter of sex into his own hand for about twenty-five years instead of always looking for a pretty girl to pass the time with.

And yet, this boy who had appeared late in his life, was a real gift. Jack liked him. They seemed to think alike about a lot of things; they laughed at the same time, scowled at the same time. He was sharp and he should probably think about college. Jack would encourage that when the time was right. So when he thought that he just should have been celibate all those years ago, he reminded himself that, had he done that, Denny would not be in his life right now.

And this young man was quality. He was respectful, cheerful, considerate…. Oh, how he wished he could remember the woman who had raised him!

"I wonder, Denny… Remember those pictures of your mom you showed me? Would you be willing to loan me one? I bet I'll remember a lot of stuff about us eventually."

"Sure," he said, grinning. "I'll dig it out for you."

Pastor Noah Kincaid was driving out of town on a sunny Saturday afternoon when he passed Lydie Sudder's house. Something just wasn't right there. He'd waved at her as he'd passed by but she hadn't waved back even though she was sitting on the porch. Noah made a wide U-turn and went back, parking in front of the little house. He saw immediately what was amiss—it was still pretty cool outside and yet she was sitting on her front porch wearing only her slip.

"Lydie?" he said, walking up to the porch.

She lifted her eyes and smiled, but there was a faraway look in them; she was dazed. Noah had spent a lot of time visiting in nursing homes and hospitals over the years and he knew Lydie was elderly, diabetic, arthritic and had a heart ailment of some kind.

"Well, my dear," he said with a smile, lifting her arm at the elbow. "We'd better get you inside and find your robe or dress. And we'll call Dr. Michaels to come take a look, see if your sugar is out of whack or something…."

"Hmm?" she said, smiling a bit. Though she spent almost every Sunday sitting up close to the front in his church, clearly she wasn't sure who he was. She stood at his urging and allowed herself to be led inside.

She was so frail, he found himself thinking. He wasn't sure of her age, just that she was white-haired, bony, elderly and felt so fragile in his grasp. He led her to the kitchen and sat her down at the table. "Just give me a second, Lydie, then I'll find your robe and slippers." He picked up the kitchen phone and called Cameron Michaels at home—it was Saturday and there would be no one in the clinic. He was quick and to the point. "Hi, Cam, I'm at Lydie Sudder's house. I found her on her porch wearing only her slip and she's out of it. She doesn't seem to recognize me."

"I'll come," he said. "Can you smell her breath?"

"Sure, but I didn't detect anything like fruity breath."

He leaned down toward Lydie's mouth; Lydie fanned her hands rapidly, trying to get him out of her space as if he were a gnat. "I don't get anything, Cam. I'm sorry, I don't know how to test her sugar levels."

"Is she agitated?"

"Only when I'm trying to smell her breath," Noah said. "Wanna hurry?"

"I'm on my way. Do me a favor and call Mel at home, get her rolling in case we have an emergency."

"Sure thing."

Noah did as he was asked and then went in search of a robe or some sort of cover-up, but he found a dress and shoes in the bedroom doorway. It was as though she'd stripped right there and had gone outside. He took the dress back to her and she was very cooperative in allowing him to help her into the dress, then the shoes. Then he sat down at the table across from her. "Well, Lydie, do you have any idea who I am?"

She smiled at him and nodded, but said not a word. "I'm Noah, Lydie. Pastor Kincaid. Are you feeling okay?"

She merely smiled faintly and drew a circle on the

table with her index finger. After just a few minutes she seemed to come back to reality. She tilted her head, frowned slightly and said, "Noah?"

It was his turn to smile. "Well, hello."

"I'm sorry, Noah, I didn't hear the door."

Oh, this was going to be hard. "How do you feel, Lydie? You seemed to be in a bit of a daze there for a while."

She laughed lightly, patiently. "I go to the kitchen, can't remember why I went, have to feel the toothbrush to see if I've brushed my teeth, burned a batch of cookies just last week. Forgetful old woman." Then she frowned. "Noah, I'm sorry. I didn't hear the door."

"Lydie, I found you sitting on the porch in your slip. You didn't seem to recognize me. I've called Dr. Michaels. He'll be here in a few moments. Meanwhile, can we check your sugar? I don't know how but I know you do it every day."

She began to tremble a bit. "Yes," she said weakly. "Oh my goodness. My slip? Oh, my heavens!"

"Don't get all upset. You weren't exposed. Only your arms were naked. You were adequately covered. I found your dress on the floor. Do you remember me helping you get into it?"

She shook her head and went to a kitchen cupboard, retrieved her testing kit and brought it to the kitchen table. She sat back down, used the kit to test a tiny drop of blood and waited patiently. "Hundred and thirty—that's okay, right? I think that's okay."

"Have you been having periods of forgetfulness, Lydie? Confusion?"

She nodded gravely. "My health has been poor for so long, but my mind has been strong. Why, Pastor? Does that seem fair? I thought the diabetes or my heart would get me first."

"It's going to be all right, Lydie," he said. "We're going to get you some help."

"We both know…" She stopped and never finished that sentence. What they both knew was that if it was what it probably was, there wasn't a lot of help for it. "You know, Pastor, how we always say God won't give us more than we can handle?"

"Yes, Lydie."

She sighed. "I wish God didn't have such a high opinion of me."

After a couple of hours of fishing in the early afternoon, Denny followed Jack back to the bar. They both walked through the back door into the kitchen to find Paige and Preacher setting up dinner, little Dana Marie in her high chair nearby.

"Jack, Noah's waiting for you in the bar—there was some problem with Lydie," Preacher said.

"Really? She okay?" Jack said, quickly washing the river off his hands.

Preacher shook his head. "Sounds like she's not completely well. Better talk to Noah."

Jack hurried into the bar, frowning with worry. Noah was sitting up at the bar with a cup of coffee and a notebook he'd been writing in. "Noah, what's going on?"

Noah flipped the notebook closed. "A couple of hours ago I was passing Lydie's house and saw that she was sitting on her porch in her slip, not fully dressed. I stopped of course. She was disoriented. I thought it might be her diabetes, so I shuffled her inside and called Cameron. Her blood pressure and sugar levels are fine—fine for her, anyway. Mel came, as well—she dropped your kids with your sister. Lydie's okay now—she got confused, but I helped her with her dress and now she is very embarrassed, but lucid. However…"

"However?" Jack pushed.

Noah took a deep breath. "She was really gone, Jack. Totally out of this world. Mel poked around her house, with her permission of course. She asked me to follow her around. What she found wasn't so good. I'm afraid there are signs of dementia, perhaps Alzheimer's. There are dirty plates with dried food in the bathtub, too many of her pans are scorched, she doesn't seem to have bathed, she might be forgetting to eat and with diabetes…"

"I wonder if she's getting her shots," Jack said.

Noah shrugged. "Apparently she got her insulin today. Not long after Cameron and Mel arrived to give her a little physical, she was perfectly lucid. She's very frightened, though. Over her physical infirmities she had some control, but over this? I've been visiting hospitals and nursing homes for a long time now, Jack—sometimes it comes and goes pretty quickly—people can be out of it one minute and back on earth the next. There are symptoms she might've chalked up to growing older. We all forget why we went to the kitchen, but crossing the street and not remembering how to get home? That's pretty serious, I'm afraid. And the problem is if she's burning up a pan of grease while she's not of sound mind, it could be a disaster. Not just for her, but for the neighborhood, if you get my drift. They might want a better assessment—Mel and Cam—but if you ask me, Lydie's headed for assisted living. At the very least."

And her only living relative, her grandson, Rick, was a newly married, full-time, working college student in Oregon.

"She isn't safe alone anymore, Jack," Noah said. "Until

something can be found for her, we're going to have to get someone to stay with her."

Jack ran his hand around the back of his neck; it had suddenly become sweaty. "Wonder if Mel can think of anyone. I guess Rick should try to get down here for a quick weekend—but someone's gotta explain about things first. How's Lydie taking this?"

"She cried," Noah said. "Broke my heart. She doesn't want to be a burden to anyone. She's a very proud woman. She's managed her way through so many difficult situations for so many years—raised an orphaned grandson, held strong while he was critical from war injuries in Iraq, suffered ill health for years, lived on the edge of poverty. All she's got is the house. She's worried about losing the house and she wants Rick to have something when she's gone...."

"Rick's better off with a degree than that old house," Jack said dismissively.

"Is this your good friend Rick's grandma?" Denny interrupted. "The old lady in that little white house down the street?"

"That's Lydie," Jack replied. "This is awful, Noah. But I should've been ready for it. She's old—her health has been poor for years. She's gotten by so well in spite of that, I think we all took her for granted."

"Left alone she could get hurt," Noah said. "She could get lost, go into a diabetic coma, burn the town down...."

"Can she be left alone at all?" Jack asked.

"Mel and Cameron will have to be the final word on that," Noah said. "When she's fine, she seems perfectly fine. I think we have to start checking on her several times throughout the day."

"Think it would help if I stayed there at night?" Denny asked.

Both men turned to look at him in surprise.

Denny just shrugged. "Not forever," he said. "I have to work during the day and I'd keep all my things at the apartment over the Fitch's garage, but for a while I could just sleep there so nothing happens during the night. So she doesn't get out and get lost, or start a fire."

"You would do that?" Jack asked.

"If it would help. I know her a little. She always talked to me if I walked by. I saw her in here a few times. Once she called me Rick. I didn't think anything about it. Old people, y'know?"

"I can't ask you to do that, Denny," Jack said. "She's my responsibility while Rick's away—I gave him my word. I have to get this figured out real quick."

"Listen, call Rick at school," Denny said. "Tell him his grandma's slipping. Her physical health is hanging in there but her mind isn't what it was, and tell him I'll stay with her at night—sleep on her couch or something—till something gets arranged for her. Tell him not to worry too much—lotta people around here to pitch in. Course you guys are going to have to check on her a lot during the day—she could just as easy burn down the house in daylight."

Jack looked almost confused. "Why would you do something like that? For someone you barely know?"

Denny smiled. "Well, I know how important Rick is to you. I know he's a Marine. Why wouldn't I help out a brother? Doesn't cost me anything to sleep on an old lady's couch for a few nights," he added with a shrug. "Tell Rick everything is going to be all right. We'll get through it."

Rick Sudder *was* able to get time off from his job and school and arrived in Virgin River less than a week later, but his return to his hometown was bittersweet. He found his grandmother in good hands with his friends watching out for her by day and a new acquaintance sleeping on her couch at night—but he knew immediately he couldn't leave her there. If a nursing home could have been found for her in one of the larger Humboldt County towns, she would still be too far away for him to check on her, to make sure she was getting the care she needed and, most importantly, to visit her regularly.

He would have to close up the house and take her back to Oregon with him.

Complicated details were being quickly sorted out; the house had already been put in his name by Lydie, who'd had much foresight in this matter long before she became confused. She had never told Rick what she had done. Ricky's young wife, Liz, had stayed behind in Oregon to try to find nursing home care for Lydie, something that could take a while, meaning they would have to keep her with them in their small apartment until a suitable spot became available. Rick already had a power of attorney so that he could act on Lydie's behalf. He packed up Lydie's things and some mementos of his childhood but, for now, the house was going to be closed up, the utilities turned off, until they had a better picture of the future.

"This is the only home I can even remember," Lydie said to Ricky.

"That's why we're not selling it, Gram," he said. "I have two more years of college, but we might get back this way."

She shook her head. "I'll never make it back here, Ricky," she said.

"You've weathered so much in your life, you never know what's coming. Let's not give up yet."

"I don't want to be a burden, Ricky. I don't want you to have to take care of me."

He laughed and hugged her closely but gently. "Didn't you raise me all by yourself? Haven't we always taken care of each other? Stop being silly and have your friends over for tea before we leave."

In the few days it took to get things in order in Virgin River, Rick stuck real close to his grandmother. Her periods of confusion were regular but fairly brief; she ran the bath and left it sitting without bathing; she boiled eggs and forgot about them until the sulfurlike smell of burned hard-boiled eggs filled the house; she put her slip on the outside of her dress and didn't notice all through the morning; she wandered around the house in the night, waking Rick. It was very apparent that she needed caretaking.

Lydie had only Medicare and Social Security, so Liz had gotten her on a list for an in-patient facility, but a medical assessment by a geriatric specialist would be needed. An appointment was set up for her in Oregon and her placement would have a lot to do with the severity of her medical situation.

"I have a feeling she's going to be able to score a pretty high ranking on that list," Rick told Jack and Denny. "She's slipping pretty fast. I didn't really make much of her forgetfulness the last time I was here a couple of months back."

"None of us did, son," Jack said. "The only important thing is that she gets good care."

"I'm going to be saying goodbye to her before too long," he said. Then he shook his head. "And yet, with her problems, I'm surprised she's made it this long." He turned to Denny and said, "Thanks for helping out, man. You don't even know us—that was cool of you."

Denny shrugged and said, "I figured out pretty fast

that that's what people do around here. If they can, they step up."

On the morning that Rick loaded Lydie and her belongings into his truck, there were quite a few people gathered around to wish her well. She was her amazing self—proud, her back straight, all primped and her disposition strong. She said her goodbyes with gentle hugs and little cheek presses, telling her friends and neighbors she hoped to see them again when in reality she knew that was highly unlikely.

Mel gave her a hug and said, "Jack and I will drive up within the month to see how you're all doing, Lydie. We'll be in touch by phone until then."

"That's so sweet, Mel. Of course, we appreciate that."

"Ricky will take very good care of you."

"He's a good boy," Lydie said.

"Well, you raised him, of course he's good."

Before getting into the truck Rick shook Denny's hand. "Thanks, man. I'm really glad you and Jack found each other."

Denny smiled. "We'll see each other again, Rick. Drive safely. Study hard."

Ten

In late April, Colin asked Jillian if she had anything she could wear to a wedding. "Why?" she asked. "Are you trying to marry me?"

"My brother is getting married in Chico in just two weeks. I have to be in the wedding—all the brothers have to be in the wedding. It's a big country club ordeal. Gee, I bet he belongs to a country club now—I never asked. Anyway, I have to wear a tux and I'd like to take you with me. There will be a lot of Riordans at this event."

"And they'll be looking me over?" she asked.

"Oh, without a doubt," he said. "They'll also be looking *me* over to be sure I'm not popping Oxys or drinking too much champagne. Come with me, Jilly. Keep me safe from them."

She tilted her head. "I did bring unnecessary clothes, but I don't think I brought the *right* unnecessary clothes. I could shop online. You're sure you really want to set them up to think you have a permanent girl?"

"I haven't told any of them about Africa yet," he admitted. "I've started getting my inoculations and I'll let them know pretty soon...."

"Oh, Colin, why haven't you taken care of that?"

"They all know I have that cabin till September, but not one of them has asked me what I'm going to do next. I'm pretty sure everyone assumes I'll find something near one of the boys, but Africa is going to throw them. I doubt they think I'm tough enough for a trip like that."

"Are you sure you are?" she asked, giving his arm a stroke.

"Strong enough and hoping Africa will show me what I'm made of, what I've still got. I'll tell them, but not till after the wedding. There shouldn't be arguing at a wedding. And Aiden has suggested a shave and a haircut."

She stood on her toes to run her fingertips through his curling locks; his hair was almost shoulder length now when it was free from his ponytail. "Maybe a little trim, but not too much. I love this hair. I love the wild man look you have. If you get any trouble about it, refer them to me."

"You'll come with me?"

She nodded. "But it worries me that you're misleading your brothers about your plans."

"Not really, Jilly. I'm just keeping my own counsel," he said with a smile. "I'll bring it out of the closet right after the wedding."

She grabbed his earlobe and gave it a tug. "Do not put me in the middle of that!"

He swung her around, laughing, kissing her. "I wouldn't do that to you, Jilly!"

"And don't think you can get away with working around the truth like that with me!"

He stopped moving. He looked down at her, his eyes dark and serious. "Jilly, if you ever get anything but the most profound truth from me, call me on it. I'll kill myself on the spot." He shook his head. "I have lots of reasons to keep things from my brothers—they're known for being in everyone's business all the time. But I'd never keep anything from you. I wanted to be completely honest with you from the start."

She was deeply touched by that, but felt a twinge of guilt. She bit her lip as she looked up at him. "I haven't exactly unburdened myself to you," she said, and they both knew what she was holding back. He'd asked her more than once what the last man in her life had done to hurt her.

"It's okay, honey," he said, touching her nose. "When you're ready. But I know you haven't lied to me. I *know* that."

Colin noticed things gradually changing in Jill's garden. He learned that tomatoes needed eight hours of sun a day and that Humboldt County in the mountains wasn't exactly known to be sunny and warm, even in spring and summer, but it was known for rich soil. Everyone in town talked about the great success that Hope McCrea had had with her garden and everyone was happy to know that Jill had brought it back to life.

Another change involved Colin—he began painting in the sunroom quite often—he preferred it to the artificial light in his cabin or the outdoors once the weather became hot in the sunny afternoon. He liked being able to look down on Jillian's work in progress and watch as she tilled, sprayed, planted, moved plants from the greenhouse into the ground, scooting around the property in her garden-mobile. The UPS truck was a daily arrival; Jilly was constantly buying supplies. After painting for a couple of hours Colin would wander down to the kitchen for a cup of coffee, then out onto the porch to take a break. If Jill saw him, she stopped work and spent a little time with him. What he liked even better was when she came silently up the stairs and sat on the floor behind him, watching him paint. More and more of his work made the move to the Victorian and it remained there. He still went out with his camera, but a lot of Colin's time was spent painting in that big room with all the windows, the two skylights and so much natural light. And many of his nights were spent in the bed he'd bought her.

There were paintings he still kept in his cabin, covered and turned toward the wall so that if he and Jillian spent a night there, she wouldn't peek. He worked on them only when he was alone. One was of a gardener wearing calf-high rubber boots, gardening gloves and a wide-brimmed straw hat—and that was all. She was turned to the side; only the lower half of her face was visible, the strong line of her jaw and her beautiful, plump, pink lips in a secret smile. Also visible was a side view of her nude body— the soft curve of her breast, the round arc of her perfect butt, her long, elegant legs, graceful arms and delicious shoulder. It was Jilly as he pictured her.

That painting's twin was the nude gardener crouched between rows of plants, small spade in hand, grooming. No one but Colin would know how perfectly each of those curves fit into his big hands, how soft that velvet skin felt against his rougher skin, how much pleasure those exquisite lips brought him.

She had become the answer to prayers he hadn't known he whispered.

After an afternoon of perfect light, Colin cleaned up his brushes, put away his paints and washed up in the upstairs bathroom. He heard a scraping sound from the room right below him and was still drying his hands on a small towel when he walked into the maid's quarters.

He found Jillian had pushed the bed away from the wall and was measuring the size of the room.

"What's going on?" he asked.

She turned toward him with her eyes glowing. "I've had an offer on my town house. I'm accepting it. I asked the Realtor to hire a moving crew to pack up all my things and deliver them to me here. It's either store them here where I live and have plenty of space, or rent a storage facility. I don't have that much—my town house is pretty small. So—we're going to make a change—this bed will go upstairs and I'm going to put my desk, credenza and shelves in here. This will be my office. What do you think?"

Colin tilted his head and frowned slightly. "Don't you want to go back there to close up your house? Pack up your own stuff? See your friends again? Because I could help manage the garden with Denny if you need to be away."

"I'm not even going back to close on the sale. Until I got settled in here, I didn't even realize how little that town house meant to me. It was no more than a crash pad. I spent all my time at work. If I end up going back there, I'm going to find something different."

"You must have friends from work you miss," he said.

She drew a deep breath and sat on the edge of the bed. "I think maybe I'm ready to tell you about it. About him. About what happened to me."

Colin sat down beside her. "Only if you want to."

"I want to. It's become kind of blurry and surreal in my mind—I still can't believe it really happened.

"He was a man on a mission. And he was relentless...." Twenty minutes later Jillian had shared with Colin many of the details about her relationship with Kurt, telling the story with brutal honesty.

"You must have been at least flattered if you were going to break rules," Colin said, pulling her closer to him.

She laughed. "Truthfully, I had promoted him because we lost a director in my department and Kurt had come with glowing letters of recommendation. I was watching him closely to see how he was holding up with his added responsibilities. He was watching me closely for other reasons. I began to get the attraction message from him and he was..."

"Tempting you..."

"I was very busy with work. I didn't have a lot of time for socializing. But, I began to see him away from work and I knew these were not just a couple of colleagues talking business over dinner. I knew what his intentions were. I warned him that it was not a good idea, but after a few months, after he continually made the excuse that we both spent so much time at work, neither of us had anyone to date and next thing I knew, I was sleeping with him and worrying about keeping it a secret from the boss." She laughed bitterly. "The boss, Harry, who was my best friend in the company. Six months after I met Kurt and one month after I first was intimate with him, he accused me of sexual harassment. He had a lawyer, witnesses, a complicated log of events that I couldn't exactly refute, text messages and emails that could certainly be construed as exploitive if it weren't for the simple fact that he'd approached me, worked very hard to seduce me and it was completely consensual. In fact, when you get down to it, *he* put the pressure on *me!* I was very reluctant! He had set me up from the beginning—he forced me out of my job and part of the settlement he asked for to keep us all out of court was to take over my position and he wanted me terminated."

"Did you fight?"

She shook her head. "We talked about fighting it, me and Harry. We both knew it was all trumped up. But in the end Harry pulled my fat out of the fire. He told me to resign, but that he was going to replace me with a consultant and would consider my resignation a leave of absence. He gave Kurt vested stock options—probably worth a lot of money, but going to court might have cost more. But Harry got a confidentiality agreement, which both Kurt and I signed, and a waiver—that would be the end of the complaint. No further suit. This was critical—I wouldn't have my reputation damaged by these phony accusations. I still have a good reputation in the industry." She fell back on the bed and looked up at him. She shook her head. "I can't believe I was so naive. So unprepared."

Colin reclined beside her, his elbow braced on the bed, his head balanced on his hand. "You never suspected?"

"Not for a second," she said. "He was cute and charming, but so wily. It never would have occurred to me that he was both lazy and predatory. He even walked me into a jewelry store once and got me looking at rings. Not that I was ready to be so serious, just a casual, fun thing. Know how I found out the truth? I walked into the boss's office for a meeting and Kurt was sitting there wearing a perfect, pathetic hangdog look—the poor victim. I was stunned. I could barely breathe."

She sat up, cross-legged on the bed, facing him. "I was devastated. Not only was I shattered that this man would betray me like that, I'd lost my *real* true love—the company I'd helped found and build."

"And tell me this—how could your mentor, your best friend, let that happen to you?"

"Because he didn't know. In retrospect, I should have confided in Harry immediately." She shook her head. "I didn't want my friend and mentor involved in my love life. In the end, he had to rescue me as best he could.

"When this accusation hit the fan, everything changed. I wanted to fight it out, but Harry saw it otherwise. I can see now that he made sense. When it was all over I left BSS, got in my car and drove. I came up here to get away, to rest and think. I didn't know I was going to discover the garden. That was an accident."

"And what did he get?" Colin asked, reaching out and running a finger around her ear, along her jaw.

"Well, not everything he wanted. He got his vested options and will make some money, but he didn't get my job. But, there wasn't a going-away party for me. That tells me he wasn't as confidential as he was supposed to be and leaked the whole thing. And that he'd charmed more people than just me."

"Bastard," Colin grumbled.

"So in answer to that first question—are there friends there? There are several I'd work with again and a few I'd consider friends, but to be completely frank I actually didn't have many close friends in San Jose—probably because I spent most of the past ten years simply working. Believe me, I won't make that mistake again."

Colin's jaw pulsed briefly and she put her palm against it. "Don't," she said. "Please don't feel sorry for me."

He gave a short laugh. "Sorry for you? God, no! Angry for you, yes!"

"But here I am and in truth, Colin, I've never felt better about anything. I'm the CEO of the backyard garden and it feels real good. No one's getting the better of me here. Well, the frost or aphids might—but I'm on top of it!" She smiled at him.

"Jilly, do you feel safe and in control now? With the garden? And with me?"

She leaned toward him for a kiss. "Yes. And you don't have to be angry for me, either. I've got that covered."

Jillian never even suggested that Colin keep her most personal information secret. She knew she didn't have to. One thing he did ask her was, "Have you talked to Harry since you left?" When she said there had just been a few emails between them, he said, "He was on your side, Jilly. I know you didn't think you got what you needed at the time, but it sounds like he did the best he could for a trusted friend—the most important thing was, he believed you."

She realized she'd been avoiding Harry because she didn't want to show her weakness by asking how Kurt was doing. There was a tiny part of her that was afraid he was thriving.

She knew how to work her way around office gossip. Too bad she hadn't thought that so necessary when she was seeing Kurt! But no way was she going to have anyone pass around the news that Jillian Matlock had called the CEO! She didn't call his office; from the widow's walk, she dialed up Harry's cell phone from her cell phone. Her name would come up on his caller ID.

"So—you're not dead?" he answered gruffly.

She laughed before she said hello. "I am very much alive and sitting on the top of a three-story, ninety-year-old Victorian house, on the widow's walk, in the middle of a forest, because I have good reception up here. The view over the forest and farms is awesome. How are you, Harry?"

"I'm grumpy. I'm told I need a knee replacement. My wife has me on a diet for my cholesterol. She wants to go on a month-long cruise. I don't think I could survive something like that. I want to send her on the cruise with her sister and go to Pebble Beach for three days. Think she'll buy that?"

She laughed at him; he adored his wife. "You'd be better off on a ship with your bad knee. Besides, you could use a vacation," she said.

"I could use a knee replacement, too, but who has time? Seriously, I don't think I can be trapped on a boat for a month. I might throw myself overboard. Jillian, how the hell are you?"

"I'm better than I've been in a long while, Harry. You'll never guess what I'm doing. I've started a very special garden...."

"Oh, God, please make this interesting soon, before I nod off...."

So she gave him the bullet points—she had started growing specialty, hard-to-find fruits and vegetables, the exotic kind that garnished meals at fancy restaurants, not something just any gardener could do.

"You going to grow in summer, read sex novels in winter?" he asked.

"You told me to relax and think. Some people go on cruises, some play golf even with a bad knee, some people go to the lake or the beach for the summer. Some even skydive for fun! And me? I'm going to spend the summer in the garden. And I'm not only relaxed, I'm having a blast! If I'm still here after September, I might buy smudge pots and experiment with a winter crop. I'm planting a lot of stuff right now just to see what works, what's strong, what's weak. I'll have an idea what's possible by late summer. I might end up with a wide variety or just a few special items. Then I'll have to decide *why* I'm doing this."

"Organic? What about bugs and worms?"

"Harry, you know about gardening?"

"Not a damn thing. These seem like obvious questions."

She had to chuckle. This was how he'd gotten so far—he knew a little bit about a lot of things and a lot about a few things. Brilliant man. "I'm doing a lot of research and, so far, things are going well. We're even making our own mulch now...."

"We?"

"I hired a hand. And I sold my town house—my goods will be delivered soon. I'm putting a little money into the garden. Call it research and development, but this is actually a low-cost operation."

When she paused, so did he. The silence stretched out. Finally, in his gruff voice he said, "You sound good, Jill."

"I am good, Harry. Is BSS doing all right?"

"All right. Stock's up. Board's a pain in my ass. One software product fuckup and recall but that's only one of our many products and we can afford to eat it." Another silence. "He's not here anymore, Jill."

"I didn't ask," she said. "He's—

"I'd like it on the record that I *didn't* ask," she said emphatically.

"He couldn't take the heat. He knew he was up against an enemy in me. Plus there was the incidental fact that he's completely incompetent. I gave him a sterling recommendation to help him out of here—the only thing that could have made it sweeter is if it had been to one of our competitors. He skipped, got a title and a pay raise. And is blessedly gone."

She actually dropped her chin and rubbed her temples. "I'm sorry. Feeling completely stupid once more."

"Aw, give yourself a break. He probably drugged your herbal tea or some damn thing. I told you, Jill—you gotta have a little balance in your life. Work hard but have some good times. Drink a few martinis here and there, have men in your life sometimes so you don't run the risk of getting lonesome, so the wrong one can't come along and trip you up."

"No chance of that up here," she said.

"Well, he's gone and we both know he's not gonna make it. He's gonna fall so hard he'll leave a very big hole where he lands…. And you're happy—just do the happy dance and come to see us. Come to the house, have a big meal, tell us about the gardens…."

"You'll be on a cruise," she said, feeling a little emotional. "Or off carbs…"

"Seriously, you're ready for your own company. You always have been. I started my first when I was twenty-eight. Didn't go that well, but I was ready and the experience was good for me. You should try it. Now's the time."

"For right now, it's time to garden. It's the strangest thing—it makes me feel… I don't know…like I'm really part of something that never stops. Year after year, the cycle of life kind of thing. In a perfect world I'd work six months a year and garden from spring to fall. Could you get into that, Harry? Put me to work from October to April?"

"Wouldn't surprise me if you made a business out of it. I always expected you to start your own company. I didn't think you'd do tomatoes, but what the hell, huh? There's money all over this world—you just have to have a nose for it. Those tomatoes smell like money, Jillian?"

She laughed through the feeling of tears that had gathered in her throat. "Sometimes they do."

"Hah! I knew it! When they're ripe, send me some, will you?"

"Sure."

"And Jill? There's one more thing and I am absolutely

not supposed to discuss this. A couple of the women from Corporate Communications who stood as witnesses in his case came to me—they realized their mistake, realized they'd been had and tricked into believing you exploited him. They now have guilt. They see the light and know they were used. They're sorry."

"Tell them to go to hell," she said, bitter.

He laughed so loud and hard it triggered a coughing fit. "Yeah," he said. "Well, I couldn't say it, but I thought it. Too little too late, huh?"

"How can I be such a hard-ass," she amended. "He tricked me, after all."

"Let him go. He's so over, the body is getting cold. Hey, if you don't come down here, I might come up there, see what you got."

"You'll be on a cruise."

"We could compromise," he said. "Three-day cruise, three-day trip to the veggie farm, three days at Pebble Beach. You know what, Matlock? I miss the hell out of you. It was time for you to take on the world, but that doesn't make it easy."

"I love you, Harry."

"Yeah, yeah… Every broad I ever gave a few million to has said that."

She laughed into the phone. "Godspeed, kid," he said.

"God bless, Harry," she said.

Jillian's town house had been a small two bedroom— around sixteen hundred square feet. Perfect for one single woman. Therefore it hadn't held a lot of furniture. Denny helped her move the bed Colin had purchased out of the maid's quarters to one of the second-floor bedrooms. When her furniture arrived, the office furniture that had been in her second bedroom went into the maid's quarters. She moved her computer and recliner from the kitchen into that room.

Her living room sectional went into the sunroom along with her big flat screen, bookcases and side tables and there was still more than enough room for Colin to paint. It became the most wonderful room—a den and studio all in one. She had come to love the smell of his paints.

Jillian put both leaves in her dining room table to make it longer and it still didn't overpower the eating area of the roomy kitchen. Her patio furniture—table, chairs, two chaise lounges—went on the back porch. Her bedroom furniture went into the largest second-floor bedroom.

She bought herself a hanging rack for clothes and filled her bedroom bureau drawers. The rack went into the third empty bedroom on the second floor, which served as one big closet. The problem with these old Victorian's—no closets. Whoever moved into this place permanently would have to invest in wardrobes.

Certain parts of the Victorian took on a look of peaceful domesticity. Colin and Jill were rarely apart and never spent a night away from each other. Colin still liked to prowl around for wildlife shots and he enjoyed painting on hilltops for a few hours here and there, but daily life saw them mostly together. In evenings, while Jill sat in the office and read the gardening blogs on the computer, Colin sat in the recliner in the same room, reading or surfing art and galleries on his laptop. Jill invited him to use her computer anytime he wished to and before long his laptop and color printer appeared to have found a permanent home in the office.

They seemed to spend most of their nights in the Victorian, which made a trip to the cabin seem like an escape out of town, a completely different environment.

"I've never had a relationship like this," she said. "I'm

thirty-two and this is the first time I've slept with a man every night. I'm kind of surprised—this is so new to me. And so natural."

"For me, too," Colin said. "I like it."

"But I hardly ever had a man in my life. You've had lots of women—I can tell."

He pulled her close and said, in all honesty, "Not like this, Jilly. Not like you."

In the bright sunshine of early May, Jillian's flowers around the house, fruits and vegetables in the open garden and flowering shrubs around the yard were in full swing. There were a few apple trees in the front of the house and the air was filled with the sweet scent of blossoms. Also bees, but for any gardener, bees were the friends who transported pollen. She'd been right about the bulbs—daffodils, tulips, lilies all bloomed in the warm sun. Jill was surprised to discover a long row of blackberry bushes along the tree line in the back meadow. When they were all ripe, there would be too many to even deal with.

It was more than a house and garden. It was a nursery.

Walking around the property she could hear the sound of the mower; Denny was running the riding mower around the expansive front lawn, a job that could take half the day. Bright sun, warm weather, plenty of rain turned the grass a dark, vivid, thick green. And plenty of it; Denny was cutting it every week. He built himself a ramp so he could load that riding lawnmower onto the back of Jillian's truck and take it over to Jack's for a little upkeep over there—Jack didn't have a rider.

Just as Jack crossed her mind, she spotted his truck coming up the drive. She took off her gloves, brushed off her knees and smiled at him.

But Jack wasn't smiling. He wore a very serious expression as he approached her. The very first thought that came to her mind was that he was bringing bad news. Her mind skittered around. Was it possible someone would call Jack to report a catastrophe involving Kelly? Had Colin had an accident? She could hear Denny's mowing so she knew he was all right. Her hand crept to her throat and she walked toward him. "What?" she asked. "What is it?"

"Well, it's a surprise out of the blue, Jillian," he said. "Caught me completely off guard. There's interest in the house."

She actually breathed a sigh of relief. Is that all? she thought. And then quickly following that she nearly gasped. "Interest in the house? But…?"

He shook his head. "I haven't listed it for sale, but I mentioned to a couple of Realtors that I'll be looking to sell eventually, probably when we have a little recovery in this god-awful economy. But real estate around here, Jillian… It's not the usual thing. Most of us are out in the country, like this house here is, and there's no point in a sign—no one's gonna see it. But sometimes some Realtor from San Francisco or L.A. will call one of our Realtors and ask if there's anything available that would work for a summer house or an oceanfront property or hunting cabin."

"And…?" she pushed, the suspense killing her.

"A couple from the Bay Area, retiring from their big companies, kids grown, they're looking for a bed-and-breakfast with a sizable acreage. Something they could run a few months of the year, which would leave them plenty of time to relax, have their family visit or travel. They like the idea of a few guests and maybe grounds that could be used for celebrations, like weddings and so on. He likes to garden. She loves to cook. The Realtor in Fortuna mentioned this place and they took a look at the outside—I guess you didn't notice them. They'd like to look inside and if it suits, they'll want to make an offer."

"But, Jack…"

"I told them it wouldn't be available until September. They think that's a good idea—it would give them the winter months to get settled in, put together some ads for their B and B, have the kids and grandkids for holidays, travel. I might even be able to put them off till October, if you need the time." He gave his chin a nod. "We're friends and neighbors, Jillian—I'm not going to run you off. I'd appreciate it if you kept in mind… I have to do right by the trust. The house is part of the trust…."

She was quiet for a long moment. Then she said, "Of course. But have you set a price? Has anyone suggested a price?"

He shook his head. "It's time to get it appraised. With the great work Paul has done here, it's going to bring a nice price. Probably just over a million."

She almost laughed but kept it to a smile. "You need to find a way to move this place to San Jose. I'm not even going to tell you what it would go for there. It would make you greedy." Jillian's little town house with no yard went for three-fifty in a bad economy. At least she hadn't lost money on it, but she didn't make much.

"I know," he said. "I just can't help but wonder who would want to come to a B and B in Virgin River. Not hunters, that's for sure. They'd be happier at Luke's or in some lean-to with an outdoor biffy where they can make noise, smoke the cigars the little wifey won't let them have at home, get up at four to beat the deer…. Who wants to come to a place like this in summer when there's no hunting? And if you're fishing, you have to change out of your wet clothes on the porch and clean your fish in the yard so you don't get someone's pretty little B and B all messy." She smiled at him patiently. "You haven't been to Ferndale lately, have you, Jack?"

"Have *you?*"

"Lots of B and B's are successful around here, especially in Ferndale. People come to relax. To enjoy the landscape, the shops, the ocean, the redwoods. Some people like to hike, to sit out on a porch surrounded by beautiful trees and flowers and just read a book. They might not have a waiting list, but they'll do just fine. Trust me."

"Well, I owed it to you to warn you. And I'm going to have to ask you to let them see the inside...."

"Sure," she said, but the very thought made her so sad. "When?"

"Right away, I guess. I'm told they drove up from the Bay Area a couple of weeks ago and saw the outside and they're ready to do business if the inside suits them."

"Just let me know," she said with a shrug. "I'll make sure I'm dressed and the dishes are done."

He made a sad face himself. "If you don't mind me asking, where will you go?"

"Oh, I have options. In fact, I can have my old job back anytime I want it. I'm just not convinced I want it." She laughed. "Harry, my boss, told me to take a break and relax. I'm not sure I'm done relaxing just yet. That whole corporate thing—it just doesn't appeal like it used to."

"I suppose not," Jack said. "I came up here after twenty in the Marines and all I brought were my rifles, fishing gear, clothes and camping equipment. And I never left. I was raised in Sacramento, no small town. But I'm just not a city boy, after all."

"Do you have to make an appointment with that couple right away?" Jill asked.

"I can't wait too long, Jillian," he said. "If this was my house, I'd do as I please. But it's not really my house. I have to do the right thing."

"Would it kill you to give me a day or two to think about what I might do next? Where I might go? Because there's a lot to do if I move—not the least of which is decide where."

"Wouldn't even make me flinch," he said. "It's the least I can do. You've taken real good care of the place for me and I appreciate it. Just call me soon as you can, will you?"

"Of course," she said. "I totally understand. I just haven't thought about my next home or job yet. I need to do that, don't I?"

"I guess so," he said. He shook his head. "Denny would work this little property forever, I think."

She had to laugh. It was huge! Ten acres, a couple of greenhouses and an enormous garden. A house with over four thousand square feet. She glanced up to the roof, feeling a little sentimental. She'd never again have another widow's walk.

She gave his arm a pat. "I'll call you tomorrow, Jack. Thanks for the heads-up."

Eleven

Jillian had gone back to her outdoor garden after Jack left. Kneeling, weeding, aerating roots, pulling a few root vegetables to check their progress, all she could do was think about the fact that this experience, her time in this house and on this land, was no longer indefinite. Even if this Bay Area couple didn't make the right offer on the property, someone else would. She wasn't the only person in the world who would find the fertile beauty of the land and the incredible refurbished space in that big old house irresistible.

She thought the most logical thing for her to do would be to return to San Jose in the fall and work for BSS again; it was work she understood, after all. Regardless of all Harry's noise about how she should take on the world, start her own company now, move on to a stronger position, the only thing that felt right was the familiar. If she had to go back to corporate life, she'd go back to a company she understood.

She couldn't be on vacation forever.

She wondered briefly if she should bite the bullet and start her next career as the owner of a B and B. That would justify staying here. With these thoughts in mind

Jill worked away for a couple hours until she heard a familiar vehicle in the drive.

Colin had brought some groceries back to the house and volunteered to make their dinner. She took him up on the offer—she didn't feel much like cooking. In fact, she rarely felt like cooking, or cleaning, or shopping for groceries. She was the kind of woman who did those things because they had to be done, not because they were fulfilling. She was the *last* person who should ever be the owner of a bed-and-breakfast.

She puttered in the upstairs bath for longer than usual. By the time she heard Colin's feet on the stairs, coming for her, she was standing in front of the mirror in the bedroom that held all her clothes. She wore pale yellow capris that tied below the knees, a white tank covered by a loose-weave sweater that fell off one shoulder, and three-inch heels.

He walked into the room and came up behind her, his hands going to her hips, a smile on his lips as he met her eyes in the mirror. "Interesting look," he muttered, kissing her neck.

She turned one ankle to get a side view of the shiny black pump. "I used to wear heels to work every day. Suits, dresses with jackets, skirts and sweater sets, even dress slacks, but I always wore heels. I liked being as tall as the men. I liked looking them in the eye."

"You liked intimidating them," he accused.

She turned in his arms. "I was a lot more girlie, that's for sure. Probably more enticing to the male eye than jeans or shorts, tank tops and Skechers."

"That might be, Jilly, but there's almost nothing you can do to make yourself sexier to me." He slid his hands around to her butt. "You're the sexiest gardener I've ever messed around with."

"You're not more turned on by the capris with three-inch heels?"

"You even turn me on in those flannel pj's pants." He grinned. "Those babies slip off real easy…."

"Jack has someone interested in the house. My party is almost over. I'm going to have to decide where I'm going, what I'm doing."

"Haven't you been thinking about it?" he asked. "Hasn't your deal with Jack always been till September?"

She nodded. "I fantasized that nothing would change and he wouldn't have a better deal than me renting here for a long time, maybe another year. Instead of thinking about where I'd go and what I'd do, I was thinking about trying out a winter crop inside shelters with smudge pots and grow lights. But… Well, it was a respite, a vacation, sort of. A break from the real world. I can't be on vacation forever."

He laughed at her. "No one works harder at a vacation than you, Jilly. Up before the sun, farming all day, studying plants and gardening online all night."

"Because it's fun," she said. "I guess the most rational thing would be to go back to San Jose and work at BSS. I should be so grateful I'm still welcome there."

"You don't sound grateful, honey."

She turned around and faced the mirror again. "I don't know how to explain this," she said, tipping one foot up on its toe and peering at the reflection in the mirror. "That corporate girl in the heels?" She looked over her shoulder at him. She gave her head a little shake. "I don't feel like her anymore."

He tightened his arms around her waist. "Who do you feel like?" he asked softly.

"I feel like a settler, like a homesteader. I feel strangely unencumbered, like a woman who never has to set an alarm clock, like someone living off the land. Like a nature kid, but I'm not. I mean, I love organic plants because they're a perfect challenge but I'm *not* one of those all-natural fanatics. I also love wearing synthetic blends, not hemp, and I'm not living off the land—I go to the grocery store. And I'm not unencumbered—I live in a huge, beautiful, restored Victorian with upkeep, with bills to pay. But I guess I can't do this forever. I have to work."

He laughed at her. "You work seven days a week. And maybe the reason you feel unencumbered is because you haven't been under a lot of pressure. The plants and your staff have been cooperating. And maybe, just maybe, you could afford to do this for another year. Even if you have to find another plot of land to do it on. Jilly," he said, squeezing her. "It's okay to do what feels good, what feels right."

"I have some money saved, but I'm only in my early thirties. If I don't add income to the bottom line, I won't have it for long."

"Why don't you think about it over dinner, honey? I bought us a roasted chicken fresh from the deli, some rice, and I tossed a salad—something I have to do until the salad in your garden is ready to pick."

There was no clock in the bedroom so Jillian had no idea what time it was when she woke. It was pitch-black outside, but her eyes popped open. She slipped out of bed, found one of Colin's T-shirts and slid it over her naked body. She found her furry slippers and went down the stairs to her office. She clicked on the computer and saw the hour was 2:47 a.m. She logged on and started skipping around the internet.

She was only vaguely aware of the sun coming up and

the faint aroma of fresh coffee. And then Colin put a cup beside her on the desk.

"So that's where my shirt went," he said, leaning down to kiss the top of her head.

She glanced at him and saw that he wore only his jeans, zipped but not buttoned, bare chest and bare feet. God, but he was a beautiful man!

"Colin!" she said excitedly. "Do you know how many organic farms and gardens there are in California?"

"A lot, I imagine," he said, smiling.

"And lots of commercial farms that concentrate on specific items, like organic berries for specially created jams and jellies, or rare, high-end-market fruits and vegetables that are used by five-star chefs in exclusive restaurants, like the stuff I'm trying to grow—the white asparagus, baby beets, teardrop tomatoes, that sort of thing. Then there's the general organic market—stuff that goes to stores and delis."

"You have a bright flush on your cheeks and your eyes are very sparkly," he said. "How long have you been up?"

"Since just after two, I think." She stood from her desk chair. "Colin, I think I can find a way to do this for a living. Maybe even a good living. At least good enough so I can get by without going back to the corporate world."

"You think?" he asked.

"A lot depends on the plants—their health, strength, reliability. Customers, especially commercial customers like delis, restaurants and health food stores want to order in advance of the season, and they want some assurance that the fruits and vegetables will come in on time and in the quantities required. So—I'll have some of those answers in the fall." She smiled. "I bet I can do this."

"I bet you can," he agreed. "But then, I have trouble imagining there's anything you can't do, if it's something you want to do."

* * *

It was a little more complicated than making a phone call to Jack; he had a responsibility to the trust he managed and couldn't just do a favor for a friend. "I have to get an appraisal," he told Jillian, "and then list the property and review the offers. I'm sorry it's not quicker or easier."

"I understand," she said. "By all means, I want you to do this the right way and at the end of the day, have no regrets. It'll all work out as it's supposed to."

"And if you don't get the property?" he asked her.

"Then I guess I'll be talking to that Realtor of yours."

"I am sorry, Jillian. You're doing right by that place and I'd like to see you in it permanently."

But Jillian didn't see this as a discouraging bit of news. She'd never been afraid to work hard for what she wanted, and right now, that ethic was coming in handy.

A week later Colin and Jillian were on the road to Chico and while they were away, Jack would be showing the house to the couple from the Bay Area.

"Births, deaths, weddings and critical injuries get a lot of attention from the Riordan family," Colin explained to Jillian as they made the drive to Chico for the wedding. "I'm afraid that I'm the one with the reputation for being a no-show most often, for making the fastest trip, shortest stay. Aiden, Sean and Luke have always been pretty tight. Aiden is actually close to everyone and the best about keeping up family relationships."

"And now he wants all his brothers to witness for him," she said.

"Typical Riordan move—gather them up, make sure everyone is front and center. I usually do what I can to resist the call—sometimes I arrive late, leave early, manage to find an excuse."

"Why do I get the sense something has changed?" she asked him.

"Because it has. I almost met my maker. My brothers, though a huge pain in my ass, came running. I wanted to kill them all, but they were persistent and it's probable that because they wouldn't let me shove them away, I got the help I needed. I'm too goddamn stubborn to do it for myself, to even acknowledge what I need. Do you know they had a conference call about me? Seriously! Paddy was the first to suspect I had a problem with painkillers and he invoked the brotherhood. Aiden was the one to get personally involved—I think he was elected because he's a doctor. And I think he put his credit card on the treatment bill. None of them will tell me if I owe anything for that. Not even Luke, and I'm pretty sure Luke would like to just shove me in a hole."

"Come on." She laughed. "Luke seems like a great brother."

"When he's in charge," Colin said with an indulgent laugh. "He's not that great when someone disagrees with him. He's a diamond in the rough—apparently Shelby sees the diamond and the rest of us see the rough."

"I so look forward to this," she said with a laugh. "Having only had one sister growing up, I can't imagine five rough-and-tumble boys. And it sounds like you're all still at it. Listen, if it would be best for you to stay at your brother's house with most of the family, I'm perfectly fine in the hotel by myself."

He reached for her hand. "You're kidding, right?"

"Really, it's a family time, and I'm not—"

"You're with me. Listen, there's no good way to ask this so I'm going to blurt it out and hope I don't fumble it too badly. Is taking you to a wedding, to a family gathering—is that going to confuse what we have going on together?"

She smiled at him; a purely indulgent smile. "You mean, am I going to hope for a change in plans?" She shook her head. "Don't mess with me on this, Colin. I'm keeping my head and my body in the present. I'm not expecting anything to change. I'm not setting up any fantasies. Spending nights in bed with you is fantasy enough…."

"You never thought about marriage? Family? All that?"

She shook her head. "In an abstract way I thought it was somewhere in my future, but there were no contenders. The first person to ever take me looking at rings was Kurt, and I was reluctant to do that—I didn't want to mislead him." She shrugged. "I told him that might be way in the future, but I sure wasn't there yet. I wasn't in love with him yet—I wasn't ready to take it that far…." She laughed bitterly. "Isn't it funny that I was the holdout and yet it never once occurred to me that he was playing me? I was worldly in business at such a young age, but in relationships? Not so much."

"Inexperienced," he said. "Which probably means you hadn't been hurt a lot."

"Not in relationships with men. I had my hard knocks in other ways—losing my dad then my mom, the usual problems with money, growing up poor, struggling on a shoestring in school, then the struggle of paying for Nana's assisted living, then her death… But men? No—only a few. Not traumatic. Don't worry, Colin—I'm not going to try anything like holding your feet to the fire for a promise you never made. I *want* you to go to Africa! I want you to find what you need, to feel whole again, to reassure yourself that you haven't missed anything! That feeling you had of being robbed? You're not ever going to feel like I was the one to rob you. Think of me as your cheerleader. But could we make an agreement about that?"

"What do you need, Jilly?" he asked, squeezing her hand.

"I need you to not ask me again. It takes a certain amount of effort to keep from thinking into the future where you're concerned. Let's not keep reexamining that."

"You're right," he said with a nod. "And I'm going to say one thing before the subject is dropped. It takes a certain amount of effort for me, too."

It made her very happy to hear that, but she said, "It's important for you to follow your plan, Colin. I could never be happy with some guy who spends his life feeling he made sacrifices for me, sacrifices I didn't ask for and that you'd eventually resent. I want you to know you did everything in life that's important to you."

"You're one in a million, you know that?" he asked, giving her hand a squeeze.

She lifted her chin. "Yeah, I know."

Colin and Jillian arrived in Chico early Friday afternoon. Colin checked them into a neighborhood hotel near the country club where the wedding would take place, dropped their luggage and followed the directions they'd been given to Erin Foley's house.

Aiden had told Colin that this was the house Erin grew up in—a comfortably large four-bedroom ranch. After Erin and Aiden met last summer they returned to Chico together; Aiden had moved into her house. And when Colin and Jillian arrived, the house was already full of people.

Colin's brothers Luke and Sean, their wives and kids were all staying with Erin and Aiden. Patrick had not yet arrived, but there was room for him there or with Erin's sister and matron of honor, Marcie. There was plenty of space left over. "Are you sure you don't want to stay with us?" Aiden asked Colin.

"Thanks anyway," Colin said. "We'll be just fine." Not long after Colin and Jillian arrived, a big RV pulled up to the house, parked along the curb and gave the horn a blast.

"There they are," Luke said. "The kids."

Jillian was introduced to Colin's mother, Maureen, and her boyfriend, George, and she quickly got the drift that they were traveling around in a motor coach, not even engaged. There were muttered jokes and chuckles about them living in sin, but the older couple seemed amused and completely unaffected.

Maureen took Jillian's hand in both of hers. "I've been looking forward to meeting you, Jillian," she said. "And I can't wait to hear all about the garden and your plans for it. I'm a gardener myself, though it's been a while."

"You know about me?" Jillian asked.

"It spread like wildfire, dear," Maureen answered with a smile.

A little while later the baby of the family, Patrick, arrived in a rented car. He had to go through bone-crushing hugs from the men, kisses from the women. A beer was pressed into his hand but before taking a drink he looked askance at Colin. Colin smiled and raised his non-alcoholic brew in a toast, bringing a big grin out of the handsome young man. Young? He was probably older than Jillian.

Jillian had expected to enjoy herself, if only because she was with Colin. But it was way more than simply having a nice time—she had a *fantastic* time! As the entire family—both Erin's family and the Riordans—gathered around the patio, kitchen and backyard, there was so much laughing she nearly had to hold her sides. Nothing was sacred; they went after each other like hungry dogs, telling stories on one another. No one was spared—even Maureen had to take her share of teasing.

The stories Jillian enjoyed the most were about the bride and groom who had met in Virgin River. "I couldn't even get to first base until I shaved off my beard and chased a bear out of her kitchen!" Aiden said.

Jillian sat up straighter. "A *bear?*" she asked. "In her *kitchen?*"

"She was baking cookies with all the doors and windows open," Aiden explained.

"Near as I can tell, Jillian only does Froot Loops," Colin said.

"Well that goes without saying," Sean said with a bad boy grin, getting a playful whack from his wife and laughter from the entire crowd.

Except Colin. He grew serious. "Jilly is outside from dawn till dark—sometimes pretty far from the house."

Then the guys looked between each other. "They're all over those mountains, Jillian," Aiden said. "Do you have bear repellent? If not, you should get some, but keep it in a safe place. Erin even used it on my ex-wife. Well, turned out she was just my ex-psychopath, but still—that bear repellant packs a punch."

"*Really?*" Jillian asked, sitting forward expectantly.

"I'll tell you all about it later," Colin promised. "I'll get her some right away. Might serve to keep all of you at a distance, too."

At five o'clock everyone headed for the club for rehearsal. Erin's attendants were her sister, Marcie, and sisters-in-law Franci and Shelby, and Aiden's four brothers were his groomsmen. The fact that they had three women and four men in their wedding party did not worry Erin and Aiden—they had the most important people in their life with them on this special day and that was all that mattered. Erin's younger brother, Drew, would walk Erin down the aisle, and her brother-in-law, Ian, would sing at the wedding. He'd rehearsed his piece once and it nearly brought Jillian to her knees, his voice was so beautiful.

The rehearsal was a quick hour filled with fun and laughter, but the surprises were really just beginning. When they all got back to Erin's house it was evident the caterers had been busy. Tables covered with linen tablecloths were set up in the backyard with lit tiki torches all around. There were flowers on the tables, china and crystal—it was magical. Members of the wedding party oohed and aahed over the delicious-looking buffet table that was laden with all sorts of food and beverages.

As she looked at all the guests milling around the back garden Jillian realized that their wedding party was made up entirely of family. There wasn't a best friend or shirttail relative among them. They were all brothers, sisters, brothers-in-law or sisters-in-law. For as much as these Riordans were at each other all the time, they were one tight clan. It made her envious.

When the party split up that night they all agreed to be dressed for the wedding and back at the country club at 2:00 p.m. Erin was a modern bride and didn't hold much with old-fashioned tradition. They were going to take their pictures in the afternoon *before* the wedding when the daylight was perfect. They'd do two hours of pictures, retire to their dressing rooms at the club for touch-ups and a little refreshment, and the wedding would take place at five.

* * *

Jillian and Colin had plans for the day of the wedding. They went out for a leisurely Saturday-morning breakfast, walked around town a bit, then went back to their motel to get ready so they could be at the club by two. Colin took his shower first—he didn't need much time and wanted to stay out of Jill's way. After cleaning up and trimming his beard, he threw on some sweats and went out to grab a newspaper and a can of cola, leaving her alone to get ready. When he returned and let himself into the room, the sight of her knocked the wind out of him.

Jillian was in front of the mirror, bent over at the waist while she dried her hair. She was wearing a pink strapless bra and a thong of a matching color. When she noticed him standing just inside the door, mesmerized, she straightened and turned off the blow-dryer. "Colin?"

He tossed the newspaper on the bed, put down his can of cola and went to her. "Look at you," he said, his voice husky.

She laughed at him. "You've seen me in a lot less."

"And every time it blows me away." He put his big hands under her arms and slowly slid them down her sides. He lowered his mouth onto hers and kissed her, tonguing open her lips, penetrating her mouth. One of his hands slid up her back and held her head against his mouth. And he moaned hungrily. "Shouldn't I be getting used to you by now? Every time I walk in the room and see you half-dressed, it's like the first time. And I start to want you like it's the first time."

While he kissed her, his fingers found the snap on that little bra and opened it, releasing her breasts into his palms. He kissed her long and hard, then dipped his head to sample a hardened nipple, smiling inside as she let her head drop back in an erotic groan. He lifted his head and stared down into her eyes, his own eyes growing smoky-dark and intense as his hands slowly ran over her hips and slid that thong to her thighs, then to the floor.

"Uh-oh," she whispered. "Are you going to make us late?"

"I'd like to make us no-shows," he said in a deep, gravelly voice.

"Oh, Colin, I don't want to make a bad impression on your family...."

"You mean the impression that I can't get enough of you? It'll be okay. We'll get there in plenty of time...."

His hands on her waist, he lifted her onto the vanity, spread her knees apart and knelt before her, kissing the inside of her thighs right before he plunged his mouth into her core. She gasped, threading her fingers into his hair, leaning away to give him all of herself. The hungry sounds he made were beautiful to her; the strength of his tongue on her, in her, drove her half out of her mind. He pulled her closer and closer to the edge of the vanity, giving himself more space, more room, more depth.

She didn't last long; her fingers knotted into his hair, she fell back against the mirror behind the vanity and she shook with an orgasm so strong her eyes rolled back in her head. Colin didn't stop torturing her for a long time. Finally he pulled his head back only to rip his T-shirt over his head, drop and kick off his sweats and stand ready between her legs.

With a hand under each side of her bottom, he pulled her toward him, onto him. He lifted her easily and her legs went around his waist. "Ahhh, Jilly..."

"Your arm, Colin... Be careful...."

"Don't worry about my arm. When I have you like this, I just about go out of my mind."

"Sit, Colin. Sit on the bed. Let me do some of the work...."

He grinned against her lips. "Now how can I say no to that?" He sat down on the edge of the bed, his hands still under her perfect butt, buried his hairy face in her neck and began to lift his hips, pumping into her, slowly at first. "God, Jilly," he whispered. "You're so perfect...."

Arms around his neck, she held him close to her, close in her, and as always with Colin, she was reaching another pinnacle quickly, gasping and grasping, tightening around him, her legs like a vise around his waist. She knew he felt it because he chuckled deep in his throat, then he plunged into her one more time and she could feel his pulsing, throbbing release.

They clung to each other for a long moment, sweating and still breathing hard. When they'd calmed and Jillian leaned away to look into his eyes, she found him smiling at her. He pushed her hair over her ear. "We're so right together," he said softly. "You just do it to me every time."

She laughed softly and said, "Ah, I believe you just did it to *me!* And now we have to start over—we need showers. And we're going to be late! Because you just can't control yourself and when you can't, I can't!"

"Your cheeks are pink, sweetheart. Flushed and satisfied."

"Get in the shower, Colin. And please hurry."

In the end Colin had to quickly shower, don his tux and head for the country club for the two o'clock pictures with a promise to come back for Jillian between pictures and the ceremony. When he walked into the hotel room later she shot him a look, held her hand up to ward him off and said, "I swear, if you touch me I'll scream! I don't have time for another shower and fix-up!"

He just grinned at her and said, "Do you just have that little pink getup on under that dress? The little bra and thong and that's all?"

"I think it would be a mistake to talk about it!"

"I'll be thinking about it all night and then when I get you back here, I'm going to undress you with my teeth."

"That's fine, as long as you don't embarrass me in front of your family!"

"Come on, sweetheart," he said. "Let's get you away from the bed. We have to get Aiden married."

The wedding was elegant, held outside in a sheltered cove. There were about a hundred and fifty guests— many of them Erin's partners, coworkers from the law firm, a few of her clients and some of Aiden's partners from his new medical practice. They spoke the traditional vows in front of a woman minister, a string quartet played, Ian Buchanan sang "From This Moment On" and, before Jillian knew it, they were walking back down the aisle. Since the pictures were already done, the rest of the evening was dedicated to a classy party. There was a champagne hour during which many toasts were made, then a beautiful meal was served, finally an incredible cake was cut. There was dancing inside the country club, but most of the guests seemed content to linger outside, visiting, listening to the soft string music that floated over the warm spring night and among the trees and flowers.

Jillian was able to spend lots of time with Colin's mother and sisters-in-law. By ten in the evening the bride, groom and most of their family were headed back to the house for coffee at the end of the day's events.

Typically, the bride and groom would be on the next plane out of town to their honeymoon destination, but Aiden and Erin didn't want to miss out on any time with the family that had traveled to their wedding, family who would have to get back to their lives by Monday. So, instead of leaving town right away, Aiden and Erin stayed and hosted a Sunday-morning brunch. The same catering service was back, this time with brunch specialties.

Most of the family would only be staying until Sunday afternoon. Colin didn't have pressing business, but Jillian had to get back to her plants. In fact, of all the Riordans, the only ones who had nothing but time were Maureen and George. They planned to stay in Chico for a couple more days, then head north for a visit in Virgin River before getting back on the road.

Before everyone went their separate ways they spent Sunday afternoon just sitting in the garden and visiting. Colin sat on a lawn chair on the far side of the lawn watching Jillian. She was sitting on the grass with Shelby and Marcie, who had their babies, both around nine months old, playing together on a blanket. The girls were talking and laughing; they'd made friends easily. Jill was animated as she laughed with the girls, played with the babies and made them giggle.

He was in awe of a woman who could look so pure and proper one moment and the next be the wild woman driving him out of his mind in his bed. This was far outside of his experience. Oh, he had lots of experience with wild bedmates, but he couldn't possibly have taken them to family gatherings. And then, of course, he'd dated some real proper girls, but hadn't met one who could hold his attention after dark.

"Usually you'd expect it to be the bridegroom who would be all fogged over, gazing at his woman…."

Colin looked up to see Aiden smiling down at him. He laughed and shook his head; he was caught.

Aiden dragged a lawn chair over and sat beside Colin. "I like your girl," he said. "Jillian's a catch."

Colin nodded. "She's pretty wonderful. I've never met anyone like her."

Aiden rested the ankle of his right leg on the knee of his left and leaned back in his lawn chair. "I take it you're feeling good? Medically?"

"Can't complain," Colin said. "Almost never have pain anymore—just the elbow sometimes." He demonstrated by stretching out his arm. It wasn't quite straight. "I keep working it, but it's still a little bent. But at least it's strong now. I have no trouble carrying heavy things, like a big duffel. I've been working with some weights."

"Don't overdo it. Take it nice and slow," Aiden advised. "So, this?" he asked, nodding toward Jill. "Serious?"

Colin gave Aiden his full attention. "Oh, I'm serious about Jill. I'm just not ready to settle down."

Aiden shrugged. "You haven't known her all that long. That could change."

"It's not about marriage, Aiden. The crash and all the bullshit that followed sneaked up on me. I was a long way from hanging up my helmet. I planned to give the Army thirty, then find a civilian flying job until the age of sixty-five, or as long as my medical held out. I screwed that up."

"True, you have issues to work through," Aiden said. "But you aren't necessarily at the end of your flying career. It's just a matter of going through all the necessary steps to get your license back."

"Aiden, I have my license back."

Aiden sat up straighter. "No kidding? Good for you! When did that happen?"

"Couple of months ago. Six months clean and sober, all healed up—I have my medical back and I'm licensed, but noncurrent. Can't fly if you're not current. I'll need check rides—but first I'll need an employer willing to set up those checks to get my license current. The Army isn't going to take me back and a civilian operation in this country won't be ready for someone like me until the last thing on my résumé looks a lot better than it does right now. Listen—it's going to be a little complicated…."

"What's going on, Colin?" Aiden asked.

"I don't think we should talk about all this here, today. It's the day after your wedding and I'm not ready to get opinions from Sean and Luke and Paddy. Not to mention our mother."

Aiden lifted a brow. "I'm ready," he said.

"Can this be just between us for now? For a few more weeks anyway?"

"As long as you're not going to tell me you are looking for work as a mercenary," Aiden said.

"Not directly, but…" He shrugged. "Never know…" Aiden leaned forward and put his forehead in his hand.

"Aw, man…"

"That's not my first choice. Like I said, I'm not ready to settle down, meaning I'm not ready for a quiet life. I'm not like Luke—I'm not going to be satisfied with some cabins by the river and a sweet little wife and baby. It's not me. It's not me *yet*, anyway. I like to be on the move, challenge myself, do the things not everyone can do. So I have some plans that will keep me moving, give me a chance to check out the possibilities."

"And these plans?"

"Well, first of all, when my lease on the cabin is up at the end of summer, I'm headed for Africa. I've never been there. I want to see as much of it as I can, but I'm planning to do two things for sure—take pictures of wildlife in the Serengeti and check out their aviation installations, see if they need any helicopter pilots. Bush pilots."

Aiden tilted his head with a nod. "That's not too shocking for me to handle. Not like the boys in this family haven't been all over the world. You're still thinking about this?"

"Nope. I have a ticket—September 1. I'm planning to give the African continent six months—I know they have safari and hunting companies that use commercial helicopters. Since a lot of their clientele are Americans, Canadians and Europeans, an American pilot might come in handy. They even have a couple of aviation ministries that regularly look for pilots, but they pretty much stick to religious guys."

"So," Aiden said, "six months and you're back stateside?"

"No telling," Colin said, shaking his head. "If I don't find what I'm looking for in Africa, there are lots of other places to explore, to experience, and while I'm at it, places where I can look for work. Alaska, Costa Rica, Australia and New Zealand, maybe India. I'm into the animals, Aiden, not the sunsets."

"What about the painting?"

"The painting is good—feeds something in me, but I'm not sure what. I think eventually I'll paint full-time, and that's one of the reasons I want to take photographs in the Serengeti and hopefully the Amazon—the pictures could keep me busy painting for a long time. But I'm not ready to give up my lifestyle to paint every day. As long as I can travel and fly, painting is good for me. As a steady diet? Just not enough."

The expression around Aiden's eyes was almost sad. "I get it," he said. "It's how you've always lived—I get that. What about Jillian?"

Colin smiled sentimentally. "You just can't imagine how incredible she is. She understands and encourages me to do this. She wants me to be sure I've done what I have to do to get my life back. It'll be hard to say good-bye, but I'm going to stay in touch with her. There's email, live video feed, international cell phones. Until we get bored with the long distance, or she meets some-one who is better for her, I'm not planning on just giv-ing her up." He shrugged. "Who knows? Maybe Jilly will get tired of her funky little tomatoes and decide to come with me? She's a risk taker at heart—she's not afraid of anything."

Aiden was contemplative for a moment before he said, "Hmm. Sounds like a good plan."

Colin sat straighter. "Seriously?" Aiden just shrugged and smiled.

"No lecture about leaving a good woman just for travel and good times?"

Aiden chuckled. "Colin, if it turns out you love that woman," he said, tilting his head toward Jillian, "you'll learn a lot more if you actually leave her than you will if you give up your plans to stay with her. I just hope your instincts and timing are real, real good because if they're not, the agony of the last year is going to seem like a pic-nic compared to trying to make a life without the other half of your heart."

Twelve

On Monday afternoon, Paul Haggerty brought a man into Jack's Bar. He grinned and said, "Jack, meet one of our new neighbors—Lief Holbrook."

Jack stuck out a hand. "How do you do. Welcome. Drink?"

"You could talk me into a cold beer," Lief said. "I'm not a neighbor yet—it's going to take a while."

"Jack, remember that vacation home I built for the rich couple? One of the first houses I finished up here after yours. Three thousand square feet with a view of the valley, about three miles northwest of your place."

"I walked through that house," Jack said. He whistled. "Some kind of vacation home. I never did meet those folks."

Paul just laughed and explained to Lief, "Up here, when there's a house under construction or in renovation, half the town walks through it, just to see how it's coming along. Then most of them make sure I have their opinion." Then to Jack, he said, "I don't know that the owners were up here more than once after it was finished."

"It's in foreclosure," Lief said. "My bid was approved, but foreclosure homes take a long time to close. Meanwhile, I came up to see if Paul could finish the office with built-ins."

"Which I'm all too happy to do, once the property closes."

"I don't think anyone but Paul ever met the folks who built it," Jack said. "What happened?"

"No idea," Paul said. "Eyes bigger than their wallets?"

"They hadn't made a payment in a year," Lief said. "I'd been on the lookout for something in a friendly small town. I knew this place was small. Now I'm just hoping I'm right about the friendly part."

"We're friendly," Jack said with a laugh. "As long as you don't cross us. So, what made you go looking for a small town?"

"Aw, a better place for my family than L.A. And, with my work, I don't have to spend much time in L.A. I can live just about anywhere."

"Family?" Jack asked.

"One thirteen-year-old daughter, Courtney. My wife is deceased. Which is very hard for Courtney, of course. We're healing—we need to step back. You know? Get out of the rush and noise, slow down, see if we can move on and get past this."

"My condolences, Lief," Jack said sincerely. "How long ago did you lose your wife?"

"It's been almost two years now, but it's not easy. Courtney's having a difficult time and I struggle to do the right thing for her, to help her get through it. She was just eleven, an awful tender age to lose a parent. Hopefully we'll be up here and moved in before school starts in September, so she can make a fresh start."

"Good luck with that. I hope it goes well," Jack said. "I do know a real good counselor, kind of specializes in middle school and high school kids. Real nice guy. A kid I've known for years, almost a son to me, came back from Iraq missing a leg and the counselor really helped him. If you ever want the name…"

"When we get back up here, I'll be in touch. I can use all the help I can get," Lief said.

Right at that moment the door to the bar swung open and in the frame stood a skinny little girl with stringy black hair streaked with pink, purple and red. Her fingernails were painted black and she wore pounds of black eyeliner and mascara. A little turquoise tank top stretched over her flat chest and above an itty-bitty black skirt, fishnet hose and black ankle boots. The whole look was completed by a sneer on her face that, somehow, didn't look in character. "Are we just about done here?!"

"Just about," Lief said patiently.

She turned on her heel and disappeared.

Jack gave the counter a wipe. "I'll find that counselor's name and number," he said to Lief.

"Thanks," Lief said in return.

Lilly Yazhi had lived in the area between Virgin River and Grace Valley since she was thirteen, which made it almost fourteen years now. But she had only begun keeping a horse at the Jensen Stables and teaching riding part-time with Annie, the vet's wife, in this past year. And it had only been six months that she'd been engaged to the vet's tech, Clay Tahoma. Lilly was Hopi and Clay, Navajo. They had much in common and their love for horses was one of many things.

She was in the stable, brushing down her Arabian mare, Blue, when she sensed him coming up behind her on silent feet. He slipped his arms around her waist and put his lips against her neck. She stood still, smiled and hummed.

"I never manage to surprise you," Clay Tahoma said. "You sense me even when you can't hear me."

"Oh, Clay? Is that you?" Lilly asked in a teasing voice.

He turned her around and looked at her laughing face. Then he wiped that smile off her face with his lips. He kissed her soundly. Deeply. His hands found her small bottom and pulled her hard against him. "I missed you last night," he said, his voice soft and hoarse. "I plan to make up for it tonight."

"Unless there's another sick horse somewhere and you have to go out again," she said.

He frowned. "That could put me in a mood. I meant to tell you, my mother called me this morning. You've made her very happy, Lilly, by agreeing to having our wedding at home on the Navajo Nation."

"I'm glad."

"It's a generous thing you do for her. The place of the wedding is your decision and I know you didn't have the reservation in mind when you agreed to marry me."

"It's important to your family," she said. "There's just Grandpa and me—you have all those Tahomas to contend with. It's a good thing we won't be using that traditional church seating of bride's side and groom's side—the bride's side would be woefully vacant."

"I love you for thinking of them. I'll find something to do for you that will make you just as happy with me. I promise. Maybe you know of something...."

She looked briefly away. "We'll talk about it sometime. Maybe when you're all soft, sweet and vulnerable. After we make love... Before we make love again..."

He smiled at her. "You can tell me now. Tell me what you want, sweetheart."

"I want you at my mercy first," she said.

"Tell me. Tell me now so I can say yes and think all day about how you're going to thank me."

She shook her head and frowned slightly. "It might be something you can't give me, Clay. It might be too much. You have your son, and Gabe is nearly an adult—he's a man already. And even though I will think of Gabe as my son, also, I think I'd like a child of my own. A child with you. But maybe it's a thing we should speak to Gabe about—it might seriously cramp his style."

Clay smiled and ran a knuckle along her jaw. "I wish it could be a little girl with your witch's blue eyes."

"If I'm marrying into the Tahoma family, that seems very unlikely."

"One can hope," he said, giving her a brief kiss.

"You'll consider it?" she asked him.

"I'll promise it. I was too young to be a father with Gabe. At the time that was a difficult passage, but now I think I'm better prepared and there's more time to enjoy a child."

"Thank you, Clay. I hoped you'd say yes."

"Lilly, I'd give you the moon if I could. Surely you know that."

"How did I find you? You're the best man. And the most beautiful."

His mouth hovered over her lips. "We need to get that wedding done soon so we can get to work on a little Nava-Hopi," he said. "I'm always hungry for you, always ready for you."

She laughed at him. "I know this. Promise me that isn't going to change too much after the vows."

"I think that's a promise I can safely keep."

Someone cleared his throat and Clay looked toward the barn doors.

"I'm sorry to interrupt," Colin Riordan said.

Clay laughed and after placing a sedate but affectionate kiss on Lilly's brow, he moved away from her. "It's
probably a good thing, Colin. You saved me from even
more unprofessional behavior." He walked around the
horse and stuck out his hand as he neared Colin. "My
fiancée, Lilly. You caught us talking about the wedding.
It tends to make me anxious."

"As in nervous?" Colin asked.

Lilly just giggled and came toward Colin, as well.
"Nice to meet you, Colin. And no, Clay isn't nervous."

"I want it official so Lilly's grandfather can stop glar-
ing at me and so my son, who just graduated from high
school, can stop teasing me."

"I think I understand. Does it happen soon?"

"Later in summer. We go home to the Navajo Nation
where I have more family than I know what to do with.
How have you been?"

"Excellent," Colin said. "I dropped by to take you up
on your offer, Clay. You mentioned you have a cousin
with a gallery. If he's willing, I'd like to talk to him, get
his advice on what to do with my work."

"Ah, the wildlife art. Of course. I think I have one of
his cards. Excuse me just a moment." Clay walked away
and left Colin with Lilly.

"Your sister-in-law Shelby is a friend of mine—we've
ridden together a few times," Lilly said. "She talks about
you and your astonishing work. How do you like the
area?"

"More than I expected to," he said. "It is really a very
special place."

"I'm glad you like it here. So, I understand you're
going to talk to Shiloh."

"Shiloh?" he repeated.

"Clay's cousin, the artist. Named for some Bible reference about the silent one or peaceful one. The Tahoma family is known for their involvement in many wars—right up to code talkers in World War II—and Shiloh came along during a peaceful time. He's a Native artist, but what's most interesting about him is that he also carries other art in his gallery that's stunning. You can read about him and see some of his works online—Shiloh Tahoma. He's regionally famous."

"You've met him?" Colin asked.

"No," she said. "I have a classical art education—I studied art history and modern art but I was naturally drawn to some of the Native artists. I will get to meet Shiloh at our wedding. According to Clay, the Tahomas are very big on births, deaths and weddings, so every relative will be there."

He laughed out loud. "That describes the Riordan family exactly. Apparently the Irish and the Native community have a great deal in common."

Clay returned with the business card. "Here you go. Call him, tell him we're friends and ask him what he recommends. Shiloh is very successful in the art community now, but he's been painting for a long time. Against much adversity, he seems to have found his niche and with that, success. You'll find him very helpful."

Colin studied the card, which was simple. It had a name, address, Web address and phone number. "Thank you. This is all new to me."

"I saw your painting. I don't know anything about art, but I don't think it will be new to you for long," Clay said. "Best of luck."

By mid-June the weather in Virgin River had warmed considerably and Jillian's gardens were beginning to flourish. Even the most delicate of her seeds had erupted into strong stalks and vines, coming alive with health and vitality, giving her great optimism. Flowers were in full bloom around the house in bright yellows, purples, reds and pinks; huge hydrangea and rhododendron shrubs added their colors of powder blue, lavender, pink and white. In the big open garden Jill clipped buds to strengthen the vines or stalks, delaying some fruit but hoping for a heavier crop when the plants were stronger. Green apples hung from the apple trees, and blackberries, still green, weighted down the bushes. The hanging baskets around the porch were sporting tomato vines and were speckled with small fruit, some already ripening.

It was during this time that Jill's sister, Kelly, said she was taking a little time for herself and wanted to drive up to Virgin River to check things out.

"Either she's way more concerned about me than she let on, or something else is going on—it's like pulling teeth to get Kelly to take time away from the kitchen," Jillian told Colin. "For at least the past ten years the only vacation of the year she'll take is one week or so with me and our two best girlfriends, and we usually plan it for early fall."

"Did you tell her you're fine?" Colin asked.

"A hundred times. I want her to come, of course—I miss her. Finding time for each other with our demanding jobs has always been difficult—having her for a week will be heaven… As long as everything is okay."

"I'm going to ask you something," Colin said. "I want you to be completely honest with me. Would this be a good time for me to be scarce? Entertain myself so you and your sister can have some time alone?"

She almost jerked in surprise. "Are you kidding? I'm sure part of the reason she's coming is to meet you! You don't have to disappear."

"Should I plan to sleep alone…?"

She laughed at him. "I think Kelly can handle the idea of us sharing a bed as long as we don't embarrass her with the sounds of our wild lovemaking." She ran her fingers over his lips. "We'll find something to stuff in your mouth."

"All right, consider this option—I've been meaning to make a road trip with my work. Lake Tahoe, Sedona, Albuquerque, Sante Fe…. I met a man while I was out painting in a pasture—a Native American guy who said his cousin is an artist with a gallery in Sedona and that Southwestern galleries were big on wildlife art. I looked at the cousin's work online, emailed him, spoke to him on the phone and he recommended some other galleries as well as his own. I've been putting out feelers, but the bottom line is that I have to show original work. Since I have to take some representative work, I have to drive." He noticed her eyes lit up. "It's going to take me a week or so. I could meet your sister, spend a couple of days here while she's visiting, then take off. You'll have some privacy with her while I'm gone, but I wouldn't be running out on you."

"You're going to do it, Colin? Get an opinion on your work?"

He nodded. "I'm curious, Jilly. But we could both be disappointed, you know. Could be I'm just a novice staying busy while my bones mend."

She shook her head. "I don't think so. But it really says something that you're going to check it out anyway."

"So you like that idea?"

"Spend a couple of days with us, two or maybe three, then head out on your road trip? I like that idea—but you have to promise to be in touch every day. I want to hear all about it. Everything, I want to know everything."

He promised. "What's Kelly like?" he asked.

"She's very beautiful," Jill said. "Maybe it's for the best you're only going to spend a couple of days with us—you might find yourself hopelessly in love with her."

He couldn't help it; his eyes got as big as hubcaps. "Whoa, Jilly! In my mind there isn't anyone on earth more beautiful than you—inside and out."

She smiled sweetly. "And this is why I let you hang around, Colin. Because you always say the most intelligent things."

As Kelly made her way toward Virgin River she couldn't help but wonder if her younger sister had found true love. Oh, she'd been told it was love with an expiration date, but would that really come to pass? If it was real, something would have to change. He would stay or she would give up her garden and go with him. Simple. If you found The One, you did what you had to do.

Fortunately for Kelly, she'd found The One. Unfortunately, he was not available to her. Professionally, they were close—he was a mentor and a good friend. They were in touch all the time and had many long discussions that always started with food and went from there. All Kelly could do was exactly what she was doing—perform as an exceptional sous-chef and try not to take these intense discussions too seriously or too personally. She tried not to let it show that he'd already swept her off her feet and she was consumed with him.

Luciano Brazzi, an Italian chef with his own restaurants and merchandising food products, was a wealthy man; a beautifully sexy man; a charismatic man who spoke to her inner chef and inner woman. He was eighteen years older than she, but it didn't seem like there was an age difference at all and she knew in her heart that he would prove to be incredibly virile. "Italians, you understand, do not grow old *there*," he once told her in a joking manner.

He romanced her with food and they often cooked together, either at her restaurant or in one of his kitchens. When they did, sometimes he would feed her, slipping a morsel past her lips. He loved to spoon tiny bites into her mouth; she fantasized about being free to let him kiss the taste from her lips. He shared his most secret recipes with her; she made some of her great-grandmother's best for him. For chefs, this was almost as intimate as foreplay.

He praised her talent and promised to help her get her own kitchen, perhaps her own restaurant—something she'd lived for and worked toward for years. If anyone could make that happen, it was Luca; he was very influential and *very* rich.

She dreamed about what the sex would be like. They would surely come together like mating cyclones. She wanted him with all her heart. They seemed completely compatible.

But there was one glitch. He was married.

Now was a good time for Kelly to be away. It was to be a busy week in the Brazzi household. Luca's children, who were either married or had been away at school, would all be at home and Luca would be completely unavailable. They wouldn't even have a phone chat, much less a cooking session.

Kelly had heard all about Colin, but she'd kept Luca to herself. Kelly had never once mentioned his full name or the details of their professional friendship. Chances were good Jillian would have heard of him or even seen his name on the side of a deli container.

It wasn't quite four in the afternoon when Kelly pulled up to the front of the Victorian. She parked and followed the drive around to the back where she thought she might find her sister—and she was right. She could see her prowling around a huge garden inside a five-foot cyclone fence with a large gate at each end. Kelly watched. Jillian would walk a few feet, crouch and examine a plant, pinch a bud or flower, stand to walk a few more feet, crouch again, and so on.

As she neared, Kelly saw that the garden flourished; some of the plants were growing tall, full and dark green. There were vines winding up parts of the fence and small trellises. Some plants were staked to hold them up, some had strong stalks, some were covered with porous cheese-cloth, some were bushy. The rows were immaculate and the color rich.

"It actually looks like you know what you're doing," Kelly said.

Jillian jumped and whirled. "Kell!" Jillian ran down the row in her red rubber boots and cargo pants, out through the gate and threw herself on her sister, hugging her hard.

Kelly laughed and returned the hug. Then she held her sister away from her eyeing her gardening clothes. "Not exactly what I expected," Kelly said, "but close. When was the last time you wore a bra or panty hose?"

"Panty hose—once. And a bra now and then. I have this sports thing on. It does the trick."

Kelly just laughed. Then she turned full circle to take in the yard—things had certainly changed since she'd first seen it almost a year ago while out here on vacation with Jillian and their girlfriends. The house was beautifully groomed, for one thing—freshly painted and sparkling in the late-afternoon sun. There were two new aluminum storage sheds nestled between big trees and a road cut through the trees out back. Just then, she saw a young man on the road driving a golf cart toward them.

When he pulled up to Jillian and jumped out she said, "Denny, meet my sister, Kelly. Kelly, my assistant, Denny Cutler."

Kelly put out her hand, but he just stared down at his. "Um," he said, wiping it on his pant leg. "Sorry, I'm kinda dusty. Nice to meet you."

"Likewise," Kelly said with a laugh.

"Grab those flats off the bed, Denny," Jillian said. "Jump in, Kell, and I'll give you a tour. This is my garden-mobile."

"This is quite the operation," Kelly said as she climbed in beside her sister.

Jillian drove them through the trees to the back meadow. There were two freestanding greenhouses and just past them, someone had begun clearing another garden plot. "We put up these greenhouses a couple of months ago and are using lights and irrigation to start plants. We've been moving half of them into the outdoor garden and leaving half inside so we can monitor the difference in growth, gestation and quality. I have another shelter ready to put up when that plot is cleared, tilled and fertilized—but the new one is made of screen with retractable panels, and it's very large. We might be trying it with smudge pots as the weather cools. Everything is experimental right now—but so far it's working exactly as I'd hoped. We have some heartier early vegetables coming through and I'm cutting lettuce, pulling a few carrots and scallions, but the special heirloom starts are another month from appearing."

Kelly gazed at her little sister in wonder. "Okay, I already know this, but tell me again how this all started."

"I remembered being here last autumn with you and

when I arrived here I just wanted to come over and see the back porch and garden, which was looking a little neglected. I was literally crying into the mud, crying over my losses in San Jose...."

"Kurt...?"

Jillian shook her head. "When you get down to it, it wasn't about Kurt. I was upset over the demise of my career, my loss of innocence, missing my mentor—all the things I had put sixty to eighty hours a week into. I was so hurt and angry, and instinctively I started digging. Next thing I knew I was sitting at Jack's bar having a glass of wine, talking about the stuff Nana used to grow and a guy at the bar asked me why I didn't grow that stuff here. He said they grow pot year-round up here—using grow lights run on a generator. He said the special plant seeds I was talking about had to be available somewhere. I found them online, I ordered many varieties and I got moving." She smiled. "I hired Denny so I could catch up with the planting season and I'm keeping him as long as I can."

"And Colin?" she asked.

"Oh, I found him painting out back here. I was sitting up on the widow's walk trying to figure out how to access this area through the thick trees when I noticed a guy had driven up here and was painting. He liked this meadow because it was large and there were no shadows from the trees. I clawed my way through to find out what he was doing here. And, little by little... Well, he's the most wonderful man I've ever known."

"When do I meet him?" Kelly asked.

"Now, if you're ready. He's here. Painting upstairs in the sunroom. Waiting for you to get here."

Thirteen

Colin had never before met a woman who traveled with spices, condiments and recipes. He supposed it should come as no surprise that Kelly had stopped at the grocery store on her way into town to buy the food she wanted to prepare and eat—she was a chef, after all. Wherever she went, she cooked. But recipes in a locked box, the case of spices and another of condiments—this was interesting. And her cases were more like tool boxes with handles so she could carry them with her wherever she went. And then there were her knives—special knives that could slice your finger off if you didn't know what you were doing. She always had a set of her own knives with her in case she'd be cooking, and if she was going to be eating, she'd probably be cooking.

After meeting Kelly and visiting for a while Colin had taken a place at the kitchen table with his laptop, watching and listening as the girls cavorted around the kitchen. Their choreography combined with chatter was interesting; they had a system for everything. Kelly was the leader in this venue: "Chop this tomato very small, no bigger than your baby fingernail. Mince the parsley and

I mean *mince*. So this Denny helps around the garden? I don't remember you telling me about him."

"This size?" Jilly asked. "Sure you do—I told you all about him. Did I tell you I thought he asked me on a date?"

Colin's ears perked up at that.

"That size is good. No way! A date?"

"I misunderstood—he was offering to take me to Jack's for supper because he thought I wasn't getting out enough. So I told him I had Colin." She shot him a look with a smile. "Now he feels better about things. He didn't really want to date me at all. Which is good because I wouldn't have considered it under any circumstances, even if I didn't have Colin. And I'd hate to fire him—he's indispensable."

"And awful young," Kelly said.

"Awful," Jilly agreed. "You still seeing that cook?"

"Chef, not cook. Preacher's a cook, Luca is a chef. We're really just friends. Friends with potential. We talk on the phone, text, email and sometimes cook together, but neither of us has much free time. Those pieces are getting too big, Jill."

"Sorry. Maybe you should find a way to have more time. Is he well-known, your chef?"

"In culinary circles I suppose he is. That's probably what attracted me in the first place. We talk food."

"Hmm. I guess that can't be any more boring than talking seeds...."

Colin laughed out loud and both women turned to look at him. "Is that so?" he asked, grinning. "Just so you know, Jilly *never* bores me."

It was interesting to him that Jilly had referred to Kelly as very beautiful, as though she could be more beautiful than Jilly. They were different enough that if you hadn't looked at their eyes and smiles you might not think of them as sisters. Jilly was tall and trim with chestnut hair that was smooth; her eyes were large and brown and, as Colin knew only too well, they could become even darker and sultry when she was getting turned on. Kelly, by comparison, was shorter, rounder, had blond hair full with loose curls and blue eyes. But their eyebrows had identical arches. Their teeth—perfect and straight—were the same shape. Their lips were different, but their smiles were alike.

It made sense to him that a gardener would be slim, muscular and tan while a chef would be more curvaceous, fuller, rounder, her skin more ivory. It didn't take much observation to appreciate how much hard work it must be to create dish after dish in a busy kitchen, yet he thought the gardening was still more physically demanding. Kelly looked like a gorgeous chef while Jilly looked like a heartstopping athlete.

He realized Jilly looked as if she could ski the Alps, jump out of an airplane, dive in a coral reef…go on a safari. Play with him by day, heat up his sheets by night, pass the quiet time in sweet camaraderie, challenge him with her wit, appreciate those qualities in him that no one else ever took the time to notice…. What was this? A mate? He saw a partner, a friend, a lover impossible to forget or replace.

He shook his head absently. Colin didn't mate. But then, according to her history and what she told him about herself, neither did Jilly. While he'd had many women and assumed he'd never settle down to one, Jilly had had few men in her life and thought that one day there might be one for the long term, but she didn't count on it. Neither of them had ever had a romantic partner who'd tempted them to a permanent relationship. He and Jill were so alike…yet so different.

There was one thing tickling the edges of his mind, however. He was falling in love with her. This was a first. He wondered if this might have happened to him long ago if he had just slowed down enough. He searched his memory, but he couldn't recall a single woman he wanted in the way he wanted Jilly. *His* Jilly. He had a very real urge to make her his so that no other man would ever touch her, so that she would always belong to him.

"Can you close up shop now, Colin?" Jilly asked him, tapping the laptop. "Kelly has hors d'oeuvres ready and then dinner."

"Absolutely," he said. "She's going to make our cooking look pretty pathetic, isn't she?"

"Oh, worse than that. She's a genius."

For the past couple of months Jill and Colin had joined forces in the kitchen at mealtime, throwing together an evening meal. It was always plenty satisfying, but certainly nothing special.

When Colin reclaimed his seat, a place mat, plate, linen napkin and water glass had appeared before him. He fingered the place mat. "Is this something new?"

"No," Kelly said. "Something from my trunk. I know Jill doesn't bother with anything as pedestrian as presentation. I brought what I needed." She put a platter in the center of the table. It looked like a sampler platter, a few bites each of mini lettuce wraps, meatballs, humongous stuffed mushrooms, little baby pears and—"Stuffed grape leaves, ground lamb and garlic meatballs, mushrooms stuffed with bread crumbs, tomato, celery and onion, baby yellow tomatoes straight off the porch, soft shell crab and broiled calamari. And—" she put down a small bowl of what looked like salsa and a small basket of sliced bread "—Nana's sweet relish and French baguette, thin sliced and lightly toasted. *Mangia!* Eat!"

Jill brought Colin an O'Doul's and a chilled glass, but he waved it away. Kelly was pouring wine that she'd brought to complement the food and he wanted to participate. For a guy who was generally unimpressed with anything fancier than a grilled steak, or a burrito, this was intriguing. He suddenly wanted to experience it all and see if he connected with this whole passion—this transporting of special spices and condiments, this chopping a tomato a certain way, this seasoning and sautéing and then presenting the whole thing on a dish that had to be on a place mat.

He watched Kelly, then put a few items on his plate. He scooped a little of that sweet relish onto a thin slice of bread, bit down and said, "Jesus," as if in a prayer. "What *is* this?"

Kelly merely shrugged. "Nana's sweet relish. She used everything in the garden. Her first mission was to feed us, but her second objective was to pass on very old family recipes—her mother's from Russia and her father's from France. Then there were some from her American husband—Chester Matlock. The beauty of Nana's recipes is that she never had access to the expensive delicacies—she only had what she could grow or buy cheap. She grew her own herbs in the windowsill and I remember she used to buy the cheapest ground meat and bring it home to grind it three more times. We had a meat grinder that was mounted on the counter—a bowl could fit under the spout. She worked hard to make her food delicious, but her first concern was that we be properly nourished."

"That starts in the garden," Jillian said. "We were very young when we came to Nana—we were the third generation she would raise. First her only child, her daughter, then her grandson, then us. And we're the only ones who have had the opportunity to take on her legacy in the kitchen and the garden."

"Now for the chicken," Kelly said as she cleared space on the table.

She served a chicken so tender and delicious, Colin had to catch himself before he let his eyes roll back in his head in a swoon. He had no idea how it might've been made.

"Marinated in virgin olive oil and saffron, spritzed in lemon, sprinkled with parsley, seared and then steamed with sliced mushrooms. The baby beans are garnished in slivered beets and almonds, the rice cooked with onions, peppers, chopped black olives and topped with paprika, the same lightly toasted baguette, and Nana's sauce— kind of a salsa made with fresh tomato, tomatillo, peppers—I brought that from home because it takes hours. It's got a kick. And I apologize—I didn't have time for dessert."

Jillian and Colin exchanged glances and burst into laughter.

"What?" Kelly asked.

"Oh, you're forgiven," Colin said. "But just this once."

For the next couple of nights, Colin's palate was indulged. His routine with his lover changed, but he wasn't unhappy about it. After a large, satisfying meal he retired to the bedroom on Jilly's second floor while the sisters stayed up way too late, drank a bottle of wine between them, talked and whispered and laughed wildly. Then they would crawl up the stairs, not quietly, and head to their beds. Jill would clamber in beside him and, even though she brushed her teeth and washed her face, he could taste the pinot on her lips—and it wasn't at all unpleasant.

By day Colin would paint, Jilly would garden and Kelly would shop, fool around in the kitchen and present them with a five-star meal. Her second night with them was Italian and her bruschetta was the most delectable he'd ever tasted. Then came an Italian chopped salad that left him weak in the knees and he wasn't even fond of salad. In fact, vegetables didn't do that much for him. Finally Kelly served an Italian dish made with eggplant, the very sound of which should have repelled him, but it was unbelievably delicious. Finally, a Tiramisu that brought tears to his eyes.

The third night brought one of Nana's traditional French meals, and again, he was helpless. Again the girls laughed through a bottle of wine while he went to bed to leave them to their reunion.

When Jill came to bed, he pulled her against him and kissed her senseless. Nothing new there. But then he said, "I hate to leave in the morning. Please, freeze the leftovers!"

She laughed at him and promised she would.

He reached down to find her panties were still on. "What's this? Is this how you plan to send me off?"

"Not exactly. I have something special for you."

"Ohhh, I like to hear that…."

She reached into the bedside drawer and pulled out a box. "It's an iPhone—the latest."

"I have a cell phone, Jilly."

"I know, but you have an ordinary cell phone—this one will allow you to pick up your emails, has a GPS for directions, an iPod for your music. You can even download audio books to listen to while you drive."

"I have to leave early, baby—how am I going to learn all that?"

"I'm going to show you how to make and answer calls before you go, how to use your GPS, and then you can play with it while you sit in hotel rooms with nothing better to do. I've already loaded my numbers and Luke's number for you—you can do the rest. You can learn how to take pictures and send them from this phone." She shrugged and looked down. "I was thinking ahead, Colin. Thinking of Africa, but not because I have expectations. But if you wanted to send me pictures from there and you're not online, maybe this will come in handy."

He put the box aside and pulled her on top of his long body. He pushed her hair away from her face. "I plan to keep in touch, Jilly, but it might be difficult from Africa. From out in the Serengeti. Even with this."

"I understand that, but I want you to have all the tools, and it's small. You can charge it in the Jeep. That way if you feel like sending me an email and the laptop doesn't work for you, maybe this phone will. Besides, it's very fun. You'll like it."

"You're fun," he said. "You and Kelly together are a hoot. Don't you girls ever fight? Like the Riordan boys?"

"I'm learning that no one fights like the Riordan boys. Kelly and I have had our little spats, but not too often. We had to stick together when we were young. Life wasn't always that easy."

"You have a division of labor. She rules the kitchen—you rule the garden."

"I know, interesting how that happened. And fortuitous, since we'd probably fight like cats if we competed in the same territory."

"And what are you girls going to do while I'm gone?"

"We're going to feed Denny one night, feed Preacher

and his family one night, go eat at the bar one night and then Kelly's on her way home."

"I like her," Colin said. "She's cute and a genius in the kitchen, and you're right, she's very pretty—but Jilly, she's not prettier than you." He slid her panties down over her hips. "You are the woman I wake up wanting, fall asleep wanting, reach for in the night. You. To me, you're the most beautiful woman in the world."

"Why, Colin," she said with a smile. "That's very romantic."

"What's strange about it is I'm not really the romantic type. I think you're doing something witchy to me."

"Ah, you found me out!"

"I'm going to love you slow tonight," he said. "Slow and deep and easy, and I'm going to take a long, long time, so no screaming and begging…." He pulled her mouth down to his and kissed her. "This has to last me as long as a week, so let me have my way."

"Don't I always?" she asked in a breath. "So far, your way is my way."

Colin had his Jeep loaded before dawn. Hearing voices in the kitchen, he went inside. Kelly offered to fix a big breakfast for the road, but Colin declined. "I want to move quickly now, get as much driving in today as I can, but I'm sorry to miss your breakfast. It's my favorite meal." Then he focused on Jilly. He smiled and touched her face. "I have my new phone plugged in. I have two phones now, two numbers, plus the laptop. Are you happy?"

"I'm happy you're taking your art on the road. I think the next step is some kind of representation, but I'm going to wait to hear what you learn from these artists and galleries you're visiting. Oh, Colin, I know this is the right thing for you to do. I know you won't be disappointed! And I'll miss you." She rose on her toes to kiss him. "I'll miss you so much, and I'm so glad you're doing this."

"You and Kelly stay out of trouble."

"When you get back, I'm going to have buds on some of the most precious fruits," she said. "You're going to have to fake excitement."

"I won't have to fake it, baby. Just don't forget about the leftovers!"

She grew suddenly serious. "Please. Be very careful driving. If you get tired or sore or—"

"Jilly, I flew a complicated aircraft in wars. I know my body, my ability, my limitations."

She smiled. "Of course you do. I can't wait to hear what you learn."

"I already can't wait to get home to you."

He kissed her goodbye and left quickly. And she stood on the porch, then walked out to the drive and watched until he passed through the trees and disappeared.

It occurred to her that this was a bit like a dress rehearsal for his departure in September. It was such a precarious balance, wanting him to live his dream and yet find a way to never leave her.

Jill kicked off her slippers, rolled up her pant legs and went to her garden in her bare feet. She walked between the rows, the dirt squishing between her toes, and admired the growth. She visited almost every plant and would visit each one again several times through the day. An hour had passed by the time she headed to the back porch with mud on her knees. Kelly was sitting in one of the chairs on the porch holding a coffee mug in both hands. She smiled at Jillian. "Okay, baby?" she asked gently.

"Sure," Jill said. "It's so important that he do this. You

saw his art. It's magnificent. He doesn't have to decide to paint full-time, but he has to know his worth. I know it's beyond his expectations."

"You love him," Kelly said.

She smiled and gave a small nod. "Let's not bring it up. It will only make him squeamish."

"But he loves you," Kelly said. "It's so obvious."

"Not to Colin," Jillian said. She sat on the porch steps and brushed the drying mud from her knees. "Trust me."

"Will you tell him how you feel?" Kelly asked.

Again she nodded. "I'll tell him before he goes, but I'm going to find the best way to do it. When I tell him I love him, I want it to feel like a gift, not a noose. I wouldn't be telling him to change him or to weaken him, but to strengthen him. I'd want to reinforce his sense of purpose."

Kelly leaned forward. "Are you sure about that? Because you seem sad."

Jillian leaned against the porch post. She shook her head. "I was just daydreaming a little. I've never had anything like this, Kell—never had a man in my bed every night, at my breakfast table every morning. When people talked about being in love I didn't even realize they meant all this laughter, this level of friendship and encouragement, this... I didn't know it was possible to have this kind of physical love. I'm sure no virgin, but I didn't know a man could love a woman this way. It's truly a miracle."

"A miracle that will be over in September?"

"No," Jillian said. Her smile was melancholy. "I'm sure it'll never be over."

While Jillian found her solace in the garden, Kelly liked to occupy herself in the kitchen. She lamented the lack of accoutrements. Jillian was competent in the kitchen but had no real interest in cooking, therefore she was short on supplies. In fact, while there was space enough for a large, double subzero refrigerator-freezer, Jack had put in a rather small refrigerator, just to keep Jill in chilled foods. The stovetop, likewise, was smaller than the space allowed. And as far as pots and pans and cooking utensils—a few pots, a few plates, a few spoons, spatulas and turning forks. Yet the cooking space was fantastic. She envisioned hanging pots above the workstation and stainless steel appliances custom-fit to the granite countertops that Paul had installed. She'd taken a flashlight and braved the cellar—nothing but cinder block and dirt, but with very little work and money, it could be an outstanding wine cellar. There were already three sinks, refrigerated drawers, warming drawers, room for three ovens—Jack had put in one—and another dishwasher to add to the one already there. This was a kitchen, once set up properly, fit for a small, elegant restaurant.

The only problem was, it was in Virgin River. There was really no one here who would want to eat in a small, elegant restaurant. A tragedy, really.

Kelly's cell phone chimed and she grabbed it. She smiled as she heard, "Ciao, Bella! How are you, my love?"

"Luca! I didn't expect to hear from you," she said. "How is the family gathering?"

"Loud. Very loud, indeed. Five children at home, their spouses, partners, boyfriends, girlfriends, even their in-laws if they have them. After Michael's college graduation celebration he announced his engagement. Not to be outdone, Bethany, age twenty, flashed her diamond. It appears there will be two Brazzi weddings in a year or less. That marries them all."

"Congratulations!"

"And of course I am in the kitchen, spoiling them and showing off. Why wouldn't I think of you and wish you were here beside me," he said. "I do miss you, Bella."

"I'll see you soon enough. For now, enjoy the family! You don't have them all together very often."

"I wanted to tell you something, Kelly. When these weddings are done, there will be some changes in my life. And, with any luck, in your life, as well."

Kelly smiled to herself. After a year and two weddings?

They began as acquaintances, then friends, then he took a position as her mentor, and finally he opened up about his deeper feelings. Kelly had grown so close to Luca in the past six months that it was no surprise she'd fallen for him, but in fact she was very proud of herself for managing, somehow, to hold him at arm's length even though he claimed to desire her madly.

Luca had been married for twenty-eight years and had five children ranging in age from twenty to twenty-seven. When their friendship began to heat up, he explained that his was a family business, that he and his wife and several employees lived in the same huge home, but his marriage had been all business for many years.

"It's still your marriage," she had replied. "And you're still all under the same roof."

"Yes, sweetheart, but a roof that covers over twelve thousand square feet, a couple of warehouses, guesthouses and a few acres. And not only have Olivia and I occupied separate bedrooms for twenty years, we've discussed the situation with our grown children! It's all geography and settlements!"

Ah, the idea of a fling with him had been so appealing! She was completely seduced by him! *Thoroughly!*

There was no one more perfect for her than a gifted, internationally known chef like Luca. Every moment they spent together, every time they talked, she was his. But she kept him back. "But until you are a single man, Luca, I am not getting further involved. It's going to be difficult enough when you're single. Your family—no matter how adjusted to the idea that you and Olivia are mostly business partners—aren't going to warm to me."

"*Only* business partners!" he barked. "She has her own love life! Has for years!"

Indeed, he had relied on Olivia to stand as his partner for the many public appearances he made, official and unofficial. And she did so willingly, he said, but it was all for show. He proclaimed theirs a discreet understanding and explained that Olivia was sleeping with a younger man, a tennis pro or something. Kelly secretly hoped it was the truth but she was no fool. And to be fair, Luca had not needed to share all those details to win her heart. She wanted him. She so wanted him. And between them, besides cooking, many conversations both on their phones and in their kitchens, there had only been one kiss.

But *oh such a kiss*. She almost fainted. Maybe she *was* a fool.

"I do miss you, my darling," he said. "When are you coming back?"

"What does it matter, Luca? You can't escape family."

"I feel better when you're near. Where I know where to find you."

She laughed, then laughed at herself because as foolish as it was, it felt so good to hear that. "A couple more days," she said. "But of course I'll be working when I get back."

"Of course. As will I. But we always manage, don't we, sweetheart?"

All this romantic, seductive talk and yet, there was nothing more between them. She wondered how long it would be before she couldn't stand it anymore and would succumb, give in, and become the other woman in his life.

She suddenly envied Jillian, even with her man poised on the brink of a departure that could be permanent. It would be so nice to have the man in her life available to her, laughing with her, loving her through the night. She would die to spend an entire night with Luca.

"Bella, I need you," he said, his voice rough in the phone.

And it made her quiver in her panties.

Several hours later, when Jillian came in for the day, showered and returned to the kitchen, Kelly handed her a glass of wine and said, "I have something to tell you. I've been holding back a bit about Luca, the chef I've mentioned."

"I can't wait!" she said, grinning. Jillian took a seat at the table with her wine, but no more had she done so than she heard the sound of a vehicle pulling into the drive along the house. It was clearly a truck and she frowned. "UPS? I'm not expecting anything." She went to the door and had reached for the knob just as the sound of Jack Sheridan's boots striking the porch floor could be heard. She pulled open the door. "Jack? What are you doing here?"

"Can I come in, Jillian? I have to talk to you right away. I've had an offer on the house."

"Of course," she said. "I'm afraid I only have nonalcoholic beer or wine to offer—"

"Nothing for me, thanks. I left Denny to help out with

the dinner crowd and I told him I'd get right back. Can
we sit down?"

Jill went to her place where the glass of wine waited
and Jack sat down opposite. "The couple from the Bay
Area liked the house." He pulled a folded piece of paper
from his shirt pocket. "The top number is the appraisal
figure, the second number is their offer." He took a breath
and looked pained. "You know how I feel, Jill. I like having you here and I like what you're doing. I just want to
say that." He slid the paper across the table toward her.

She stared at it for a second before she unfolded it. The
top number was $1,245,000.00. Their offer, the second
number, was $1,300,000.00.

She lifted her eyes to Jack's face. "They really want
it, don't they?"

He gave a nod. "According to the Realtor, they've been
looking for about a year. This house seems to meet their
requirements, but it's the land that tilts the price. Ten
acres is a nice spread for a B and B. They'd have room
for horses or whatever for guests. If there's any thinking
to do, you should do it in the next day or two."

"Right," she said. She stared at the small paper and
felt the threat of tears gather. She looked over her shoulder at her garden. She took in the flood of lilacs and hydrangea bordering the backyard.

"Just give me a call, Jill," he said, standing.

"Sure," she said. She had bought one piece of property in her entire life—the town house. She paid three
hundred thousand.

"I'm pretty surprised by the appraisal, but I shouldn't
be. If times were better, it would've been even higher."

"I know," she said. She looked up from the paper and
smiled weakly. "They must be pretty well fixed, this
couple from the Bay Area."

"They're older than you, and they retired early. They're in their fifties, old enough to have amassed some money, still young enough to be able to run the place for a good while."

And she thought, *But I'm thirty-two. If this works out, I'll be running the place for a long, long time. If it doesn't work out, I'd have to sell. Maybe in a few years the economy will be better and it would go for more. Or maybe the economy will be worse, interest rates even higher and it'll be a huge loss.*

"Just let me know," he said.

"Thanks, Jack. Nice of you to drive out here." He went to the door.

The problem was, she had had a number in her head—just over a million. She'd gotten used to that number and was seeing it as a hundred thousand an acre with a free house on the land. The thought of herself going back to the corporate world in panty hose and shiny black pumps made her grimace. But the thing that shifted her mind very quickly was the thought of wanting to keep Colin's easels standing in the sunroom, ready, for whenever he might come back.

"Kelly! Get me a pen!" She jumped up and ran to the back door. She opened it and yelled, "Jack! Jack, come back here!"

She grabbed the pen out of Kelly's hand and sat back down, scribbling on the paper. She'd refolded it by the time Jack was standing in the kitchen again. She passed it to him.

He was slow to open it and when he did, his eyes rounded in pure shock. He looked at the paper, at Jillian's eyes, back at the paper.

"You sure?" he asked.

"Sure," she said, giving a nod.

"This is quite a big move, Jillian. Have you thought about this? Carefully?"

"That's my sister," Kelly said, though she didn't know the financial details. "She likes to charge into things. Impetuous. Impulsive. She moves on things real fast."

And suddenly Jillian let go a laugh, a big, belly laugh. She'd just realized a few things—important things.

"Sure you can do this?" Jack asked.

"Yes, Jack. I'll qualify. But this is confidential information, right?"

"Right. Of course. Well, I guess you've made a decision about that city job," he observed.

She laughed. "I guess I have."

Written on the page was: $1,500,000.00.

"This might be a little crazy," Jack said. "Shouldn't you inch up to this number? I mean, give them a chance to push you up to this number?"

"I think it makes sense to be perfectly clear. I'm not screwing around. I'm serious. I'd prefer not to be challenged by a counteroffer."

He whistled. He stuck out his hand to shake. "Good luck with this. I'll let you know what the response is."

"Thanks, Jack."

He slipped that folded piece of paper into his shirt pocket and left. By the time the sound of the departing truck motor was fading, Kelly was standing behind a kitchen chair across the table from Jillian, holding her own glass of wine.

"Big business?" Kelly asked. "Did you bet it all?"

"Not all, but a nice share. You know what I just realized? When I act on my gut instinct, I do pretty well. I'm seldom wrong. Going with Harry right out of college, many rapid-fire PR decisions, right up to falling for Colin in the space of a few days… It's when I don't act fairly quickly, when something I can't quite identify is cautioning me, that's when something is wrong. That happened with Kurt—it took me *months* to give in to him! *Months!* Somewhere in my gut I knew there was something wrong, I just didn't know what.

"Once I made up my mind about the garden, I knew right away I wanted to expand and do it on a grand scale, and I knew I wanted to do it here. I don't want a bidding war on the house and land," Jill said. "I'd be very surprised if I didn't just win. I topped the other potential buyer's offer by a couple of hundred grand."

Kelly went pale; she sank weakly into the chair. She knew her sister had made lots of money at BSS, but *lots* to Kelly was far, far less than that! "Are you kidding me?" she asked in a whisper.

"Nope, that's a fact." She held up her wineglass for a toast. "Now. What were you going to tell me about Luca?"

"Hmm? Oh," Kelly said. "Nothing. Nothing. You'll like him, I'm sure of it."

"I can't imagine not liking someone you care about."

Fourteen

Colin had planned from the beginning to visit Shiloh Tahoma's Sedona gallery first. It wasn't quite what he expected—it surpassed his expectations. It was a bit off the beaten tourist track for one thing. The sign posted above the shop said, simply, Art. On the glass door, stenciled in gold, it said, The Navajo. Colin stood on the sidewalk for a long while, just looking in the front window at the paintings displayed—Native American men in traditional costume, braids or flowing hair, Native women alone and with children, natural settings, chiseled faces, exquisite shadows, stunning renditions.

Colin had looked the artist up online and felt he was somewhat familiar with his work, but up close and personal these paintings were magnificent. Colin didn't want to go inside. He felt like an imposter, a fraud. This artist was beyond his wildest imaginings.

"May I help you with something?"

In the shop's doorway stood a beautiful Native woman with traditional long, straight black hair and high cheekbones. "I…ah… I'm here to see Mr. Tahoma."

"Is he expecting you?"

"I think so. I'm Colin Riordan."

"Of course," she said, smiling. "Come in. He's in the back. I'll take you."

Colin had only a moment to glance through the storefront on their way to the rear of the gallery; there were many more items than just the incredible oils—there were trinkets, dream catchers, mobiles, photographs, postcards, books, stacks of prints, painted rocks, turquoise. Lots of turquoise. There was a glass case that appeared to hold silver jewelry.

But he passed all that as he followed the young woman. The storefront was actually small, but they came to a very large back room. It was a workroom, paintings in progress everywhere. There was a kitchenette, table and chairs, bathroom, lots of shelves and cabinets.

"Dad, Mr. Riordan is here." Dad? Colin wondered.

A very tall Native man with a long black braid hanging down his back turned from a work in progress, but it wasn't the usual Native art. It was a wildly colored abstract of a Native mother and child. Colin stared at it openmouthed. He had no experience with abstract art; he had no idea if it would be considered as good, but he loved it. His surprise was complete.

"It's nice to meet you in person, Colin," Shiloh said. He wiped off his hands and stretched one toward Colin. "Let's have coffee and talk."

"I'm interrupting your work," Colin apologized.

"It'll keep. I want to hear about your painting. How do you take your coffee?"

"Just a little milk," he said. But what he thought was— what's to talk about? After seeing the paintings in the front of the showroom, he was completely intimidated— this man was a master. And forget about Colin's wildlife art, what he really wanted to know was why this Navajo was painting in two completely different genres.

But Colin held his tongue and accepted a cup of coffee and a chair at the table in the back room. "Your daughter is a lovely young woman."

"Thank you. She's twenty-three, an accomplished artist in her own right though she's still experimenting a great deal. I have three daughters, aged seventeen, twenty and twenty-three. They all help out here from time to time but it's Samantha's true passion. She wants her own gallery one day."

"This painting," Colin said, indicating the abstract. "I didn't see anything like this out front. It's a completely different approach to Native art. Are *you* experimenting?"

Shiloh shook his head as he stirred a mug of coffee for Colin. "This is something I love and believe myself to be good at, but because I'm Navajo and can produce competent Native renditions, this is what people who know me, who know my store, want from me. I'm not making complaints—I'm good at Native art and it holds a special place in my heart. It's the first thing I ever sold and I'm marginally famous in some art circles for it. I'm happy to provide it and I do my best. But the abstract is unique and makes my heart beat a little faster." He shrugged his shoulders. "Who knows why."

"The paintings on display in the front of the gallery are so good, I didn't want to come inside. Remarkable work."

"Thank you. It pays the bills. I ship my other work like this to Los Angeles." Shiloh sat down across the table from Colin. "When did you first notice that you could draw?"

Colin took a sip of his coffee. "Six?" he answered. "Something like that. You?"

Shiloh smiled. "About six, I think. When I first showed an inclination, my parents had me painting symbols on artifacts to be sold to tourists visiting the reservation. My family were ranchers. They did whatever they could to make a living, but no one ever considered fine art. That would have been out of their realm of experience.

"And where do you like to paint?" Shiloh asked.

"I like to be on the top of a hill in the natural sun, but I have a sunporch that works. It's in the house of a woman I'm with. Even though it's good, I still go outside to paint if the conditions are right. And I prowl around with a camera to get shots of wildlife."

"Some of the pictures you sent by email interest me—they're very good."

"I've never shown them to a professional before. After seeing your work, I can't believe I had the nerve. But after all the painting, I find the animals work best for me." He grinned almost shyly. "If you're ever in the market for aircraft, I'm not bad at those. I did a wall mural of a Black Hawk once."

"And where will you go with this personal best of wildlife art?" Shiloh asked.

"First? I'm going to Africa to shoot the Serengeti—big game. Lions, gazelle, tigers, elephants, et cetera. And the landscape they live in. Then all I intend is to get better."

Shiloh leaned back in his chair and asked, "How did you get from age six to the Serengeti?"

"Thirty-four years?" Colin asked.

He nodded solemnly. "I hope you won't take thirty-four years to tell it, but don't leave out the important things."

"And how will I know which things are the important things?"

Shiloh smiled lazily. "You'll know."

So Colin began. He spent fifteen minutes on his high school art, his Army career and part-time drawing and painting. Then he spent forty minutes on his crash, rehab and temporary residence in Virgin River. And finally, Jillian's insistence that he try to find out if his work was worth anything. And his reluctant agreement that he should know.

"I assume you have supplies with you?"

"Like painting supplies?" Colin asked.

Shiloh gave a nod. "So you could stop along the way if you found the perfect spot or if something interested you."

"Yes."

Shiloh Tahoma stood. "Then let me take you to a favorite place."

"Do you want to see my work before you waste a lot of time?" Colin asked.

"It won't be a waste of my time," he said. "You're parked on the street?" When Colin nodded, Shiloh said, "I'm in a white SUV. I'll come around from the back and you can follow me."

Colin was left standing in the studio while Shiloh Tahoma left by the rear door. A little confused as to what purpose this would serve, he found himself slowly leaving through the front. Samantha was standing in the gallery talking to a man who might be a customer, a neighbor or a friend. She paused in conversation to look at Colin; she tilted her head and smiled. "Your father," Colin said. "He wants to show me a place. To paint, I think."

Samantha smiled and let her chin fall in an accepting manner. Then she went back to her conversation.

By the time Colin got behind the wheel of his Jeep, Shiloh was beside him in his SUV, waiting. Colin followed the Navajo for about thirty minutes out of town, into the desert, into the red rocks of Sedona, up a mountain road and finally the artist pulled over. For the entire time he was driving Colin wondered what this was all about. Would there be a test of some kind? Did the man want to see what he could do? What were the Native's expectations of him?

But when the SUV stopped right along a deserted cliff with an amazing view, Shiloh got out and lifted up his hatch. When Colin got out, as well, Shiloh said, "We have a couple of hours of good light at best. Get out your gear and let's just slap some paint around."

"So you can see what I can do?"

"I imagine I'll see what you can do when I look at your work later. I just hate to waste good light."

Seriously? Colin thought. We just sip some coffee, drive into the desert, slap around some paint?

But he had looked up Shiloh Tacoma on Google and knew he was a respected Native American artist who also sometimes taught at the university. He might be a bit weird, but still—he was at the top of his game. So Colin went along. He pulled out an easel, his paints, a palette, a collection of brushes, some turpentine, some rags. He set up and with charcoal, outlined his brand-new, completely unplanned and uninspired painting. And he decided he'd just throw it all out there and pretend. He outlined the monstrous red rocks, but he didn't fill them in. Instead, he left the charcoal outline and drew a very large mountain lion lying on a lower shelf of rock. And that was what he went after with paint a half hour after starting.

"I usually paint alone, but I think we have a few things in common."

"Like what?" Colin asked.

The Navajo shrugged. "We've had our hard times and we both used art to help us get stable again. Mine weren't like yours. I never crashed anything. But the mother of my daughters died. It was very difficult."

Colin looked over at him; the man continued to paint and didn't gaze back. "I'm sorry," Colin said.

"Thank you. I have a good woman in my life now. My daughters like her very much. It takes away the sting. I'm not very wise about these things, but I think if you paint and draw when life gets hard, it means you're an artist in your soul." He shrugged. "Maybe I just made that up. What's your goal for your art?" he asked.

Colin chuckled. "To get decent at it."

"I see. To make money?"

"I have a pension from the Army. Not much, but enough. I just would like to be good. What's the point in giving it so much time if you're not good at it?"

"Are you accustomed to being very good at everything you do?" Shiloh asked.

"Generally. I suppose."

"You must think you're good or you wouldn't have called me."

"I wondered how far from good I was, but it was the woman in my life who insisted I find out if there's any worth in my paintings. She thinks they're brilliant, but she's biased." He laughed and shook his head. "She's gardening on a large scale—special fruits and vegetables, the rare kind that fancy restaurants buy in limited quantities for garnish—odd peppers, heirloom tomatoes, white asparagus, beets the size of cherry tomatoes.... I guess she's an artist, too."

Shiloh looked at him, lifted his chin and smiled. "You believe in each other. That's nice."

Then they were silent for a long time, painting. It was by far the strangest time Colin had ever spent. Then, almost two hours into the exercise, Shiloh put down his brush, looked at Colin's painting and said, "Nice. I'll see your other work now. I assume it's in the Jeep?"

"It is," Colin said. "Crated and covered. I'd prefer to set it up in your studio with decent lighting."

"We'll get to that," he said. "Open up a couple for me. Your favorites."

For a moment Colin felt the enormous pressure of finding his best, but he dismissed that immediately. He thought this whole audition could be a waste of time. He might get some encouragement, but it was doubtful he'd get anything more. "Three," Colin said. "Here? Now?"

"Here," he said. "Now."

Colin's shoulders shook with silent laughter. He was a bit confused.

"Quickly," Shiloh said. "Before we lose the light. Need help?"

"Please. Open this one," he said, passing a large canvas draped in protective cloth. Colin used a box cutter to remove a cardboard crate from another. He intended to show Shiloh the buck, the herd and the eagle.

When all three were open, two large canvases leaned against the rear bumper while one stood up in the back of the Jeep.

For the first time since he'd met the man, Shiloh smiled and his eyes were warm. "Splendid. Now we'll have dinner at my home and talk."

Kelly made gourmet pizza for Denny and he raved about it; he said it was heaven. Then while Denny helped Jack serve a dinner Preacher had made earlier in the day, Kelly fixed a special menu for Preacher, Paige and the two little ones. For the appetizer, she prepared the same tray she had originally made for Colin and Jillian—her sampler.

"I have to learn how to make these stuffed grape leaves. And the stuffed mushrooms," Preacher said, inhaling the food. "Do you think anyone at Jack's would eat them?"

"They'll eat anything that's good, John," his wife said.

Their first course was cream of pumpkin soup, then salad, then chicken Parmesan with anchovies, black olives and asparagus tips. For dessert, her special lemon cake with coffee. He raved through the meal, then finally sat back in his chair and rubbed his belly. "Oh, my God," he said most reverently. "I think I'm beginning to see the problem with full-time work in a diner. As the cook, I almost never sit down to a full meal. I taste all day. I'm never stuffed and never hungry. I just ate like a pig!"

"I can't wait to see what you make for me tomorrow night," Kelly said.

"Well, I'm torn between a Thanksgiving dinner or a Christmas dinner, my true specialties," he said. "Thanksgiving is turkey with all the trimmings, Christmas is duck. I have a couple of ducks in the freezer from January. They'd be better fresh, but you'd get the idea."

"Duck!" Kelly said. "How will you prepare it?"

Preacher straightened proudly. "I've made a few adjustments in a recipe I found—it's awesome. Be surprised."

"I can't wait!"

"One of these visits, we'll have to have a cook-off," he said.

"We will do that one day, whether here or in San Francisco. Chefs in mutual admiration entertain each other that way."

The next day Preacher made ribs, corn, beans, coleslaw and corn bread for the bar crowd's dinner while he prepared his special duck dinner for Kelly and Jillian. He planned to feed them in the kitchen at his workstation.

When Kelly and Jillian arrived at Jack's, they sat at

the bar to enjoy a glass of wine while Preacher put the finishing touches on his dinner.

"This cooking competition has Preacher all wound up," Jack told them. "I've never seen him more excited. He told me to try to keep you busy for another twenty minutes."

"Jack," Kelly said in a whisper. "Are you capable of sneaking me a sampler of his rib dinner?"

Jack leaned close and whispered back, "No. No way he'd let me do that. He told me not to let you have anything to spoil your taste buds before dinner. He even asked for this particular wine for you. I think he's been researching again. Eat his duck then ask him for a sample. He'll let you taste the ribs after you've had his dinner."

She smiled. "That's exactly what I would have done! God, I love the way he runs this place." To Jack's flummoxed expression she amended, "I meant the two of you, of course."

Jillian laughed. "Don't let her kid you, Jack. Chefs always think they're running the whole store. They allow that the owners and managers might contribute something, but not anything of particular importance."

"Yeah, that's kind of how it sounds around here." While Kelly and Jillian made small talk with Jack as they waited for Preacher to be ready, Kelly happened to see a man on the far side of the room, seated in the corner. He was alone as far as she could tell and there was something about him—something either familiar or engaging. She liked his looks, that much she knew. He appeared to be a big guy; his hair was a reddish-blond and he had a bit of stubble on his face. She realized she was strangely attracted to him, even though she didn't consider herself available for attraction. He was the guy on the Brawny paper towel package. And though she was staring at him, he wasn't looking her way. He was watching a young girl at the jukebox and he wasn't smiling.

Just then the girl left the jukebox and came to the bar, boldly inserting herself between Kelly and Jillian. "Got any cool tunes?" she asked with a curl of the lip.

Jack leaned on the bar and looked over at her. "Well, let's see, Courtney. This is a bar. That means the over-twenty-one crowd. That means what's in the juke *is* cool. I guess you're outta luck."

She glared at him briefly and then muttered, "Lame." Then she turned and stomped out the door.

The Brawny man came over to the bar, but he didn't rudely interrupt anyone's conversation. Rather, he stood at the end of the bar and waited for Jack. He pulled out a couple of twenties and Jack moved down to get them.

"Let me get you some change, Lief," Jack said.

"Forget it, Jack. Thanks for dinner. Exceptional. Tell the cook those are the best ribs I've ever had."

"I'll be sure to tell him," Jack said.

When the man left, Kelly turned to Jack. "Was it my imagination or was that young girl a real *B.I.T.C.H?*"

Jack was scowling. "You don't need any imagination to come up with that."

All the way back to the house after dinner, Kelly raved about Preacher's duck, wild rice, creamed onions and asparagus with Hollandaise sauce. She'd also tried his ribs, beans and corn bread. Being a seasoned taster, she hadn't stuffed herself. "He's one of those natural cooks," she told Jillian. "He trained himself and knows exactly what to do, when to do it and how to do it. He has an expert palate. I'm impressed. And his stuff isn't real fancy, but it's exactly right for that bar. *Exactly.*"

"I may never walk again," Jillian said with a deep moan. She was not an expert taster and had overeaten.

"When we get home, I'm going to get all my stuff together and loaded into the car. I'm heading back to the city early. I want to get my driving done by afternoon."

"I understand. But it was such a good week. I'm fifteen pounds heavier, but really..." She sighed deeply. "I'll help you get packed up tonight. Moving around will be good for me."

They folded Kelly's clothes together in her bedroom. "Tell me how you met this guy you've been seeing," Jillian asked.

Kelly didn't have to think. "It was a charity event, a huge thousand-dollar-a-plate event that was held at my restaurant and our chef de cuisine, Durant, was a participant. Luca is not only well-known in the area, but also part owner of the restaurant and he was one of the star chefs. I had already met him, but we became better acquainted, started talking food and menus and voilà—friends. That was almost six months ago and we've been in touch since—sometimes we cook together."

"Chefs," Jillian said. "Weird. I don't get together with gardeners and talk vegetables...."

"Yet," Kelly said with a laugh.

There was a chiming sound from down the hall. It was Jillian's cell phone. She looked at her watch—it was after nine. "I wonder who'd be calling me."

She ran down the hall and grabbed up her phone. "Colin?" she said. "Have you learned the iPhone?"

"I have things to tell you!"

"I can barely hear you! Wait, just stand by a minute. Let me see if I can get better reception." She ran out of her room and up the stairs to the widow's walk. Getting out the trapdoor created a racket, but she emerged into the star-filled night. "Can you hear me?" she asked him.

"I know where you are," he said with a laugh. "You're on the roof."

"Oh, that's so much better. Where are you?"

"In my car, headed back to Virgin River."

"Already? At night?"

"I never went farther than Sedona, Jilly," he said. "I went to Shiloh Tahoma's gallery. He calls it a shop or a store, but his oils and prints are on display in the front and it's every bit a gallery—they're awesome. Of course, he's been serious for a long time, since he was just a kid. First thing he said to me was, 'Let's go slap some paint around.' I thought it was a test of some kind, but I think he really wanted to paint for a while. Then he looked at three of my paintings and said, 'Nice.' Then he took me to his house and I had dinner with his family—a wife and three daughters. It was just a simple house, but the art in it was unbelievable—the man is a master. And he collects masters. I wish you could have seen it all."

"When was this? Today?" she asked him.

"Yesterday. Last night. He offered me a bed for the night but I just didn't want to impose any more than I had. So he told me to come back first thing in the morning and I was at his shop at eight. He had a lot of questions for me—like what did I know about lithographs and prints, that sort of thing. Stuff I remember from art in school and stuff I read about over the years, but barely understood and haven't worked at. He suggested that when I have more work and can offer prints, he had a guy who could set up a website for me, if I felt like doing that. He sells numbered prints on his site, but never sells his originals that way. To make a long story short, he told me I should talk to dealers, maybe agents, look at some other shops, but he offered to hang my work. And get this, Jilly—I asked him if I was good enough for my work to hang in his gallery and he said, 'Not quite. But in five or ten years you're going to be outstanding.' He said he thought my work would sell, though, and there was an advantage in being first, and he knew it was nothing but luck, me having run into his cousin in Virgin River."

"And what then? What did you do?"

"I left him all my work and signed a simple three-paragraph contract that said he'd give the work six months and take fifty percent. He said if I checked around I would learn that fifty percent is high, but that I am also unknown and he has bills to pay. He's so practical, so logical. And he asked me—if I did any painting in Africa, would I send him photos. Then we had lunch, shook hands and I started driving. I've been driving for eight hours and I'm still so wired I wonder if I'll ever sleep. I've been driving, doing reruns of this in my head for eight hours, wondering what happened."

"Colin, are you sure he'll be fair with your work? What if there's no money? Or what if he doesn't give it back?"

"If that happens, Jilly, it will be the most remarkable lesson of my life, and the lesson will be that I don't know anything about a man who strikes me as the most down-to-earth, honest, ethical man I've ever met. It would mean I know nothing about human beings and better never trust another one again."

"Oh, Colin, you sound so excited!"

"He said it would take him a few days to hang the work—it has to be just right. But he said he'd email me a picture of the shop so I could see where he put them." He laughed. "Then he showed me how to take pictures with the phone and email them or text them from the phone.

The only joke he made—he said it was hard to believe I flew a complicated helicopter in combat and couldn't use an iPhone."

She laughed. "Colin, I don't think it was a joke!"

"It was an experience, all right. Makes me want to paint even more. It doesn't make me want to fly less, but paint more." Then his voice quieted some. "Are you all right, Jilly? Is your sister still there?"

"Kelly is leaving early in the morning. Shouldn't you be stopping for the night?"

"That ship has sailed," he said. "I'm somewhere between Las Vegas and Reno, out in the middle of the desert. I pass another vehicle about once every ten minutes. There's nothing on the road and I'm headed home. Talk me home, Jilly."

Home. She tried not to take that particular word too seriously. She was sure he had only meant *back.*

"I don't think my battery will last that long, and I don't think my news is as exciting as yours, but I'll tell you what's going on around here." So she told him about the meals they'd had and what she was saving for him. She explained that Denny was going to be a little scarce—he was taking Jack's place at the bar over a long weekend so Jack, Mel and the family could drive up to Oregon and check on Rick and his grandmother. She gave him the farm report—what was blooming, what had buds, what was coming in. Then she talked a little bit about the stars—from the rooftop they were incredible.

And she told him she'd made a bid on the house. "If it works, I think I'm settling down," she said.

"Farming for a living," he said.

"If I can. I believe I can."

"I believe you can," he said.

He described the black desert south of Reno and every

now and then he'd remember another thing he'd learned from the Navajo artist. "I plunked down six hundred dollars on my charge card for one of his new paintings—not one of the traditional paintings but one of his Native abstracts. I'm not sure what he could have sold it for, but I bet thousands. He insisted six hundred was enough—and I know I barely paid for the canvas and paint. Will you hang it in your house for me?"

They had talked for a long time before Jillian's phone started to beep. "Colin, I'm running out of phone juice," she said. "Are you all right to drive without me talking you home?"

He laughed a little. "You know what? I can't remember doing this before. Talking to a woman for over an hour on the phone."

"You can't possibly expect me to believe that," she said. "I know you've had a million women!"

"Not like you, Jilly. I was always looking for women who would take me to bed. It never occurred to me to look for a woman who would take me to heart."

Colin had been back in Virgin River for three days when Jillian got the call from Jack.

"I hope you were serious," he said. "There's no counteroffer. It's yours."

She beamed. "Oh, I was serious," she said. "Thank you so much, Jack. I hope you are as happy as I am."

Fifteen

Denny Cutler had become a family man in a manner of speaking. He'd been "adopted" by the Sheridan family. He had dinner with the family at the Sheridan home about once a week. He'd play with the little kids, pushing them on their swings, chasing them around, helping them to get washed up for dinner and in their pajamas. From time to time he helped out at the bar, serving, bussing, hauling crates of glasses, cleaning out the ice chest. On weekends he would go out to the river with Jack for a little guy time. It wasn't his first experience with an older male role model—there had been his mom's onetime boyfriend, Dan Duke, also a very nice guy who seemed to genuinely care about Denny. Jack, however, was special to him. There was that blood bond.

While Jack was away checking on Rick and his grandmother, Denny worked double time. He stayed at the Sheridan house at night, minding the dog. Then he checked in with Jillian early in the day and got any particularly heavy work done around her gardens and greenhouses, but he was at the bar by noon so he could tend bar, serve and bus, making sure Preacher was covered. Jack had made sure supplies were in stock before he left, so in the afternoon when things were quiet at the bar, Denny took a run out to Jack's house to let the dog out, did any chores that needed doing like hauling trash to the Dumpster in town. Then he was back at the bar before the dinner hour.

Mike Valenzuela helped him serve drinks and dinner and kept him company, but Denny was managing very well. His days were long and productive and he was proud of what he could do. In fact, when he thought back on his life, he thought maybe he'd reached a real high point. He was very attached to Jack and Mel, liked the town and the folks who dropped in, and he was into Jillian's farm in a big way. The only things really missing for him were a place of his own that was a bit larger than the room above the Fitch's garage. And a female; he'd like to have a serious girl in his life. Jack might've avoided commitment till he was forty but Denny didn't necessarily want that life. He'd like a steady girl, plans for a family, the whole drill. There was nothing like that on the horizon, but Denny kept his eyes peeled.

Jack was back in the bar late Monday. "Well, stranger, welcome home," Denny said. "You just get back?"

"At about five," Jack said. "I got Mel and the kids settled and came to town to see how everyone was holding up."

"I don't think we're ready for you to retire, but we got along all right," Denny said.

"The dog's alive and the house and yard have been kept real nice. Thanks, Denny. I really didn't expect all that."

Denny laughed. "You didn't expect me to keep the dog alive?"

"I noticed you did a little trimming and cutting in the yard. You didn't have to do *that*."

"It's the least I can do, Jack. Besides, I was glad to help out, and you know that."

"You always do just a little more than you're asked. You—"

"Jack, it's the least I can do!" Denny said. "You know what I prepared myself for? For you to say, 'Kid? I don't want a kid, for sure not now!' But you didn't say that." He smiled. "You've been awesome about this. And no kidding, I know I sneaked up on you with the news you're my father."

Jack rubbed the back of his neck. "That's a fact."

"I've been meaning to ask—you about ready to do that blood test?" Denny asked.

Jack lifted a brow. "Want a little confirmation?"

"I'm good. But I thought it might give you some peace of mind. Since you were the one who mentioned it."

"That came from Mel, and since it came from Mel, I'll ask her where she thinks we should go. How's that?"

"Anytime you want," he said. "This life? It's pretty close to perfect. Not much missing," Denny said.

"What's missing, if you don't mind me asking."

"I could make do with a girlfriend," he said with a handsome grin.

"You're probably in the right place. They drop like flies around here."

Denny laughed and said, "How's Rick getting by?"

Jack shook his head in some bemusement. "Better than I expected. Lydie's living with them in that little apartment and it's working. They put her in the bedroom and Liz and Rick are on the pullout sofa. Lydie's on some medication that's slowing her down a little, but helping with those spells of delirium and anxiety. They have a facility lined up for her and should get her in within a couple of months—hopefully before the next semester of college starts for him. They've taken her to see it several times, trying to get her familiar with the place and, even though a lot of the patients are way worse off than she is, she seems to accept the idea. Lydie has always been brave about things like that. She's always said she doesn't want to be a burden."

"But is she happy at all?"

"Well, there's an upside for her. They have activities going on at the facility and not only is she closer to Rick and Liz, but once she's a resident there, they'll be able to visit her a lot more often than when she was in Virgin River. Lydie likes to stay busy—she likes playing cards and bingo and stuff. And Rick can swing by and spend a little time with her most days on his way home from school or work. He was going to go to school all summer, but he's taken it off to see about Lydie. They're doing real well with a batch of big adjustments—that's the best anyone can ask."

"Sounds like it's gonna work out the best it can," Denny said.

"Yeah. Sad time for Rick, but it's not like it's unexpected. With what Lydie's gone through healthwise, we're all real lucky she's had what she considers to be a good, long life. That's all anyone wants."

Denny's chin dropped briefly. He couldn't help but think about his mom; she had always seemed strong and healthy, yet was taken from him way too soon. "Yeah."

"Listen," Jack said, pulling something out of his shirt pocket. "Here's a little something for your work…." He slid a check, folded in half, across the bar toward Denny.

"Don't even think about it," Denny said with a laugh. "It's a favor for a friend. You'd do the same for me."

"Not exactly," Jack said, trying to push it toward him again. "I'll help out where I can, son, but if you get the flu or something, don't expect to see me out at Jillian's spreading chicken shit on her fancy plants."

"I'll be sure to tell her that," Denny said, pushing the check back. "Get rid of it, Jack. We don't have that kind of relationship."

"I always paid Rick…."

"I don't work for you, Jack. I just help out sometimes. Friend to friend."

Jack was touched and it robbed him of words for a moment, something that didn't often happen with Jack. "You know what, kid? The day you showed up here? That was one of my luckiest days. Thanks."

June passed in a warm rush and by the first of July, Jillian was pulling and picking some of her earliest vegetables. The Roma tomatoes were healthy, deep red and delicious. Her miniature beets were in, as were carrots, scallions, leeks and some of her small eggplant. Together with Denny, they lifted one end of the fence and rerouted the pumpkin and melon vines so they wouldn't overtake the garden; they could grow their large fruit outside the fence. Deer and bunnies wouldn't bother with hard-shelled fruit.

"What does a person do with this?" Denny asked her, holding up a box of eggplant.

She smiled and said, "Kelly can make you fall in love with it. When I was little, we survived off Nana's garden and didn't know for years how truly rare and valuable some of the things she grew were. But this, sliced and with red gravy and cheese? Heaven. If I cooked, I'd show you. But… Tell you what—let's put together a nice big box for Preacher and see what he can do with it."

"How'd you survive on it? The plants are only fresh

in July and August—with some September crop—that's only two or three months of the year."

"She canned. She reused the same jars year after year and she bought new seals for just pennies, and through the winter we ate what she'd grown in the summer. She had recipes for relishes, salsa, sauces, vegetables and so on and Kelly is the proud owner of all those recipes now. My nana's canned carrots were to die for. Pickled asparagus—the end of the earth. Onions and peppers— astonishing. That's exactly why I'm sending some of this stuff to Kelly—she'll know better than anyone if I'm on the right track here."

"The Russian Rose isn't in…"

"It's green and it's heavy, almost too heavy for the stalk, as is the Purple Calabash. Give 'em three more weeks and I bet we hit the jackpot."

"But, Jillian," Denny said, "I don't think we're making it with the asparagus…."

She laughed. "It takes a good three years to get an asparagus bed, but once you achieve it, you've got asparagus forever. Cover it, deprive it of sunlight, and it's white. It's a natural companion plant for tomatoes—it repels the tomato beetles." She smiled at him. "Check out those brussels sprouts. By the end of September—by pumpkin time—I'm going to have a lot of them."

"But…" She eyed him and noticed he was frowning slightly. "Is it *working?*" he asked.

"Yes!" she said emphatically. "Yes, Denny! It's working! Oh, I think I missed the boat on a few plants, but most of this stuff is coming in strong. And there are lots of things I haven't tried yet."

"But… But can you make money?"

She laughed at him. "The most important part of the equation isn't how much money you can make right away.

We already know if it's done right there's money in it. Right now the important thing is, can we develop the product! That takes commitment. It takes patience and determination. When I went to work for BSS we had investment seed money, some support staff and some software engineers. We had a business plan and a product in production—accounting and money management programs. Five years later we had one of the biggest IPO's in the industry."

"IPO?"

"We were selling our software products at a profit and took the company public—Initial Public Offering. We'd been in business long enough to turn a consistent profit and did that with a skeleton crew and inventors. Now, for this garden, look at it this way—we need to know what we can grow, whether it's desirable and delicious, who wants it, how much it brings the company, and then we concentrate on the most profitable crop. You know why we can afford to do that? Because it's me and you and we're concentrating on a good balance between generic and the rare, exotic stuff. And because we understand that this takes time and dedication."

"Right…" he said.

"Ultimately, this farm will have to expand. But that's something to worry about when we've perfected the product."

"Expand to where?"

She tilted her head. "First we'll clear the back meadow, then the land to the east, then we might terrace down the hill to the west. One thing at a time. Come on—let's cut open some Sugar Baby watermelons and see where we stand."

"Sure," he said, going outside the fence to pluck one. "Largest or smallest?"

"Hmm. Grab one right in the middle. We're going to collect a couple from each plant type for tasting—then we'll put together a large box for Preacher to work on. Maybe for the Fourth of July picnic in town. Damn, I wish I was a baker like Kelly—the rhubarb is coming up and my great-grandmother's rhubarb pie was to die for."

Denny chuckled. "Well, I think I'm glad you're the farmer. It never once crossed my mind to do something like this and now I keep hoping those other jobs I applied for don't come through anytime soon. At least not while we still have harvesting to do."

"We'll be harvesting straight into October, young man. And in September it's time to plan the winter garden. We're going to see what we can produce in greenhouses. These small, portable eight-by-twelves are functional and cheap, and if they serve our purposes, I can invest in large custom shelters like you would see in an established commercial farm. But, one thing at a time."

One of the first things Jack had added to his bar when the building was complete was a large brick barbecue. It allowed Preacher to turn steaks and hamburgers outside and host summer gatherings in the big yard behind the bar. He and Preacher had initiated the annual Fourth of July barbecue just a couple of years ago. They had added some picnic tables and had plenty of space, especially with the bar, porch and churchyard next door. They filled a couple of big plastic trash cans with ice and added canned sodas, beer and bottled water. There were several vintners in the area and some would bring wine, uncork the red and let it breathe on picnic tables; uncork the white and chill it in the ice. If they moved a few tables from inside the bar and set up a buffet outside, people filled them with potluck items. As for Jack and Preacher, their job was to turn burgers and dogs on the grill. All day long.

Even though they had the picnic tables, people tended to bring their lawn chairs and blankets—there would never be enough seating. And it didn't take any time at all for events like this and like Buck Anderson's end-of-summer picnic to become traditions. "I could use your help around the grill, if you're not too busy," Jack told Denny. "Especially since Rick isn't going to be here this year."

"I bet you really get to missing him," Denny said.

"I sometimes miss his company, but he's in a good place in his life. It's a lot easier on me than getting a phone call from Iraq that he's in a hospital in Germany and might not make it. Right now he's healthy and happy, even with Lydie declining. I can live with that easy."

So Denny was posted at the grill with Preacher and Jack, sometimes running back and forth to the kitchen for more buns and meat to grill. And Jack was grateful to have him there, helping out. Jack figured he'd been damn lucky with the people in his life. He had good, solid extended family in his dad and sisters, he had his Marine brothers, he had Mel and the little ones, he'd discovered Rick when the boy was only thirteen and now—Denny.

Jack kept an eye on the gathering crowd—even Aiden and Erin Riordan had decided to make the drive up from Chico for a mini reunion. It made him grin to see Colin and Jillian arrive holding hands—that guy must be down for the count. All the usual suspects were present—Paul Haggarty and his family; the town minister and his family; his sister Brie and her husband and daughter; Cameron and Abby Michaels with their twins....

And then the couple he'd been watching for. Darla and Phil Prentiss came walking from down the street; Phil was carrying their little son, Jake. Jack's glance shot to his wife and watched as Mel slowly rose from a picnic table and moved toward them. Her back had been to the road and it was as if some kind of maternal radar had tipped her. She was smiling as her arms reached out for Darla and after the women hugged, Mel automatically reached for that baby.

Mel was smiling, laughing, cuddling the baby. He let out his breath in a long, even sigh. This was the way she acted with every baby. She loved babies.

Almost a year ago Mel had it in her head she needed another baby. It was quite a trial for them, a real strain on their marriage. First she wanted one of their own with a surrogate, then she met a young couple looking for adoptive parents for their baby and Mel was all over that. It took her a while to get things into perspective— they had a good marriage and a couple of kids. And her good friends, Darla and Phil, had been trying to adopt and here was this very special young couple, Marley and Jake, needing parents for the baby that was coming while they were unmarried, too broke and too young.

Mel had seen the new baby before today, but Jack had to admit he held his breath each time Mel came in contact with the baby she more or less passed over to Darla and Phil. He hoped they'd survived that passage and Mel was now content with life as it was for them. He thought so, but he'd learned not to take things like women's emotions or whims for granted.

He reached into one of the big buckets, fished out a beer, held it up and gestured toward Phil. Phil spotted him, smiled, gave his wife a kiss on the cheek and headed toward Jack. Phil took the beer with one hand, reached out to shake Jack's with the other. "Gotta love a mind reader," Phil said.

"I'm a bartender," Jack answered. "I figure you either

need to drink or talk. So, how's parenthood treating you these days?"

"Well, let's see. Jake wakes up about five times a night and neither one of us has it in us to let him cry himself to sleep. I guess that means it's going pretty well. For him, anyway." He took a slug of beer. "Let me ask you something, you being an experienced father. Is this going to pass before he goes off to college?"

"Couldn't tell you. Now that both my kids are out of cribs and in their big beds, they don't cry so much, but they wander into our room and sneak in with us. Sometimes Emma has a nighttime accident...almost always on my side."

Phil laughed loudly at that.

"Something I've been wondering, Phil. That young couple, Jake's biological parents, do you know if they're doing all right?"

"We haven't heard from them in a few months. They're in Oregon working and going to school as far as I know, unless they're back in California for the summer. I'll tell you this—it was real hard for them to go after the baby was born, until I said something like, 'I reckon there's no law that says the boy has to be eighteen before he knows about his biological parents. It should be whenever he asks, provided he's old enough to understand the answer.' That seemed to ease things up for 'em."

Jack pondered this for a moment. "That was a generous thing to say," he said. "And naming the kid after his biological father—that had to have made the boy proud."

"We liked the name. And it was Darla who said it might help the young father trust us a little more. Trust that we'd keep our word and be sure they're informed about their child."

"I'm glad this worked out, Phil. I hate to think I'm

going through the rigors of fatherhood alone." He grinned. "Misery loves company."

"Well, get this—we still have our application for adoption out there. I don't know if it'll bring anything—these things tend to happen if they're supposed to. But if we get another one or two, we won't complain."

"Good for you, man. I hope you get a bunch of 'em."

"Thanks." Then he shook his head sentimentally. "That Darla—she's so fantastic with little Jake. Any kid who gets her for a mom has it made. Darla always says the best thing you can give a child you love is happy memories and a foundation they can be proud of."

Something like a bugle started to sound inside Jack's brain. He barely heard as Phil continued to brag about his wife.

"We were young when we got married—God must've given her to me because I guarantee you I wasn't smart enough to know what I was doing."

"Right," Jack said absently. "I mean, you're still not all that smart," he added with a smile. Then he dug into that big can and pulled out his own beer. *Suddenly he remembered her. He remembered Susan. Like it was yesterday.*

Colin Riordan was standing around with his brothers Aiden and Luke in a little group that included Brett on his father's hip, talking about the fact that Maureen and George had taken the motor coach north to Vancouver, looking for some cooler temperatures in July.

"So—Erin wants you all to come out to the cabin for dinner tomorrow if you can get away—we'll grill some salmon. We're staying until next Sunday. Marcie and Ian might come up for a long weekend—it's still up in the air for them. And Erin wants to see this big house of Jillian's."

"I'm sure that can be arranged," Colin said. "Her garden—I swear, it ripens as you watch. Maybe you can talk her out of some vegetables."

"You still have your cabin?" Aiden asked.

"Sure," he said. "I'm mostly at Jillian's, though. Two reasons—she has a dynamite sunroom on the second floor—a great place to paint. And she's busy with the farm all day long, especially now that they're watching every plant to see if it's ready. Well," he added, "three reasons—that's where Jill is." Then he smiled. "Oh, by the way, Luke, I already mentioned this to Aiden but haven't told you yet—in a couple of months I'm taking off for Africa."

Luke actually spewed a mouthful of beer and started choking. "Africa?" he finally got out when he recovered.

"Yep. I'm all booked on a couple of safaris in the Serengeti—mainly to photograph big game for models. But I'm also going to check out some of their air cargo and touring companies." He shrugged. "I might get in some flying time over there."

"Jesus, how long are you staying?"

"About six months."

"And then?"

"Depends. If I have a flying job I like, it could be longer. Or I could go somewhere else. I'm going to have to get something on the résumé that looks a little better than rehab if I ever want to work in this country. I'm thinking they don't look too closely when hiring bush pilots."

"Man, aren't you just full of surprises," Luke said.

"And that gallery owner I told you about? The one I left my paintings with? I gave him your address. I don't expect a check, but hey. You never know. When I figure out where I'm going to be, I'll get you an address."

"I'm sure I'll visit. But I'm not planning to live around here. You knew that."

"Yeah, but does Jillian know that?"

"Sure. She understands. I need to fly. I need to do things like go to Africa. I'm not ready to retire."

"You sure she understands?" Luke asked. "You two look pretty tight."

"I'm crazy about her, but… Look, I didn't say anything about Africa because even though I had the ticket I was still limping and I know you, Luke. You were going to give me a lot of shit about it, about not being ready. I'm ready. And I really need a little action."

"Have you seen a doctor?"

"More or less," he said with a shrug. "I've been getting my shots. For travel, you know."

Luke looked at Aiden. "And you knew about this?"

"I think it's a good idea," he said without answering the question. "Colin wants to see if there's something left from before that accident—something he can still recover. Flying for one thing. Not just flying, but exciting flying. I feel better about Africa than Afghanistan when you get down to it."

"And everyone knew but me?" Luke asked.

Colin smiled at his brother. "Only you and Aiden know. I should call Mom, Paddy and Sean. But there's plenty of time—I leave September first."

"Aw, Colin, you can't really be leaving Jillian," Luke said. "Listen, that might be your biggest mistake right there. You're a whole new man since you found her."

"We'll be in touch," he said. "In fact, she even got me the newest iPhone just in case I have trouble with email in some places. She wants to see whatever pictures I get. And I haven't figured it out yet, but I think there's a live video feed between cell phones. And the travel agent I used said they have disposable international cell phones—like we used in Iraq and Afghanistan. Who knows—maybe she'll visit me, I'll visit her. But I agree with you—she's good people." He turned to look at Aiden. "When do you want to bring Erin over to see the house and gardens?"

"In a couple of days. After we have dinner at the cabin?"

"Great. I'll see what I can do to pilfer some of her homegrown stuff to add to the dinner. She's starting to pull salad out of the ground most nights. I'll go tell her." When Colin walked over to where the women sat on a blanket and talked, Luke turned to Aiden and said, "Big mistake. Big."

Aiden just smiled. "Me knowing that and you knowing that doesn't mean a thing. The person who's going to have to find that out is Colin. And trust me, there's no telling him."

"I'm going to have a talk with him," Luke said.

"Ah, listen, Luke. Let it be. It's not going to matter. Especially coming from you."

"The hell!"

Aiden lifted one dark, expressive brow. "You're the guy who almost let Shelby get away. Don't act like you know what you're doing now. If she hadn't come back from Hawaii and wrestled you to the ground, you'd probably still be one sick, messed-up, half-suicidal son of a bitch. I'm saying let him do what he's going to do. If you're going to be there for anyone, consider being there for Jillian. If she cares about him half as much as it appears she does, his leaving isn't going to feel too good."

Sixteen

It was very rare for Jack to have any kind of issue and not seek the counsel of Melinda, but on this occasion he was going to forge ahead on his own. He made plans to go fishing with Denny on Saturday. "Not so much biting out there yet," he told the young man, "but the weather's been perfect and you never know, one of the big ones might be lurking, waiting for some die-hard like me."

Between the Fourth of July picnic and the following Saturday Jack did a lot of thinking, a lot of remembering. He thought he might've been a little preoccupied, a little on the quiet side, but no one seemed to notice. He thought he'd make good use of the week trying to mentally put all the pieces together, but in point of fact the pieces fell into place immediately when Phil Prentiss had said, *Give the kid a foundation he can be proud of....*

Susan Cutler had said almost the same thing. She'd said, *I wish it had been you, Jack, because you're a man a little girl or little boy could be proud of....*

There were some major reasons he hadn't been able to place her. First of all she'd been about thirty in the picture Denny gave him, the one of them together when Denny was a little tyke about six or eight years old, and she'd been brunette. The Susan he'd known had been blond. Another reason—he'd been concentrating so hard on a woman he'd been sexually involved with and he really, arrogantly, thought he remembered them all. At least any that had become serious on the woman's part. It wouldn't have completely shocked him to learn there was one he was so briefly involved with that she'd slipped his mind, but he thought that any woman who felt that strongly toward him would have left an imprint on his mind. And yet another reason—he hadn't really known Susan's last name. He might've heard it once, twice at the most. And did he like her? Oh, he thought she was great! But he had never dated her. She had a guy in her life. A guy who was making her life miserable.

Jack and Denny staked out a little piece of river on Saturday and began casting. Fly-fishing was a quiet sport for the most part and Jack waited a long time to begin talking.

"This place has a reputation for father-son talks," he said. "Rick wasn't really my son, but I thought of him like you would a son. He counted on me like a kid would a father, that's for sure. This was the place I brought him when he was sixteen to tell him not to mess with his four-teen-year-old girlfriend. He promised me he wouldn't, but I gave him some condoms anyway."

"How'd that work out for him?" Denny asked.

"He got her pregnant." Denny just whistled. "Then I brought him here to counsel him about not giving in to panic. I told him to come to me with his issues, that I could probably help him somehow, but that he shouldn't be crazy enough to try to marry some young girl just because she was pregnant, only making one problem into several problems. By that time they were fifteen and seventeen, so…" Jack paused. "So, they ran away to get married."

"I know Rick's married, but I guess I didn't realize he'd been married as a teenager."

"He wasn't. I caught up with them, stopped them. He married Liz, the same girl, last fall. That baby from their teenage years, that baby was stillborn. It was horrible for them. They stayed together—all through his Marine career, all through his war injuries and disabilities. They've had a rough road, but they love each other a lot. Needless to say, I don't have a real good track record with the advice I give out on this river…."

"You oughta give yourself an A for effort, Jack. Sounds like you tried to do all the right things."

"You know, probably the only reason I really thought of Rick like a son was because of his young age when I found him. Just a kid, not even close to grown-up. With you, it's different—you're a man. Even without that letter your mom left, even if that hadn't become a consideration, we were bound to be friends. We think a lot alike. And it goes without saying—I'm proud of you, Denny. Proud of your actions, your behavior. Proud of your ethics. We were gonna be friends who just keep getting to be better friends. You've been there for me and my family in an outstanding way. Not only am I attached to you by now, Mel and the kids are, too."

Denny performed a beautiful cast and said, "I told you, Jack—if you can't think of me as your son, I get that. I mean, you don't remember my mom, which isn't your fault. And even without that, I like you and the family."

"Denny, I remember your mother. It came to me all of a sudden at the picnic this week and I remember her very, very well. And… Denny, I'm not your biological father."

When Denny turned to look at Jack, Jack met his eyes. Clearly Denny was shocked speechless.

"Here's how it was, son. Your mom cut my hair every single week—she worked in the barbershop at the PX. I was a dedicated young Marine and I never let much hair cover my head. It wasn't a quick friendship, but I liked her right away—she was awesome. She looked a little different back when I knew her—different than the picture you showed me. Her hair wasn't brunette like in the picture. But now I know exactly why you turned out so great—Susan was the best. She was positive, friendly, happy all the time. I never let anyone touch my head but her. Not only did she do a real good job, I liked talking to her. We talked about our families, our ambitions. I was determined to make a name for myself in the Corps. She wanted to settle down, have a family. Then one day she wasn't so happy and I took her out for some coffee, let her talk and found out she was in a bad relationship.

"We got to be real good friends, Denny. I was willing to do just about anything to help her get out of that bad situation—anything but marry her. I knew you were on the way and she was definitely worthy of a good solution, but I had my family—my parents and sisters—to consider. I couldn't marry her just to help her out. My family would have higher expectations of me. They'd expect me to be a dedicated husband and father and I wasn't ready. I didn't love her that way. I would have ended up disappointing her, you and my whole family. But I laid it all on the line—I offered to help her financially, to help her get that guy out of her life for her, anything that would work. And then I got my orders. She slapped on a cheerful face, told me everything was going to be fine, her parents were on her side and she had all the help she needed. She also said she wished she'd have met me first—that

I was the kind of man her child would be proud to have as a father." Jack took a breath. "I had no idea what that might mean in the end. And now I understand why she did what she did. And I understand why you turned out to be a fine young man."

Denny was quiet for a long time. Finally he let out a breath with the word, "God."

Jack gave him some time to absorb all that. He fished awhile, grateful nothing bit; he didn't want to be distracted. When Denny didn't speak, Jack said, "I don't see that it changes anything."

"It changes everything," Denny said at once.

"No, Denny, it just alters a few biological facts, but the important things are the same."

"My mother lied to me," he said. "My mother *never* lied. And she implicated you when you had nothing to do with me."

"She reinvented your past. I know she had a reason. Probably a good one. And from what you told me, she didn't expect you to hunt me down. She just wanted to give you some comfort. I'm good with that."

"Because you don't know the guy, Jack. If he's my true father, I have issues to worry about."

"Why? Because he wasn't a good guy? What's that have to do with you? You're a good guy. And I have witnesses."

"She made you a part of her drama and—"

"Stop right there. The Susan I knew didn't have drama, she had survival instincts."

"For all the good that did her," Denny said with a bitter tone.

"I don't think there's a lot we can do about serious illness, son."

"You don't have to call me that," he said, anger at the edges of his voice.

"Okay, listen up, kid. Last year Mel had it in her head we had to adopt a child. She just wasn't done having children, but she'd had a hysterectomy so her body was done. When you came along she reminded me that we were ready to take on a child with different biological parents and she never doubted for a second that we'd accept that child as our own. She thought we—you and me—should do the blood work, if for no other reason than to know who was a potential candidate if anyone in the family ever needed help, like a bone marrow transplant. But she reminded me that the outcome of the blood work didn't really matter in relationships. Relationships are connections you make. What that means, Denny, is you don't have a connection with the man you always knew as your father because he was indifferent and cruel. You don't owe him anything, either—let him go. You're free to create your own family. Think about that."

"Let me tell you what's different, Jack. I came here to find you, thinking you were my father, thinking that meant I belonged here. I don't belong here."

"You do if you want to. I came here not knowing a soul and I dare you to argue I don't belong here."

"It's different and you know it. I'm sorry. It was all a lie and I'm sorry."

"Okay, I understand that you're disappointed. Suck it up—we're still good friends. You're still important to the family, to the town, to a lot of people."

"Yeah. Maybe, until they find out the truth."

"I haven't said anything to anyone about this."

"You have to tell Mel," Denny said.

"Of course I'll tell Mel," Jack replied. "But I don't see why anything has to change between us. I don't see why we have to alert the town. Give your mom a break here, kid. She had a dying wish. I don't know if it was as much for you as for herself. She regretted that relationship. The only thing about it she didn't regret was you. She wanted you. She loved *you*. She raised you right."

"Yeah? Maybe so. But even considering that, I don't feel like living a lie."

"I know you're offended. It wasn't what you expected," Jack said. "How about you just remember, it doesn't have that much to do with us. We were friends for months before you laid this on me."

Denny reeled in his fly. "Yeah. I understand. Listen, if it's all right with you, I think I might be done fishing for today."

Jill and Colin attended a great salmon dinner at Erin's cabin; Jill brought a nice assortment of salad vegetables to contribute. Of course she already knew that she got along very well with Colin's family, so no surprise there. And she not only offered a tour of the Victorian, she threw together a light dinner and invited them all to stay, including Denny.

But the real excitement in the weeks following the Fourth of July picnic came in the form of harvesting some of her most precious fruits and vegetables. The Russian Rose was in. Not quite as large as her nana used to get, but big, dark, delicious and beautiful. There were teardropshaped yellow tomatoes—a bush in the garden, a hanging basket on the porch. She had baby melons, miniature eggplants, a variety of colorful peppers, red lettuce, red brussels sprouts, tiny beets smaller than cherry tomatoes. Jillian and Denny boxed up some of her best samples of most rare and beautiful fruits and vegetables and shipped them off to Kelly via overnight express; she would know if they were just the sort of thing that high-end restaurants could use. Since they were free, Jill didn't have to worry about licensing her farm and crop.

The rare heirlooms aside, she had a delicious assortment of organic fruits and vegetables—her zucchini, yellow hook squash, cucumbers, carrots, leeks and scallions were out of this world and she made baskets of them daily to be taken to Preacher. She even shared some of her rare lot with him; she couldn't save it or eat it all. She did photograph everything, however.

Jillian and Denny were at the outside edge of the fenced garden gathering their crop in a wheelbarrow, separating what she wanted to eat and what she wanted to send to town.

"Don't you want to take it to him, Jillian?" Denny asked her.

She shook her head. "No, go ahead. You were as much a part of growing it as I was, and don't you usually stop there after work anyway?"

"Sometimes," he said with a shrug.

The way he glanced away and shrugged wasn't the first time she noticed that he might be a little quieter than usual. In fact, he'd been less excited than she had expected. "Hey, is something wrong? I thought you were all keyed up for the harvest! And this is just the beginning."

He just ducked his head shyly. She grabbed the sleeve of his shirt and pulled him back to face her. She tilted her head and gave a sharp nod, urging him to answer.

"Yeah," he said. "It's better than I expected. You've got something, Jillian. I don't know what it is, but if you stick a seedling or starter in the ground and nurse it along, it returns the favor and gets big, beautiful and strong. I never thought I could get so jazzed about that."

"Unless we want it small, precious and rare," she said with a smile. "What's up with you?"

"Aw, I don't know…"

"Spit it out," she demanded.

"It's too soon to say, really."

"Say it anyway!"

"You know I like this, right? And you know it's been working, right? At least I think so. But Jillian, I don't know if it's going to work for me in the long term. I'd never run out on you during your harvest, especially your first harvest, but I think I'm going to have to get serious about finding something more permanent. And no offense, something that has more security and benefits and pays a little… Sorry, but a little better. I've been kicking around going home."

"Home?"

"San Diego," he said. "I grew up there."

"I thought you'd decided to relocate?"

He shrugged and looked away again. "I don't know if that'll work."

"But Jack's here," she said, because everyone knew the story about how this young man had come here to find his father.

"Nothing stopping me from visiting sometimes," he said.

Jillian shook her head. "Something else is going on here. Something—" She stopped talking as she was distracted by the sound of a vehicle. She automatically assumed it was Colin in his Jeep, then remembered the Jeep was already here as Colin was in the sunroom painting. She squinted toward the drive that ran along the side of the house and recognized the BMW convertible. "Aw, shit," she said. "Christ on a crutch. Son of a bitch."

"Um, I take it you're not happy to see this guy?" Denny said.

"You armed? If you're armed, just shoot him right now!"

"Jillian, maybe you should just take a few deep—"

But Denny watched as she stormed away, toward the BMW. A man got out and stormed toward her. He was about five-ten, blond, tan, slender, dressed like a city boy. But he had a sneer on his face. It was nothing to the grimace Jillian had on hers.

There was a part of Denny that thought it would be best to give her a little space to deal with whatever this was. Clearly it was private. It might be an old love affair gone sour. Hell, it could be an ex! But he just wasn't comfortable letting the kind of blind rage he saw on Jillian's face, matched by Mr. BMW, go without some backup. So he moved toward what was certainly going to be a conflict, but he tried to go slow to let her have her privacy and fast enough to intervene if necessary.

"Kurt! What the hell are you doing here?" Jillian stormed. "This is my property and I want you out of here!"

"Get off your high horse, Jillian! I'm here to tell you I'm going to sue your ass for everything you *think* you've got!"

"I believe you missed that opportunity, you jackass! We settled. Now get the hell out of here before I find a pitchfork and—"

"We had a confidentiality agreement, Matlock, and you violated it! And for that you're going to pay! And pay *large!*"

She couldn't quite stop the stunned expression that floated across her features. "Huh? I didn't do any such thing."

"Oh, yeah, you did. They told me at Intel that word leaked about my... Now, what did they call it? Transgres-

sions! That's right, transgressions. I didn't have a real big
fan club, they said. And since they weren't very attached
to me, they invited me to leave. No package, by the way.
No one else would have done that! Only you!"

For a second she was shocked. But then she started
to laugh. She laughed so hard she doubled over. So, the
women Harry wasn't supposed to mention? They went
after him! She straightened and wiped at her teary eyes.
"Why, Kurt," she said, humor in her voice, "is it possible
you lied to more people than just me? Possible you used
more women than just *moi?* Because I haven't talked to
anyone, Kurt!" She laughed some more. "I've been gardening!"

He stepped toward her, his posture and expression
threatening. "You lying bitch! You're nothing but a lying
bitch." And then he shoved her and she stumbled backward a couple of steps. But she recovered and was right
back in his face.

"Hey, hey, hey," Denny said, inserting an arm between
the two of them.

Kurt suddenly smiled meanly. "What's this?" he
asked. "You doing the pool boy, Jillian? Just your speed.
A liar and a slut!"

She pulled back an arm and slapped him across the
face with all her might. He actually moved back from
the blow. It left a red patch on his face.

His hand went to his cheek and he wobbled a little bit.
"That's assault and battery! I'm going to file charges and
you're going—"

The back door to the house crashed open and slammed
shut, but by the time the noise reached the side yard
where they all stood, Colin was upon them. He moved
Jillian out of the way, pushed past Denny, grabbed Kurt

by the front of his shirt and landed a blow to his face that knocked him three feet back and right on his ass.

"No, *that's* assault and battery," Colin said, towering over him. "Want to go a few rounds? You look kind of little, but I could promise to go easy."

"Seriously," he said, holding his face and struggling to his feet. He moved backward, out of Colin's reach. "You're going to *jail*."

"*Seriously*," Colin mocked. "You might have a little trouble with that. But, hey, go for it. We'll hash it out with the sheriff, if you can find him, if he has time to deal with a little bitch slap. Things work a little different out here in the mountains, sweetheart." He grinned at the slight, blond man. He winked. "They have work to do. They don't have a lot of time to screw around with little boys and their whining. Out here when men get into it, they just fight." He raised a hand. "Best of luck, asshole. Now get the fuck out of here before I get mad!"

Kurt took several steps toward his BMW, still holding his cheek and jaw. He turned back toward Jillian and at that moment Colin draped an arm over her shoulders. He was at a safe distance, so he lobbed a few nasty insults. "This guy know you're just a low-class, blue-collar whore who slept her way up? Just a poor girl who came from nothing and brought it with her?"

Jillian just smiled. She shook her head.

"You'll regret this, Jillian," Kurt said. "I'm going to sue you."

She shrugged. "Knock yourself out."

"You'll be sorry."

"I highly doubt it."

Once Kurt was gone, Jillian brought Denny into the kitchen. Of course Colin followed, listening.

"You deserve an explanation about that," she said. "Would you give me a pass on that? It was both personal and professional and… Well, and embarrassing. I misjudged him and it cost me."

"Sure," Denny said. "Total pass."

"Thanks. Here's what I want to say about your situation. I wouldn't think of getting in the way of you taking a better position. It would be selfish of me because I have no guarantees for you. I have ideas, of course. Ideas that I might not be able to bring to fruition. When you're starting a company, or a farm, as the case may be, you always have to fly high and loose. I have to plan to succeed while keeping my alternative options in my vision. And by that I mean—I'm not going to be a fool. The minute this doesn't seem to be working and I can't see a solution, I'm not throwing good money after bad. You with me so far?"

"I think so."

"Okay, I have ideas. I'm buying this property and I'd like to farm ten acres of organic fruits and vegetables, much of it dedicated to specialty items. It'll take me some more time. It'll take buyers. But it's looking like it's going in the right direction and I'll continue to develop my line. I don't want a lot of employees—I'll want to supervise my own gardens, watch my plants. But I will want a farm manager. If I reached that point tomorrow, that person would be you and the position would come with higher pay, benefits and about as much security as you'd get anywhere. That is to say, job security is always at some risk. After all, I lost a job with a company I helped to build, and I never saw that coming." She smiled. "You probably had more security with the Marines."

He smiled back. "You're not planning to send me to war, are you, Jillian? I'm not going back that way."

"I'd appreciate it if you wouldn't talk about my plans. I'll keep you informed, show you my business plan as it evolves, as I make changes. But it's sensitive information. Can I count on you to keep it to yourself, Denny?"

"Sure, but—"

She held up a hand. "I only tell you this so you have a few options to weigh. Pretty iffy options, I know. Still, there's no reason for me to keep that from you—we've worked together since March, almost five months. I trust you. If I manage to grow this little farm, you will be my first choice for a manager. But, if you have to follow other opportunities?" She shrugged. "That's the chance I'm taking." She leaned toward him. "I have one piece of advice—choose work you love over everything else. Especially over money."

"Yeah," he said. He stood up. "I'll take those veggies into town for you."

"Want a sandwich before you go?" she asked. "I'll make you one."

"No, thanks, Jillian. If I give Preacher food, he'll give me food." He smiled at her. "I'll think about everything."

"If you get the right phone call, Denny, I understand. That was our agreement from the start."

Denny gave her a brief salute, then left the house. She watched him from the window as he transferred the vegetables from the wheelbarrow to a couple of boxes and put them in the back of his truck. She still stood in front of the kitchen windows until he'd pulled away. Then she turned toward Colin. "I worked like a mule all day and was holding up pretty well, but the last fifteen minutes did me in. I feel like an eighty-year-old woman."

He stepped toward her with a smile, wrapping his arms around her waist. "You were great. You didn't take any of Kurt's shit."

"What were my choices? I think I need to get a shower."

"Sure, but tell me first—when he called you a blue collar whore, you smiled at him. Why in the world would you smile at him?"

"I was never a whore. That would've been easy—I was a slave! I worked so hard for Harry, even he couldn't believe it. But blue-collar? A poor girl who came from nothing?" She chuckled. "Oh, he has no idea! Blue-collar would've been a promotion! My nana took in ironing. Me and Kelly—we got free breakfast at school. We were a couple of the poorest kids there and qualified. Nana had food stamps but also did odd chores like wash, sold her vegetables, then later sold some of her canned stuff, always keeping back enough to feed us. She bought our clothes at secondhand shops. Poor? We were so poor, we envied the church mice. On top of that, she was our *great*-grandmother. She was elderly when she got us all. And she was a full-time nurse to our invalid mother." She shook her head and just laughed. "Honestly, I don't know where Kurt came from, but he never came from anything as tough as that. Now, I really need a shower."

"Want someone to wash your back? I mean, since the farm manager has gone to town?"

"Who's going to wash my back when you're photographing the Serengeti?"

"I won't leave without making sure you have a good brush with a long handle."

Seventeen

Jillian did the logical thing following Kurt's surprise visit—she called her attorney and reported the threats. "I'll let you know if I hear anything," her lawyer said. "But if you haven't had any contact with him or his new employers, I imagine the threats were empty. And you haven't talked to anyone at BSS?"

"Just Harry Benedict. He's a very old friend and we discussed his wife wanting to go on a cruise and my new business venture."

"Could Kurt Conroy have designs on your new business?" the lawyer asked.

"I doubt it," she said. "I've invested thousands and haven't earned a dime. And it's not in software or public relations—I'm growing vegetables."

The lawyer began to laugh. "Is this funny?" she asked.

"It's funny trying to picture Conroy suing you for breach of confidentiality or libel only to win a vegetable garden. I'll let you know if I hear anything, but I predict you're safe. And with any luck he'll invest his settlement money in more attorney fees that bring him no results."

As a courtesy, Jillian put in a call to Harry. When she got to the part about Colin decking Kurt, sending him flying through the air and coming up threatening assault and battery, Harry started to laugh so hard he had to hang up and call back when he was under control. When he did finally return the call he said, "You've just experienced the true downside to being the CEO, Jillian. Our hands are tied. We're expected to be professional. I would have loved to punch his lights out. So—did the sheriff show up?"

"Nah. And I'd be real surprised if I hear from Kurt again. He thinks I have a big bodyguard now."

A little over a week later when Denny brought the wheelbarrow around for Jillian to fill with some fresh picks, she took stock of his expression and said, "Hey, Denny—do we have unfinished business?"

"Huh?"

"Obviously you're still really struggling with this job thing. Maybe I can help. I can maybe scare up a little more pay for you. I could shop around for some kind of benefit package that would make you feel a little more comfortable. Or I could do for you what Harry did for me—cut you in on the action. A profit share when we make some money—I don't think we're that far away. Or—"

"Aw, Jillian, it's more than the job. I should've just told you when I found out. I thought I was going to get right with this, but it just keeps bothering me."

She felt suddenly alarmed. Something was wrong! "What is it? Tell me!"

"I'm surprised Jack hasn't said anything to anyone. He's just letting everyone think everything is the same between us, but—"

"Did you two have a fight or something?"

"No. It's just that Jack finally remembered all the details about my mom. Turns out he's not really my father. He was just a good friend of my mom's, that's all."

She just looked at him for a long moment, studying his eyes, the downturn of his mouth. "Denny, Denny... Are you so disappointed?"

"Well, yeah. And maybe a little embarrassed..."

She shook her head. "You don't have to be embarrassed. It's not like you made it up. And besides, even if Jack's not your dad, you two seem to have a real nice relationship. Right?"

"Right," he said. "Course, a lot of that might be because he thought... You know..."

"Oh, I don't know about that, Denny. I don't know Jack real well, but he seems like a genuine guy. Is that what's got you all upside down about job possibilities?"

"In a way," he said with a shrug. "See, that was my whole reason for coming up here—to get to know Jack, then tell him. Might be I came up here for nothing."

"But you said you like it here. You said you like working the garden. And Jack's not exactly the only friend you've made. We're friends—more than just friends. Colin's your friend. You're on good terms with most of the town, aren't you?"

"Guess so," he said. "But, you know, I just don't want to be in the way."

"You're not in the way of anything. Lots of us are real grateful you came along. I know what it's like, you know. To not have much family. I only have my sister—that's the entire Matlock clan. But I have a lot of good people in my life—you being one."

"That's nice of you to say, Jillian...."

"Listen, young man, everyone has their hard knocks and disappointments. Everyone, not just you. I know for you this is a big one, but it might help to wrap your head around what you *have*, not what's missing. Because my way of seeing it, you have a lot. And I don't think Jack would pretend to like you if he didn't."

"Probably. I know what you say is right. I might need a little time, but I'm trying."

She reached out and put a hand on his shoulder; she gave a squeeze. "I'd like you to please try to list me on the 'have' side. You're more than just my handyman, Denny. You're like a little brother. Like a partner."

He cracked a smile. It might've lacked some of his wellknown youthful enthusiasm, but at least it was a smile. "You are definitely on the 'have' side, Jillian. I'm real grateful we met."

"That's a start," she said. "Keep working on that."

Through the end of July Jillian pulled bushels of beautiful, healthy organic vegetables from her huge garden. Some of her first specialty items she sent to Kelly in samples and Kelly was most impressed. Besides a farmer's market or roadside stand, Jillian had not yet isolated a market, but she was studying the possibilities. And to that end she announced to Colin and Denny over lunch one day, "I'm heading for the state fair. Just for a couple of days. Denny, you should come with me—there are lots of produce competitions and displays. And Colin, there are art competitions and exhibits. And all this is not to even mention junk food and rides."

"What about the plants?" Denny asked.

"The weather forecast is excellent and they're hearty—they'll be fine for two days. This is important. We have to see what the competition is up to."

"But when?" Denny then asked.

"Tomorrow. We leave at 5:00 a.m." Then she looked

at Colin and smiled. "Is this train leaving the station without you?"

"Not a chance," he said.

"That's what I like to hear. Will you drive? You have plenty of room for the three of us."

"It would be my pleasure," he said, giving her a bow.

Jillian and Kelly had gone to the state fair when they were teenagers, but money was too tight, their nana too elderly and mother too infirm for the family to go when they were younger. Once they were driving and had a cheap used car they shared, they were allowed to make the trip to Sacramento together on their own. Then later, when she was an executive, she attended much bigger events than an ordinary old state fair. But always, in her heart, she longed for the thrill of it. She wanted to see Best Of Show horses, bulls, even chickens. She loved the displays of flowers, the clowns, the rides, even the sideshows.

She tried to remain calm and businesslike as she ventured there with her two men—her boyfriend and her assistant—but inside she was giddy as a ten-year-old girl. She felt the excitement rise inside her; it was a bubbling joy. There would be breathtaking flowers, for one thing; at the peak of summer in California everything was in full, glorious bloom. Someone would win a blue ribbon for the biggest cucumber or pumpkin. And this was a dairy state—there would be a lot of cheese, ice cream, shakes and yogurt booths. She remembered a huge cheddar wheel carved into a woman's face from her last trip to the fair!

Even though she was there for the produce exhibits, she had no intention of missing a thing. She couldn't contain her enthusiasm once they had parked the car. "We'll check out the vegetables and flowers, and I want to see the art since I already know how wonderful Colin's is, but I can't wait to see the prize-winning bull! Or the biggest pig! Denny have you ever been to the fair?"

"Can't say I have, Jillian," he answered with a chuckle.

"They'll have everything here. Probably a two-thousand-pound wheel of cheddar, a two-hundred-pound pumpkin, a zucchini that can feed a small town, but then they'll also have crafts, jewelry, even furniture. This is California—there will be redwood furniture displays. And a huge wine and home brew competition, and wine tasting. But also rides, and contests, and prize booths. If you were here with a girlfriend you'd have to spend your last dollar trying to win her a stuffed dog and by the time you actually get the dog, you've spent more than the stupid toy is worth. And we do *not* leave without a ride on the Ferris wheel. Then, since we have more than one day for this excursion, tonight we'll dance. You'll be free to actually pick up pretty young girls! As long as you're ready to hit the fair again bright and early in the morning."

Denny laughed at her. "Sounds like great fun, Jillian."

Colin put an arm around her shoulders and pulled her against him. "I think you should seriously consider motherhood. Or maybe camp director. Or prison guard?"

"I'm not listening to you," she said. "What I want to come away with, besides a good time, is what they're growing and entering in competition or putting on exhibit. I want to know the names of the most well-known organic farms and where they're shipping their fruits and vegetables. I want pictures. I want details." Then she grinned. "And I want chili, corn dogs, candy floss, popcorn, barbecue and I want to hear some good, live country music."

Colin looked over her head at Denny. "She's going to throw up on the Ferris wheel."

Colin didn't have compelling reasons for tagging along on the state fair run, however he was leaving soon and didn't feel like being away from Jilly. And, also because he would soon be gone, he wanted to make her happy while he could. Even the promise of the art exhibit didn't sway him much, though it should have—it was most impressive and took several hours of his first day there.

However, he was immediately so glad he hadn't let himself miss this, and not because of the fair, but because of what the fair did to Jilly. It was like taking a little girl in a grown-up costume out on the town. She was animated, fascinated, enthralled. Her face would light up when she saw something unexpected or surprising, and absolutely everything seemed to fill her with awe and delight. The prizewinning hogs made her gasp and laugh; the biggest bull on the property had her peeking out from behind Colin. She almost lost it when Denny, a decorated Marine Corps sharpshooter, couldn't sink a moving tin duck to win a stuffed toy.

Colin snapped a few pictures of fruit and vegetable displays for her, but then marveled at the focused and engaged way she interviewed those growers she was lucky enough to meet. She had a million questions ranging from business licenses to best markets; sometimes she took notes in her little notebook, but other times she was just thoroughly engaged, listening raptly. That might have been his favorite part, watching her do that.

But no, his favorite part had to be her runaway laughter! If something caught her humor, she let it all go and laughed and giggled like a girl. Her happiness was not only infectious but mesmerizing. It truly glowed from somewhere deep inside her; pure joy lit her up. Her glee while she stomped her foot, clapped her hands and shouted during a square dancing demonstration was like a runaway train. She was pure child; complete woman.

Then again, watching her concentrate was pretty powerful to him, the way her forehead wrinkled a little bit between her pretty brows, the way she would breathe through her slightly parted lips, completely absorbed.

There were other things that held him hostage. He loved holding her hand as they walked from event to event. Listening to her sing along with the band as they danced under the stars late at night; she was slightly offkey, which seemed perfect. She continually pointed things and people out to him and he was always surprised by her perception. "See that couple over there? She has on a gray tank top and he's wearing a bright red T-shirt and cowboy hat. They had a fight about something on the way to the fair—they're miserable.

"Aw, look at the young lovers! Can't you tell they're completely full of each other?"

He was completely full of Jilly.

He felt a nagging urge to call his married brothers and ask, "Is this it? Is it the real thing when you can't stand to have her out of your sight? Or even four feet away?" He wouldn't, of course. He wasn't prepared for the answer. He had a feeling he was going to find out just how real this thing he had with Jilly was when he left her. He thought it might have the impact of a sledgehammer between his eyes.

But he knew he'd have to go, experience his personal truth, or he'd forever wonder.

"When I was a little girl, the state fair was a magic

place for me and Kelly," she said, telling him about their first day there. "It was out of our reach when we were little, so it was like a fantasy that the other kids talked about but we believed we might never experience. We had it so built up in our heads that by the time we finally made it to the fair, it was like a dream that came to life. Colin, thank you for doing this with me. I think you're part of the reason the magic was recreated for me. It's only the third time I've ever been to the fair and the best one I've ever had."

"And when you went to the fair as a teenager, did you find a boy to hold your hand, buy you corn dogs until your stomach hurt, dance in the dirt to a country-western band and take you back to the hotel and make love to you for hours?"

"No," she said with a laugh.

"Then the magic of the fair is just beginning, Jilly."

It was nine o'clock the following evening before they finally started that five-hour drive home. Denny insisted she take the front seat beside Colin; he was going to nod off in the backseat anyway.

"I hope you got the phone number from that pretty girl you were dancing with," she told Denny as they all climbed in.

"I have all the phone numbers," Denny reported.

"I hope you can remember who goes with them," Colin said with a laugh.

And not long after that brief conversation, Denny was snoring in the backseat and Jilly's head rested on Colin's thigh while she slept. Every few moments his hand would drop to her head to run through her silky hair or to her shoulder to caress her arm.

He never so much as yawned. He was determined to get his precious cargo home safely.

* * *

Jillian learned a great deal from the internet and from the people she had met at the state fair. There was work to do, work that required organization. While she continued to bring in a plentiful harvest through the month of August, she also registered a trademark, applied for a business license and filled out forms to be approved by the Department of Agriculture county branch. Maybe she couldn't zero in on her specialty market this week or this month, but she could begin to develop her reputation.

During that late summer when the weather was hot and steamy, she spent many nights with Colin in his little rented cabin along the creek. That wonderful old Victorian she'd just purchased didn't have central air-conditioning. The cabin, buried under the tall trees in the forest was cool. There were such wonderful sounds deep in the woods from the calling of birds, a quack or a honk from a Canada goose, not to mention the rippling of the brook over the stones. She loved her big house, but she also loved his little cabin, the first place they'd ever had a full night together. She liked the mornings sitting in his doorway, watching and hearing the forest come alive at dawn, frequently observing wildlife visit the creek for a drink. It was a magical place. In fact, it seemed like everywhere she went around this area was filled with dreams. Fantasies. Unimaginable beauty.

While Denny continued to tend and harvest, Jillian registered her trademark—Jilly Farms. All natural, all organic, all delicious. All sentimental. No one but Colin had ever called her Jilly.

It was as much because of Colin as her own personal and business needs that she was so glad she wouldn't be making a territorial change right now. It was as if leaving the Victorian was as hard as having him travel to

Africa—she wanted that sunroom there in case he came home to paint. She put a healthy sum down on the property and the bank approved her loan immediately. She owned Jilly Farms.

All this made her late summer extremely busy. She had paperwork to file to allow her to sell her produce, appointments with an inspector from the Department of Agriculture and loads of produce to harvest from her garden. Since she owned the property, she was ready to get another large garden plot cleared, mulched and ready before the winter cold. She started early and worked hard all day, keeping lists of things she had to do in preparation for a season change, and for this she was so grateful. It kept her mind off the fact that in just two weeks Colin would be leaving.

"I have a surprise for you," Colin said. "I stopped by Luke's today and there was a letter for me. The eagle and the buck sold—Shiloh sent me twelve hundred dollars."

"Oh my God!" she said. "That means they sold for twenty-four hundred!"

"The eagle for eighteen and the buck for six. The point is, they sold. I'm pretty surprised."

"You shouldn't be, Colin. They're awesome. You're awesome."

"My fan club," he said, kissing her nose. "There's a lot going on for both of us right now. You're busy with the farm. I have Riordans coming to Virgin River for a gathering before I go. I know this transition with the farm, getting inspected and licensed, demands your time and attention. You're under no obligation to take time off for their visit."

"I want to be busy. I'm trying very hard not to do a countdown in my head. But of course I want to see your family. Who's coming?"

"Everyone but Patrick—he's spending another three months in the Gulf. I'm not real keen on this—I'd rather have a quiet couple of weeks with you, but this was the price of convincing my mother and George they'd cramp my style by heading for Africa, too."

She grinned largely, shaking her head. "I love that woman. Nothing intimidates her."

"Tell me about it. And Jilly, I'm selling the Jeep. I ran an ad. If it doesn't move before I leave, Luke will take care of it."

Her heart plummeted. "Of course," she said very softly. This was something she hadn't even considered, yet she should have. It was a very expensive late-model Jeep Rubicon. Why would he keep it if he wasn't coming back permanently? If he was only coming back for brief visits? Yet for some reason, selling his vehicle felt so final, so resolute. He was really leaving for another continent, for another life, for at least six months. And if his trip proved successful, it would be for much longer. If there was any doubt about that, he'd probably store the Jeep with her or his brother. "Yes, I suppose you would have to. If Luke's too busy, I could take care of that for you."

"He doesn't mind. I have a favor to ask."

"Sure."

"I'd like to pack up the cabin," he said. "I don't have much there anymore—it all seems to move over here anyway. Would you let me stay here until I leave? I could clear out now and have that behind me. Luke will store everything I'm not taking with me."

"Or… You could leave your stuff here. I have three floors, five bedrooms and an office." She laughed lightly. "I knew there was a reason I wanted to buy this place."

He smiled but shook his head. "It's okay. He's got it."

"Colin, are you declining my offer to store your things in case my life changes while you're gone? Or in case yours does. So we're not obligated?"

"Not really," he said. "But we know that could happen."

She shook her head. "I suppose. But not for quite a while. It's more likely your life will change and six months will turn into six years."

"Not without seeing you, Jilly. I promise. The longest it will be before I visit you is six months. Unless…"

"I know," she said. "Unless I tell you otherwise, but I still believe it would more likely be you telling me *otherwise*."

"I have something for you. Stay here in the kitchen and I'll be right back."

Jillian took a lot of deep breaths. She'd almost lost it at the mention of the Jeep, the packing up of the cabin, the fact that this was, indeed, coming to a close. She hoped she could hold it together; she didn't want to send him off thinking only of herself. Truly, in her heart, she wanted him to find everything in his world that brought him a sense of fulfillment and happiness. She didn't want the man she loved to feel a sense of loss. He *deserved* to have his life back.

And she deserved to have a man who felt he had everything important in his life, including her.

But she was doomed to tears. And she dreaded that. It would weaken them both just when they needed to be strong and resolute.

He came back carrying two covered canvases. She recognized the size and covers; these paintings had been covered and turned toward the wall at his cabin. He pulled out two kitchen chairs and propped the canvases on them for viewing. He pulled off the covers to reveal two paintings that were now framed in black frames with gold piping. Both paintings featured the same subject: a nude gardener in two different poses.

She covered her mouth and couldn't keep the tears from gathering in her eyes. They were exquisite. "Colin," she nearly squeaked.

"I think they should go in your bedroom, but of course you're the final word on that. Wherever you want them, I'll hang them for you."

She reached out a hand toward them, not really wanting to touch them but so much wanting to feel them. She had suspected he was painting something for her since he wouldn't let her see them, but she had expected more wildlife. These were not only personal, but simply stunning. "The bedroom," she said in a breath. "Of course the bedroom."

"I'll hang them tonight. And then we can go to the cabin if you…"

"I want to sleep under them. We can go to the cabin tomorrow night. Colin, you couldn't possibly have given me anything I would love more."

Luke was host for the gathering of the Riordan clan during the third weekend in August. By the time the big motor coach pulled into the cabin compound, the small RV park behind the cabins was complete. There was now plumbing and electric hookup available. Maureen and George were able to christen the new addition with their RV. There was still some cosmetic work to be done; Luke planned to do some planting around the individual walkways and patios next spring. But it was clean, functional and ready.

"Perfect," George said.

"Fantastic!" Maureen announced. "We could stay here for months!"

"That would be wonderful," Shelby exclaimed.

"Why don't you just shoot me," Luke muttered to Colin.

"No good deed shall go unpunished," Colin replied with a laugh.

Luke was impressed as he watched Jillian; she was in good humor, laughed easily, glowed when Colin as much as looked at her. She lavished her stunning vegetables on everyone and the first day of the gathering Maureen immediately commandeered Shelby's kitchen to prepare as much as she could. Jillian seemed to swell with pride at Maureen's praise of her garden.

Luke knew that neither Colin nor Jillian would be prepared for the extended family that would show up to wish Colin well. Shelby's Uncle Walt and his girlfriend, Muriel, were present for a big barbecue on Saturday, along with the Haggerty clan, George's protégé and the town minister, Noah Kincaid and his family. Franci's mother and her boyfriend drove over from Eureka and yet another reunion took place. Jillian brought baskets of freshly harvested vegetables every day; no one went away empty-handed.

Luke was completely impressed by her spirit and generosity. He thought, for the hundredth time, that Colin was a damn fool to leave her.

I just have to get through the next week, Jillian kept thinking. Just one more week of being positive, wishing him everything good on his journey, and then if she had to cry when he was gone it wouldn't hurt anything. But Jill was just a little afraid that her throat would ache and her eyes would sting for the rest of her life from the strain of holding back emotion.

Eighteen

The end of August remained warm and sunny, which continued to nurture Jill's gardens. Her melons were coming in large and strong and the pumpkins were so beautiful that she began to plan a pumpkin patch giveaway. She decided she'd put up notices in the bar and church for local families to come out and pick their own pumpkins, free, for Halloween. She'd get Denny's help to decorate the house and yard. The leaves would begin to turn in a couple of weeks, and there was a feeling of fall in the mountain air as September approached. There was plenty of occasional light rain and the only tending needed was a bit of weeding and harvesting. If one thing had been made perfectly clear in six months of gardening, it was that she could grow fantastic produce. Her business license was granted, her trademark registered, and the county commissioner of agriculture assured her that her crop met all the standards and her registration would be approved.

Colin packed up and shipped to Sedona those few paintings he had completed since meeting Shiloh Tahoma. Shiloh had sent another check and was happy to hang whatever new work Colin sent him. Additionally, Colin sent a very nice wedding gift to Clay and Lilly Tahoma—in part gratitude for making that connection for him.

Then, too soon, the day came. Jill was more than willing to drive Colin all the way to San Francisco for his flight, but he had made other arrangements. Luke would drive him to an airport shuttle pickup in Fortuna. "I want to say goodbye to you, leave you on your back porch and go. Even though we both know this is how it should be, I don't expect either one of us is going to like it too much. Especially the morning we say goodbye."

When they had their last night together, Colin's large duffel and camera case packed and ready, Jill took herself to a remote place in her mind. She thought about the pure happiness she'd had for months and it brought her comfort. She thought about the hundreds of thousands of soldiers who had left their families to go to faraway lands where they'd be willing to risk their lives for their homeland. Surely this could not be as difficult.

She concentrated on Colin. They made sweet, slow love and she wondered how she would endure without this in her life; she wondered *how long* she would have to make do without it. Then they rested, curled around each other. She didn't sleep and suspected he didn't, either. In the morning they shared the shower and one last and more frantic coupling. As he was emptying himself inside her, her legs around his waist and his lips against her neck, he whispered, "I don't know how I'll manage even a day without you."

Any other woman would have taken that moment to say, *Don't go! Don't go! Let me be what you need! Stay with me!*

Not Jill. "You'll have to manage," she whispered back. "You're going to renew your strength, to get your life back. You'll send me wonderful pictures. And you'll come to see me when you can." Then she sighed and added with a whisper, "I'll be right here."

They were having coffee on the back porch, the sun barely up when Luke pulled into the drive. They both stood up. It was time. Colin grabbed his duffel, tossed it in the back of Luke's truck along with his camera case. But then, of course, he went back to her as she stood on the top step of the porch. He stood one step below her, giving them equal height, and with his arms around her waist, he kissed her deeply.

She had saved the words. She had never intended that her feelings would manipulate him or attempt to change him. "You should know something, Colin. I love you. Please travel safe. And in all the exciting things you do, please take care."

"Of course I will," he said, showing no surprise. "I love you, too, Jilly."

She smiled. "I know. I felt it."

"I knew it, too," he said. "You showed me every day. Every night. That's perfect, when you think about it—we both knew, both felt it, never really had to say it."

She smiled and touched his cheek. "Send me pictures. Let me know you're having a wonderful time."

"I'll call or email when I get there. Will you take pictures of the garden? Of the pumpkins? Those monster squash?"

"I will," she said with a laugh.

"I think you have some blue-ribbon pumpkins there," he said, giving her nose a gentle little kiss. "I'll miss you."

"I'll miss you so much, Colin, but I want you to have everything. *Everything*, Colin. I want you to be one hundred percent fulfilled. I don't want there to ever come a day when you mutter I *should have* in disappointment."

"Six months will go by quickly," he said.

"Sure it will." But he'd never misled her about the length of his absence. This trip would be six months, but after that he would try other countries, other possibilities. If he found a satisfying, fulfilling flying job, he was only coming back here for visits. Colin had wanderlust and hungry adrenaline; he needed to keep moving, keep challenging his easily bored spirit. How many years would this passionate love last with a short visit every six months?

"Take care. Watch out for Denny. He feels like a little brother to me."

She laughed a little. "I told him that, too. Don't worry about Denny. He's in good hands."

"Goodbye, Jilly," he said. "I'll talk to you soon."

"Soon," she echoed.

And then she watched him get in his brother's truck and disappear down the long drive.

Jillian did what she did best—she concentrated on the garden. Of course, she wasn't as lighthearted or joyful. She was in mourning, though she fully expected it to pass soon. After all, she'd had many losses in her life and she'd weathered them well. At least Colin was perfectly fine, just not in her home or her bed.

She was a little quiet for a while, and Denny asked her if she was doing all right and she said that of course she missed Colin, but that was to be expected.

It was two days before there was contact from Colin. She received two emails. One was a group mailing to her and everyone in his family describing the long flight, the connecting flights in a couple of small prop planes from South Africa through Mozambique to Tanzania. He included pictures he'd taken along the way. He explained that once he hooked up with his safari group, he would very likely be out of touch for a while. And he also mentioned that before leaving on safari he had already made arrangements to take a tour of Mount Kilimanjaro. He'd decided against any mountain climbing, but was booked on a helicopter tour! He wished everyone well and told them not to worry if they didn't hear from him.

The second email was more personal.

Jilly, I'm not too far from where my brother served in that disaster that was Somalia. I was so young then. If you'd asked me even five years ago if I'd ever be interested in this place, I would have said no! Yet what I've seen of this continent so far is heart-stopping in beauty. I can't wait to get to the park, to the safari. It could be as long as weeks before I can send pictures, but I picked up a couple of international cell phones. I'll try to call, though I'm told communication is limited. Meanwhile, tend your prizewinning crop and think of me sometimes.
Love, Colin

She spent more time indoors after that, while Denny did some chores around the gardens. Not surprisingly, she did some crying. She'd gone from mourning to grieving, not only missing him but letting go of the expectations for a life with him that she'd hidden deep in her heart. She had been lying to herself that she was going to be able to let go without a fight.

After ten days some pictures came. Rhinoceros, elephants, cheetah, apes, even a lion! And the email that accompanied the pictures—which he sent to the entire group was short but exuberant. He was filled with excitement and exhilaration. She could feel the energy in his words.

At first it made her heart soar with happiness, that he reached out to her. She reveled in the pictures, looking at them over and over, reading and rereading the brief email. But there was no second, more personal note this time. And there still had not been a phone call. Her heart began to ache.

"Denny," she said to him one Friday morning, "I need a little personal time. Take a week. Full pay, of course. Visit friends. Look up some of the state fair girls you met. Do chores around town. Whatever. I just want to tend my crop alone. I need a little time by myself and I don't want to hide in the house or make you uncomfortable."

"Are you going to be okay, Jillian?" he asked her. "Is there anything I can do to help?"

"I'll be fine. Just missing him a little more than I thought I would." She forced a smile. "My gardens heal me, but there could be some… Well, there could be some emotion I'm not real comfortable sharing with anyone. Please, just give me a week and then I'm sure we'll be squared away. I'll see you a week from Monday."

"Listen, if there's anything you need—"

"I apologize, but I just want my house and yard to myself for a little while. Solitude and my plants make me feel better." She shrugged. "I have experience with it."

She could tell Denny was reluctant to leave her alone, but he was such a sensitive guy, he gave her what she asked for. She felt so bad—she hadn't even shared the most recent pictures with him! And of course Denny would be interested in what was going on with Colin, as well! But somehow she just couldn't. She promised herself that when he came back to work in a week, she'd be all straightened out and they'd look at the pictures together.

Once Denny was gone, she let it go. The crying she'd

been holding inside for God knew how long came flooding out of her. Her tears fell on many plants; she let them run down her cheeks and fall onto her T-shirt. She talked to him, though he was thousands of miles away. *Colin, oh Colin, is it everything you wanted, everything you imagined and needed? Does every cell in your body scream that this was the right thing to do? Do you think of me sometimes?*

I think of you all the time... All the time...

Because she was clearly depressed over Colin's departure, Kelly had taken to calling her several times a day, worried about her. Jillian had never hidden herself from her sister, but she didn't take most of those calls. She had her cell phone hooked to her belt even in the garden, even though the reception wasn't great in the trees. If it was her sister she often let it go to voice mail while she was grooming and tending the plants. She could return those calls later, but she couldn't bear the thought of missing a call from Colin.

Then, before Kelly had to go to work, Jillian would climb up onto the widow's walk where the reception was superb and dial up Kelly. She had always been able to tell Kelly everything. She was painfully honest about how much she missed him, how lonely her days and nights were, how afraid she was that she'd never get to feel that kind of love and romance again. Through tears she described Colin's two emails, how magnificent the pictures, how enthusiastic the updates. He was happy, that much was clear.

"Did you always think that at the last minute Colin would either stay or compromise in some other way?" Kelly asked.

And Jillian was again in tears. "I did," she admitted. "Plus, since I always knew it was right to encourage him to follow his dreams, I never thought I'd go to pieces like this! Why would he want someone who couldn't support him any better than this?"

"You're asking a lot of yourself," Kelly said. "Very hard to let go of a man you love. Can't you give yourself a break?"

"I'm going to get past this," Jill said. "You're going to think this sounds awful, but I want a man who says, 'If I died tomorrow in your arms, I would feel there was nothing in my life I'd missed.' Very selfish," she added. "I want to be his end-all, be-all. He's my everything. I want to be his everything, too."

"Would you give up Jilly Farms?" Kelly asked.

"See? There you have it! Maybe that's why I'm crying! Because what I really want is that neither of us has to give up anything! And yet, feel that we have everything!"

"Don't worry, kid. This is going to pass. It just takes time."

"Yes," Jill said. "Yes, time. I guess at least six months."

Denny sat at the bar, nursing his beer.

"Dinner tonight?" Jack asked him, giving the bar a wipe.

"I'm thinking about it."

"Haven't seen too much of you lately. Things busy at the farm?"

Denny took a swallow. "I haven't been to the farm. Things are kinda slow and Jillian wanted some time to herself. I think Colin being gone really bites for her."

"I imagine," Jack said. "They looked pretty tight."

"I don't think that even touches it. I think he was crazy to give her up, but I have to admit, I envy him a little. At least he had a plan."

"So," Jack began, "where have you been, if not working?"

Denny shrugged. "Lots of fishing. Not much catching."

"Alone?" Jack asked, lifting an eyebrow.

Denny casually lifted his beer. "I guess I needed some think time. Just like Jillian."

"Listen, son, it hasn't escaped my notice that you've been giving yourself lots of think time ever since—"

"You don't have to call me that. Son."

Jack was struck silent for a moment. Then he frowned. "All right, *Dennis*," he said. "You've been all upside down since our day at the river. That was weeks ago now and I figured you'd come to terms with it. I know you're disappointed. Hell, who wouldn't be? But it is what it is and we go on from there."

"As far as I can tell, you haven't told anyone the truth."

"I told you, Denny. It doesn't make any difference. We're exactly the same as we were. I don't like you any less and I assume you don't like me any less. You said you weren't looking for a kidney, anyway." Then Jack tried a smile. It didn't seem to break the ice much. "Denny," he said, leaning close. "Family isn't what we're stuck with. It's what we make it."

"Sometimes it's what we're stuck with," he argued.

"Think again, bud. When you've got some asshole with your DNA, you give him a real wide berth and forget to send the Christmas card. Pretty soon he gets the message that DNA isn't enough."

"Maybe not, but you can't fake DNA."

Jack took a deep breath. "I never did score real high on reassuring angry young men. At least when Rick came home without his leg, I knew some things to do. But—"

"What did you do?" Denny asked.

"I *drove* him to physical therapy so I could be sure he went and I personally delivered his sorry ass to the counselor because if he wasn't going to talk to me, he was damn sure going to talk to someone." He lifted a brow and the corner of his mouth. "You need a ride to the shrink?"

"I don't need you to feel sorry for me," he said, grimacing.

"I don't feel sorry for you," Jack said. "But I am starting to feel a little fed up. I didn't cut you off when it turned out we weren't as connected as you thought. I just can't figure out why you wouldn't return the favor."

"I thought I made it clear, Jack. You don't owe me anything."

"Well you owe me a few things," Jack said. "When I put myself out for a friend, a brother, I expect acknowledgment if nothing else. Trust would be good. Maybe a little goodwill. Or how about this? How about my friend doesn't act all pissed off all the time, like I just don't measure up? You know, I told you the truth because it's what you deserve. You expected *me* to bail out, but I never expected you to!"

Denny was quiet for a moment. Then he slowly drank about half his beer, put a couple of bucks on the bar and stood. "Sorry, Jack. Looks like I disappointed you from the start and I just can't stop." And then he turned and walked out of the bar.

Jack scowled blackly, insulted to his core. Then he picked up the money and threw it over the bar. "Buy a fucking drink in my fucking bar?" he muttered, rubbing a hand along the back of his neck. "No fucking way."

He turned around, steamed.

Before the door closed on Denny, Luke Riordan walked in just in time to see the bills flutter to the floor.

He stopped short for a second, then he bent to pick up the money. He put it on the bar just as Jack was turning back. "Lose something?" Luke asked.

"Yeah," Jack said. "Maybe." He gave the bar a wipe. "Taking a Brett break?"

"Yeah, he's teething. Shelby said I looked like I'd had about enough. Beer?"

"Sure." Jack put one on the bar.

Luke took a drink. "She's a wise woman, that wife of mine," Luke said. "So, Denny mention how things are going out at Jillian's?"

"Not sure I can answer that, but she gave him a week off. She said she needed some time alone, or something like that."

Luke sat up straighter. "She's not alone enough with my brother in Africa?"

"Sounds like she's missing him. No news there."

Luke was quiet for a long moment. He didn't lift the beer again, but he frowned. Then he put his two bucks on the bar and stood. "Gotta go. Thanks, Jack."

Jack was completely aggravated. "Doesn't anyone finish a beer around here anymore?"

It was just a little after four in the afternoon when Luke made the turn onto the drive that led up to the Victorian. Colin had been gone three weeks. Luke wanted to kick himself for not coming over sooner. He had called Jillian the first week and she said all was well, though she missed him. Ironically, so did Luke! The second week he had run into Denny at the bar and the young man said Jillian was a little on the quiet side—no big surprise. But there were no problems to report.

But Luke hadn't seen her since Colin left and there was simply no excuse for that. Even though Colin had stupidly left her for six months of fun and games on another continent, this was Colin's woman. It was an unspoken commitment the Riordan men had—they looked after each other's families. Jillian was as close as it had ever come with Colin.

Luke pulled along the house to the rear, expecting to find Jillian in the garden. But she was right there on the porch, feet drawn up under her in the chair, multicolored quilt wrapped around her shoulders, big furry slippers sticking out.

He flashed a brief grin as he got out of his truck, but the grin slowly faded. She didn't look so good. And she was still wearing her pajamas. It was doubtful she'd dressed this early for bed. More likely, she had never dressed for the day. Maybe more than one day.

He stepped up onto the porch, looked at her gaunt, tear-stained face and said, "Aw, honey..."

That's all it took for her shoulders to begin to shake with the strain of barely audible sobs. "Don't," she said in a tense whisper. "Don't you dare tell him!"

"Here," he said, reaching for her hand. She had little choice but to comply and he pulled her to her feet, then took her chair and brought her down on his lap, holding her like a small child. "It's sure no crime to cry when you miss someone," he said.

She leaned her head against his shoulder and sobbed. "It *is*," she choked out. "Because I understand what he needs. I *do!* This is *so* important to him. This is what I want for him. To feel like he's one hundred percent again, to feel like himself again!"

"That doesn't seem to be working for you, Jillian," he said. "You're falling apart."

"That's why you can't *ever* tell him! The thing he loved best about me was that I was strong enough and loved him enough to encourage him to go, to do what he had to do. If going was what he needed, I wanted him to do it."

"Ever consider telling him what *you* need?"

She shook her head. "What I want, you mean? What I don't want is a man who did what some woman asked of him even though it left something empty and unfulfilled inside him. That would be like asking him to give up what he needs just so I can be more comfortable. I couldn't do that to Colin...."

"Jill, you should have told him you love him."

"Of course I told him I love him. That I love him and want him to have everything he needs. Luke, that accident—it cost him more than any of us can relate to. It left not only his body broken, but his spirit, too. If he doesn't get that back, what good is he? To me or anyone? I love him. I want him to be whole again."

Luke snorted. "He looked all right to me."

She shrugged her shoulders. "I thought he was in good shape, too. But I can't count the number of times he told me he just wanted to fly again, to challenge himself again. He told me painting was good, but too tame. He's forty years old and since he was twenty he's been flying, traveling, skydiving and who knows what else. He said he'd be ready to slow down someday, but he wasn't about to let that accident and the problems that followed do it for him." She looked into Luke's eyes and a fat tear ran down her cheek. "I sure wasn't going to be the second thing in his life to force him to settle for less. To live a life that didn't suit him, that didn't give him a sense of value. Do you have any idea what it's like when a man feels like a failure?"

Oh, let's see, Luke thought to himself. He'd been in three Black Hawk accidents in his career, the first one in

Mogadishu and it had been pretty serious. He had been young then and had come home to his pregnant wife only to learn the baby she was having wasn't his. So long ago. Suicidal tendencies had followed that…. Years of living on the edge to avoid living an authentic life. And later, after finding Shelby, almost losing her out of the sheer stupidity of believing he couldn't deserve her. "He's such an idiot," Luke muttered. "I thought I had the franchise on that."

"You must promise you won't ever tell him you found me like this," she said. "I don't want him to come home because I need him, because I'm pathetic. I want him to come home because this is where he wants to be. Do you promise?"

He wiped a tear off her cheek. "I promise. Have you heard from him?"

"Just the emails. The same ones you got. And there was one short one just for me. Two weeks ago."

"No phone calls?" Luke asked.

"He's in the jungle, Luke."

"Don't they have some kind of communications?"

"I don't know," she answered. "He told everyone not to be worried if he was out of touch. I just wish… It would have been nice to hear his voice before he went into the wild. You know."

"Do the two of you have some kind of plans for after this? Like when he comes back? Because…"

But she was shaking her head. "He said he'd keep looking for a good flying job, an exciting flying job. Something that can compete with flying for the Army, I guess. If not Africa, maybe New Zealand or Alaska. And he said he'd paint, but he couldn't be happy just painting. I think I'm smart enough to know he couldn't be happy on a farm where the most exciting thing that happens is the first Russian Rose tomato comes in."

"He had no idea what's next for him? Because he never suggested to the rest of us that this was just the beginning... He said six months...."

She shook her head. "Unless he found that flying job he's looking for," she said. "He said he told you all that if he found something he liked, it could be longer than six months."

"Yeah, I guess he said something like that."

"Maybe that's what's so hard now. He might find he does just fine without me, that it's time to move on...."

Luke started to laugh. "Funny?" she asked.

"Yeah, it's funny. I really thought I was the biggest blockhead in the family. Good of Colin to outshine me in this area. Remind me to thank him."

"Sure," she said. "Can I show you something private?"

Luke frowned. "I don't know if I want to see anything private. Could be embarrassing..."

"You'll get over it, Luke. You might not know all about your brother. Come with me," she said, getting off his lap. She let the quilt drop in the other porch chair and walked through the kitchen and up the stairs.

As Luke followed her, he was vaguely aware that she'd grown thin. Well, she didn't have much to spare to begin with, but it seemed she'd been more solid before Colin's departure. He followed her into the bedroom and there, over the bed, were two large oils. Nudes. A woman in a big straw hat that hid most of her face. Only the curve of a breast or roundness of her butt were visible, but just the line of the jaw and tilt of the smile made these portraits out to be Jillian. And the Jillian in the paintings was much rounder, fuller, more muscular than the one who stood before him, her pajamas hanging off her trim frame.

"He gave me these before he left. They were a complete surprise."

"My brother painted these?" Luke asked, though he knew the answer.

She nodded.

Luke shook his head. He whistled. "I was never exactly jealous of this, that he could do this. I don't have any interest. But damn. I wonder if that pain-in-the-ass brother of mine has any idea how much he has to be grateful for." He turned to look at Jillian. "I kind of doubt it. He's got a gift, but he's not all that bright."

Jillian laughed in spite of herself. "Stop. He's very smart."

"Aw, you and Shelby, always sticking up for him. I don't get it."

"You're both good guys. I don't know why you don't get along better."

"Because he's a blockhead and a pain in the ass," Luke said. "Now you get a shower and get on some jeans. I'm taking you home to dinner and don't argue. We're not going to say anything to Colin, should we ever hear from that lowlife idiot again, but you're obviously not eating. Probably not sleeping much, either. Waste of your time, crying over that asshole if you ask me, but this is gonna get fixed. Don't tell Shelby I said this, but she's not a great cook—but tonight is pot roast and she hardly ever makes it inedible. There will be plentiful wine with it and dessert which, thank God, she bought. The food and wine will go a long way to helping you sleep. I'm going to make sure you eat and sleep until you get back to your old self."

"You don't have to do this, Luke…."

"But I am. You think you're the first person whose heart hurt? Aw, hell, Jillian—the Riordans are famous for it. Since we can't change Colin, we're gonna have to get you on your feet."

"It's pretty embarrassing," she said. "I didn't want anyone to—"

"To care about you?" he asked. He took a step toward her. "I think my brother made a mistake. I think he's going to regret it—taking off like that. I think it's possible he's an idiot savant and this is just something he *got*, this painting thing. But he should have planned ahead better, made sure you were willing to wait for him while he did whatever it is he thinks he has to do. There should have been an expiration date on this ego-feeding thing he has going on. But the man who painted those," he said, glancing over his shoulder, growing serious and even respectful. "That man worships you. It's obvious."

Jillian smiled sentimentally. She knew that. Colin loved her. But would that ever bring him back to her?

"Now let's concentrate on getting you back on your feet. You have a farm to run. My wife loves getting your vegetables. She hardly ever screws up salad."

Nineteen

Luke brought Jillian to his house, fed her, plied her with good red wine, dessert and left her in Shelby's expert hands. For three days Shelby carried food and understanding to Jillian at the Victorian, or forced Jillian to come to her house. Jillian might not have eaten otherwise. They talked about their men and experiences with them, about how much they loved them and how much it could hurt while waiting for them to figure out their heads. In that time Jillian began to sleep better at night, regain her appetite and cry less often. She also became very close to Shelby.

Who would figure Luke could be capable of knowing how to help heal a woman's broken heart? But in an abstract way, he'd been responsible.

"It's strange that Luke, such a clumsy romantic, came to you to help," Shelby said. "But these Riordan men. They have so much conflict between them and yet they do all they can for each other. Aiden came to me. He flew all the way to Hawaii to find me, dry my tears, prop me up. His mission was to try to explain why Luke was so impossible to reach."

"And did he?" Jillian asked.

"He did. But you've met Aiden. It doesn't take long to figure out how wise and sensitive he is—I guess he has to be as a woman's doctor. Who would guess Luke could be sensitive enough to do the same thing?" She smiled. "I'm glad you got to see that, Jill. I'm glad someone besides me knows how really special my Luke is."

In no time Shelby was harvesting right alongside Jillian, taking home great quantities of delicious and precious vegetables and melons.

And Jillian was feeling stronger and more confident. She wasn't missing Colin any less, but she realized she had to fill her life with more than grief and worry. There were people in her life who would be friends. And there was her work—she vowed to focus on her own ambitions while Colin experimented with his.

She took pictures of some of the crop and she fired off a few emails for Colin to receive whenever he was able to next make an internet connection.

She was no longer sobbing and losing weight, thanks to Luke and Shelby. But she still thought about Colin constantly. She slept on his pillow, inhaling that special scent that grew fainter by the day, and she dreamed about him. She had taken to lying down in the afternoon for a while to make up for the sleep she lost at night. But she was on the mend. For the first time since he left almost four weeks ago, she believed she would survive no matter what came next.

Jillian was ready for some semblance of normalcy, but it was not to come quickly. On the morning she would have expected Denny to return to work with her, he crept silently up her drive, tiptoed onto the back porch and slipped an envelope in the crack of the back door. It wasn't even 6:00 a.m. but she happened to be up. She'd been awake since five, on the heels of another vivid

dream about Colin, and since she was awake she wanted
to see the sun rise over the tall trees that surrounded the
house and gardens. Because of that, the only light on in
the big Victorian was the little red light on the coffeepot.
Denny would have assumed she was still in bed.

She thought about snatching open the door and calling out to him, but instead she simply slid the envelope
inside, opened it and looked at the contents. There was a
handwritten, folded piece of paper for her and a sealed en-
velop upon which Jack's name was written. Her note said,

> Dear Jillian, I'm sorry to be leaving you without
> notice, but after giving it a lot of thought, I've de-
> cided to go back to San Diego. I enjoyed working
> with you, but I think I'll find more opportunities
> in the city where I grew up. Thank you for every-
> thing and I hope you're very successful. And if you
> would please give the enclosed letter to Jack, I'd
> appreciate it. Thank you. Denny

That's it? she asked herself. After all we've done? This
was *all* wrong, she thought. That Denny would leave her
like this, knowing how much he liked the gardens and
how alone she was at the moment, that was bad enough.
But sneaking his letter of resignation in the predawn
hours? Leaving a letter for Jack rather than talking with
him? Slipping away before anyone could say goodbye?

She picked up the phone and called the bar, hoping
that line would ring into the house. She supposed if no
one picked up she could find Jack or Mel's number by
calling around, though it was awful early for that.

"Jack's Bar," a gruff voice said.

"Preacher?"

"That's me," he said, sounding fully awake and alert.

"It's Jillian. Listen, something very weird just happened—"

"You all right?"

"Fine. But I was sitting in the kitchen, in the dark, waiting to see the sunrise, when Denny slipped a note in the door and took off. The note says he's leaving and asked that I give a letter to Jack for him. It's in a sealed envelope, Preacher. Denny is sneaking away for some reason. This makes no sense."

"Crap," Preacher said. "Thanks, Jillian. I'll take care of it. Don't worry."

Preacher called Jack and Jack called Jo Ellen Fitch, Denny's landlady, while he was pulling on jeans and boots. "Jo, sorry about the early hour…"

"I'm up, Jack. I start early."

"I need you to check and see if Denny's around. He left a note for Jillian saying he's leaving town."

"Leaving town?" she echoed. "He didn't say anything to me. Why wouldn't he say anything to—" She stopped talking and Jack could hear her opening her door. "What in the world…? Jack? There's an envelope in my door and there's… There's money in it. It's the balance he owed for the rest of the month. He paid by the week and—And, his truck seems to be gone. You want me to read the note, Jack?"

"Never mind. That's all I needed to know. I'll get back to you later." He put the phone on its base and muttered, "Son of a bitch!"

Mel sat up in bed, her hair all a mess. "What in the world is going on?"

"Denny bolted. He left notes for Jillian, Jo Fitch and one for me. Says he's going home."

"And where are you going?" she asked.

"Possibly all the way to San Diego. Can you get the kids together without my help before going to the clinic?"

"Sounds like I'd better be able to," Mel said. "What are you going to do?"

"I don't know yet," he said. He leaned down, gave her a kiss and said, "We don't do things like this. We don't leave *notes!*"

Denny figured it was all for the best, that he just head back to a life he understood and felt comfortable in. He knew people in San Diego. Maybe not a ton of people, but he still had a few friends there. And it was true—there probably were more opportunities for him, jobwise. He hated to leave Jillian's farm, though. He'd begun to have visions of what it might become—like one of the hottest, most productive organic farms in northern California. Just listening to her talk about it day in, day out, he thought that a couple of years from now it would be incredible. Fantastic. He was sorry he'd miss it.

He trundled along down highway 36 toward 101, which would take him south. He'd drive as far as possible today, maybe all the way. He turned up the volume on the iPod and let rock music fill the cab of his truck, but the next thing he knew there were headlights from the rear blinding him, a truck horn blasting and some lunatic following too close. "Jesus," he muttered, looking for a wide space in the road to get to one side so this idiot could pass him.

That happened pretty quick and Denny pulled over on a widened shoulder and the truck behind him shot past. But he stopped ahead of Denny and backed up, blocking him in. Mystery over, it was Jack's truck. And Jack jumped out and stomped back to Denny's truck.

"Oh, brother," Denny muttered.

Jack stood in the middle of the road. He stared at Denny, hands on his hips. And Denny thought, *Might as well get this over with.* He got out of his truck. "I explained the best I could," Denny said.

"I wouldn't know about that," Jack said. "Heard there was a letter. I haven't seen it."

"Then why are you chasing me down?"

Jack took a step toward him. "Because I want you to look me in the eye and tell me where I went wrong with you."

"Huh?" Denny said, confused.

"Six months before you laid that father business on me, I was your friend. I kind of saw myself as a mentor, at least until you covered me with your body to keep me from being killed by falling liquor bottles during an earthquake—that made me wonder who was mentoring who. I don't remember ever putting any stipulations on the friendship, either. Far as I knew, we thought a lot alike, acted a lot alike I thought it was the Corps. Then I thought it was just one of those things. Then I thought I was probably your father and that would explain it. Whatever it was, it was working just fine. Just a couple of guys. To tell the truth, I thought you had a similar connection with Preacher, with Jill, with Mel."

"Look, Jack, it wasn't your fault, okay?"

"I *know* it wasn't my fault. It wasn't anyone's fault, Denny. It just worked out the details were not the same as we thought."

"It was someone's fault, just not ours! My mom! Maybe she had all the right reasons and maybe it was because she was sick, maybe it was because she was worried about me, maybe it was—"

"Maybe it was because we were close, me and your mom," Jack interrupted. "Maybe she hoped I'd look out for you, if the worst happened. She wasn't my girl-friend—I wasn't her boyfriend. We weren't lovers. We were better than the kind of lovers I had back then, when I was twenty and really couldn't think like a man. We were good friends. I thought I told you—I knew you were *there!* Inside her! I said I'd do anything to help her get out of that bad situation! I'd give her money, get her a safe place to live, and because I was twenty and big and built and ready, I would'a been so happy to go over to her place and beat the living *shit* outta that guy who wasn't good to her, but—" He stopped suddenly. "That wasn't the kind of thing I'd offer to do for a stranger, for someone who meant nothing to me. Just look me in the eye and tell my why that isn't enough for you. Why you'd take off in the dark of night."

"I came up here to find my father," Denny said. "I thought you were my father. I didn't mean to mislead you, Jack. I was so sure...."

"So? What's that got to do with anything? So there were a few details to sort out. Not your fault you didn't have all the information."

"Yeah, but I was looking for a place to *belong*," he said. "I was looking for a connection. Everything back home seemed like it faded away. After my mom was gone, after breaking up with my girl so she wouldn't worry about me in Afghanistan, after a lot of my friends moved on... With a father somewhere, there was a con-nection somewhere." He shook his head. "I don't really belong here, Jack. Any more than I belong anywhere."

Jack frowned. "You feeling sorry for yourself?" he asked.

"What if I am?" Denny answered defensively.

Jack laughed, but there was no humor in it. "I thought I knew you better than that." He rubbed a hand along the back of his neck. "I guess I could adopt you. It'd be awkward, you being well over twenty-one, but if you need some kind of legal—"

"Shit," Denny said, "don't you get it? I was looking for the real thing, not some pity thing!"

"Then grow up!" Jack stormed. "Friendship with me has always been *real*. No one has ever doubted my word before this! No one has ever needed a signature or a blood test or a sworn statement from me! No one has ever doubted my commitment! You'd let down a whole town just because you can't seem to trust me to stick by you?"

"I'm not letting down a town...."

"A goodly part of one. Running out on Jillian at one of the toughest times in her life, that's not real neighborly. We kind of got used to you coming around, hanging out with the family. My dad feels like he got himself a grown grandson—I doubt the way he feels about you is likely to change when the details come clear. Preacher—he treat you like you don't belong? We put you on a little old lady's couch to keep her safe at night—we don't do that with someone we don't have a lot of confidence in. Kind of looks like everyone but you felt you belonged."

"It was artificial, in a way," Denny said.

"Hey, it was from the heart, son. The best I had to offer, anyway. But if that's not what you're looking for, it's all I got. You'll do what you have to do. Maybe you can feel a stronger connection somewhere else."

"I'm sorry if I let you down."

"You did, son. I like the way things are between us. Liked the way it was before I thought I was your father, after I realized I wasn't. All the same to me."

"It's not enough," Denny said.

"It was enough for me."

"I'm sorry. I was afraid of what would happen if I made a mistake. Guess this is what happens."

Jack put out his hand. "Nothing ever changed as far as I was concerned. I wish you good luck. I'd like it if you kept in touch. That connection might take a lot longer to leave me than it does you."

Denny took the hand. "Sure," he said. "Of course I'll be in touch."

"Drive carefully."

"Jack, there's that letter I left, trying to explain…"

"Yeah, I know. I'll keep it. But I'm not reading it."

"Why?"

"Because we looked each other in the eyes and talked. Sometimes it's what you feel, what you say to each other that weighs more than some sworn statement. This is more real to me. Goodbye, son. Take care."

Jack checked in with the principle characters—Mel, Preacher, Jillian, Jo Fitch. He explained he'd caught up with Denny, tried to convince him to stay but failed. He also said Denny was doing what he wanted to do and that he was traveling safely.

Jillian delivered the sealed letter addressed to him later that morning. "Thanks," he said. "Need help looking around for someone to work in the gardens?"

"I'll be all right for now. I might have to hire someone in a week or two to clear another big plot so I can mulch it, get it ready for spring. I could wait till spring, but I like tenderized soil."

"You might be able to talk one of the Bristols or Andersons into that, if that's all you need. They'll be plowing under some fields anyway. Let me know."

"Thanks. Otherwise, there's just harvesting to finish. I'll be pulling and picking everything as the last of it continues to ripen. I can handle it. Luke's helper, Art, might want to come over and work. He's capable if I show him what to do. I'll talk to Luke about that."

"Good idea. Hear anything from Colin?"

"A couple of emails, some amazing pictures of wild-life. I'll try to remember to forward on to your email if you write down the addy for me."

"That'd be great." He put the sealed envelope in his back pocket. "You doing all right?"

She smiled. "I'm a little lonelier now than I was yes-terday, but I'm all right. First Colin, then Denny." She shrugged. "Not everyone is content with the same old thing."

"If you need me for anything, call," Jack said. "Not a good time for you to feel overwhelmed…"

"Speaking of overwhelmed, I'm growing some of the biggest pumpkins in the county. I'm going to make up a poster for free pumpkins, decorate the house and grounds and hold a pumpkin picking party. When that comes around, I might need a little help."

"Could be fun. We might get Preacher to load up the barbecues and make a day of it."

"That would be awesome," she said. "You know, I've had my ups and downs…more ups than downs… But this *is* a good place for me."

"Yeah. I guess not for everybody, though—like Denny for example."

"I know," she said. "*You* going to be all right?"

"Yeah. I'm disappointed, but that's the way it goes."

She covered his hand with hers. "Hey, call if you need me. I'm a good listener."

"Thanks," he said. "We'll be fine around here. Plenty to do to keep us busy."

It being Virgin River, it didn't take long for the word

to get out regarding Denny's clandestine departure. All day long, as people stopped in the bar for lunch or pie and coffee or a drink, they asked. "Hey, did I hear Denny took off for San Diego? He didn't like it here?"

"San Diego is home for him, remember," Jack said.

"I thought he was getting to think of this as home," someone said.

"Apparently not quite," Jack said.

"Think we'll be hearing from him?" someone else asked.

"Of course!" Jack said, though he felt sadly doubtful. Their goodbye had felt very final.

At around two in the afternoon, when the bar was typically quiet, Mel walked across the street from the clinic to check on Jack. "Try not to be too upset with Denny, Jack. Young men are driven by all kinds of things. It probably doesn't have anything to do with the realization that you're not related by blood."

"I've decided it's a good thing," Jack said. "I'll miss the kid, no question about it, but if he'd stayed here just because he thought I was his biological father, it might not have been enough for him. You know? He should do everything he feels an itch to do and not be held in some little town by DNA."

She leaned across the bar and kissed him. "Very wise," she said.

But Jack wasn't feeling wise. He felt like he was compensating. Compromising. He'd started to feel like one of the luckiest guys alive. Not only did he have a perfect little family, the best friends in the world, but he had a couple of amazing young men like Rick and Denny who looked up to him, felt that he was more than a friend, thought of him as worthy of being their father. Now they were both away doing what young men had to do to get their lives together. He wanted to just count his blessings, but he was a little disappointed. He went from slightly overwhelmed by his good fortune to a cup less than half full.

Until about four that afternoon. The door to the bar opened and who should walk in but the prodigal son. Denny wore a hangdog expression, hands shoved in his pockets, eyes downcast.

Jack quickly picked up a spotless glass and his towel, as a means of keeping his hands busy, to keep from grabbing the young man up into a fierce hug. He wasn't sure he was able to keep the grin off his face, however. "How far did you get?" he asked Denny.

"Almost all the way to San Francisco," he said.

"What turned you around?"

"Just some little, insignificant thing. Turns out the guy that really is my biological father not only never married my mother, never tried to support us after he left, but he also never once tried to have a relationship of any kind with me. I got in touch with him when my mom died. He said he was real sorry to hear that. That guy was my father, and he always seemed to ignore the fact. You, on the other hand, seemed real sorry to learn you weren't my father."

"True," Jack said with a nod. "Once I got used to the idea, I liked it. You and Rick, a couple of guys a man would be proud to claim."

"I'm sorry I've been such a pain in your ass."

"Sons. I believe it's one of those predictable things."

"I do like it here," Denny said. "I did feel like I belonged. I felt like you were at least a father figure. You didn't have to make me feel that way, but you still did."

"Don't *should* on me, and I won't *should* on you," Jack said.

Denny laughed. "I hope you're not too pissed."

Jack put down the glass and rag and walked around the bar. He got real close to Denny. "I'm a little pissed, but I think I can get over it. People have been asking about you all day. They seemed disappointed that you were gone."

"Really?"

"And Jillian needs help."

"I'll get right out there and try to explain."

"And I need you, too. No particular reason."

Denny's eyes clouded a little. "Thanks, Jack."

Jack grabbed a fistful of the kid's shirt and pulled him hard against his chest, wrapping a big arm around him, hugging him closely, pounding his back. "You don't ever have to thank me, son. You just have to be who you are. I'm good with that."

Colin sent Jillian a picture of Mount Kilimanjaro with a note that said,

Someone else can climb her. But isn't she spectacular? Nice pumpkins, baby. Love, Colin.

That message made her laugh so hard that Denny came to the kitchen to ask her if she was all right. She couldn't bring herself to share his email, but not sharing made her feel guilty. Really, she still wanted the man all to herself!

Although Halloween was still a few weeks away, she had Denny begin decorating. They had filled up the back of the truck with hay bales, lanterns, spiders and witches to hang from the trees, and since Jillian hadn't grown gourds, she bought them along with straw horns of plenty. When the holiday drew near, she'd carve her own pumpkins for the front porch. Being out here in the middle of nowhere, there would be no trick-or-treaters, but she'd be ready for the pumpkin pickers.

Nice pumpkins, baby.

She missed him, but with a kind of joy and possessiveness in her heart. She knew he thought about her. The picture of the mountain had not been sent to everyone, but just to her.

Jill liked to go up to the widow's walk every afternoon and look at her grounds from that great height; she liked to watch Denny at work. He was staking scarecrows in the pumpkin patch. She was so glad to have him back.

She enjoyed watching the advancing color of the leaves, still just in the early stages. And then she would lie on her back on the roof, bask in the warm afternoon sun and fantasize about that first time they made love on the roof. She could remember every single touch, every kiss, every sweet word Colin spoke. She smiled to remember half their clothes disappearing off the top of the house because they'd been so lost in pleasure, in sweet satisfaction.

Sometimes she actually dozed while she thought about her gardens, her harvest, her faraway lover. Life was not as perfect as it was when Colin was here, but it was good. She wasn't feeling sorry for herself; she wasn't losing weight or prowling the big house in search of memories and solace late at night.

After a nice half-hour stretch in the sun, she sat up and looked down at the grounds, the garden nearly plucked naked, the lilac, rhododendron and hydrangea bare of flowers. Her six months had been well spent. She planned to experiment through the winter with smudge pots, grow lights and inside irrigation in the greenhouses to see what could be done during the off-season. She stood up and was able to see Denny driving the garden-mobile through the trees to the back meadow where two greenhouses stood.

Her hands on her hips, faced toward the back of the property, she heard a piercing whistle. She turned and looked down in the opposite direction and saw a mirage…. It was a man in fatigue pants, long-sleeved green Army T-shirt, camel-colored vest and straw cowboy hat. He carried a great big duffel and a worn brown leather camera case.

"Now I'm just hallucinating," she murmured to herself.

He dropped the duffel and camera case and waved his arms at her.

"Dear God, if I'm crazy, can I please *stay* crazy?" And then she scrambled, stumbling, breathing like a marathon runner, down three flights of stairs to the front of the house. She burst out the front door, crossed the porch, leaped off the porch stairs and ran like her pants were on fire across the yard and down the drive toward him. She was crying as she ran; he was laughing as he walked toward her, his arms open to catch her. She flew into his arms with such force she caused him to laugh harder and stumble backward while he grabbed her. Her arms went around his neck, her legs around his waist and she shut him up with her lips.

"God, oh God, oh God," she said as she took possession of his mouth. His hands were running up and down her back; she grabbed his hat off his head and threw it, plunging her fingers into his hair. "You're here," she whispered, kissing him, wanting him, holding him so hard he might never get away.

"Yeah," he finally said against her mouth.

"It was supposed to be six months!"

"I know," he said. "What was I thinking, huh?"

"Why didn't you tell me you were coming?"

"By the time I could call you, I was in San Francisco. I woke up one morning in a small African village and thought, this isn't working without Jilly. And I bought a ticket home. You have no idea what I had to go through to get here on such short notice. I've been on way too many props, flying over the jungle. I was in San Francisco before I could have called you." He grinned. "Right then I decided to surprise you. See if you acted like you were happy to see me."

She looked over his shoulder. There was no car. "But how did you get here?"

"An airport shuttle, then I hitched."

She whacked him on the shoulder. "You should have told me you were coming! So I could have been ready! Cleaned up and pretty!"

He lifted her with hands under her butt. He shook his head. "I like you dirty," he said, laughing. "You couldn't get any prettier, Jilly. And I just can't make it without you."

"Is this just a visit? Are you leaving me again?"

"Maybe," he said. "But never for long. And if you can find times the farm doesn't need you, maybe you'll come with me. I'll paint while you grow—we'll travel when we can. Maybe I'll get to be a better painter and Shiloh can send me money for plane tickets." He held her up with one hand and with the other, he smoothed her hair back away from her face. "Did you miss me?"

"A little bit," she said with a shrug.

"You have tears running down your cheeks," he said with a grin. "I think you missed me more than a little."

"You never called me! You barely emailed me!"

"I was in the jungle. And I missed you so much my whole heart felt broken. I don't ever want to miss you that much again."

"And the flying?"

He gave a shrug. "I took a chopper up, just to see how it felt. Felt pretty good. But not as good as being with you." He leaned his forehead against hers. "Not as good as being inside you. I think it's time I made a few minor changes."

"Minor?"

"Might slow down, just a little…. Maybe I'll take short trips—like a week or two. Maybe you'll come, too, if you want to. Maybe we'll admit this thing we have is perfect, not worth messing around with. And stay together forever. If you're interested, that is."

She glanced away. "I could think about that."

He buried his face in her neck. "Think fast," he growled. "I might peel your clothes off in the driveway!"

She leaned back and put both her palms on his cheeks, staring into his eyes with heat. "Are you done fooling around now? Are you mine now?"

"I am totally and helplessly yours. I'll get a tattoo if you want. I'm in love with you, Jilly. Like I've never been in love in my whole, stupid life."

"And you feel you have your life back?" she asked him.

"Not exactly like that," he said. "I feel like I have a whole new life, one I didn't even realize was waiting for me. You're everything I need, Jilly. Without you? I can't even think about it."

"But what about your adventure? Do you need more adventure to feel like you're alive?"

He kissed her, long and hard, and then in a throaty whisper he said, "You're my adventure, Jilly. You're what I need to feel alive."

* * * * *

#1 *New York Times* Bestselling Author

ROBYN CARR

**Love comes unexpectedly in
Thunder Point, Oregon...**

Grace Dillon was a champion figure skater before she moved to Thunder Point to escape the ruthless world of fame and competition. And though she loves her quiet life running a flower shop, she knows something is missing. She could use a little excitement.

High school teacher Troy Headly appoints himself Grace's *fun coach*. When he suggests a little companionship with no strings attached, Grace is eager to take him up on his offer, and the two enjoy... getting to know each other.

But things get complicated when Grace's past catches up with her, and she knows it's not what Troy signed up for. But Troy is determined to help her fight for the life—and love—she always wished for but never believed she could have.

Available now, wherever books are sold!

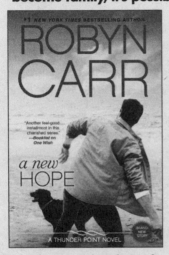

**Return to Thunder Point with
#1 *New York Times* bestselling author**

ROBYN CARR

**and discover a town where hard work and
determination make dreams come true.**

Professional triathlete
Blake Smiley has traveled the
world, but Thunder Point has
what he needs to put down
roots. There he can focus on his
training without distractions.
That is, until he meets his new
neighbors.

Lin Su Simmons and her teenage
son, Charlie, are fixtures at
Winnie Banks's house as Lin Su
nurses Winnie through the realities
of ALS. A single mother, Lin Su is
proud of taking charge and never
showing weakness. But she has her
hands full coping with a job, debt
and Charlie's health issues.

When Charlie enlists Blake's help to escape his overprotective mother,
Lin Su resents the interference in her life. But Blake is certain he can
break through her barriers and be the man she and Charlie need.
Slowly, Lin Su realizes Blake just might be the man of her dreams.

Available now, wherever books are sold!

Be sure to connect with us at:

Harlequin.com/Newsletters

Facebook.com/HarlequinBooks

Twitter.com/HarlequinBooks

MIRA®

www.MIRABooks.com

MRC1749

From #1 *New York Times* bestselling author

ROBYN CARR

comes the story of four friends determined to find their stride.

Gerri can't decide what's worse: learning her marriage has big cracks, or the anger she feels trying to repair them. Always the anchor for friends and family, it's time to look carefully at herself.

Andy believes lasting love is out of reach. When she finds herself attracted to a man without any of the qualities that usually appeal to her, she starts questioning everything she thought she wanted.

Sonja's New Age pursuit of balance is shattered when her husband walks out. There's no herbal tonic or cleansing ritual that can restore her serenity—or her sanity.

But BJ, the newcomer to Mill Valley, changes everything. The woman with dark secrets opens up to her neighbors, and together they get back on track, stronger as individuals and unfaltering as friends.

Available now, wherever books are sold!

#1 *New York Times* bestselling author

ROBYN CARR

examines the lives of three sisters as they step beyond the roles of wife, mother and daughter to discover the importance of being a woman first.

Clare Wilson is starting over. She's had it with her marriage to a charming serial cheater, and with the support of her sisters, Maggie and Sarah, she's ready to move on. Facing her fortieth birthday, Clare is finally feeling the rush of unadulterated freedom.

Then a near-fatal car accident lands Clare in the hospital, and her life takes another detour. While recovering, Clare realizes she has the power to choose her life's path. The wonderful younger police officer who witnessed her crash is over the moon for her. A man from her past stirs up long-buried feelings. Even her ex is pining for her. With enthusiasm and a little envy, her sisters watch her bloom.

Together, the sisters encourage each other to seek what they need to be happy. Along the way they all learn it's never too late to begin again.

Available now, wherever books are sold.

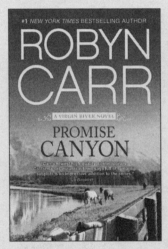

REQUEST YOUR FREE BOOKS!

2 FREE NOVELS
FROM THE ROMANCE COLLECTION
PLUS 2 FREE GIFTS!

YES! Please send me 2 FREE novels from the Romance Collection and my 2 FREE gifts (gifts are worth about $10). After receiving them, if I don't wish to receive any more books, I can return the shipping statement marked "cancel." If I don't cancel, I will receive 4 brand-new novels every month and be billed just $6.49 per book in the U.S. or $6.99 per book in Canada. That's a savings of at least 19% off the cover price. It's quite a bargain! Shipping and handling is just 50¢ per book in the U.S. and 75¢ per book in Canada.* I understand that accepting the 2 free books and gifts places me under no obligation to buy anything. I can always return a shipment and cancel at any time. Even if I never buy another book, the two free books and gifts are mine to keep forever.

194/394 MDN GH4D

Name _____ (PLEASE PRINT) _____

Address _____ Apt. # _____

City _____ State/Prov. _____ Zip/Postal Code _____

Signature (if under 18, a parent or guardian must sign)

Mail to the Reader Service:
IN U.S.A.: P.O. Box 1867, Buffalo, NY 14240-1867
IN CANADA: P.O. Box 609, Fort Erie, Ontario L2A 5X3

Want to try two free books from another line?
Call 1-800-873-8635 or visit www.ReaderService.com.

* Terms and prices subject to change without notice. Prices do not include applicable taxes. Sales tax applicable in N.Y. Canadian residents will be charged applicable taxes. Offer not valid in Quebec. This offer is limited to one order per household. Not valid for current subscribers to the Romance Collection or the Romance/Suspense Collection. All orders subject to credit approval. Credit or debit balances in a customer's account(s) may be offset by any other outstanding balance owed by or to the customer. Please allow 4 to 6 weeks for delivery. Offer available while quantities last.

Your Privacy—The Reader Service is committed to protecting your privacy. Our Privacy Policy is available online at www.ReaderService.com or upon request from the Reader Service.

We make a portion of our mailing list available to reputable third parties that offer products we believe may interest you. If you prefer that we not exchange your name with third parties, or if you wish to clarify or modify your communication preferences, please visit us at www.ReaderService.com/consumerschoice or write to us at Reader Service Preference Service, P.O. Box 9062, Buffalo, NY 14240-9062. Include your complete name and address.

ROM15

ROBYN CARR

32897	DEEP IN THE VALLEY	___ $7.99 U.S.	___ $9.99 CAN.
31772	ONE WISH	___ $8.99 U.S.	___ $9.99 CAN.
31742	PROMISE CANYON	___ $7.99 U.S.	___ $8.99 CAN.
31733	MOONLIGHT ROAD	___ $7.99 U.S.	___ $8.99 CAN.
31728	A SUMMER IN SONOMA	___ $7.99 U.S.	___ $8.99 CAN.
31724	THE HOUSE ON OLIVE STREET	___ $7.99 U.S.	___ $8.99 CAN.
31702	ANGEL'S PEAK	___ $7.99 U.S.	___ $8.99 CAN.
31697	FORBIDDEN FALLS	___ $7.99 U.S.	___ $8.99 CAN.
31644	THE HOMECOMING	___ $7.99 U.S.	___ $8.99 CAN.
31620	THE PROMISE	___ $7.99 U.S.	___ $8.99 CAN.
31599	THE CHANCE	___ $7.99 U.S.	___ $8.99 CAN.
31590	PARADISE VALLEY	___ $7.99 U.S.	___ $8.99 CAN.
31582	TEMPTATION RIDGE	___ $7.99 U.S.	___ $8.99 CAN.
31571	SECOND CHANCE PASS	___ $7.99 U.S.	___ $8.99 CAN.
31513	A VIRGIN RIVER CHRISTMAS	___ $7.99 U.S.	___ $8.99 CAN.
31459	THE HERO	___ $7.99 U.S.	___ $8.99 CAN.
31452	THE NEWCOMER	___ $7.99 U.S.	___ $9.99 CAN.
31447	THE WANDERER	___ $7.99 U.S.	___ $9.99 CAN.
31428	WHISPERING ROCK	___ $7.99 U.S.	___ $9.99 CAN.
31419	SHELTER MOUNTAIN	___ $7.99 U.S.	___ $9.99 CAN.
31415	VIRGIN RIVER	___ $7.99 U.S.	___ $9.99 CAN.
31385	MY KIND OF CHRISTMAS	___ $7.99 U.S.	___ $9.99 CAN.
31317	SUNRISE POINT	___ $7.99 U.S.	___ $9.99 CAN.
31310	REDWOOD BEND	___ $7.99 U.S.	___ $9.99 CAN.
31300	HIDDEN SUMMIT	___ $7.99 U.S.	___ $9.99 CAN.

(limited quantities available)

TOTAL AMOUNT	$ _____
POSTAGE & HANDLING	$ _____
($1.00 for 1 book, 50¢ for each additional)	
APPLICABLE TAXES*	$ _____
TOTAL PAYABLE	$ _____

(check or money order—please do not send cash)

To order, complete this form and send it, along with a check or money order for the total above, payable to MIRA Books, to: **In the U.S.:** 3010 Walden Avenue, P.O. Box 9077, Buffalo, NY 14269-9077; **In Canada:** P.O. Box 636, Fort Erie, Ontario, L2A 5X3.

Name: _____
Address: _____ City: _____
State/Prov.: _____ Zip/Postal Code: _____
Account Number (if applicable): _____

075 CSAS

*New York residents remit applicable sales taxes.
*Canadian residents remit applicable GST and provincial taxes.

MIRA®

www.MIRABooks.com

MRC0915BL